THE SWISS SPY

ALEX GERLIS

STUDIO 28

Published by Studio 28, 28 Haymarket, London SW1Y 4SP.

ISBN: 978-1-78292-510-1

The Author

Alex Gerlis was a BBC journalist for more than 25 years before leaving in 2011 to concentrate on his writing. His first novel, *The Best of Our Spies* (2012), is an espionage thriller set in the Second World War and like *The Swiss Spy*, based on real events. *The Best of Our Spies* has featured prominently in the Amazon bestseller charts and has received some 400 Amazon reviews. His third novel is also set in the Second World War and will be a sequel to *The Swiss Spy*. He is also the author of *The Miracle of Normandy*, published in 2014 as a non-fiction Kindle Single. Alex Gerlis lives in London, is married with two daughters and is represented by Gordon Wise at the Curtis Brown literary agency. He is a Visiting Professor of Journalism at the University of Bedfordshire.

Alex Gerlis

Contents

List of main characters

Henry Hunter
Also known as Henri Hesse

Marlene Hesse
Mother of Henry. Formerly known as Maureen Hunter

Erich Hesse (deceased)
Husband of Marlene and stepfather of Henry

Louise Alice Hunter (deceased)
Aunt of Henry Hunter

Captain Edgar
British spy master

Hon. Anthony Davis
Cover name for Edgar

Patrick O'Connor Jr
Cover name for Edgar

Christopher Porter
Edgar's boss

Basil Remington-Barber
British spy chief in Switzerland

The Swiss Spy

Sir Roland Pearson
Downing Street intelligence chief

Madame Ladnier
Contact at Credit Suisse, Geneva

Sandy Morgan
British spy in Lisbon

Rolf Eder
Austrian, working for the British in Switzerland

Franz Hermann
Berlin lawyer and British agent. Codename Hugo

Frau Hermann
Mother of Franz Hermann

Werner Ernst
Generalmajor in German Army High Command

Gunter Reinhart
Official at the Reichsbank, Berlin. Married to Gudrun

Rosa Stern
First wife of Gunter Reinhart. Married to Harald Stern

Alex Gerlis

Alfred Stern
Son of Gunter Reinhart and Rosa Stern

Sophia Stern
Daughter of Rosa Stern and Harald Stern

Alois Jäger
Berlin lawyer

Katharina Hoch
British agent in Stuttgart. Codename Milo

Dieter Hoch
Brother of Katharina Hoch

Manfred Erhard
Contact in Essen. Codename Lido

Gertraud Traugott (deceased)
'Aunt' in Essen

Telmo Rocha Martins
Official in Portuguese Foreign ministry

Dona Maria do Rosario
Secretary at Portuguese Legation in Berlin

8

The Swiss Spy

Viktor Krasotkin
Russian spy master

Father Josef
Priest at St Hedwig's Cathedral, Berlin

Michael Hedinger
Official at Bank Leu, Zürich

Anatoly Mikhailovich Yevtushenko
Russian émigré in Interlaken, Switzerland

Tatyana Dmitriyevna Yevtushenko
Wife of Anatoly

Rozalia Anatolyevna Yevtushenko
Daughter of Anatoly and Tatyana

Nadezhda Anatolyevna Yevtushenko
Daughter of Anatoly and Tatyana

Nikolai Anatolyevich Yevtushenko
Son of Anatoly & Tatyana

Prologue: London, 22nd June 1941

'It looks like it's started. You'd better come over.'

It was dark in the room and he was unsure if the vaguely familiar voice next to him was part of a dream or was real and, if so, where it was coming from.

'Are you there Edgar? Can you hear me?'

He realised he was holding the telephone in his hand. He must have picked it up in the middle of a dream in which he'd been surrounded by men even taller than him, all wearing black uniforms with gleaming smiles. The menace that accompanied them had suddenly vanished at the sound of a shrill bell and a man calling his name.

'Edgar! Are you there?'

He switched on the bedside lamp and leaned back on his pillow. It was Christopher Porter. Annoyingly, his cigarette case was not on the table.

'Yes sir.'

'At last. I imagine I've woken you up?'

'At two o'clock in the morning? Whatever makes you think that?'

'You'd better come over. Looks like it's all started.'

'Not another false alarm, I hope.'

'I don't think so: you'd better come and see for yourself.'

He dressed quickly, not bothering to shave. Just as he was about to leave his flat he noticed a half-glass of whisky on the sideboard. He hesitated for a moment then drank it. *If what Porter says is true, this may be the last chance for a drink for some time.*

There was a light drizzle as he hurried down Victoria Street and by the time he crossed Parliament Square the rain had turned heavy, causing him to run down Whitehall. The city was enveloped in the darkness of the blackout, which meant he stepped in a few puddles. By the time he arrived at the entrance to the heavily guarded basement beneath Whitehall his light summer suit was quite drenched, his socks were soggy and he was breathing heavily. He joined a small queue of people waiting to be allowed in. The pervading smell was that of rain, sweat and cigarette smoke. He edged his way to front of the queue, ignoring the muttering behind him.

'Who shall I say it is again sir?' The army sergeant glanced anxiously at the men behind him.

'I told you: I was telephoned just before and told to come here. I really do not expect to be kept waiting. You understand?'

The sergeant hesitated: he had strict orders about who he was to allow into the basement and what accreditation they needed. This man was trying to barge his way in. At that moment the door to the basement opened and a man tapped him on the shoulder.

'Captain Edgar is with me: be a good chap and let him through please?'

Five minutes later they had descended several flights of stairs and passed through a series of guarded doorways. Now they were on a narrow platform overlooking a large and brightly lit operations room, its walls covered in huge maps. Men and women in a variety of uniforms were either on the phone, writing on bits of paper or climbing ladders to adjust markers on the maps. Another platform to their left was crowded with senior officers.

'So this is it sir?'

'Seems to be: it all started just after midnight, our time that is. The Germans launched air raids against key targets in the Soviet-controlled sector of Poland. Soon after that their land forces crossed the border. Hard to be too precise at the moment, but everything we're picking up seems to indicate this is a major invasion. Some reports say that over 100 German divisions are involved. Other reports say it could be nearer to 150.'

'Reliable sources?'

'Bletchley say they can barely cope with all the radio traffic: noisiest night of the war, they say. Plenty of good stuff coming through Helsinki too. The Finns are pretty much in bed with the Germans now as you know; wouldn't be surprised to see them joining the party. They're also well plugged into all kinds of sources in Russia. Close proximity and all that. Stockholm station is sending broadly the same message. Morgan sent three messages from Lisbon last night saying he thought it was imminent – two different sources apparently, one particularly good one in the Ministry of Foreign Affairs.'

Edgar showed no reaction, as if nothing he was being told was news to him. He felt in his pockets and realised he'd forgotten to bring cigarettes.

'What does the front look like?'

Christopher Porter pointed to an enormous map of Europe opposite them. 'Starting up there in the north – where that red diamond is – they've certainly crossed into Latvia. Probably the 4th Panzer Group, we know they were in that area. Then all the way down the border, as far south as the Ukraine. Looks like the Romanians may be involved there, possibly the Hungarians too. See Brest on the map… there? That's where the main thrust may well be, though it's a bit early to say for sure. Between there and Lublin: north and south of the Pripet Marshes.'

'Quite some front.'

'Well, if they've really attacked from the Baltic to the Black Sea, that's well over a thousand miles. Extraordinary if they manage to pull that off.'

Edgar stared at the map for a good five minutes. 'He's crazy, isn't he?'

'Who is?'

Edgar looked down at Porter, surprised. 'Hitler. He's left it far too late. Look how far they are from Moscow, over 600 miles. Talking of which, much noise coming out of there?'

'Nothing official. Apparently there's talk of their High Command having sent out some kind of alert about an invasion some three hours before the Germans attacked, but we can't confirm that. Obviously didn't have any effect. Certainly there was a very noticeable increase in radio traffic in and out of Moscow last night, but then we know the Soviets are prone to getting quite noisy every so often. All in all, it looks like they were caught by surprise.'

'Well,' said Edgar, removing his jacket, 'it wasn't as if we didn't warn them.'

* * *

Alex Gerlis

Chapter 1: Croydon Airport, London, August 1939

A shade after 1.30 on the afternoon of Monday 14th August, 20 people emerged from the terminal building at Croydon Airport and were shepherded across a runway still damp from heavy overnight rain.

They were a somewhat disparate group, as international travellers tend to be. Some were British, some foreign; a few women, mostly men; the majority smartly dressed. One of the passengers was a man of average height and mildly chubby build. A closer look would show bright-green eyes that darted around, eager to take everything in and a nose that was bent slightly to the left. He had a mouth that seemed fixed at the beginnings of a smile, and the overall effect was of a younger face on an older body. Despite the heavy August sun, the man was wearing a long raincoat and a trilby hat pushed back on his head. In each hand he carried a large briefcase; one black, one light tan. Perhaps because of the burden of a coat and two cases, or possibly due to his natural disposition, he walked apart from the group. At one point he absent-mindedly veered towards a KLM airliner before a man in uniform directed him back towards the others.

A minute or so later the group assembled at the steps of a Swissair plane, alongside a board indicating its destination: 'Service 1075: Basle.' A queue formed as the passengers waited for tickets and passports to be checked.

When the man with the two briefcases presented his papers, the police officer responsible for checking looked through them with extra care before nodding in the direction of a tall man who had appeared behind the passenger. He was also wearing a trilby, although his had such a wide brim it wasn't possible to make out any features of his face.

The tall man stepped forward and impatiently snatched the passport from the police officer. He glanced at it briefly, as if he knew what to expect, then turned to the passenger.

'Would you come with me please, Herr Hesse?' It was more of an instruction than an invitation.

'What's the problem? Can't we sort whatever it is out here?'

'There may not be a problem sir, but it'd be best if you came with me. It will be much easier to talk inside.'

'But what if I miss my flight? It leaves in 20 minutes.'

The taller man said nothing but gestured towards a black Austin 7 that pulled up alongside them. By now the last passenger had boarded and the steps were being wheeled away from the aircraft. The short journey back to the terminal was conducted in silence. They entered the terminal through a side door and went up to an office on the second floor.

Herr Hesse followed the tall man into the small office, which was dominated by a large window overlooking the apron and the runway beyond it. The man took a seat behind the desk in front of the window and gestured to Hesse to sit on the other side .

'Sit down? But I'm going to miss my flight! What on earth is this all about? All my papers are in order. I insist on an explanation.'

The man pointed at the chair and Hesse reluctantly sat down, his head shaking as he did so. He removed his trilby and Hesse found himself staring at one of the most unremarkable faces he'd ever seen. It had the tanned complexion of someone who spent plenty of time outdoors and dark eyes with a penetrating stare, but otherwise there was nothing about it that was memorable. Hesse could have stared at it for hours and still had difficulty picking it out of a crowd. The man could have been anything from late-thirties to mid-fifties, and when he spoke it was in grammar-school tones, with perhaps the very slightest trace of a northern accent.

'My name is Edgar. Do you smoke?'

Hesse shook his head. Edgar took his time selecting a cigarette from the silver case he'd removed from his inside pocket and lighting it. He inspected the lit end of the cigarette, turning it carefully in his hand, admiring the glow and watching the patterns made by the wisps of smoke as they hung above the desk and drifted towards the ceiling. He appeared to be in no hurry. Behind him the Swissair plane was being pulled by a tractor in the direction of the runway. A silver Imperial Airways plane was descending sharply from the south, the sun bouncing off its wings.

Edgar sat in silence, looking carefully at the man in front of him before getting up to look out of the window for a full minute, timing it on his wristwatch. During that time he avoided thinking about the other man, keeping any picture or memory out of his mind. When the minute was up, he turned around and sat down. Without looking up, he wrote in his notebook:

Complexion: pale, almost unhealthy-looking, pasty.
Eyes: bright-green.
Hair: dark and thick, needs cutting.
Nose at a slight angle (left).
Smiles.

Build: slightly overweight.

Nervous, but sure of himself.

A colleague had taught him this technique. Too many of our first impressions of someone are casual ones, so much so that they bear little relation to how someone actually looks, he had told him. As a consequence we tend to end up describing someone in such general terms that important features tend to be disregarded. *Look at them for one minute, forget about them for one minute and then write down half a dozen things about them.*

A man who at first glance was distinctly ordinary-looking, who in other circumstances Edgar might pass in the street without noticing, now had characteristics that made him easier to recall.

You'll do.

'There are a number of things that puzzle me about you, Herr Hesse. Are you happy with me calling you Herr Hesse, by the way?' As Captain Edgar spoke he was looking at the man's Swiss passport, as if reading from it.

'Why wouldn't I be?' Hesse spoke with an impeccable English accent that had a hint of upper-class drawl.

'Well,' said Edgar, tapping the desk with the passport as he did so. 'That's one of a number of things about you that puzzles me. You're travelling under this Swiss passport in the name of Henri Hesse. But do you not also have a British passport in the name of Henry Hunter?'

The man hesitated before nodding. Edgar noticed he was perspiring.

'I'm sure you'd be more comfortable if you removed your hat and coat.'

17

There was another pause while Hesse got up to hang his hat and coat on the back of the door.

'So you accept you're also known as Henry Hunter?'

The man nodded again.

'Passport?'

'You have it there.'

'If I were in your position Herr Hesse, I think I'd adopt a more co-operative manner altogether. I mean your British passport: the one in the name of Henry Hunter.'

'What about it?'

'I should like to see it.'

Henry Hunter hesitated.

'For the avoidance of doubt, Herr Hesse, I should tell you I have the right to search every item in your possession: the British passport please?'

Henry lifted the tan briefcase on to his lap, angled it towards him and opened it just wide enough for one hand to reach in. He retrieved a thick manila envelope, from which he removed the passport and handed it to Edgar who spent a few minutes studying it.

'Henry Richard Hunter: born Surrey, 6th November, 1909; making you 29.'

'Correct.'

Edgar held up the Swiss passport in his left hand and the British passport in his right, and moved them up and down, as if trying to work out which were the heavier.

'Bit odd, isn't it? Two passports: different names, same person?'

'Possibly, but I very legitimately have two nationalities. I cannot see...'

'We can come to that in a moment. The first thing then that puzzles me about you is you have a perfectly valid British passport in the name of Henry Hunter, which you used to enter this country on the 1st August. But, two weeks later, you're trying to leave the country using an equally valid passport, but this time it's a Swiss one in a different name.'

There was a long silence. Through the window both men could see Swissair flight 1075 edge on to the runway. Edgar walked over to the window and gazed out at the aircraft before turning back to face Henry, raising his eyebrows as he did so.

'Any explanation?'

Henry shrugged. Edgar returned to the desk and reopened his notebook. He took a fountain pen from his pocket.

'We can return to the business of flights in a moment. Let's look again at your different names. What can you tell me about that?'

'Will I be able to get on the next flight? There's one to Geneva at three o'clock I think. It would be most inconvenient if I didn't get back to Switzerland today.'

'Let's see how we get on with the explanation you're about to give me, eh? You were telling me how you manage to have two nationalities and two names.'

Henry shrugged, as though he could not understand why this would require any explanation.

'Terribly straightforward, really. I was born here in Surrey as it happens, hence Henry Hunter and the British passport. My father died when I was 14 and a year or so later my mother met a Swiss man and married him fairly soon after. We moved to Switzerland, first to Zürich and then Geneva. When I was 18, I became a Swiss national, and for the purposes of that I used my stepfather's surname. In the process, Henry became Henri. So you see, there's really no mystery. I apologise if it turns out to have been in any way irregular as far as the British Government is concerned: I'd be happy to clear matters up at the British consulate in Geneva if that helps. Do you think I'll be able to make the three o'clock Geneva flight?'

'There are a few more questions, Mr Hunter. I'm sure you understand. What is your job?'

Henry shifted in his seat, clearly uncomfortable.

'I don't have a career as such. My stepfather was very wealthy and had property all over Switzerland. I travel around to check on them – keep the tenants happy and make sure they pay their rent on time, that kind of thing: nothing onerous. I also did some work with a travel agency and a bit of translation. I've managed to keep busy enough.'

Edgar spent a few minutes flicking through his notebook and the two passports. At one stage, he made some notes, as if copying something from one of the documents. He then consulted a map he'd removed from his jacket pocket.

'You said that your stepfather was very wealthy...'

'... He died a couple of years ago.'

'And where did you live?'

'Near Nyon, by the lake.'

Edgar nodded approvingly.

'But I see you now live in the centre of Geneva, on the Rue de

Valais?'

'That's right.'

'And how would you describe that area?'

'Pleasant enough.'

'Really? From what I remember of Geneva that's rather on the wrong side of the tracks. Overlooking the railway line are you?'

'To an extent, yes.'

'Well, either one is overlooking the railway line or one is not?'

'Yes, we do overlook it.'

'Sounds rather like a fall from grace. Wish to tell me about it?'

Edgar selected another cigarette and he had smoked most of it before Henry began to answer. He appeared to be distressed, his voice now much quieter.

'After my stepfather died, it transpired he had another family, in Luzern. Of course, with hindsight that explains why he spent so much time in Zürich on business; my mother never accompanied him on those trips. The family in Luzern, it turned out, were the only legitimate family as far as Swiss law is concerned and therefore had first claim on his estate. I don't fully understand why, but my mother's lawyer assures us there is nothing whatsoever we can do about it. The property by the lake near Nyon turned out to be rented and the various bank accounts my mother had access to were more or less empty. We quickly went from being very comfortable to very hard up: hence the flat by the railway line. We've only been able to survive as we have because my mother had some funds of her own, not very much, and her jewellery: fortunately there was quite a lot of that. She's had to sell most of it. I do as much freelance translation as possible at the international organisations, but work isn't easy to find at the moment. These are difficult times on the continent.'

'As one gathers. So the purpose of your visit back to England – to get away from it all?'

'Family business, friends. That type of thing.'

Edgar stood up and removed his jacket, draping it carefully over the back of his chair before walking to the front of the desk and sitting on it. His knees were just inches from the other man's face. When he spoke it was in a very quiet voice, as if there was someone else in the room he didn't want to hear.

'*Family business, friends. That type of thing...* What you need to know Mr Hunter is that we already know an awful lot about you. We have, as they say, been keeping something of an eye on you. It would save a good deal of time if you were to be honest with me. So please could you be more specific about the family business you mentioned?'

'You said "we". Who do you mean by "we"?'

Edgar leaned back, pointedly ignoring the question.

'You were going to tell me about your family business, Mr Hunter.'

'My aunt died in July. She was my late father's elder sister. I was attending her funeral.'

'My condolences. Were you close to her?'

'Not especially, but I was her closest living relative.'

'And you are a beneficiary of the will, no doubt?'

'Yes.'

'And how much did you inherit, Mr Hunter?'

The Swissair DC-3 was now beginning to taxi down the

runway. A tanker was turning around in front of the building, filling the room with the smell of fuel. Henry shifted in his chair.

'By the sounds of it, I suspect you probably already know the answer to that.'

Edgar had returned to his chair and leaned back in it so it tilted against the window. As he did so, he crossed his arms high on his chest, staring long and hard at Henry.

'What I'm curious about, Mr Hunter, is whether my answer is going to be the same as yours. How about if I endeavour to answer my own question and you stop me if I say anything incorrect?'

'Before you do, could I ask whether you are a police officer?'

'No.'

'If you're not a police officer, what authority do you have to question me like this?'

Edgar laughed, as if he found Henry's remark to be genuinely amusing.

'Mr Hunter. When you find out on what authority I operate you will very much regret asking that question. So, shall I tell you my version of why I think you came over here?'

Henry loosened his tie and turned around in his chair, looking longingly at the door, as if he were hoping someone would come in and explain the whole business had been a terrible misunderstanding.

'Louise Alice Hunter was, as you correctly say, your late father's elder sister and you were indeed her only surviving relative.' Edgar had now opened his notebook and was referring to it as he spoke. 'She was 82 years of age and had been a resident in the Green Lawns Residential Home near Buckingham for nine years. The matron of the home informs us that you dutifully came over to visit her once a year. You visited her last November and then again in May, shortly before she died. On each of those visits you were accompanied by her solicitor. Am I correct so far?'

Henry said nothing.

'I shall assume then that you will point out if anything I say is incorrect. Your aunt died on the 24th July and you flew here on the 1st August, which was a Tuesday, if I am correct. You travelled straight to Buckinghamshire, where the funeral took place last Thursday, which would have been the 9th. So far, nothing remarkable, eh?'

Henry nodded.

'But this is where an otherwise very ordinary story does become somewhat less ordinary: sordid, perhaps. I am now relying on a statement kindly provided by a Mr Martin Hart, who, as you're aware, is your aunt's solicitor and the man who accompanied you on your last visits to your aunt. According to Mr Hart, your aunt's estate amounted to a not insubstantial eight thousand pounds, all of which was held in a deposit account administered by Mr Hart. You are indeed a beneficiary of that will; the main beneficiary most certainly, but – crucially – not the sole beneficiary. There were bequests totalling some one thousand pounds to various friends, staff and charities, but after Mr Hart had deducted fees due to him and duty was paid to Exchequer, you would expect to receive a sum of just under six thousand pounds: certainly a handsome sum. Does this sound correct to you?'

'If you say so. You do seem to know a good deal more than I do.'

'But there's a small problem, from your point of view. That

money could only be passed to you once probate was granted, which could take many months, perhaps even up to a year. We've already established you and your mother have serious financial problems. Your inheritance would restore you to a position of financial security. You would once again be wealthy. However, waiting for probate is bad enough, but with the very likely – some would say imminent – possibility of war, you had a quite understandable concern that you may not be able to get that money out of England and into Switzerland for quite a long time. I...'

'... You're making a number of assumptions here, Edgar. What makes you think I've done anything improper? I...'

'Mr Hunter, who said anything about doing anything improper? I certainly didn't. But, as you raise the subject, let me tell you what the most obliging Mr Hart has told us. According to him, he was prevailed upon by you to cut a few corners, as he put it, and to ensure the entire funds of the deposit account were released straight away. This is not only improper, it is also illegal.'

Henry shifted in his chair and pulled a large handkerchief from a trouser pocket to mop his brow. Edgar had now removed a pair of reading glasses from a crocodile-skin case and, after polishing them for longer than necessary, he began to read from a document he'd extracted from the desk drawer.

'According to the best legal advice available to me, there's no question that both Mr Hart and you committed a crime, namely conspiracy to defraud. My learned friends tell me that on the evidence they've seen, a conviction would be extremely likely and a term of imprisonment would almost certainly ensue. They say there is ample *prima face* evidence to show you have conspired to defraud His Majesty's Exchequer of the duties owed to it from your great aunt's estate and you had conspired to prevent the other beneficiaries of the will from receiving the money bequeathed to them. Fraud, Mr Hunter, is a most serious criminal offence. Confronted with our evidence Mr Hart has, as I say, been most co-operative. He claims that due to a health issue, as he describes it, he allowed himself to be persuaded against his better judgement to release the funds. He admits he received a much larger fee than he would ordinarily have expected. Apparently...'

'It's not as bad as it sounds, I have to tell you.' Edgar was taken aback by how forceful Henry was sounding. 'I told Hart that if I was able to take the money to Switzerland while I could, then I'd be in a position to return the money owed to the exchequer and the other beneficiaries very soon, certainly before probate would ordinarily have been granted.'

'Really? I think you and Mr Hart cooked up a somewhat clever scheme whereby you were counting on war being declared. Mr Hart believed that, in those circumstances, he could apply to be granted a stay of probate until such a time as you were in a position to claim. In other words, Mr Hunter, he would use the war as an excuse: pretend to keep the money in the deposit account until after the war, whenever that is. Except, of course, the money would not be in the deposit account, it would be with you in Switzerland. Apparently, he – you – may well have got away with it had not the matron at the home overheard some conversation about it between yourself and Mr Hart, and contacted the police.'

'It would all have been paid back, I promise you. Once I

deposited it in Switzerland, I would have transferred what I owed back. It seemed easier to send the money back from Switzerland rather than wait for probate then have it transferred from London.'

'Really? All we need to do now is find the money, eh Hunter? Do you want me to hazard a guess as to where it could be?'

Henry sat very still and stared across the airport as Edgar stood up and walked around the desk. Once in front of Henry he bent down to pick up the two leather briefcases and placed them both on the desk.

'Keys?'

Without saying anything or diverting his gaze from the runway, Henry reached into the inside pocket of his jacket and produced a set of keys, which he handed to Edgar.

It took Edgar a full 20 minutes to remove all the bundles of banknotes from the two briefcases, assembling the different denominations in separate piles. Not a word was exchanged during this process, which Henry watched with some interest, as if he had never seen so much money before. By the time Edgar had finished, there were four piles: one comprised the bundles of ten shilling notes, another the one pound notes, then five pound notes and ten pound notes. The pile of the large, white fives was by far the largest.

Edgar stepped back from the desk and stood beside Henry. The entire surface of the desk was covered in money.

'I've only of course been able to do an approximate count, but I'd say that there's seven thousand pounds there. Would that be correct, Mr Hunter?'

'More or less. I think you'll find it's more like six thousand, eight hundred pounds. Mr Hart claimed rather late in the day he needed another two hundred pounds – for expenses, apparently.'

'Two hundred pounds doesn't seem to me to be very much considering the impact this is likely to have on his professional career.'

'It's all been rather rushed, Edgar. As it was such a large sum of cash we had to withdraw it from a main branch of the Midland Bank in the city. We were only able to get hold of it this morning.'

'Yes, I'm aware of all that Mr Hunter.' Edgar was still standing next to Henry, with a hand on his shoulder. 'In a moment some colleagues of mine are going to come and take you away. I shall look after the money and all your possessions. We shall meet again in a few days.'

* * *

A few minutes later, Henry Hunter had been escorted from the airport in handcuffs by three uniformed police officers. In the office overlooking the runway, Edgar removed his tie, lit another cigarette and dialled a London number from the telephone nestling between the bundles of banknotes on the desk.

'It's Edgar.'

'I thought it might be you. How did it go?'

'Very much according to plan.'

'Good. We're on then?'

'Yes. Indeed. We're on, as you put it Porter.'

'And what's he like?'

'Rather as we were expecting. Not altogether the most agreeable of types, but then that's hardly a disqualification in our line of work, is it?'

'Too true… and, um, any hint at all of… you know?'

'No, none whatsoever. He was rather impressive in that respect, I must say. Had one not been aware, one would really have had no idea at all.'

'Splendid. What now?'

'I think he needs a few days on his own. It ought to be easy enough after that.'

* * *

Alex Gerlis

Chapter 2: London, August 1939

It was early on a blazing hot Monday afternoon – one of the first truly hot days that August – when Edgar stepped out into Whitehall and paused for a good minute or two on the pavement to enjoy the sun. There was an uncharacteristic bounce in his step as he strolled up Whitehall to Trafalgar Square where he caught the number 12 bus and headed west. He needed some time to think and what, he thought, could be a more pleasant place to do that from than the top deck of a London bus?

He stayed on the bus until Notting Hill Gate then walked over to Kensington Park Road, taking care as he did so to ensure he was not being followed. He was about to walk, but a number 52 bus came along and he decided to hop on. He stayed on the bus until it was halfway down Ladbroke Grove. He waited a full five minutes at the bus stop to ensure his tail was clear then headed north-west to where the grandeur of Holland Park petered out to a series of plain and forgettable buildings. He passed a grocery shop with a long and excited queue outside it and briefly wondered whether he should join it, as one did these days, but a glance at his watch made him realise he needed to hurry.

Edgar paused outside a small alley, allowed an elderly lady to be pulled past him by a pair of yapping terriers then entered the alley. At the end of it he pressed a bell and a large iron gate swung open. He was now in a small courtyard: a policeman saluted and unlocked a door and from there Edgar descended three flights of stairs before finding himself in what was, to all intents and purposes, a small police station.

* * *

Minutes later he was sitting in a stuffy windowless room in the basement with a police inspector. 'What I would like to know is what his general mood is like: what he does; how he behaves; what he says – that kind of thing, Inspector Hill. I'm sure you know the score.'

The inspector removed a notebook from the top pocket of his uniform jacket and flicked through a few pages.

'Let's see then… in a pretty bad mood when he arrived here on Monday night, shouting the odds, insisting he had a right to a lawyer. Shut up once he'd had something to eat. Next day he was on again about a lawyer. We kept him in his cell until Wednesday afternoon when he was brought in here and I read him the riot act: told him that under emergency regulations he had no right to a lawyer. He asked for a copy of those regulations and I told him it was in the post, which didn't seem to reassure him. Thursday: he's still making a fuss so we bring in a couple of the plainclothes boys as you suggested and that does the trick. They tell him he's being done for conspiracy to commit fraud and that if he pleads guilty and is terribly lucky with the judge he may get away with five years. Otherwise, he can double it.'

'And how did he take that?'

'Very much as we would have hoped: a few tears before bedtime. He begged to be able to send a telegram to his mother; told anyone who'd listen that there had been a terrible misunderstanding and he'd happily donate the money to charity.'

'And I presume you then did as I asked?'

'Of course: plainclothes boys returned on Friday morning and he provides us with a neat statement, confessing all. I have it here.'

From a drawer in the desk between him and Edgar the inspector produced three closely typed sheets of paper, each signed with something of a flourish. Edgar carefully read then re-read the statement.

'Signed on Friday 18th August, good: and since then?'

'We allowed him to stew over the weekend. Other than being brought to this room and into the corridor outside his cell for exercise a couple of times a day, he's been locked in his cell all day. He hasn't seen daylight in a week. Even so...'

'You're hesitating, Hill.'

'It's just I would have expected someone like him to be even more affected by his ordeal. According to the guards he doesn't sleep well, and he's unquestionably shaken and has signed the confession, but he has a resolve about him I wouldn't have expected. When he was first brought here he was a nervous character: quite jumpy. But I warn you Edgar, there's a certain steel about him.'

'We'll see, shall we? Anyway, well done Hill. Good work. Better bring him in.'

Despite what the police inspector had said, Henry Hunter looked more worn in the week since Edgar had last seen him, although his smile was still in place. He had lost a bit of weight; dark rings had appeared around his eyes along with two or three day's growth of beard. He appeared to be relieved to see Edgar.

'I thought we may meet again.'

'How has your week been, Hunter? Treated well?'

'Well, I haven't been tortured, if that's what you mean. But they wouldn't even let me have a newspaper and I can't believe I'm unable to see a solicitor or contact my mother. Is that right?'

'Depends on what you mean by "is that right?", Hunter. What's *correct* is you've not been able to contact either a lawyer or your mother, whether that's *in order* is entirely another matter. You'll discover in due course that we have very good reasons for pursuing this course of action. We have, incidentally, taken the liberty of sending her a telegram in your name saying that all is well and she's not to worry.'

'Can I ask, Edgar, whether this a regular police station though? I do seem to be rather... isolated.'

'It is a police station, although you are at present the only person in custody in it. I understand your predicament has been explained to you by some officers here?'

'Yes. Conspiracy to commit fraud apparently and if I'm very, very lucky I shall get away with five years in prison. I've signed a statement.'

'And did they add that if you're found guilty or plead guilty then all of the money we found in your possession will be confiscated? After the other beneficiaries and the duty have been paid, you'll be left with nothing.'

'They didn't mention that, no.'

'So all in all, Hunter, a bit of a mess eh?'

'So it would seem.'

A long silence ensured during which Edgar lit a cigarette and wrote some notes in his book.

'I'm told the prison regime is likely to be especially harsh during wartime. Most prisoners are required to undertake quite onerous physical labour.'

Henry said nothing, unsure how he was meant to react.

'However, there is an alternative Hunter. There is a way of avoiding prison and even keeping most of your money. You'd be able to return to Switzerland and see your mother again.'

Henry's eyes lit up and, suspicious as he was, he found it hard to suppress a thin smile.

'Tell me more.'

'Before I can do that I need to know for sure whether you're interested or not.'

'Yes, of course I'm interested.'

'Very well then. This is, to all intents and purposes, the point of no return. Once I tell you what the alternative is, your options really are very limited. Do you understand that?'

Henry nodded.

'I work for a Government agency whose purpose is to gather intelligence. As you're no doubt aware, this country is perilously close to war with Germany. We urgently need to expand and improve our intelligence networks across Europe; they're in a pretty woeful state at the moment. As strange as it may seem, Mr Hunter, you are very well placed indeed. You have genuine Swiss and British passports, and are fluent in German and French.'

Henry leant forward, his hands touching the desk, eager to hear more.

'What would you require me to do?'

'I had hoped I'd made that apparent Mr Hunter – Henry. To help us gather intelligence.'

'Be a spy?'

'Correct.'

Outside in the corridor a metal gate slammed shut and there was a murmur of voices passing by. Henry laughed.

'A spy? You must be joking: what on earth makes you so sure I'm up to this?'

'We aren't: we'll give you some training, of course, but our priority is to get you back to Switzerland. That's where we need you to be. For us, your dual identity and your ability to move around what may be enemy territory as a Swiss national are invaluable. And don't forget, we have a hold over you.'

'Which is?'

'If you turn down our offer, the alternative is a lengthy spell in one of His Majesty's prisons. Furthermore, there is the question of the money.'

'You mean my aunt's?'

'Yes, the six thousand pounds that's legally yours but which you'll lose as a result of the court case. However, if you agree to work for us then not only will there be no court case but you'll also receive the money: all six thousand pounds of it. A bank account will be opened in your name at the Quai des Bergues branch of Credit Suisse in Geneva. If you accept my offer, the sum of five hundred pounds will be transferred to that account immediately. Thereafter, we'll transfer a further one hundred pounds a month into that account for as long as you work for us.'

Henry frowned, trying to work something out. 'Hang on. At that rate, it could take, I don't know, years for me to receive all my money!'

'Henry, you're not obliged to take up our offer. We cannot *force* you to be a spy. Look, it may be a while before we call upon your services, but if you undertake any specific mission successfully then we can consider advancing further lump sums of five hundred pounds. And of course, we'll cover any expenses you may incur.'

'How about if you were to advance a thousand pounds? My mother and I have considerable debts to clear.'

'Henry: you really aren't in a position to negotiate.'

'Will there be any danger – you said something about "enemy territory"?'

Edgar laughed, standing up as he did so, stretching himself.

'Of course there'll be danger: plenty of it, I imagine. What's the point of being a bloody spy otherwise! But if you ask me, even with that risk of danger, it's still a more agreeable lifestyle than ten years hard labour here.'

'Ten? I thought it would be five if I pleaded guilty?'

'Believe me Henry. If you decline my offer and this goes to court, it'll be ten years. Come on now…' Edgar tapped his watch. 'What's it to be? Are you coming with me, or shall I leave you here with the police for the wheels of justice to start rolling?'

Edgar had expected more questions, more hesitation and more signs of nerves, but with what seemed to be barely a second thought, Henry Hunter clapped his hands and allowed his thin smile to become a broad one.

'All sounds most interesting Edgar. I'm ready to join you.'

* * *

Chapter 3: to France and Switzerland, November 1939

Henry Hunter's training as a British agent had been entrusted to a classics don who had moved from a crumbling Oxford college to a crumbling country house somewhere north of London for the purpose of training his special scholars, as he liked to call them. He never tired of telling them that the transition from teaching classics to teaching espionage was a natural one.

'Classics,' he would say, 'are all about war, human failings, chance and intrigue: not so very different to spying.'

Captain Edgar had visited the country house once a week to check on Henry's progress. He was taking his time: physical fitness was an issue, as was his radio training, but he was regarded as a brilliant map reader and became proficient with a revolver. It was only towards the end of October that the classics don conceded he was more or less ready.

'My opinion is that the characteristics of a spy are innate. It is a skill one is born with: it is, I believe, part of someone's personality. You see, we all too often make the mistake of taking someone who appears to have all the attributes of a spy then train them in the specifics of the job. They could fly through the training with an A-plus, but that wouldn't necessarily make them a good spy. Some of those A-plus types make hopeless spies once they're out in the field. A truly effective spy will have some personality flaw or such like which marks them out from others. They are used to walking in the shadows, on the other side of the street, slightly apart from the crowd but not so much so that people would notice them.'

'Very interesting, but does Hunter make it as a spy?'

'Good heavens, yes, Edgar. I don't think I've ever come across someone quite so well-qualified. The most dangerous moment for a spy is when they make that transition from what one might call "normal society" into the world of espionage. For the vast majority of people that can be too great a wrench, they have too much to lose. But if you feel you've never really been part of society, that you've always been on the margins of it, then you're a natural spy. I've rarely come across such a good example of this than Hunter.'

* * *

A week later, Henry and Edgar were being driven down a lane on a moonless night when Henry chose to break the uneasy silence that had accompanied them since leaving the country house.

'Can't see a bloody thing in this dark Edgar – and what's happened to all the road signs?'

'I appreciate that you have been holed up in the country for the past three months or so Henry, but it can't have escaped even your attention that we're now at war with Germany, even if it doesn't actually feel like it. Hence the blackout.'

'And the road signs?'

'No need to help any German spies who are lost, is there?'

'Can you at least tell me where we are, Edgar?'

'No.'

'You're treating me like I'm a bloody prisoner.'

'Which but for the grace of God and my own good offices, Hunter, you actually would be – and for many years. Don't forget that.'

'How could I? You know how grateful I am to you.'

'Less of the sarcasm if you please, Hunter. I can tell you we've been driving south and we're now in Hampshire, which is as much as you need to know.'

'Any particular part of Hampshire?'

'Obviously, Hunter, but you don't need to know any more than that. In any case, you'll be gone within a day or two. Look, we've arrived: better go and get some sleep. We'll start the briefing first thing in the morning.'

* * *

First thing in the morning for Edgar was around two hours earlier than Henry had hoped it would be. It was still dark when he was woken by a knock at the door, followed by the sound of a key turning in the lock and a stiff bolt sliding open. The soldier who woke him – the same one who'd escorted him to the room the previous night – announced he would need to be ready in ten minutes.

Edgar was sitting at a long table in a large office, the room already wreathed in smoke. He was wearing a coat and a high window was open, letting in the cold morning air and the distinctive smell of recently turned soil. The table was crowded with files and documents. As Henry entered the room, he was followed in by another soldier bearing a tray with a pot of tea, toast and boiled eggs.

Henry had little appetite, but Edgar tucked in. He ate in silence for five minutes while Henry nibbled on a slice of toast and sipped the weak tea.

'Right: now we begin! Tonight, Hunter, you will begin your journey back to Switzerland. I need to be very clear and you need to fully understand that from now on, you are working for British Intelligence. It's a role that carries few rewards and privileges, other than that of serving your country. On the other hand, you'll find this life that has been chosen for you will have plenty of responsibility and not a few dangers. There'll be long periods of tedium and you'll find the fact that you can't confide in anyone makes it a most difficult and stressful existence. I need hardly tell you the world of espionage is not one of glamour or excitement. The most common emotions are boredom and fear.'

Henry nodded. This was not the first time he'd heard this, but now his return to Switzerland was imminent he began to feel nervous.

'I'll spend the next few hours briefing you. I shall remind you of what is expected of you. I'll tell you everything you need to know.'

And so it continued for many hours. As noon approached and the sun became brighter, sandwiches were brought in along with a couple of bottles of beer. Edgar began to appear more relaxed than Henry had ever seen him.

'Usually in these situations, Hunter, one spends a good deal of one's time making sure someone in your position is absolutely familiar with their new identity. In your case, however, the Henri Hesse identity is so good, there'd be no merit whatsoever in furnishing you with a new and false one.

'You leave tonight, Henry. I know that flying is your preferred method of travel around Europe, but I'm afraid that now we're at war there are no more civilian flights to either France or Switzerland, so you're going by boat. A troopship, the *SS Worthing* is leaving Southampton this evening. She's taking a contingent of the Royal Fusiliers over the Channel. She'll dock at Cherbourg early tomorrow morning and you'll travel from there to Paris. You will stay in Paris tomorrow night then travel by train the following day to Geneva, using your Swiss identity. Do you understand?'

Henry nodded.

'Good. Your mother is expecting you: send her a telegram from Paris giving details of your arrival. Once you arrive, you'll tell her as little as possible. All the letters you wrote while you were being trained have been sent on to her, along with two payments of one hundred pounds into her own bank account. As far as she's concerned, you were staying at a guest house in Fulham while you were sorting out your aunt's will. That was the address from where your letters were sent.'

'It's going to be hard to convince her why those financial arrangements took so long.'

'But not as long as it could have been, eh? Don't try and explain too much. Just tell her it was far more complicated to transfer money out of the country than you'd realised and in the end you had to settle for it being paid in instalments. The initial five hundred pounds deposit and the two hundred pounds she has been sent should ensure you can now lead a more agreeable lifestyle, along with the one hundred pounds per month, of course.'

'When will I be contacted Edgar? How will I know what to do?'

'Within a day or two of your arrival back in Geneva you are to go to the Quai des Bergues branch of Credit Suisse, where we've opened an account in your name as promised. You are to ask for an appointment with Madame Ladnier. Under no circumstances are you to see anyone else there. Madame Ladnier is a senior clerk there and looks after new clients. You are to go through paperwork with her, then she'll activate the account and you'll be able to access the money. Madame Ladnier is, very indirectly, a contact of ours, but you must never discuss intelligence matters with her: she is no more than a conduit, a messenger if you like. However, if you need to contact us urgently, you can do so through her. You can do this either at the bank, which is preferable, or on her home telephone number – she will give that to you. That, you understand, is most irregular, so please do be discreet. If you need to contact us urgently, simply tell her you need to change some Swiss Francs into Italian Lira. If there are any changes in your circumstances, you must inform her. Do you understand all this?'

Henry understood. Edgar got him to repeat it.

'When we make contact with you, it won't be through Madame Ladnier. It could be in anything from a couple of weeks to a few months. Depends on what we need you to do. Chances are that the first job will be something relatively straightforward, probably within Switzerland. Shouldn't be anything too dangerous; a warm-up, if you like. What will happen is this: you'll be approached in the street by someone asking for directions to the Old Town. What is it you call it in Geneva?'

'The *vieille ville*'.

'They'll be carrying a copy of the previous day's edition of the

Tribune de Genève. In reply to their question, you're to ask them if they'd prefer to walk or to take the tram. They'll tell you they'd prefer to walk if you can point them in the right direction. You'll explain you are walking that way and they're welcome to follow you. Take any route to the Old Town. At some point after entering it, they'll overtake you. You're not to acknowledge them, just carry on walking at the same pace, but now you're following them. When you see them place the *Tribune de Genève* in a waste bin outside a building, you are to enter the building and wait. If no-one has approached you after five minutes, you leave the building and return home. But if someone joins you and introduces themselves as Marc, you are to go with him. He will take you to meet your main contact. At that moment, your new career will have begun. Please repeat all of this to me Henry.'

* * *

Edgar's briefing finished just after 1.00 and Henry was escorted back to his room. Edgar urged him to try and get some sleep: it was going to be a long night and he shouldn't count on being able to sleep on the boat. In his room he saw a case had been carefully packed for him, along with his two briefcases. A change of clothes was laid out on the bed. Edgar explained that everything had been carefully checked to ensure nothing incriminating was in his possession in case he was searched.

He was woken at 4.00 and the soldier who had been looking after him told him a bath had been prepared. By 4.30 he was back in the office where his briefing had been held that morning. The soldier carried his bag and Henry carried his own briefcases. Edgar was nervously fiddling with his leather gloves.

'There's a train from Cherbourg at 10.15 in the morning, which you're to take to Paris. You're to go to the telegram bureau inside Gare Saint-Lazare as soon as you arrive and send a telegram with the following message to this address.'

He handed a slip of paper to Henry. The message read: 'Arrived safely Paris stop regards to all stop.'

'Memorise that and destroy the paper. Then go to find a hotel and, the next morning, take the train to Geneva. You know your way around Paris?'

Henry shrugged. 'I've been once or twice.'

Edgar pointed to the table. 'Here are your British and Swiss passports, which we've been looking after for you. Here's a receipt for the guesthouse in Fulham to show you've been staying there since the middle of August. In this envelope is more paperwork than you could imagine from various firms of solicitors and the Midland Bank relating to the release of money from your aunt's estate, including a terribly helpful letter from the bank explaining the money can only be transferred legally to a foreign country in instalments. Can I ask, is your mother the inquisitive type?'

'Do you mean, is she nosey?'

Edgar laughed. 'Well, yes.'

'She could not be more nosey, if I was honest. Always poking about in my things.'

'Good. Don't show all these letters and documents to her, then, just leave them for her to find. It'll be much more convincing that way and she then ought to believe your account of why you were kept here for so long. It's essential she never suspects what you're up to, do you understand?'

Henry nodded.

'Hang on, before you put all that in your briefcase, here's some more money: twenty pounds worth of French francs which ought to be more than enough for your hotel tomorrow night and the ticket to Geneva, plus meals. And here in this envelope is fifty pounds worth of Swiss Francs, which ought to cover any expenses you may incur in the foreseeable future in Switzerland.'

At five o'clock a car pulled up outside the building and the two men left the office and walked quietly to it. Edgar helped Henry put his cases in the boot then joined him in the back.

'I thought you'd like me to see you off.'

* * *

Henry Hunter boarded the SS *Worthing* in Southampton before the troops embarked and was taken straight to a tiny cabin in the officers' quarters, which had a bunk and little else. The captain came in and told him he was to remain in the cabin for the duration of the voyage.

They docked in Cherbourg just after seven the next morning and at nine o'clock the captain came into his cabin. He was safe to leave now, all the troops had disembarked. A taxi was waiting on the quay to take him to the station.

Henry was shocked at how France had changed. Everywhere there were troops – British as well as French – and people looked pinched, worried and in a hurry. None of which were characteristics he'd usually associate with the French. Normally the train journey would have been jolly, with people chatting. Now, it was quiet. People stared out of the windows and said little. It was as if a whole nation was wrapped in its own thoughts, unwilling to share its fears.

The train pulled into Gare Saint-Lazare just before three o'clock: the journey had taken longer than scheduled due to a lengthy and unexplained stop outside Caen. If Cherbourg had been quiet and the train silent, Gare Saint-Lazare was not. Half of Paris seemed to be leaving through the station and the other half arriving into it. He found the telegram bureau and sent the message to London. He had little doubt he would be watched at the station: requiring him to send the telegram was a good way of ensuring that. He then walked out of the vast concourse of Gare Saint-Lazare and away from Clichy and its temptations.

The further you walk the harder it is for you to be followed.

So he headed south then east, down Boulevard Haussmann where the elegant shops and straight lines afforded him plenty of opportunity to observe every angle around him. He entered a leatherwear shop to look at wallets and a *tabac* to buy matches, and in Boulevard St Martin he joined a long queue in a *patisserie* to buy an almond croissant. The ten-minute wait allowed him enough time to be certain no-one was following. He decided to look for somewhere to stay around Republique and found a small hotel by the Canal Saint Martin, where he took a comfortable room with its own private bathroom overlooking, as requested, the front of the hotel. He then spent an hour sitting by the window, behind the half-open shutters, observing the street below. When he was as certain as he could be that no-one had followed him and no-one was watching from the street, he closed the shutters and drew the curtain. After a bath and a rest he left his room at six thirty.

Had anyone checked in since his arrival, he asked the *patron* at reception? He was not sure if a colleague was joining him or not. The *patron* shook his head. He understood, he said, with a knowing and even conspiratorial look. Henry wasn't sure what it was the *patron* understood, but he slipped him a generous few francs for what he said was an already excellent service and explained he may be back late, perhaps very late. Would the *patron* be so good as to let him have a key? *Of course.* And would he also be able to perhaps slip a note under his door to let him know if his friend arrived, or indeed if anyone else checked in or even asked for him? Naturally, said the *patron*. *It would my pleasure.* Henry knew that, this being Paris, the *patron* would assume that Henry was conducting an affair: in such circumstances it would be his pleasure, indeed his duty as *patron* to do whatever he could to assist.

Henry walked out into the bitter Parisian night air, where a wind had swept up the nearby Seine and was settling over the city. He waited in the entrance of the hotel for ten minutes and, once he was certain he was alone, he headed south, turning up the collar of his coat as he did so.

The real danger of being a spy is that which you court yourself.

He headed in a south-easterly direction, away from his destination. On the Rue de Crussol, just before it crossed Boulevard Voltaire, he found a telephone kiosk. The call lasted no more than 30 seconds, much of which was taken up by a pause by the person who had answered the phone.

Very well. You know where to come. Give us one hour. Be careful.

So he walked down Boulevard Voltaire then found a tiny café in the Passage Saint-Pierre Amelot. There were four two-seater tables, crammed into a space where three would have been a tight squeeze. One of the tables was occupied by a young couple. Henry took a vacant one, making sure he faced the door. He remained there for half an hour: dinner was a bowl of soup with bread and an excellent omelette.

It took him 20 minutes to reach his destination from the café. The Marais was once swampland, then home to the aristocracy and now, as far as Henry could tell, in an advanced state of decay. It was the kind of area of which people would say it had known better days, though no-one alive could remember those better days. But Henry liked the anonymity of the Marais, with its obvious edge of danger that meant people hurried along and avoided each other. It wasn't relaxed and given over to enjoyment of life, like most other parts of Paris. It had its different groups; the Jews and their synagogues and little shops around the Rue de Rosiers; those too poor to have their own place and living with others in large crumbling houses; the prostitutes who couldn't make it in Clichy; the gamblers, the drinkers and the anarchists.

He knew the area very well and picked up his pace, darting up and down little alleys, doubling back on himself, pausing in darkened doorways and making it impossible for anyone to follow him. He emerged into the Rue de Bretagne and slipped into the entrance of a large grey building with enormous shuttered windows and waited. On the wall inside the entrance was a series of bells, one for each of the 20 apartments. Under the bells someone had drawn a small circle in pencil. On the opposite wall they had drawn a square. It was safe. He pressed a bell and went straight up to the top floor.

* * *

'You look very well. You've lost weight.'

'Yes, thank you Viktor.' Henry hesitated. He was about to return the compliment, but realised nothing could be further from the truth: the other man was bigger than ever, his face heavily lined and his large nose even redder. Viktor had greeted him with an embrace and had held him in it for a while, which made Henry feel less than comfortable. As he slowly emerged from the hug, the man held him at arm's length by the shoulders – one hand on each – as if to admire him. For a moment Henry feared the man was about to kiss him on the cheeks, as he was wont to do. He was always nervous in the Viktor's presence, not least after a long gap, as now. Anyone looking at him would have noticed that, for a brief moment, his thin smile had disappeared.

'I wasn't sure we'd ever see you again. Come, sit down. We have much to talk about.'

They were speaking in French, neither man's native language, which added to a formal, even tense air in the room. Two other men stood either side of the window, keeping watch through half-open shutters. Another man entered the room and announced it was all clear: no-one had followed him. He was sure of that.

'What will you drink? I seem to have everything here. Whisky?'

'No, not for me, thank you.'

'Really? That's the first time I've known you to turn down a whisky. What have they done to you?'

The man's look of concern broke into a broad grin as he poured himself a drink and pulled his chair closer to Henry's. 'This really has been a most unexpected development, most unexpected. And you're certain they suspect nothing?'

'I'm as certain as I can be,' said Henry.

Viktor shuffled his large frame around in the chair to make himself comfortable. From a side table he picked up a large notebook, expensively bound in brown leather. He produced a pencil from his top pocket and sharpened it with a penknife that came from another pocket, allowing the shavings to gather on the front of his jacket. He made a few notes before looking up at Henry and smiling, as if checking on him once again.

'We have two hours, maybe three. You need to tell me everything.'

* * *

Henry returned to the hotel just before one that morning. There was no note under the door from the *patron*. Despite his exhaustion, he slept only fitfully and woke at seven o'clock. He checked out of the hotel an hour later, stopped for a coffee and croissant nearby then caught a tram on the Boulevard du Temple down to the Gare de Lyon. He managed to book a good seat on the ten o'clock train to Geneva where he found himself in a carriage with six other passengers: a formally dressed Swiss businessman who tutted loudly if anyone came too near him; an elegantly dressed, elderly

French lady who spent most of the journey smiling wistfully out of the window and did not remove her leather gloves once during the journey; and a couple with their son and daughter who were, as far as Henry could tell, a year or two either side of ten. They seemed to be overburdened with suitcases and other bags, some of which they had to keep in the corridor. When the children spoke, which was not very often, they did so with strong Parisian accents. The parents spoke to the children in accented French, but to each other in what sounded to Henry like Polish and also a strange version of High German he'd never heard before. From what he could tell, they were anxious about crossing the border. The wife kept asking the husband if all the paperwork was in order. *I hope so. Who knows?* Whenever one of the family spoke, the Swiss businessman looked annoyed. On more than one occasion he caught Henry's eye, hoping to share his disapproval with him.

The journey was uneventful until around a quarter to six when the train pulled into Gare de Bellegarde, the last station in France before the Swiss border. For around ten minutes, the train just stood still, with no apparent reason for the delay. The businessman looked at his watch and shook his head. The French lady continued to look out of the window, smiling. Then they heard voices, working their way slowly down the train. Through the window Henry could just make out the shape of gendarmes patrolling along the tracks. The voices grew nearer and the parents looked even more anxious. *Everything will be alright?*, the wife asked the husband, in the strange German dialect. *I have no idea*, the husband replied. *Speak in French now: only in French.*

Five minutes later, two Swiss border guards and a French

gendarme entered the carriage. 'Papers please,' he said. 'A routine check: we'll have you on your way in a minute.'

Henry showed his Swiss passport. One Swiss border guard showed it to the other and they both nodded. 'No problem Monsieur Hesse.' Nor was there any problem with the businessman and the elegantly dressed lady. But for the family, it was different. Both guards looked at the papers in some detail and shook their heads, passing various documents to the bored-looking gendarme behind them.

'These papers are not in order,' one of them said to the father.

'But I was assured there would be no problem.'

'Well, there is. You have no valid papers here allowing you to enter Switzerland. It is not possible.'

The husband and wife exchanged glances; the wife nodded. *Do it.*

'Perhaps I could have a word with you in the corridor?' He gestured towards the children. *Away from them, please.*

Henry could just make out the man pleading with the guards, both of whom looked stone-faced. 'Perhaps I could pay for the visas now, I have the funds?' Henry could see the man open his wallet and attempt to press a wad of banknotes into the hand of one of the guards, who refused to take it.

'You are denied entry to Switzerland. You have to leave the train now,' he heard one of them say. Henry noticed the other guard grabbed the banknotes.

'You are in illegal possession of Swiss currency. We are confiscating it.'

The gendarme shrugged. *This is not my problem.* The father came back into the carriage, crestfallen and defeated. His wife was doing her best not to cry and the children looked frightened, as if they knew what was happening. The gendarme helped them to remove their cases. The elderly lady looked shocked and the businessman annoyed as baggage was removed from around him. A minute or so later, Henry watched as the family emerged onto the deserted platform and the train slowly began to move again. The businessman shook his head and muttered the word 'juifs'. The lady had stopped smiling.

The train pulled into Gare Cornavin just before seven o'clock. On the short walk home Henry was hit by the icy blast from the nearby Alps, bouncing into the city from the lake. Despite this and the burdens he now carried, he had the most unusual sensation of arriving somewhere he could call home.

* * *

At around the same time that Henry Hunter's train was leaving Gare de Lyon, Edgar took a call on a secure line in his office. It was Hurst from the Paris station.

'Well done Edgar, you've found a bit of a star there. He didn't half give my chaps the run-around.'

'You didn't lose him, did you Hurst? There'll be all hell to pay if you did.'

'Come on Edgar, you ought to know my boys better than that. He's very good, but in the end he made the mistake of assuming one can only be tracked from behind. We managed to keep tabs on him all last night, but only just.'

'Where did he end up?'
'The Marais, as we suspected he would.'
'And the people he met up with: you're sure of who they are?'
'Yes sir, we're absolutely certain. No question about it.'

* * *

Chapter 4: from Marseilles to Moscow, December 1939

Early in the afternoon of the first Monday of December a large man wearing a long, dark coat and a smart black fedora marched with surprising agility up from the *vieux port* in Marseilles to his *pension* overlooking the port and the Mediterranean beyond it.

He was Russian, but for the purposes of his visit he was a Swedish shipping agent from Gothenburg. He had been hanging around the *vieux port* for a few futile days, hoping to make contact with an Algerian who had apparently contacted a Communist Party official in the city with the promise of some secret documents of an unspecified nature. The Party official had now disappeared and the Algerian never showed up. It was the nature of the job he reflected, as the *pension* came into sight: unlike the fishermen he had been watching that morning selling their catch on the Quai des Belges, a spy had to become used the prey only occasionally succumbing to the bait.

He had decided to remain in Marseilles for another day or two; a ship was due in from Greece and Greek crews always offered the opportunity of good contacts. But when he returned to his *pension* there was a telegram waiting for him, sent from the main post office in Gothenburg.

'Mother ill stop return home soonest stop'

The Russian rarely allowed himself the indulgence of emotion, but he did that afternoon, sitting quietly in his room for a few minutes after he had packed and contemplating what a summons home could mean. He had survived, as he liked to see it, various such calls over the past few years, but feared his luck could not hold out much longer. A sensation of fear swept over him and it took the remains of the vodka by the side of the bed and a cold bath before he came to his senses. *I have done nothing wrong: No one in the service is indispensible, but I am closer to it than many.*

An hour later he had checked out of the *pension* and stopped at the main post office to send a telegram to Gothenburg to the effect that he was so concerned about mother he was returning home: **love to mother stop**. Then he headed to the port office, where he found the captain of a Turkish steamer leaving that evening for Istanbul who was more than happy to take a passenger, especially one who was offering to pay so generously. *We have a light load: with luck we should arrive on Saturday; maybe Sunday.*

The steamer duly arrived in Istanbul early on the Saturday evening and the captain took his passenger straight to the house of his wife's cousin, who sailed his trawler in the Black Sea. *Yes*, said the cousin. *He would be setting off as usual on Sunday morning: yes, he would be happy to sail to Odessa first; yes, that is very generous. Thank you sir!*

Odessa was a day and a half's hard sailing from Istanbul and, encouraged by the Russian's generosity, the skipper made it there late on the Monday afternoon. He went straight to the railway station: the night train to Moscow was leaving at a quarter to midnight. He had time to send a telegram announcing his arrival then find a café where he could eat familiar food and get used to hearing familiar languages around him once again.

It was past midnight when the train noisily pulled out of the station and, as the final leg of his voyage began, the fear that had struck him in Marseilles returned. It kept him wide awake until they reached Kharkov in the early hours of the morning, turning his stomach into knots and making his heart beat fast. Along with the fear came the doubt: *should I have stayed in France? I could so easily have disappeared from there.*

The train was held in Kharkov for three or four hours. As usual, there was no explanation and no complaints from his fellow passengers. He left the train to send another telegram to Moscow: he didn't want them to think he wasn't coming.

By the time dawn broke on the Wednesday morning they were approaching the outskirts of Moscow and the train slowed down. The Russian tried hard to compose himself. The cruellest part of this job was not the loneliness or the danger or the stress of swapping identities every few days: that was all to be expected. No, the worst part – the part he could never come to terms with – was that the one place you could call home, the place you risked your life for and suffered all the hardships on behalf of – was the place you feared most. He would have no idea whether the day that had just begun would end with a bullet to the head in the basement. It had happened to so many others, after all. But then he pulled himself together as he remembered what they instilled into all the new recruits: *Never question; never discuss; never hesitate.*

The train pulled into Kursky station at eight o'clock and he was met on the platform by two young men who escorted him to a waiting car, which he decided was a bad sign. It was a glorious day in Moscow and he began to feel quite emotional on the short journey. He resolved if he survived this trip and was sent back into the field, he would make plans. Next time he was summoned back, he'd disappear. He had worked for the service since 1920; he had outlived all those he had been recruited with and many more recruited after him. He knew he was good, but he also knew that he was not indispensible. What mattered most was that he did outlive his luck and now he feared this had run out on him.

The car drove straight into a basement, which he decided was another bad sign. He could feel his whole body trembling as he walked with his unsmiling escort to the lift. If it went down into the basement, he knew that was the end. Moments later they emerged onto the fifth floor and he had to bite his lip to stop tears of sheer relief. He was steered into a large office where there were half a dozen of them waiting, all of whom seemed to be pleased to see him. From that group, a familiar figure emerged and hugged the new arrival.

'Viktor: welcome home.'

* * *

He had been so well received that for a day or two after his arrival in Moscow he wondered whether this was some kind of elaborate trap. But it wasn't: they were clearly very pleased with him, but most of all they wanted to know about Henry. *Who would have thought it? Tell us everything? Does he realise how important he could be – do you realise how important he is? We need to handle him carefully.*

After three days in Moscow he was taken to one of the dachas outside the city that the service used. For the first time in years he could relax in the silence. A woman came in every day to cook and clean, and a younger woman arrived every evening and stayed with him until the following morning. The service could be brutal and cruel, especially to its own, but it knew how to look after those it was especially pleased with.

Viktor stayed in the dacha for a week before travelling to Stockholm and from there by sea back to France. But not once during that time was he ever in doubt that he owed all this to Henry. *Do you realise how important he is*, they had asked?

But Viktor certainly didn't need anyone to tell him how important Henry was. An agent he had recruited had in turn been recruited by the British.

Do I realise how important Henry is?

Important enough to have kept me alive.

* * *

Chapter 5: Switzerland, 1929–1930

It was a filthy evening sometime in late January 1929 when Henry emerged from the pink-stuccoed building on the university campus. The rain swept into Geneva from every direction: the Alps, the lake, France. He paused at the end of the flight of steps, already drenched and wondering whether to dash into the Old Town through Les Bastions or go back into the building and wait for the rain to abate.

He was still debating what to do when he felt a hand on his shoulder.

'You are deciding whether to brave the rain? Me too: who knows when it will stop? When it rains like this in Geneva it feels like it will rain forever.' It was the last speaker at the meeting, a handsome man in his late twenties with piercing blue eyes, thick black hair which touched his collar and a distinctive Parisian accent. Henry had never heard anyone quite so charismatic and mesmerising. He wore no tie but had a silk scarf wrapped stylishly around his neck, and when he spoke it was about the injustices in Europe and around the world, and how only the Communist Party had the answer. Henry had felt the hairs rise on the back of his neck; tears had even come to his eyes. 'Europe is in crisis: capitalism is in crisis. The solution is in our hands – your hands,' he had told the 30 or so people sparsely arranged around the large lecture hall.

'My name is Marcel by the way.' The Frenchman's hand was still on his shoulder as he gently steered him back into the building. The meeting had taken place in the Law Faculty and Marcel guided Henry through its corridors until they found a deserted seating area on the first floor. Marcel unfurled his silk scarf, revealing a white shirt with two or three buttons undone. He smiled at Henry, his teeth white and perfectly straight.

'Maybe in ten or 15 minutes the rain will stop, but it's good to talk. Are you a member of the Party?'

'Not yet,' replied Henry. 'I'm thinking about it.'

'Tell me why?'

It was a while before Henry replied, during which time the noise of the rain beating on the windows grew heavier. *When it rains like this in Geneva it feels like it will rain forever.*

'I live in a privileged and bourgeois world,' said Henry eventually. 'I've visited Germany and seen areas where people have no jobs and little food. Even in Switzerland, you can go from a rich area to one nearby that's completely different and that just seems wrong to me. My mother and my step-father are always saying a civilised world relies on having some people making money and others working for them. They say the reason why people are poor is they're lazy and feckless. They blame unemployment on trade unions and socialists. I always find I disagree with whatever they say about politics and the people they seem to despise the most are communists. That got me thinking. If my mother and step-father are so opposed to communism, then maybe it can't be that bad. When I saw a notice for this meeting in the library, I thought I'd come along. I'm reading a lot about it at the moment.'

'Really? Tell me, what are you reading?' Marcel leaned forward, genuinely interested.

'I've read *The Communist Manifesto*, of course, and all three volumes of *Capital*, though I can't pretend I found that easy-going. Now I'm reading *The Origin of the Family, Private Property and the State*, but it's even more difficult.'

'I understand, Engels isn't the easiest person to read, but his ideas – they're excellent, do you agree?'

'I do.'

Marcel edged his chair a bit closer to Henry's. 'I can tell from your accent that you're not from Geneva.'

'No, I lived in Zürich for a number of years. We moved to Geneva last year.'

Marcel switched to German. 'And can I ask what you do; are you a student here at the university?'

'No... not yet. My mother isn't keen on me being a student. She thinks I'll end up mixing with people she disapproves of.'

'Like communists?'

'Like communists.'

'I suspect you're not a native of Zürich either? I'm not Swiss myself: I'm from Paris. I can always tell when someone isn't Swiss: they have more... warmth.'

Marcel patted Henry on the knee. *A friend: someone to trust.*

'Actually, I'm originally from England.'

'Really, where?'

'I was born in a place called Woking; it's not far from London.'

'And how did you end up in Geneva?'

'It's a long story and a rather boring one, I'm afraid.'

'No, no – not at all. People's stories are always more fascinating than they realise. Do tell me.'

Marcel edged his chair even closer to Henry's and looked at his companion in admiration. 'Please tell me, Henry!'

'Well, as I say, it's not terribly remarkable. My father was an accountant and a good deal older than my mother. He died suddenly in 1923. My mother was still in her early forties and, though we weren't rich, my mother had aspirations to wealth. She inherited a life-insurance policy upon my father's death and, as far as I can recall, she set about spending it – furs, jewellery – that type of thing. We spent most of that summer on the French Riviera and in Antibes she met a Swiss businessman, Erich Hesse. She married him later the same year.'

'Rather quick?'

'Indeed: indecent haste was how people described it. But my mother was quite unashamed about it. She disliked England and what she described as a provincial lifestyle. She wanted glamour and wealth, and Erich Hesse offered all that. In the short period following the death of my father, she'd quickly become accustomed to a certain standard of living, so, Herr Hesse was an extremely attractive proposition: financially at least. I ought to add he was also quite a bit older than my mother. He was 65 when they married.'

'So you moved here to Switzerland?'

'Yes. To Zürich at first, this was where his business interests were. We lived there for around five years and moved here last year.'

'Why the move to Geneva?'

'My stepfather has property here, though he has all over Switzerland. I think the main reason was my mother: she always said she found Zürich rather stuffy but she loves Geneva and the area around it. We live by the lake, close to Nyon.'

'And how did you become so fluent?'

'I turned out to be something of a natural linguist,' said Henry. 'I'd never really fitted in well in England. I didn't excel at school and I was bad at sport, so I was bullied a bit. I managed to make myself more popular by impersonating teachers – I was rather good at it and the other boys loved it. I was always playing pranks, phoning teachers and pretending to be the headmaster, that kind of thing. When I arrived in Switzerland at 13, I discovered my talent for impersonation was a godsend for learning languages: not so much the vocabulary and the grammar, which I found easy enough, but in imitating the accent and the nuance of speech. In Zürich I became fluent in German and Swiss-German, and since moving here my French has really come on.'

Marcel nodded and smiled in the right places. He was sympathetic and friendly, someone Henry instinctively felt he could trust. To his surprise, Henry found himself opening up even more to this stranger: the coldness of his mother; his lack of a relationship with his step-father; his loneliness; his boredom; his curiosity about the world around him and his frustration at not being able to satisfy that.

Marcel switched to English, but only after he had looked carefully around the empty room and moved his chair so close to Henry's that they were touching.

'You're clearly very interested in communism, Henry.'

'Yes.'

'So, are you going to join the Party?'

'Probably. I'm a bit nervous about what my mother and step-father will think. I know it's nothing to do with them, but, if they found out, they'd throw me out of the house. But they won't need to know, will they?'

Marcel said nothing. He leaned back in his chair and looked Henry up and down.

'You don't have to join the Party, you know.'

'What do you mean?'

'What matters, Henry, is that you believe in the cause, that you believe in communism.'

'I'm not terribly sure I follow you.'

Marcel paused while a man and a woman walked by, their shoes reverberating long after they had passed on the wooden floor. The rain now sounded as if it had turned into a storm. Marcel lowered his head and only raised it very slightly when he spoke again.

'Henry, if one truly believes in the cause, then there are many different ways of serving it. Joining the party and attending meetings have their place, but for someone such as yourself, there may be other ways… better ways in which you can help the cause more effectively.'

'I'm still not really following you. Why are you so interested in me?'

'Because it's clear you believe in the cause and that you are a man of many parts, not all of them obvious ones. You have a natural caution about you, along with an inquisitive mind. You speak three languages. You have a Swiss passport and a British one. And the only person who knows that you are interested in the

Party, that you came to the meeting tonight, is me.'

'There were other people at the meeting.'

'Sure, but do any of them know who you are, do they know your name?'

Henry shook his head.

'Exactly. For the time being, can I ask you not to join the Party or attend any meetings? In a few weeks, maybe two or three, possibly longer, I will approach you. We will meet and I may be able to introduce you to people who share our views. In the meantime, I ask you not to discuss this with anyone.'

'But how will you know where to find me?'

Marcel patted Henry's knee. 'Don't worry: finding you will not be a problem.'

* * *

Marcel found him in late February, around four weeks after they had first met.

He was in the library at the university, where he spent most weekdays. It got him away from his mother and step-father, and away from Nyon and the home overlooking the lake. He tended to arrive at the library around 11 in the morning and leave around four. On Marcel's advice he had stopped reading political works ('there's no need to draw unnecessary attention to yourself') and was now working his way through the French novelists. On this particular day he was finding it hard to concentrate on Zola's *Thérèse Raquin* so in the middle of the afternoon he went for a stroll along the corridors, past the crowded notice board where he had first spotted the handwritten poster advertising the Communist Party meeting. When he return to his desk he noticed that his copy of *Thérèse Raquin* was closed, with a slip of paper poking out of the last page he had been reading. It was a card from a bar on the Place de la Taconnerie and in neat handwriting, '*Ce soir. 6.*'

The bar was in the shadow of St-Pierre cathedral and was little more than a dimly lit cellar. It was hard to make out the few other customers. Henry had arrived in good time – well before six – and for 30 or 40 minutes he sat on a small table facing the entrance and contemplated what he may have let himself into. Until that evening, he had decided that Marcel was just an enthusiast who had perhaps become carried away. He was, in Henry's opinion, unlikely ever to contact him again and he'd come to the conclusion this was very much for the best. Whatever serving the cause in different ways meant, it was not for him.

He did not notice Marcel until he slid into the chair opposite and greeted him warmly, placing two empty glasses on the table and proceeding to fill them both from a bottle of red wine while holding the cork between his teeth. He gestured for Henry to drink and it was only when they had both finished and he had refilled their glasses that he spoke.

'I've come from Paris this morning, which is why I'm late. How have you been keeping my friend? Tell me what you're reading.'

They chatted for a few minutes and by the time they were finishing their third glass of wine Marcel suggested they go for a walk. They left the bar in silence. By now, a grey mist had descended on the Old Town and the cathedral was only just visible in front of them. They walked in silence along the deserted streets, as if they were the only people in the city. They turned into Rue Verdaine, then Marcel placed an arm in front of Henry, gesturing for him to wait. They stood still for a while: ahead of them they could just make out the sound of footsteps. Marcel glanced at his watch, angling his hand to try and catch what light there was from the street lamp. He nodded and then looked straight at Henry.

'You do believe, don't you?' When Henry did not reply but only looked at him as if he did not understand, he repeated the question. 'In the cause, I mean. You still believe in communism?'

'Of course.' *What else can I say?*

'Good.' Marcel started to walk forward again, very slowly. He placed a hand in Henry's back so he would join him. 'You'll find that if you believe, that will help. It's difficult enough even if you do believe, but impossible if you don't. Don't allow yourself to harbour doubts. If you force yourself hard enough, it'll work. Trust me.'

Marcel said nothing more, but continued to walk on slowly. They had not gone very far when they passed an alleyway on their left and Henry noticed Marcel peering into it. In the shadows he could just make out a bulky figure standing still at the far end of the alley. They carried on walking, but now Henry could hear footsteps behind them. They reached the corner of Rue de la Vallée and Marcel stopped. When they turned round a large man was standing a few yards behind them. He was wrapped in a long, black coat, its collar turned up to conceal the lower half of his face, with much of the upper half hidden by the brim of a large fedora.

Marcel placed a hand on Henry's shoulder: 'attends!' *Wait.* He walked over to the man and they spoke for a minute, no more than that. They weren't speaking French or German. As far as Henry could tell, it was Russian or Polish. When they had finished talking, Marcel turned and beckoned for Henry to join them.

The three of them stood together for a moment, not a word being exchanged. Then, as if on a signal, Marcel turned and walked quickly away, back along Rue Verdaine.

It was the last time Henry would ever see him.

* * *

As Marcel disappeared into the mist the man in the long, black coat and hat moved off in the other direction, making it clear Henry should follow him. Halfway down Rue de la Vallée, he stopped by a parked Citroen and opened the rear passenger door, allowing Henry to enter first. The driver turned around and nodded, and without a word being exchanged, they drove off.

The car drove fast through the Old Town, the speed and the mist making it difficult for Henry to work out where he was. As far as he could tell, they were heading south through Champel but then he noticed they were heading back into the city, driving along the banks of the River Avre. Soon they were in Jonction, a working-class district Henry was quite unfamiliar with. The driver stopped for a while, his eyes fixed on the rear-view mirror then started again. Less than a minute later, he braked suddenly then reversed hard into a narrow alleyway, stopping alongside a large wooden door. Henry was guided out of the car, through the door and quickly up a flight of steps into a small attic room which smelt of gas and cabbages.

Once he had closed the shutters and turned on the fire, the large man looked Henry up and down, his head slowly moving as if checking him out from every angle. He gestured to a pair of chairs in front of the fire and removed his fedora, revealing a lined face that showed no hint of emotion. Once Henry had sat down, the man unbuttoned his coat and lowered himself onto the chair opposite. He addressed him in French, which he spoke with a heavy Eastern European accent.

'English is your first language, yes?'

Henry nodded.

'And you also speak French and German?'

'Yes, though I'm more comfortable with French.'

'We shall speak French in that case, I understand it better than English. Two foreigners speaking French; they would like that in Paris.'

'Henry Hunter.' The man removed his overcoat and took out a brown leather notebook from one of the pockets. From his top pocket he withdrew a pencil and began sharpening it with a penknife, letting the shavings fall on his shirt before he blew them away on to the floor. He squinted as he checked the notebook, the pencil now lodged in his mouth like a cigar.

'I know everything I need to know about you, Henry Hunter.'

'Not too much I hope!' *A nervous laugh.*

Over the course of the next hour the man delivered a quiet monologue. He told Henry things about himself he had thought no-one else could possibly know, and other things he had long forgotten or hardly been aware of. He gave him the name of the maternity home where he was born; revealed the names and addresses of family members long forgotten or never heard of; informed him of the name of the accountancy firm for which his father worked and described in some detail his routine, such as it was, in Geneva: when he left home in Nyon, his route into the Old Town and to the library. He knew the name of every book he had taken out. He knew the names of the bars in the Pâquis he liked to hang around in, where he cut a lonely figure as he eyed the working girls without ever quite managing to sum up the courage to approach them. When he had finished, he smiled for the first time, displaying a set of large teeth, half of which seemed to be made of gold. Henry sat incredulous.

'You can call me Viktor, by the way.' A long silence, during which Henry wondered if he was meant to say anything, but he had no idea what.

'Marcel tells me you were about to join the Swiss Communist Party?'

'Not quite: I attended one of its meetings. I told him I was thinking of joining, nothing more than that. We had a nice chat after the meeting and he mentioned something about not joining or attending meetings. He said there were better ways I could help the cause. I was not altogether sure what he meant.'

'You will work for me Henry Hunter: that is how you'll help the cause. You are a communist, yes?'

Henry thought. 'Yes, I suppose…'

'You are ideal Henry. You have two nationalities and three languages. Most people in Europe have just one of each. You are the kind of person who people do not notice too much, if you understand what I mean – you don't stand out.'

'What does working for you entail, Viktor?'

'It means what Marcel said: it is another way of serving the cause.'

From a nearby rooftop a clock struck eight. 'Look, I ought to be getting a move on. I should have been home ages ago and my mother will be getting worried. Perhaps I could think about things for a few days?'

Viktor was smiling again, displaying even more gold teeth than before. When he smiled he looked friendly, but the second the smile disappeared his demeanour became cold and menacing. 'No, no, no Henry Hunter,' he said, shaking his head. 'It doesn't work like that, I'm afraid. I'm not advertising a vacancy at a Swiss bank, I'm not looking for a man to deliver cheese. You are already working for me: you started working for me the moment we met.'

* * *

For the best part of a year, Henry was little more than a messenger for Viktor. At first this amounted to taking an envelope from – say – Geneva to Paris then stopping off in Lyons to deliver another one on the return journey. Even Henry, normally naïve, came to realise these errands were tests. About once a month the errands would coincide with meeting Viktor, usually in Paris but sometimes in other cities. He was, he realised, being trained: Viktor would talk at length in either English or French about what helping him really meant. He explained the rudiments of espionage: the need to fit in to any environment or circumstance without being noticed; the need for discretion; the ability to see and remember everything;

how to assume different identities to the extent that you became that person for however short a period; the importance of thinking of not just one step ahead, but two or even three, and at the same time not forgetting what you'd been doing before, your cover story.

At no stage did Viktor actually say who he worked for, although over a period of time Henry came to understand that he worked for Soviet intelligence or possibly Comintern, but he was never totally sure which branch it actually was. Henry's instincts told him the less he knew the better. Viktor began to talk about the 'service' and that became how they referred to who his new employers were.

There was a travel agency in Geneva's Petit-Saconnex that was a front for Viktor's operation and Henry became a courier for them. It provided a perfect cover for his trips and meant his mother, though curious and somewhat dubious as to whether a travel agency was the right job for her son, did not question his frequent absences.

In the spring of 1930, Viktor introduced Henry to a German called Peter and a week later Henry accompanied him to an isolated farmhouse in northern Germany, somewhere between Hamburg and Bremen. There were five other recruits there; two German men; a French woman and a Dutch couple. All were a few years older than him.

On the second day at the farm the six recruits were taken to a shed and shown a litter of puppies. *Choose one each: it can be your companion while you are here!* Having a dog will make your stay here easier, they were told. Henry chose the smallest of the litter, a black puppy that he named Foxi. He'd take Foxi for walks two or three times a day and, as with the other recruits and their puppies, they became inseparable.

For the next six weeks they were trained in what Peter described as field craft. They learnt how to create and use secret message drops; how to follow people without being noticed and in turn spot if they were being followed and how to lose the shadow. They learnt unarmed combat and how to use a series of handguns; there was even instruction in making bombs and other forms of sabotage. And in the evenings, there were lectures: ideological instruction was how they termed it. Any hint of doubt about commitment to the cause was spotted and eliminated. By the end of the first week, everyone fully understood that working for the cause in the way they were meant there was no room whatsoever for discussion: without total commitment and utter loyalty, they would fail.

Never question; never discuss; never hesitate.

And along with this there were individual sessions. Henry spent hours with first an elderly German man and then a younger Polish woman. They were intent on teasing anything personal out of him. The German man seemed to be a psychiatrist of some sort, asking a series of apparently unrelated questions and making extensive notes. He seemed to be preoccupied with Henry's relationship with his mother.

Everything about the Polish woman looked severe: her manner, the heavy glasses and the way her hair was pulled into a tight bun. She insisted he tell her everything about his personal life. Had he ever had a girlfriend, for instance? Henry had blushed and muttered something about there being one or two, but nothing serious. Had he ever slept with a woman, she asked – or a man?

Henry was so shocked that he readily told the truth. No, he had never slept with a woman. The thought of sleeping with a man, he said, had simply never occurred to him.

That night he lay in bed, unable to sleep as he tried to make sense of what was happening to him. He felt trapped, drawn into a life he'd never have willingly chosen, but one which did at least offer some prospect of excitement. He had just drifted to sleep when he was woken by someone sitting on his bed and turning on the bedside lamp. It was the Polish woman. Her hair was now loose and she'd lost her glasses, and was wearing bright red lipstick and perfume that smelt of lemons. Henry found himself unable to say anything.

She leant over and brushed his face with her hand then gently pulled his head towards hers and kissed him. 'How can we let you go out into the world and not know what to do with a woman?' she said softly. 'That would be… risky.'

Henry opened his mouth to speak, but she placed a finger inside his lips, holding it in there for a few moments before pulling it slowly away. She stood up and removed her dressing gown so she was totally naked. Then she stood still for a moment, her eyebrows raised, inviting Henry to look at her, silhouetted by the bedside lamp. Through a gap in the curtain on the other side of the bed, the light of the moon lit up the front of her body.

Had she not remained with Henry for an hour after they had made love, he would have readily passed it off as one of his more pleasant dreams. But they lay there together and every time he tried to say something, which he felt he ought to do, she placed a finger on his lips and shook her head – her long hair brushing his bare shoulders. As the first hint of dawn peered through the half drawn curtains, she climbed out of bed and got dressed. 'We never discuss this, you understand? This was something you needed to do: there is a saying that there are more secrets to be found in a bed than in a safe. For your first time you were quite good Henry, but next time remember you don't need to rush so much. Try not to think about what you're doing: it will come naturally, it's the most natural thing we do. At least next time won't be your first.'

Henry was confused, but at the same time quite pleased with himself.

Never question; never discuss; never hesitate.

On his penultimate day at the farm, Henry was walking with Peter and Foxi in the woods, when the German turned to him and handed him a pistol.

'Shoot her,' he said, pointing at the puppy.

'What!' The puppy's eyes looked up at him, full of joy.

'The longer you wait the harder it will be.'

Henry fiddled around with pistol, hoping that at any moment Peter would stop him.

'Get on with it. You do as I tell you.'

Henry felt himself drift into a trance and, as if from above, he saw himself call Foxi over and cuddle her, allowing her to lick his face before placing the barrel of the gun behind her ears and pulling the trigger.

Afterwards Peter held out his hand for the gun and Henry did all he could to stop himself crying. *Never question; never discuss; never hesitate.*

When he returned to Geneva after six weeks, he felt emotionally drained: there was now nothing his new masters did not know about him. It was as if they possessed his soul. He had come to understand, even before the trip, that Viktor had been putting him through a process which meant there was no going back. Whether he liked it or not, he was now committed to the cause. He knew that his views on communism were now quite immaterial.

By the end of 1930 the errands, as Viktor liked to call them, became more serious: clandestine trips to the more dangerous corners of Europe; fleeting encounters with wary women and frightened men; switching identity before hurrying out of the country. There were even some trips to Britain, where he used his Henry Hunter identity to enter and leave. He was seeing Viktor at least once a month, probably nearer to once every three weeks. Viktor always allowed plenty of time for their meetings; it was if he enjoyed them. During the course of these meetings it became apparent Viktor worked for Comintern and he would reminisce about the Revolution and his early days as an agent. He would describe to Henry the dangers he foresaw in Europe. Above all, he seemed to show a genuine interest in Henry that neither his mother nor his step-father did. He clearly cared and Henry found himself being frank with Viktor in a way he was unable to be with anyone else. Viktor began to refer to Henry as *synok*.

It was the Russian for son.

* * *

Alex Gerlis

Chapter 6: Switzerland, 1931

The event that would change Henry's life forever took place in the summer of 1931, but its origins came earlier that year in Paris. At the beginning of March, Henry was summoned to the French capital, to one of the safe houses Viktor used in the Marais. Unlike his usual meetings with Viktor, this one was more charged and stretched over a period of days. Viktor wanted to satisfy himself that no-one – 'not a single soul', as he put it – could have an inkling as to what Henry was up to or who he was working for. It took four days and three nights of what amounted to an interrogation for Viktor to satisfy himself of this.

A week later, Viktor came to Geneva – the first time he'd been there for some months. Over a long dinner in a private room at the back of a seedy Armenian restaurant in Grand-Lancy, Viktor talked politics. What did Henry understand about events in the Soviet Union, about the dangerous and counter-revolutionary activities of Trotsky and his mad followers? Henry replied truthfully that he knew little, but his allegiance was with Comrade Stalin. Traitors such as Trotsky and his ilk were a distraction.

Viktor had nodded in agreement then spoke well into the early hours of the morning, fortified by an endless supply of strong Turkish coffee and plenty of vodka. Viktor patiently explained the aims of the Left Opposition, how their arguments may have had some merits in their early days, but they had deviated seriously from the correct socialist course charted by Lenin. Henry needed to be clear there was no room for what Viktor described as a bourgeois indulgence. Henry said he understood and was grateful to Viktor for explaining matters so clearly: he had no doubt Trotsky and his few remaining followers were enemies of the Soviet Union and of socialism, but surely the matter had been dealt with? Had Trotsky not been expelled from the Soviet Union?

It was one in the morning now and when the exhausted *patron* returned with more coffee, Viktor dismissed him sharply in Russian.

'I told him to leave us alone *synok*. What I am about to say now is most important. Trotsky is indeed living in exile in Turkey and most of his supporters in the Soviet Union have seen the error of their ways – or at least claim to have done so: even Zinoviev and Kamenev. Others have been dealt with. But the danger posed by Trotsky and those of his followers that remain still exists. There are powerful supporters of Trotsky dispersed around Europe and as long as they are able to operate, they pose a threat to us, which we cannot tolerate: we cannot put at risk the achievements of the Revolution. You understand that?'

Henry nodded.

'So dealing with them is a priority for our service.'

Henry nodded again: *of course*.

A long silence followed, during which Viktor removed his jacket, loosened his tie and looked at Henry in a quizzical manner, as if expecting him to say something. Henry shifted in his chair, unsure of how to react.

'This is where you are going to perform a vital role for the Service, *synok*.'

* * *

Henry Hunter spent the first two weeks of July 1931 in a large house on the outskirts of Neuchâtel, overlooking the lake. He had been told to expect to be away from Geneva for at least a month, possibly a good deal longer. As far as his mother and step-father were concerned, the travel agency he'd been working for had acquired a new branch in St Gallen and, as Henry spoke good Swiss-German, he was being sent there for a while.

Viktor accompanied Henry to the house and remained there for the first two days. Peter, the German who had taken him to Hamburg for his training the previous year was also present. For two weeks, Peter helped Henry assume a new identity. Just before the end of the fortnight in Neuchâtel, Viktor returned and after a couple more days, he finally satisfied himself Henry had now become William Jarvis.

According to his much-used British passport, William Jarvis had been born in Norwich and was, at 26, a few years older than Henry. After graduating from Cambridge, Jarvis had become a teacher and had moved to Switzerland for a year thanks to a legacy from a recently deceased and much-loved uncle. His aim was to travel and do some occasional teaching, should the opportunity arise.

That opportunity happily arose in Interlaken.

'They've been advertising for an English tutor on and off for weeks: they'll be delighted a proper Englishman who also happens to be a teacher applies,' Viktor had told him.

'But I'm not a teacher!'

'You don't need to be. They want someone to improve their children's conversational English, that's all.'

The night before Henry travelled to Interlaken, Viktor had given him his final briefing.

'Anatoly Mikhailovich Yevtushenko.' The three of them were sat around a finely polished table in the dining room near Neuchâtel and Viktor had almost ceremonially placed a photograph of a distinguished looking man in front of Henry. 'Anatoly Mikhailovich Yevtushenko, born Kazan in 1884: bourgeois family, but became active in socialist politics when he was at university in Moscow. He became a lawyer and was one of the very early members of the Russian Social Democratic Labour Party, which you may or may not know was the forerunner of the Communist Party. He was active in the October Revolution and began to rise through the ranks of the Party. However, in around 1923 or 1924, he became a confidant of Trotsky and since then the two have become close. In 1924 Yevtushenko took up a position in the finance department of the Party. In early 1928, not long after Trotsky was sent on internal exile, Yevtushenko and his family disappeared while on holiday in Crimea. We lost track of them, but a few months ago we discovered that they were living in Interlaken.'

Viktor nodded at Peter, who opened a folder and produced a series of photographs that he laid out in front of Henry as if dealing from a deck of cards.

'This is Yevtushenko's wife, Tatyana Dmitriyevna,' said Peter. 'We understand she suffers from a debilitating lung condition, which may well be the reason why they are living in Interlaken. This is Rozalia Anatolyevna, she is 17. Nadezhda Anatolyevna is 14 and this is the son, Nikolai Anatolyevich. He is 11.'

'And that's their house?'

'Indeed. A very fine house as you can see, but also a very secure one. This wall runs all around it and is 12 feet high. It is not altogether unusual for houses to have such security in Switzerland: people like their privacy and Interlaken is a wealthy town.'

Viktor moved the photographs away from Henry. He wanted him to concentrate on what he was about to say. 'We have been watching Yevtushenko very closely. We have come to the conclusion he is an important source of finance for Trotsky and his movement, something the Service has long suspected. We know now that in the few months before he escaped from the Soviet Union, Yevtushenko channelled large sums of money from Moscow into Swiss bank accounts. Only he has access to them. We don't know exactly how much money is in these accounts, but we believe it could well be in the region of eight hundred million Swiss Francs. As well as the family, these three men live in the house – Peter...'

The German produced a series of photos, blurred shots of three different men. 'They are guards, all Russians. They stay in the house and vet whoever comes in or even approaches it. A local woman and her daughter act as housekeepers: they arrive early in the morning and do the cleaning, cooking and shopping. They leave in the middle of the afternoon. The family very rarely leave the house and, when they do, they are always accompanied by a guard.'

Viktor took over speaking now. 'Approximately once a fortnight, Yevtushenko leaves the house and travels first to Bern and then to Zürich. He always leaves early in the morning and arrives back late in the evening. And he's always accompanied on these trips by two of the guards. We know that in Bern he visits the Swiss Volksbank and in Zürich he goes to the Union Bank then to the

Eidgenössische Bank. Our assumption is that, once there, he's able to transfer money from the accounts he controls to those of Trotsky's supporters around Europe or even to Trotsky himself. Our aim is very simple: that money was stolen from the Party and we want it back. In the process, we can starve Trotsky of the funds that are keeping his miserable movement going.'

'And my role is...?' Henry sounded confused.

'To become the family's English tutor, *synok*, and become trusted by them. That may take weeks. Once that happens, we'll be able to move to our next stage.'

'And what does that involve?'

'You'll find out then *synok*,' said Viktor.

Never question; never discuss; never hesitate.

* * *

It had all gone according to plan, as things tended to do in Switzerland, especially when they were organised by Viktor. William Jarvis had taken the trouble to write from England to reserve a room at an inn in the centre of Interlaken. He was on the top floor with a small balcony, from which he could see Lake Thun to the west, Lake Brienz to the east, the mountains of the Jungfrau and the Grindelwald to the south, with the Harder Kulm and Emmental beyond it to the north. Henry, who now had to think of himself as William, had decided this could turn out to be a pleasant enough task.

He waited until his second day in Interlaken before enquiring in the bookshop about the discreet sign in their window seeking an English tutor and that afternoon he telephoned the number the bookshop owner passed on to him. Two days later he walked through the town and crossed the River Aare, and there on the north bank found the house on the very edge of the rising forest. It was a perfect position, separated from neighbouring houses by trees and surrounded by a high wall, with the front gate set into it. Next to the gate was a small window. Two large men searched him after he rang the bell and he was then led through to a library

Both Anatoly Yevtushenko and his wife Tatyana were in the room, but the interview was conducted by the husband in passable German. His wife, he explained, did not speak the language. Tatyana Yevtushenko was a thin woman, with skin so pale it was the colour of chalk and, even on a warm July day, she was dressed for winter. Anatoly Yevtushenko told William Jarvis the family had moved around Europe but had settled here in Switzerland. 'Because of my business,' he said, in a tone that made it clear he did not need to elaborate. For the most part, they educated the children themselves, he explained, but they did require the assistance of tutors from time to time.

Please tell me about yourself, Mr Jarvis.

William Jarvis remembered what Viktor had told him: *tell him just enough, not too much… he will be clever, he will spot any mistakes… concentrate on how much you would enjoy tutoring his children rather than talking about yourself. Avoid sounding too fluent: be slightly hesitant with dates.*

Anatoly Yevtushenko spoke to his wife every so often in Russian, evidently giving her the gist of what he'd been told.

'Are you interested in politics, Mr Jarvis?'

'I'm afraid not sir. I do hope that isn't a problem?'

'No, not at all. And what about foreign affairs, do you follow those?'

'Only what one reads in *The Times* sir, but I have to tell you my main interest is literature. I would rather read a good book than a newspaper!'

And so it went on. After a brief conversation with his wife, Anatoly Yevtushenko offered William Jarvis the position of English tutor to his children. They agreed the fee and that he would come for two hours every morning. They would review his position after two weeks.

At the end of the first week William Jarvis was summoned into Anatoly Yevtushenko's study.

'How long do you plan to stay in Interlaken for, Mr Jarvis?'

'A few months, possibly. I hope to learn to ski, so I suppose I'm in the right place. It depends on whether I can find work to help pay for my stay.'

'Well that's why I've asked to see you. The children adore you: they absolutely insist we keep you for as long as possible. For reasons that are too complicated to explain, our life is an isolated one and my wife and I worry about the effect of that on the children. Already we can see how you've been able to help brighten their lives. From now on, we'd like you to spend an hour every day with each child and to stay for lunch, which will be a further opportunity for you to converse with them in English.'

This was the routine for the next month. William Jarvis would arrive at the house at 11 o'clock every morning apart from Sunday and ring the bell on the wall. The heavy metal gates would eventually open and one of the guards would search him before another would lead him through to the library. He would spend the first hour with Nadezhda, who was by far the brightest of the three children. Nikolai would have the second hour, which was hard work as the boy completely lacked discipline, but seemed pleased to have William read simple stories to him in English. Then he and the three children would eat lunch together, speaking only English during the meal.

After lunch, he would teach Rozalia for the final hour. Very quickly, he came to appreciate this was the part of the day he most looked forward to. At first he had seen Rozalia as little more than a child but, on her own, away from her parents and her sister and brother, she was more of a young woman. Her thick, long brown hair fell well below her shoulders and she was constantly sweeping it away from her face. Her skin wasn't as pale as her mother's, but she'd certainly inherited her complexion from her rather than her father. What she had got from him, though, were dark brown eyes, with an almost unblinking gaze.

They would spend much of the time in the garden, wandering around, talking in English but more often than not slipping into German. Her German was not too bad and she did her best to ignore his attempts to speak in English. She was, Henry realised, desperately lonely. She had fled her home country and was now trapped in a house surrounded by high walls. So she confided in Mr Jarvis, as she called him. He found it hard to do other than lend a sympathetic ear and assure her if she was patient her life would change for the better. He told her about life in England and what he had seen of Europe on his travels.

Call me Roza.
Very well – and do call me William.
What is a short form of William?
Bill, I suppose – or Billy.

Roza preferred Billy, and so she and Billy became friends. When they did read from books she would sit so close to him that their bodies touched. Roza had a habit, a mannerism even, of touching his arm and allowing her fingers to briefly hold him by the wrist. He'd noticed her doing this to the others too, so he did not imagine she meant any special affection for him, but once or twice he tried to return the gesture – placing his hand on top of hers. She would smile and wait until she had once more swept the hair from her face before gently removing her hand. He knew what Roza wanted more than anything else was companionship. William's story was that his mother had died when he was young and his father had remarried. This struck some kind of chord with Roza, whose eyes would fill with tears when he told her about being sent to boarding school at the age of six and how his stepmother did not like him. Henry worried he may be getting too close to Roza, but then Viktor had told him to make sure that he became trusted.

He knew that he was developing feelings for Roza, but he also knew he wasn't in a position to do anything about them. She would never be allowed to leave the house without a guard and, at home, there were always others around. One morning, after he had been there for a month or so, the downstairs toilet was being repaired and he was told to use the bathroom upstairs, which he would normally never do. When he opened the bathroom door, he was met by the sight of Roza, who had just stepped out of the bath. Despite the steam and the fact that she was mostly covered by a towel he caught a glimpse of her breasts, smaller than he had imagined them but perfectly shaped, with locks of her dark, wet hair hanging between them. There was a brief moment when neither of them said anything or moved, then he said 'sorry' and swiftly shut the door before hurrying downstairs. Neither of them ever said a word about it, but that afternoon she was even friendlier towards him.

On Sundays – the only day on which he did not go to the house – Henry would take the bus from Interlaken to Thun, where he would meet Peter in a park. They would walk while Henry would recount what had happened during the week and Peter would ask a series of questions, occasionally pausing to write something in his notebook. Once he took Henry to a small apartment above a shop in the centre of the town, where Henry was told to draw detailed plans of the house.

In the middle of August, he arrived in Thun on a Sunday to be taken straight to the apartment by Peter. When they arrived, Viktor was waiting with three Frenchmen, who were introduced as Lucien, Claude and Jean-Marie: the conversation that followed – which lasted well into the evening – was conducted in French.

'*Synok*: Peter tells me that sometimes you and Roza are allowed to leave the house?' Viktor was sitting directly across a narrow table from Henry, watching him carefully. Despite the stifling August heat the Russian was wearing a heavy jacket. The three Frenchmen were lounging back in their chairs and one of them had a revolver in a shoulder holster.

'Well, yes and no. Roza has a lot of spirit, she feels like a caged animal in that house, but her parents won't allow her to go into the town, certainly not without a guard. However, behind the house is a small, private wood, just for the residents of the nearby houses. It has a fence around it.'

Peter handed a map to Viktor, pointing to a circled area. 'Here?'

Henry picked up the map and studied it. 'Yes, here. You can get into it from a door set in the garden wall. Her father agreed we can go for a walk in there, so long as it's just for a few minutes and we promise not to leave the wood. The guards have the key: At first they'd come along to let us out and then in again, but now they don't bother. I have to collect it from them and return it afterwards. I am trusted.'

'And tell me *synok*: when do the housekeepers leave – is it still in the afternoon?'

'Yes. They make the lunch then prepare the evening meal. They're usually gone by three o'clock.'

The Frenchmen and Peter all asked questions and Henry must have described the layout of the house a dozen times. Viktor then outlined his plan. It was clever and audacious and by the time he had finished, Henry felt quite sick.

* * *

Two more weeks. Viktor had decided that another two weeks would help ensure William Jarvis was even more trusted by the Yevtushenkos and this was important, because if they didn't trust

89

him then the plan wouldn't work. The two weeks was also important because Anatoly Yevtushenko's last trip to Bern and Zürich had been just a few days previously. The timing had to be right.

The agreed date was the 1st September, a Tuesday. On the Thursday before that Peter had arrived in Interlaken and rented an apartment on the east side of the town, close to Lake Brienz. Henry checked out of the inn and moved in with Peter.

William Jarvis arrived at the house just before 11 o'clock on the Tuesday morning. By now the guards were more relaxed with him, even quite friendly. He went through to the library and had his lessons with Nadezhda and Nikolai. By the time they went into the dining room for lunch he was feeling sick with nerves and anticipation. He hardly ate anything, but no-one seemed to notice. He managed to keep the children distracted by playing 'I spy'. After lunch he went to the guard's room at the front of the house to collect the key. The guard who spoke the best German handed it to him, with a warning to make sure he locked it properly.

He and Roza wandered into the garden, with Roza struggling to count to 100 in English. That was the way it worked: complete a task such as counting or naming the days of the week or months of the year and they could go into the woods as a reward. Roza became marooned in the seventies, but Henry announced that was good enough. He unlocked the garden door and they spent the rest of the hour walking. Henry kept glancing around, expecting to see people hidden amongst the trees or beyond the fence, but it was as deserted and silent as always, apart from the sound of water rushing on the Aare below them.

'Are you alright Billy?'

'Yes thank you Roza, why do you ask?'

'You're very quiet.' She had switched to German now. 'You keep looking around and you didn't eat any lunch.'

'I'm fine thank you Roza. I slept badly last night, that's all. Look, you really must speak English. Please try.'

'Why? What's the point? We'll never visit England. We'll never leave this house. I am a prison, Billy,' she said in English.

'I am a "prisoner", Roza. That's what you meant to say. A prison is a building in which the prisoners are kept. I'm sure you'll get to visit England one day.'

They spent much of the hour with Henry doing his best to sustain some kind of conversation in English. But, as ever, Roza was wrapped up in her thoughts. When they went back into the garden Henry told Roza to go on ahead while he made a play of locking the garden door. It appeared shut, but he kicked a stone against it just in case the wind blew it open. After he returned the key to the guard's room, he went into the library, pausing on the way to remove the bolt on the side door that opened into the garden. His hands were shaking so much he feared the sound of the bolts being removed echoed around the house.

They'll need to move: I told them the guards usually check the garden door soon after I lock it.

Roza and Nadezhda were in the library. He would hang around for a few minutes, as he had started to do lately. He could hear Nikolai playing upstairs and the two local women leaving the house. Anatoly was in his study and he imagined the mother would be asleep upstairs. From the corner of his eye he imagined he caught a movement in the garden, but he did not want to look up. A few moments later and there were some sounds from the front of the house, nothing too noticeable at first but then it became more of a commotion and first Nadezhda then Roza looked up. Seconds later there was the sound of shouting down the hall then three loud popping noises followed by a scream, and the sound of Anatoly shouting and then scuffling in the hall. The door to the library burst open. The first person inside was one of the Frenchmen, followed by Peter and behind him Viktor and another of the Frenchmen frog-marching Anatoly into the room. The girls screamed and Viktor shouted at them in Russian, waving his revolver at their father's head as he did so. The message was clear: *shut up or I shoot.*

Viktor pushed Anatoly into an armchair and gestured for the girls to sit on the floor. They could hear movement upstairs. 'Go and see what's going on,' Viktor told Peter in French. Shortly after that one of the other Frenchmen appeared in the room, dragging Nikolai in with him by his hair. Tatyana followed as if in a trance, with Peter bringing up the rear. Nikolai was shoved to the floor next to his terrified sisters while their mother was guided to a chair opposite her husband. Viktor addressed the family in Russian, then in French told Peter to see what was happening at the front of the house. When he reappeared it was with the third Frenchman and the two of them were dragging along one of the guards. He appeared to be badly wounded: he was groaning and his chest was covered in blood.

'What about the other two?' asked Viktor.

'Dead,' said the third Frenchman.

'And him?' He was nodding at the injured guard.

'Took one in the chest.'

'Finish him off.'

The Frenchman had been holding a revolver by his side. Now he knelt down by the guard and yanked up his head, forcing the barrel of the gun into his mouth. As he did so, the guard seemed to become fully conscious, his eyes opening wide, clearly terrified. The three children screamed and were only silenced when Viktor shouted at them. When the Frenchman pulled the trigger, the guard's head slumped. There followed a long silence then the sobbing of the three children. Tatyana sat very still, clearly in shock and seemingly unaware of what was going on. Henry noticed Anatoly was staring at him.

Viktor spoke to the family in Russian, pointing at Anatoly and waving his pistol around. They all nodded. *We understand.* Then he spoke in French. 'I'm going to separate them now.'

He pointed to the three Frenchmen. 'I'll take Anatoly into the study; he and I have much to talk about. One of you will come into the study with me, the other two had better keep an eye on the rest of the house – make sure one of you stays in the guardroom, we need to keep an eye on the front. Peter, you stay in here. William, you too: try to keep the children distracted. You'll need this.'

It was only when Viktor handed a revolver to Henry that it dawned on the family he had betrayed them. From the shocked look on the faces of the children and the glare of hate on that of the father, Henry realised that, until that moment, they must have thought he too had been caught up as a victim in this nightmare.

Anatoly was hauled up by one of the Frenchmen, who handcuffed his hands behind his back before marching him out of the room. As he passed Henry, Anatoly stopped and looked Henry straight in the eye before spitting out '*du Bastard!*'

None of the children wanted anything to do with their tutor. They ignored all his attempts to talk in English. Nadezhda spent most of the time quietly sobbing, sitting on the floor by her mother's chair. Little Nikolai looked confused and terrified, while Roza stared at him with blazing eyes. 'You were the one person I thought understood me, you were someone I trusted,' she said in German, in a quiet but angry voice. 'You know what will happen to us now, don't you?'

'Everything will be all right Roza, don't worry.'

'You think so, do you Englishman? In that case you have no idea who is it paying you.' She shuffled over to him, lowering her voice even more. 'They will kill us all, you realise that?'

Peter leaned over from the nearby chair where he was sitting, 'Shut up' he shouted at Roza. He turned to Henry and spoke in French: 'Don't talk with her anymore.' From the study there was the sound of raised voices in Russian, mostly Viktor, but Anatoly too. The afternoon turned into evening and one of the Frenchmen brought food into the library, but apart from Nikolai, none of the family ate anything. When it began to turn dark, Viktor called Henry and Peter into the kitchen.

'He finally understands we mean business. I think he realises he has no alternative but to do what I say. There's a train to Bern at 7.20 tomorrow morning: Lucien and Jean-Marie will go with him. He'll be at the Swiss Volksbank when it opens and I've agreed he can telephone here to reassure himself everyone is safe. Then he'll transfer all the funds from the Swiss Volksbank. After that, they'll travel to Zürich and repeat the procedure at the Union and Eidgenössische Banks.'

'How do we know he'll transfer all the funds under his control?' asked Peter.

'We can't be totally sure, but we know from following him that these are the only three banks he's ever visited. I managed to persuade him to show me what documentation he had and the accounts amount to just over nine hundred million Swiss Francs: that's more than we estimated. They will be very pleased. By tomorrow night that money will be in accounts controlled by the Party.'

'And what happens then Viktor?' The German looked nervous, playing with his watch strap and biting his finger nails, glancing first at Henry and then back at Viktor.

'We'll see. I've told him he'll be brought back here and that a few hours after we leave the town we'll phone the local police to release them.'

'Roza told me that they're all going to be killed,' said Henry. 'Why would she say that?'

'Don't worry about it *synok*. We know what we're doing.'

'But...'

Peter leaned over the table and grabbed Henry's forearm, very tight. 'Don't you remember anything? We just do as we're told. This isn't that stupid game you play for days at a time in England, understand?'

Never question; never discuss; never hesitate.

Viktor told them both to shut up. They would keep Anatoly apart from the rest of the family that night. Two of them would guard him while the others stayed with Tatyana and the children in the library, taking it in turns to sleep. Anatoly was made to telephone the housekeepers: *you aren't required tomorrow, please take the day off – we'll see you as usual on Thursday.*

Anatoly was woken up at six in the morning. Henry had been with him in his bedroom along with Peter for the past few hours and was surprised that the Russian had slept at all. They watched while he washed, shaved and dressed. When he was ready, he turned around and addressed them.

'Tell him I want to say goodbye to my family before I leave.'

They called Viktor up and there was a short exchange in Russian. The result was that, as Anatoly came downstairs, he went into the library and hugged each member of his family, but said nothing other than a word or two in Russian to each one. When he had finished hugging the last one, Nadezhda, he turned sharply and swiftly left the room. As he passed him in the hall Henry noticed the Russian's eyes were filled with tears.

* * *

Viktor spent much of that Wednesday in the study, behind Anatoly's desk. The first phone call came at 9.30: it was Lucien at the Swiss Volksbank. Peter brought Roza through from the library and put her on the phone to her father. *Yes, we're alright. When are you coming home? What are they...?* The phone was snatched back from her. Thirty minutes later and Lucien rang again. The money had been transferred. They were now on their way to Zürich. The next phone call came at a quarter to one. It was Jean-Marie to say they had arrived in Zürich and were about to go into Eidgenössische Bank. This time, Nadezhda was brought in from the library to assure her father all was well. Henry was in the study when Jean-Marie rang again at 1.30 to say the transfer had been made; they were now on their way to the Union Bank.

'Wait: ring me back in half an hour. I need to make a call first.'

Viktor dialled a Zürich number and, after a short conversation in which he said no more than a few words, a large smile filled his face, displaying the familiar gold teeth. 'Good news, *synok*. The funds from both banks have already been transferred to our account in Credit Suisse. Before the close of business today they will have been spread among various untraceable accounts across Europe. We are better at capitalism than the capitalists!'

By three o'clock the business had been done. Nikolai had spoken to his father before the transaction at Union Bank then Lucien rang to say it had been completed.

'Is Yevtushenko in the room with you?' Viktor was speaking with Lucien. 'Right then, don't say anything, but when I have finished say out loud you will be on the 4.15 train from Zürich and you expect to be back in Interlaken by eight o'clock, you understand? You know what to do, Lucien... I will see you in Paris.'

Viktor paused while Lucien spoke then placed the phone back on the receiver, holding onto it for a while after putting it down. He sighed and loosened his tie.

'All good, *synok*. The transfers have taken place. Moscow will be delighted. Now, Trotsky has no more money.'

Henry nodded. 'Is Anatoly on his way back here, Viktor?'

The Russian peered at him as if the sun was in his eyes. 'Tell Peter to come in. You stay in the library with Claude.'

* * *

The longest half hour of Henry Hunter's life began very soon after that.

He was in the library with Claude, keeping an eye on Tatyana and the three children when Viktor appeared in the doorway. He spoke in Russian, and Roza and Nadezhda both raised their hands. Viktor pointed at Nadezhda and gestured upstairs. 'I've asked if they want an opportunity to use the bathroom,' he said to Henry in French. Viktor closed the library door as Nadezhda went upstairs. Viktor said nothing but glanced at his watch then up at the ceiling, his back against the closed door. After five minutes he spoke to Roza. *Your turn.* She brushed past Henry, looking through him as she went past, pulling her cardigan tightly around her shoulders and across her front.

Ten minutes later, with no sign of either of the girls, there was a knock at the door. Viktor opened it slightly to reveal Peter on the other side. The German nodded briefly but said nothing. Viktor nodded his head approvingly and briefly gripped Peter's shoulder in a friendly manner.

'Go into the guard room,' he said to Henry, 'and tell Claude to come here. You remain there; keep an eye on the road. Don't leave until you're told to.'

From the guard room Henry could see the front gate and the quiet road beyond it. The silence was pierced by a scream, one that was loud but stopped short by a popping noise then the sound of something falling. Henry wondered whether to go and see what was happening, despite Viktor's instructions. Next came the sound of Nikolai shrieking and another popping noise, followed by two more. After that, more silence.

The door to the guardroom opened. Peter was standing there. 'You're to go to the library.' When he got there, Viktor and Claude were standing in the middle of the room, revolvers in their hands. The body of Tatyana was thrown back in her chair, her eyes and mouth wide open and a large wound on her forehead. Prostrate on the floor in front of her was Nikolai, two wounds visible on his back and a large pool of blood emerging from under him.

Henry was too shocked to move and for a while could say nothing, until he noticed Nikolai's back moving.

'He's breathing Viktor! Nikolai's breathing.' Henry felt himself swaying. Claude walked over to the boy and with his foot turned him over. Nikolai was breathing very slowly. His face was white, but his eyes were moving as if he was having trouble focussing. Claude looked up at Viktor: what do you want me to do?

Viktor held up a hand: wait. 'Henry, you finish him off. It is a tradition in our service: everyone on a mission should take part.' The Russian pressed his own revolver into Henry's hand: the barrel was still hot. Henry's hand was shaking so much that the gun was waving around.

'Be careful with that thing, please Henry. You'd better use two hands' said Viktor. 'And be quick. We need to get out of here.' Henry breathed in deeply. *Never question; never discuss; never hesitate.* He calmly walked over to Nikolai and knelt down by him.

The boy's head moved slowly towards him, his eyes locking onto Henry's as his mouth opened, allowing a trickle of blood to slide down his chin.

'Come on, quick,' said Claude. Henry released the safety catch and placed the revolver against Nikolai's temple. He noticed he was trying to say something: hearing him say something – anything – would be more than he could bear. When he pressed the trigger he felt the splatter of blood and flesh on him before he heard the sound. It had been no harder than shooting his puppy. Claude hauled him up.

'Good. Well done. We need to move now.'

* * *

They left the house just before four o'clock, after trying to make it appear as if a robbery had gone dreadfully wrong. They opened the safe and made the study look as if it had been ransacked. Henry went upstairs with Peter to help find any jewellery. As they walked past the bathroom Henry stopped suddenly. A girl's leg was poking out of the door. Its shoe had fallen off and was upside-down on the carpet in front of him. Peter pushed in front of him as he tried to open the bathroom door, placing himself between Henry and the door.

'You don't need to come in here.'

'I want to see,' said Henry, barging his way past the German.

The bodies of Roza and Nadezhda were sprawled on the floor, on top of a pool of dark blood that had spread around the room. The heads of both girls were jerked at an unnatural angle, facing each other, their eyes open and full of fear. Roza's hand had reached out to her sister's, her fingers clutching one of Nadezhda's wrists.

'What...'

Peter had now pushed past him and was drawing the curtains. He smiled at Henry and pointed at the girls and made a cut-throat gesture.

Henry stood in the doorway for a minute, watching as Peter hauled the bodies of the two girls into the bath then threw towels onto the floor to soak up the blood. He was shocked to realise how un-shocked he felt. His main concern was he should be careful not to step in the blood.

Henry left the house as normal through the front gate and headed into town, crossing the river and towards Interlaken West train station. He was halfway down Bahnhofstrasse when the car pulled up. Peter and Claude got out and walked towards the station. Henry climbed into the passenger seat next to Viktor.

They drove north towards Bern, but were well past Thun before either of them spoke. 'You realise there was no alternative, don't you *synok*?' Viktor turned briefly towards Henry, who shrugged. 'We couldn't afford to have any witnesses.'

Henry said nothing. *Never question; never discuss; never hesitate.*

Instead of driving into Bern, they stopped briefly in Köniz then took the road towards Lausanne. It was only then that Henry spoke. 'What happened to Anatoly?'

'I think you can guess *synok*.'

'Did he know what was going to happen to him?'

'I'd imagine so: he's been an *apparatchik* all his adult life. He knows how we work. He'd have known what to expect.'

'So why did he co-operate then?'

'Because I promised him that if he did, we would spare the children.'

'And he believed you?'

Viktor said nothing for a while as he thought about Henry's question. The headlight of an approaching bus caught the Russian's gold teeth as he turned to reply.

'Probably not, but what choice did he have? He wanted to believe that I – we – would spare the children and his wife. Look, you're asking too many questions *synok*. You did well, just leave it at that. You are one of us now. You should be happy.'

Later that night, once he had arrived home in Nyon and lay in his own bed for the first time in weeks, what most shocked Henry was the realisation of how much he agreed with Viktor. He was now one of them. He was happy. But he knew it had come at a terrible, terrible price. When he had returned from Germany the previous year he knew they had taken possession of his soul.

Now they had destroyed it.

That night, he had the dream for the first time.

* * *

Chapter 7: Berlin, January 1940

On a foggy winter's afternoon in the middle of January, a tall man with a stooped bearing that gave him a misleadingly academic air left his office at the Reichsbank on Werderscher Markt in the centre of Berlin, by the canal. It was 5.30, somewhat later than most other people he worked with. The later he left work, he reasoned, the later he would arrive home and that suited him fine.

Gunter Reinhart had developed a habit of leaving the enormous complex through different exits on different days. Had someone been observing him, which they would have no cause to do, they might be suspicious. But he did not vary his routine for reasons of security; the truth was far more prosaic than that. It afforded him the opportunity to take different routes home and on each of those routes lay various bars, where he could further delay his arrival there. At least it gave him something to think about during the afternoon.

There was no point in leaving through the Unterwasserstrasse exit because beyond that was the canal. He liked the anonymity and slightly rougher edge to the bars round Leipzigerstrasse, but that was further from home. Leaving through Französischestrasse meant heading towards the Unter den Linden, which one could never accuse of offering anonymity. He would, he decided, leave through Kurstrasse and find somewhere to stop off around Jägerstrasse.

These days, stepping out into the street after dark was like descending into a tunnel. Reinhart had mixed feelings about the blackout that descended upon Berlin at dusk. On the one hand, it conferred an atmosphere of privacy on the city. You felt you were in your own world. On the other, there was no question it made life more difficult. There were no street lights, buildings were dark and the trams moved around like ghost trains. Cars had just a small strip of paper over their headlights. Any lights that were allowed were covered in blue paper, while low-level red lamps marked danger spots such as roadworks. Then there was the phosphorous paint: gallons of the stuff liberally sloshed on the pavements and road surfaces to give pedestrians and drivers some chance of knowing where they were. The effect was quite eerie and unsettling. Berlin at night looked as if it was deserted. There were reports of numerous traffic accidents and people being killed from walking into things or falling over in the blackout. The sister of one of the secretaries in his office had died when she stepped off the platform at Kaiserhof station. And then there were the rumours. Berlin thrived on rumours anyway; they had been part an essential part of its pre-war diet. Now, rumours were disseminated in more hushed and guarded tones. The latest was that a murderer was taking advantage of the blackout and had already killed a dozen young women. There had even been oblique references to it in the newspapers. Naturally, the police said they suspected the person responsible was Jewish; or Polish; or both.

The few people who moved around the city at night did so tentatively, as if wading through water. Some had taken to whistling or coughing constantly so as to alert others to their proximity and thus avoid bumping into them. But that was something of a forlorn hope: it was impossible to avoid other people.

Even though this was a route he knew very well, on nights like this, when there was no moonlight, Gunter Reinhart could not find his bearings. Just after the intersection with Friedrichstrasse, he came across a group of men silently beating up a man on the ground. He paused for a moment, taking in the surreal nature of what he was witnessing before he decided to cross the road. He had learned to keep well away from trouble. Suddenly, a long black car swept passed him and stopped. Very quickly, the man who was being attacked was bundled in.

Six months previously he would have been shaken to the core by what he had seen, but now it was quickly forgotten. He was more concerned with finding somewhere to drink. Looming out of the dark, he spotted the dim blue-covered sign for *Das Potsdamer Taverne*, a bar he used to visit at least twice a week, though recently it had become something of a favourite haunt for a group of young SS officers. Given that the whole point of going to the bar was to relax, they were the last people he'd want to find in there.

He walked slowly down the steep steps to the basement, clutching on to the iron railings and keeping a careful eye on the dabs of phosphorous paint on the steps. The bar had a low ceiling which caused him to stoop. Through the blue-brown cigarette smoke he could see perhaps half a dozen other customers spread out: all alone, all smoking, all drinking quietly, all sitting as far as they could manage from each other. Like him, they were avoiding going home. There was no sign of the SS, or indeed anyone else in uniform.

The barmaid caught his eye as he waited to order a drink.

'How are you?' she asked. 'I haven't seen you for a while.'

'A week perhaps? No more than that. I was in here last week.'

The kind of conversation repeated in bars around the world, between barmaids and husbands who would rather not go home.

She was a friendly girl with broad shoulders and hair that looked as if it had been dyed yellow. His wife, in her usual waspish manner, would describe her in the unlikely event of her ever meeting her by saying that she had seen better days, but she had friendly eyes and a seductive voice, with a distinctive Bavarian accent. She kept glancing at him as she pulled the beer, her eyes darting around. He started to move away, hoping to find a seat on his own. She held up her hand. *Wait a moment.*

When she had finished serving another customer she leaned over to talk quietly to him.

'A man was in here asking about you.'

Eight words no-one wanted to hear in Berlin in 1940.

'What man?'

'I don't know, I've never seen him here before. He was very polite and well-spoken. A Berliner definitely: wore a nice coat.'

'When was this?'

She leant back as if trying to calculate the answer.

'Last Thursday, I think: and then again yesterday – Monday.'

Gunter Reinhart pulled up the stool next to him and sat on it. This was bad news. Who could possibly be coming into a bar to ask about him? People knew where he worked and where he lived.

'And what did you say?'

'He seemed like a nice man, but I didn't want to say much. On the other hand, I didn't want to lie. I just said you come in here every so often: about once a week these days. Was that alright?'

Not really.

'Did he say anything else?'

'Wait'. The barmaid knelt down and emerged with her handbag, which she rummaged through. 'Here, I've found it. He said that if you come in, I'm to give this to you.' She handed him a book of matches with *Das Potsdamer Taverne* on the front. He looked at it for a while, puzzled.

'Open it.'

Neatly written inside were two dates.

Den 8 Juni 1901

Den 4 Oktober 1929

'Are you alright?'

Gunter Reinhart was evidently not alright. The hand holding the book of matches was shaking and the other was gripping the bar tightly. Beads of sweat had formed on his forehead. He could feel his chest tightening.

'Pardon?'

'Are you alright? You look shaken.'

He put the matches in his top pocket and drank most of the glass of beer in one go. He pushed the empty glass towards her and nodded for her to refill it.

'I'm fine, thank you. Did this man say how I could contact him?'

'He said he'd be here at six o'clock every Thursday and Monday night until he was able to meet up with you.'

Reinhart stayed in the bar for another hour and three more beers before he decided to walk all the way home to Charlottenburg. It was a long walk, but he needed the time to compose himself. He crossed Hermann Goring Strasse, which people would quietly joke was almost as wide as the man himself, and into Charlottenburger Chaussee, the Tiergarten an enormous void on his left.

Despite the brisk night air and absence of British bombers, he found himself becoming increasingly tense rather than composed. He had continuously checked the dates before leaving the bar. There was no question about them.

Why on earth would someone write the down the birth dates of his first wife and his eldest son, especially now they were no longer in Berlin?

* * *

The following morning, Reinhart took extra care on his journey into work to ensure he wasn't being followed, not that he was sure what he was meant to do. He was a banker: his knowledge of subterfuge was limited to the world of finance. He could move funds from one bank account to another without leaving a trace, but he had no idea how to walk from one place to another without being spotted and, in any case, he towered above most other people. It wouldn't be hard to follow him. When he arrived at the Reichsbank he casually enquired of his secretary – maybe a bit too casually – whether anyone had been asking for him: *perhaps over the past few days?* His secretary assured him that no-one had been asking after him. She looked appalled at the very thought that someone might have enquired of him and she would not have passed the information on.

His head of department informed him that Funk wanted to see

them both the next morning: he wanted an urgent and up-to-date report on some of the new Swiss bank accounts. 'You're not to worry,' he assured his head of department. 'The information will be ready.' Pulling it all together was at least a distraction for Reinhart, but it did mean his head of department fussed around him for the rest of the day. He was a rotund man whose suit was always too tight, with bad breath and clothes that reeked of mothballs. He had been promoted from his natural level as an assistant bank manager somewhere near Magdeburg simply due to a longstanding loyalty to the Nazi Party and as a consequence was now utterly out of his depth.

The next day – Thursday – followed a sleepless night. The meeting with Walther Funk proved to be but a two-hour distraction, even something of an amusement. The President of the Reichsbank, who doubled as Hitler's Minister of Economics, was someone else who'd been promoted because of service to the Nazi Party rather than any kind of financial competence or knowledge. Reinhart produced a series of complicated balance sheets and lengthy lists of transactions. Funk was impressed and confused in equal measure, but unable to own up to the latter.

The afternoon went slowly and, as the sun disappeared over Berlin, Reinhart wondered whether he was being led into a trap. Maybe he had been a bit too clever by half. Maybe he'd upset one too many of the Nazi Party bosses at the top of the Reichsbank, who felt they had cause to distrust him. *Gunter Reinhart, the man who knows everything about the Swiss accounts: time to put him in his place.*

Das Potsdamer Taverne was as quiet as the previous night. He nodded at the barmaid and she smiled, slightly shaking her head: *not yet.*

There was a tiny table wedged into a corner behind the bar, and Reinhart took a seat there. He waited as the bar became quieter and was just wondering how long he should stay when he caught sight of a man who looked vaguely familiar and seemed to be glancing in his direction. The man remained at the bar, toying with a glass of beer. A few minutes later he appeared at Reinhart's table.

'Do you mind if I sit here?'

Reinhart was almost certain this man was a friend of his first wife's family, a lawyer – specialising in banking and finance, rather intelligent and a bit too liberal for his liking: Catholic. First name Franz, if he remembered correctly. He doubted, though, this was the man who had gone to such lengths to meet him. After all, bumping into an acquaintance in the centre of Berlin was hardly the most remarkable of coincidences. The man produced a packet of cigarettes, took one out and placed it in Reinhart's hand.

'Would you like a light?'

Reinhart hesitated. The man reached into his pocket and found a book of matches, one with *Das Potsdamer Taverne* on the front. As he opened it he casually angled the packet so that Reinhart could clearly see it. Again, two dates were handwritten on the inside of the packet.

Den 8 Juni 1901

Den 4 Oktober 1929

This time it was in the unmistakably familiar handwriting of his first wife. The man shifted his chair even closer to Reinhart and when he spoke again it was in a quieter voice.

'You remember me, Gunter? Franz Hermann. Just act normally, don't speak too loud or too quietly. Smile occasionally.'

'I remember you Franz. I guess it was you who's been asking about me here?'

Hermann nodded.

'What's it all about? You've given me a couple of sleepless nights.'

'I fear I'm about to give you many more. You see...'

He paused. A couple of Luftwaffe officers had come into the bar and moved noisily towards them, looking for somewhere to sit. Franz waited until they moved away.

'Good, this is not a conversation we'd want them to overhear. Stop looking so worried Gunter; you'll draw attention to yourself. Just relax and smile: we're friends who've met in a bar. Don't look like you're being interrogated by the Gestapo. When did you last hear from Rosa?'

Gunter frowned, trying to remember.

'There was a letter from Paris in October. She sent it at the beginning of October but I didn't receive it until the end of the month: it came via a friend of hers in Switzerland and then through my brother.

'How come?'

'I don't know if you're aware, but I remarried soon after Rosa and I divorced. Far too soon, as it's turned out. But we have children and it's a situation I'm stuck with. Gudrun won't tolerate me having any contact whatsoever with either Rosa or Alfred. As far as she's concerned, I have nothing to do with them. It's safer she thinks that: she's become a devoted Nazi, like the rest of her family. The fact I was once married to a Jew and had a son with her is a terrible thing in Gudrun's eyes. I've had to promise her I have no contact whatsoever with Rosa and Alfred, that I've disowned them. Have you heard from her Franz: is everything alright? What about Alfred?'

'Gunter, unless you keep your voice down and act normally, we're going to have a serious problem. Do you understand? Drink some of your beer. Try to look relaxed.'

Gunter nodded and composed himself. 'I understand, but is there any news?'

'For the time being, they're safe.'

'And they're still in Paris?'

Hermann lowered his head and talked a little more quietly.

'A smile please Gunter, you need to smile. We're old friends meeting for a relaxed drink. Good, that's better. You need to prepare yourself for what I'm about to say. They're safe, for the time being: Rosa, Alfred and little Sophia. But I don't know for how long. They're in hiding you see. Here in Berlin.'

* * *

Gunter Reinhart had to wait three days before he could see his son and his ex-wife, along with her young daughter. Having to wait that long was bad enough, but visiting them on a Sunday presented added problems. Sunday was the day his wife demanded his undivided attention, but he insisted he had work commitments that were none of her business and he was able to slip out of the house once they returned from church.

'They're living with my mother in Dahlem: near the Botanischer Garten,' Hermann had told him at the bar. 'My mother has become quite unwell, unable to look after herself. She insists on staying in the old family home. She needed someone to live in and look after her and, luckily, with her qualifications and experience, Rosa is ideal. She'll tell you the full story. On Sundays, my brother-in-law drives over from Brandenburg and takes her back to their house for lunch. She leaves at 11 in the morning and they bring her back around four, so that doesn't leave much time.'

Not much time.

'There's no reason to think anyone will suspect what you are up to, Gunter,' Franz had warned him, 'but be careful. Assume you're being followed and take basic precautions: walk at an even pace, don't keep looking behind you – that kind of thing.'

So he walked at an even pace across Spandauer Strasse and caught the S-Bahn at Westend. He did as Hermann had advised: making sure he got onto the busiest carriage and watching out for anyone getting on at the same time as him. The train worked its way south at a Sunday pace. At Schmargendorf, he changed to the U-Bahn then headed south again, getting off at Podbielski Allee.

He wasn't far now: he had not seen his son or Rosa for nearly six months. He had assumed they were out of the country. His excitement at seeing them was mixed with the shock they were still in Germany.

From Podbielski Allee, he headed down Peter Lenne Strasse towards the Botanischer Garten. He had memorised Hermann's instructions. *'Write nothing down.'*

At the end of the road, he turned left into Königin-Luise-

Strasse, across the square then continued along Grunewald Strasse. 'You know Kaiser Wilhelm Strasse, Gunter? Runs off Grunewald Strasse. Turn into there: first right is Arno-Holz Strasse. The white house on the corner is where my mother lives. I'll be there from 12. If the curtains are drawn in window directly above the front door, it's safe to approach, but please only do so if you believe you've not been followed. Otherwise, head down to the Botanischer Garten at a leisurely pace.'

He did as instructed. In other circumstances he would have enjoyed his walk on what had turned out to be an unseasonably warm afternoon. The house was as Hermann had described it, the front garden deep and heavy with trees, the walls white and in need of repainting and above the front door, a window. The curtains were drawn.

He looked around him once more, but the streets were deserted. He had not been followed. He unlatched a noisy iron gate and walked down the path. As he approached the porch, the front door opened and behind it he could see Franz Hermann, silently ushering him in.

They stood together in the dark hall of a silent house.

'Are they here Franz?'

'Upstairs. Take your shoes off.'

Gunter ran up the stairs. On the landing, waiting for him in the gloom, was his ex-wife and their son. Behind them, peering out from behind a door was Sophia, Rosa's daughter from her second marriage.

Alfred flung himself at his father, holding him tight and burying his face in his chest. Gunter could feel the warm tears seeping through his shirt and vest. Rosa came up to him and held his face, kissing him tenderly on each cheek, her hand cupping the back of his neck. He could feel tears welling in his eyes. Little Sophia waved at him. He waved back.

He held both Rosa and Alfred, unsure of what to say. *The only family I ever wanted.*

It was 2.30 by the time Gunter and Rosa were able to be alone in a small room on the top floor of the house. Franz had told them he would wait with the children and keep an eye on the front. Gunter would need to be away by a quarter to four to be safe. He and Rosa sat quietly for a while, holding hands.

'I thought you were in Paris, Rosa? '

He was trying hard not to sound angry.

'We were. I wrote to you at the beginning of October. Did you get the letter?'

He nodded. She shrugged.

'Harald was meant to join us in the middle of October: he'd remained in Berlin because he needed to make a few arrangements. The idea was he'd get what money he could out of the business, which wasn't much, and transfer it to Switzerland. Then we'd have something to live on and, together with the money you gave us, we may be able to get to America.'

'That was the idea.'

'I promise you that was the plan. As you know, Harald had been forced to sell the business to two of his managers for a fraction of what it was worth. Both of them were men who were friends of his, who he'd always helped in the past. They'd always said they'd help him and one of them did, but the other refused. I don't know exactly what happened, but from what I can gather Harald was reported to the Gestapo for trying to get money out of Germany, which is illegal for a Jew. I suspect the manager he'd fallen out with reported him. So Harald was arrested and taken to Sachsenhausen – it's a special camp for prisoners of the Nazis. Have you heard of it?'

'Of course I have – near Oranienburg. Are you sure he's there?'

'Believe me, I'm sure. Terrible things happen there. I don't like to think about what he must be going through. I know he's still alive, or at least he was two weeks ago, but I don't know what state he's in.'

'So why on earth did you come back here? What were you thinking of, Rosa?'

'I don't know what I was thinking. Please don't be angry with me. I thought if my husband was in prison here then I should come back to help him. I thought I could get him released.'

'But Rosa, what about Alfred – and Sophia?'

'I know Gunter. But remember, we left Germany for France in July. I'd no idea how bad things had become. In Paris I borrowed some money from my cousin and I sold all my jewellery. I thought I could pay a fine or a bribe or something like that and get Harald released. But when I went to the police station they confiscated my passport and wanted to know where I was living. I gave them the address of the old flat in Pankow we were staying at and they only let me go because I had papers showing I was registered there. I knew they'd come for us, but fortunately, I'd left the children with my old colleague Maria in Kreuzberg while I went to the police station. When I left, I went straight to Kreuzberg, picked up Alfred and Sophia then contacted Franz. He took us to his house for a few days then came up with this plan for us to move in here with his mother. It's worked out well: the old lady is almost deaf and can't climb the stairs, so as long as the children are quiet and stay upstairs they are alright and she's no idea they're here.'

'And she doesn't suspect you?'

'She's been told I'm a nurse from the north whose husband is in the Navy. Of course, I don't let on I'm a doctor. I can use all my skills to keep her alive: if she dies, we'll have to leave the house. I have some papers Franz managed to get showing I'm from Bremerhaven, but they're not good enough to travel with. Franz comes round most days. The old lady has very few visitors other than that: one or two friends who pop in for an hour every so often, but they always call first. Franz's sister doesn't know the truth about me, and I think she's just grateful someone is looking after her mother so she doesn't have to.'

'And the children?'

'It's terrible for them here; they just have to stay upstairs all day. Poor Sophia has no idea what's going on, other than her father is in prison and she has to keep quiet all the time. Alfred understands, of course. That makes it worse, I suppose. He misses you terribly Gunter.'

Gunter sat for a while with his head in his hands, deep in thought.

'Why didn't you contact me before now – I mean, once you got back to Berlin?'

Rosa looked at him long and hard. *You don't know why?*

'Gunter – you always said I wasn't to contact you directly. You

117

said Gudrun doesn't allow it. I didn't know what your situation was, whether it was safe. I also thought you'd be angry with me. I was hoping we'd find a way back to France: Franz was going to see if he could find false papers, but it's impossible. We're trapped here in Berlin.'

Rosa was weeping now, her trembling hand holding Gunter's.

'I should never have divorced you Rosa, I was...'

'Don't blame yourself Gunter. We agreed it was for the best.'

'No, I was being selfish. The three of us should have left after that damn law was passed.'

They sat in silence for a long while.

'It's 3.15 Gunter. Franz says you're to leave soon. Please spend some time with Alfred before you go. He misses you so much.'

'I don't know what to do Rosa. Do you need food or money?'

'Yes, but what we really need is to get out: even if you can just save Alfred. As far as the Nazis are concerned, he's only a half-Jew. Could you take him, would Gudrun not understand?'

Gunter laughed. 'Understand? Even if I said you'd abandoned Alfred and I'd found him in the middle of Berlin, she wouldn't want to know. When we got married she made me promise I would never, ever have anything to do with the two of you again. Frankly, I wouldn't put it past her to turn him in. Her brother, Norbert, who has all the intelligence of a field mouse but with less of the personality – he's now a big shot in the Nazi Party in Bergdorf, which says everything you need to know about them. The fact I was once married to a Jew is a terrible secret in that family. Gudrun insists the children aren't allowed to know about it.'

'But what are we going to do, Gunter?'
'I don't know Rosa. Give me time, I'll think of something.'

* * *

Chapter 8: Geneva and Bern, June 1940

'*Do nothing unusual and certainly nothing that's likely to draw attention to yourself.*'

For eight long months Henry had followed Edgar's advice, leading an unremarkable existence. The waiting to be contacted was tedious and living with his mother even more so. The fact he was now in control of the purse strings was more than she could bear. It was 'intolerable', she announced during a dramatic argument on the night he returned. She could not understand why he had returned with so little of the aunt's money.

He explained their predicament once more, very clearly and very slowly.

'Remember it was your clever idea to bypass probate and for me to attempt to bring all the money back here as soon as possible,' said Henry. 'That proved to be simply impossible – and illegal: I could have ended up in prison. I've told you what happened: I had to go to London and stay there for all that time to sort out the money. I was tangled up in reels and reels of red tape, then war was declared at the beginning of September, which made matters almost impossible. The British Government simply don't want to release money overseas, they say they can't be sure whose hands it'll end up in. You ought to be grateful I managed to get anything out at all and return in one piece.'

'But it's our money Henry!'

'My money actually – and not all of it as it turned out. In the end, the authorities accepted my explanation that there'd been a misunderstanding over the Will. I was fortunate. Then it took a few more weeks for probate to be granted. After that, I had to obtain agreement that the money could be released, but, as I told you, I don't get it in one sum. You were advanced 200 pounds. I'll be able to access a further 500 over the next few days and the rest will come through at the rate of 100 pounds per month. It's not the amount we'd hoped for, mother, but it's enough for us to be able to live far more comfortably.'

Since the death of her second husband, Marlene Hesse's perfectly formed world had steadily unravelled. She now accepted the changed situation with the minimum of grace. At least they had been able to afford to rent a larger apartment in a much more respectable location just off Quai du Mont Blanc, which was some consolation.

But the wait to be contacted was considerably more trying than his mother. Two days after his return, Henry had gone as instructed to the Quai des Bergues branch of Credit Suisse and made an appointment to see Madame Ladnier later that morning. In a small office in the basement she went through the details of the account, before handing him a folded piece of paper. *My home telephone number: I only give this to special clients and then only to be used in particular circumstances. You understand?*

After that, nothing. As soon as they moved into their new apartment he went to see Madame Ladnier to give her the details. She assured him the matter would be dealt with. He was desperate to ask her if there was any news, but managed to restrain himself.

He began to follow a routine, in the hope it would make it easier for whoever would approach him: leaving the apartment at a certain time, returning to it at a certain time, an afternoon walk, the shops...

Christmas came and went, celebrated mostly in silence with his still-embittered mother, and January brought the snows down from the Alps, but still no contact. By the end of the month, he'd started to wonder if he would ever be contacted and decided this would be no bad thing. Perhaps they'd forgotten about him: at least the money was still appearing in his account. There was the occasional contact from Viktor and he always told him the same: no news. Loyalty was proving to be a most complicated business.

At the end of February, he received a phone call from Madame Ladnier. Could he come into the bank to sign a document? *You aren't to worry*, she assured him. *They've told me to tell you that you will be contacted in due course, but it may take a few months. Remain patient – and discreet.*

The same happened at the end of April: *they want me to assure you that you've not been forgotten. Be patient. It shouldn't be too long now.* Viktor was not surprised when he told him: *there's no rush synok – that's how people like us operate.*

On the last Tuesday in June, Henry left the apartment off Quai du Mont Blanc as usual at 9.30. It was already a warm morning, with a light breeze skimming over the lake. As he headed south for a brisk walk before breakfast a woman swept past him before slowing down and studying a map. As he drew alongside her she looked surprised, then spoke in French with a Provençal accent, much faster than the Swiss.

'I'm sorry sir, I appear to be lost! I'm looking for the Old Town. Do you know the way?'

It was so natural, so matter of fact, that Henry was taken aback and thought this couldn't possibly be the contact, who he'd assumed, would be a man. It must be a coincidence, he thought, but then he noticed she was carrying a copy of Monday's *Tribune de Genève*. It took him a moment to compose himself.

'Of course. Would you prefer to walk or take the tram?'

She smiled. 'I'd prefer to walk if you are able to show me the way to go.'

Another smile and a slight hesitation before Henry replied.

'Well, I'm walking to the Old Town myself now. If you wish, you're most welcome to follow me.'

She smiled and theatrically held out an elegantly gloved hand. *Lead on.*

'Take any route to the Old Town.'

Henry tried to walk at a normal pace, unsure what a normal pace felt like. He crossed the Rhône at the Pont des Bergues, allowing himself a glance behind to check the woman was still following. He crossed the Rue de la Rôtisserie into the Old Town and soon after that the woman overtook him: it was now his turn to follow her. She walked through alleyways, crossed roads, waited on corners and eventually they emerged onto Rue de l'Hôtel de Ville. Her pace did not change, other than when she paused briefly at a shop window. Henry was wondering how long this would go on for, but then they crossed into the Grand-Rue and there on the corner was the Brasserie de Hôtel de Ville and outside it a waste-paper bin, into which she dropped her copy of *Tribune de Genève*. She carried on walking, but Henry knew his rendezvous would take place here. He entered the café.

You're to enter the building and wait. If no-one has approached you after five minutes, you are to leave and return home.

He glanced at his wristwatch and the clock on the wall. Within two minutes a man entered the café, smoking a cigar and greeting two people sat at a nearby table. He shook hands with the barman and walked straight over to Henry.

'I am Marc. Would you care to join me?'

If someone joins you and introduces themselves as Marc you're to go with him. He will take you to meet your main contact. At that moment, your new career will have begun.

Henry nodded. Beside the bar was a door that Marc opened: *after you.*

A narrow staircase twisted and turned to the top of the building. When they reached a small landing, Marc gestured for him to wait then knocked three times on a polished oak door.

'It's me, Marc. I have the delivery.'

Henry heard a bolt being drawn then the door opened. It was a corner room, expensively furnished with an ornate fireplace and a thick carpet: one wall was taken up with a floor-to-ceiling bookcase, many of the volumes leather-bound. On a French-polished sideboard there was an exquisite cut-glass decanter with matching glasses on a silver tray. Next to that was another tray, with a teapot and various cups.

The door was opened by a dapper man in his sixties who was wearing a three-piece suit. His iron-grey hair, going white at the sides, was slicked back, slightly longer than Henry would have expected.

'Ah, Hunter: welcome! At long last. Welcome indeed. Sorry about all this John Buchan stuff. Not really my idea: seems to be the form these days. Apparently we can't be too careful.' It was a distinctly upper-class drawl.

'Now do come in and make yourself at home. My name is Basil by the way, like in the Swiss city.'

'Pardon?'

'Basle, Hunter. The Swiss seems to find it amusing, or at least they would do if they allowed themselves the indulgence of a sense of humour. Basil Remington-Barber. There's an 'Hon' that goes in front of the name if you're a stickler for that kind of thing. As far as the Swiss are concerned, I'm a commercial attaché at the British Embassy in Bern. As far as you're concerned, I run the station out here in Switzerland and if you're still confused that means I look after all intelligence matters from our place on Thunstrasse. Thought it'd be a quiet place to wind up my career. Had rather expected to have retired by now, but I'm told there's a war on and someone in London has decided I'm indispensible: helps I speak the lingo I suppose, all of them as it happens. Had hoped to be hacking my way round some of Scotland's easier links courses by now, but there we go.'

With that, he switched to Swiss-German, alternating between it and German. 'Now, tell me Hunter, are you raring to go or had you been hoping we'd forgotten all about you?'

'Well, I can't really say. I imagine that…'

'Bit of both probably, perfectly understandable – not knowing is the worst part. Sorry about the delay, but the good news is – the waiting's over. The fall of France has rather spurred London into action as far as I can gather. We have a little errand for you. But first of all, let's have some tea: milk and sugar?'

Henry relaxed a bit now. The civilised serving of tea and the promise of a little errand sounded quite acceptable, perhaps even fun. What was it Edgar had promised? *Chances are the first job will be something relatively straightforward, probably within Switzerland. Shouldn't be anything too dangerous; a warm-up, if you like.*

The Hon Basil Remington-Barber took a while to serve tea, fussing first that Henry's and then his own tea was neither too weak nor too strong. When he was satisfied everything was just right, he leaned back in his armchair and addressed Henry through the steam rising from his china teacup. Henry was beginning to enjoy his morning. His pleasure was to be short-lived.

'We understand you're very familiar with Stuttgart, Hunter?'

'I beg your pardon?' Henry felt his throat tightening.

'Stuttgart, the German city?'

Henry placed his teacup down on the side table next to him. His hands were beginning to shake and he needed to cover that up, so he folded them on his lap, crossing and then un-crossing his legs as he did so.

'Yes, I know it.'

'Been there often?'

'Once or twice.'

'Really?'

Henry shrugged. *Not sure.*

'*Quite* a few times, we understand Hunter.'

'Well, possibly…'

'Something you omitted to tell any of my colleagues back in England?'

Henry hesitated for longer than he knew he should. 'Forgot rather than omitted, I'd say.' He was not convinced by his own answer. Nor was Basil Remington-Barber, who shook his head in mild disapproval. 'I rather know the feeling; I seem to forget the odd thing these days. My wife tells me I'm starting to remind her of how her father was just before he went completely potty! The old boy had to be locked up after he shot one of his gamekeepers: thought he was a pheasant, apparently. The point is, though, that not mentioning Stuttgart is a rather important omission. Perhaps you'd like to tell me about it now?'

Henry tried to sound as casual as possible, hoping to convey the impression that his knowledge of Stuttgart was really nothing very important, the kind of thing one could so easily forget.

'There's not an awful lot to say. My stepfather had some property in Stuttgart. I used to pop up there every so often to keep an eye on things for him.'

'How often would "every so often" be, Hunter?'

'I really couldn't say. Once or twice a year, maybe.'

'My very strong advice, Hunter,' Remington-Barber had now dispensed with the bonhomie, 'would be you're totally honest from now on. You see, your first mission is to go up to Stuttgart and the more we know about your familiarity with the city, the better. I do hope you understand that.'

Shouldn't be anything too dangerous; a warm-up, if you like.

'Edgar implied my first mission would be within Switzerland.'

'Did he now? Well, that's Edgar for you: an officer but not quite a gentleman. Grammar school, I'm told. Now, tell me all about Stuttgart.'

'My step-father had a fair amount of residential property in Stuttgart, in the best areas: quite a lot in Gänseheide to the east of the city centre and more in the north, Azenberg and Killesberg mostly. He had local agents that looked after them, but he liked me to go up there once a quarter to check everything was in order and to oversee the transfer of his rental income back to Switzerland.'

'So you visited Stuttgart four times a year.'

'Yes.'

'For how many years?'

'Seven or eight, possibly more.'

'Mathematics was never my strongest subject, Hunter, but I make that somewhere in the region of 30 visits to Stuttgart.'

'If you say so.'

'I do. So you're very familiar with the city?'

'I suppose so.'

'Speak the local dialect?'

'No, though I do understand it.'

'And where did you stay?'

'Usually at Hotel Marquardt in Schlossplatz.'

'That is certainly quite an omission, Hunter. Don't worry too much; I'm sure you're about to more than make up for it.'

* * *

Henry Hunter could never quite see the point of Bern. It was a pretty enough place, with an undoubted medieval charm and the River Aare leant a certain picturesque drama to the city as it twisted through the centre. But in a typically Swiss way it was rather too aware of its virtues; a little bit too smug. For the past 90 years or so the city had been the capital of Switzerland and now all roads led to it and, in the case of Henry's journey there on a windy Wednesday morning, so did the trains.

At the end of their briefing the previous day, the Hon Basil Remington-Barber had told him to get a move on. Henry had rather imagined this meant by the end of the month, possibly within a fortnight.

'A fortnight? You must be joking Hunter. No, this week. Get up to Bern tomorrow, sort out your visa then I'll give you your precise instructions.'

He explained to his mother he was visiting friends in Basle for a few days and took an early morning train to Bern, arriving at the station in Bahnhofplatz just in time for lunch. Henry had been pleasantly surprised when Remington-Barber suggested he book into the Schweizerhof, the best hotel in the city and no more than a short stroll from the station.

'Rather goes against the grain Hunter and certainly pushes the expenses, but the point is you have to stick to your role: as far as the Germans are concerned, you're an affluent Swiss gentleman who wishes to travel to Stuttgart on business. Such people stay at the Schweizerhof, I'm afraid. Make sure you're seen out and about in the hotel. There are something like 115,000 people in this city and I think if you took the spies away, it'd be less than 100,000. Most of the spies hang around the Schweizerhof, so it's good to be seen, just being yourself. Book yourself in for two nights. I just hope London buy it.'

Make sure you're seen out and about in the hotel. Once he had checked in and changed he went down to the restaurant. The restaurant manager asked him to wait at the bar, where he found himself alongside two very formally dressed, middle-aged men speaking in German. The two Germans greeted him correctly, almost standing to attention as they did so.

'What brings you to Bern?' they asked. Henry explained he was from Geneva but was here in Bern to arrange a visa: he was hoping visit Germany soon on business.

'Whereabouts?'

'Stuttgart.'

'Very good. Is Herr Hesse likely to be in Berlin at any time in the future?'

'Maybe. You never know!'

'You must look me up if you do,' said one of the men. 'There are so many misunderstandings about Germany these days. I'm sure you're not one of those people who thinks nothing but bad of Germany; we are, after all, of the same race, yes?'

Henry nodded enthusiastically. *Indeed.*

'But if you're ever in Berlin, I could introduce you to people. You'll be pleasantly surprised. I'd be happy to be of service.'

With that he presented Henry with a card, bowed slightly then left. Henry looked at it:

Alois Jäger
Rechtsanwalt
181 Friedrichstraße
Berlin

A Berlin lawyer; you never know.

* * *

The next morning, he visited the German Embassy on

Willadingweg. As he planned his journey there he remembered Remington-Barber's instructions.

'Whatever you do, Hunter, keep well away from where we are in Thunstrasse. There's a good chance you may be seen, the Germans pretty much keep a permanent watch outside our place. You know how you are to get hold of me.'

He breakfasted at the hotel, returned to his room briefly then strolled casually through the Old City, past the Münster – the enormous Gothic cathedral, over whose main entrance the sculpted participants in the Last Judgement gazed down at him, trying to decide whether he was wicked or virtuous.

He crossed the river on Kirchenfeldbrücke and soon found a taxi which took him to the German Embassy, located in a residential street in the east of the city. A large swastika hung limply over the entrance, which was guarded by half a dozen armed German soldiers. In the street outside were two Swiss policemen.

He had expected a short delay, but not the queue that greeted him. The visa office, the man in front of him explained, did not open until 11. It would close for lunch at one, re-open again at three and then close at five. The man looked up and down the queue. They do not hurry, he told Henry, but with some luck you may be seen sometime around four. Then you will have to return tomorrow to collect the visa.

He had been standing in the queue for an hour and a half when he heard a familiar voice behind him; Jäger, the Berlin lawyer.

'My dear Hesse, what are you doing in the queue? Come with me.'

To the obvious annoyance of the people in front of him, Henry was removed from the queue and escorted straight into the Embassy.

Wait here.

It was 1.15 now and the visa office had closed for lunch. Ten minutes later and Jäger emerged from it with a clearly reluctant man in tow.

'Hesse: Herr Soldner himself will look after you. You could not be in better hands. He has volunteered to curtail his lunch break in order to deal with your visa.'

It was evident that Herr Soldner was no mere clerk, as much as he looked like one. As they marched through the ground floor of the embassy to his office on the third floor, colleagues greeted him with a 'Sieg Heil', which he returned enthusiastically. His office was well appointed, overlooking the gardens at the rear. There was a portrait of Hitler on the wall and a large photograph on the desk of Herr Soldner shaking hands with some officers in black uniforms. Next to that was a smaller photograph of Herr Soldner with what he assumed was Frau Soldner and their children. On his lapel was a swastika badge. He gestured for Henry to sit down, removed his spectacles then read through Henry's form, nodding at times, making notes in the margin in places.

'Please explain the purpose of your visit to Stuttgart, Herr Hesse.'

Henry spoke in standard German, repeating the story he and Remington-Barber had agreed.

'My step-father had some business interests in Stuttgart, property mostly. Unfortunately, he died two years ago and I want to ensure there are no outstanding liabilities. Tying up loose ends, if you like.'

'Do you have any bank accounts in Germany, Herr Hesse?'

'No.'

'Do you have friends in Stuttgart?'

'More like acquaintances – business contacts.'

'Their names please.'

Henry gave the names of the two lawyers they dealt with, along with the three agents who handled the various properties.

Herr Soldner wrote each name down. He then laid down his pen and put on his spectacles.

'The last name you gave me, Herr Hesse – one of the agents.'

'Bermann?'

'Yes: first name please.'

'Heinz: Heinz Bermann.'

'A friend of yours?'

'As I say, more of an acquaintance, a business associate.'

'When did you last see Bermann?'

'Last time I was in Stuttgart, some three years ago.'

'And were you planning to see him this time?'

'Possibly.'

'Do you realise that if you did so, Herr Hesse, that would be in breach of the conditions of your visa?'

'Really... Why's that?'

'The very strong likelihood is that Bermann is a Jew, an enemy of the state.'

With only the briefest hesitation, Henry slapped his thigh in annoyance.

'You don't say! Well that would explain a lot Herr Soldner. I didn't want to say too much before I went there but we never totally trusted this Bermann. We always suspected he was being less than honest with us. That was one of the reasons for my visit, to find out whether he owed us money. Typical.'

'If he's still in Stuttgart, Herr Hesse, he will no longer have any assets in his own name.'

He wrote on a plain sheet of paper and attached it to the visa application, placing the complete document in a tray.

'Your passport please Herr Hesse.'

He handed his Swiss passport over to the German.

'Please wait in the reception on the ground floor. I will call you when I'm ready. You'll understand I need to make some enquiries.'

* * *

'The one thing we could get unstuck on is if they delve too far back,' Remington-Barber had told him. 'The only problem would be if they found out either you or your mother also has British nationality.'

'That'd be most unlikely. My mother hated being Maureen Hunter, she thought it sounded common. She's always regarded becoming Marlene Hesse and taking on Swiss nationality as the height of sophistication, and I'm certain she hasn't used her English name or British identity in 17 years. Also, remember we moved from Zürich to Geneva after she married. I became a Swiss national in 1927 and, as far as the Swiss authorities are concerned, I'm Henri Hesse.'

134

'Well, the Germans would have to dig very deep indeed to find all this out and they're only going to do that if they suspect anything. Obviously, we hope they don't.'

Obviously.

* * *

An hour later Adolf Hitler was once more staring at Henry Hunter, who was attempting to remain as calm as possible after being summoned back to Herr Soldner's office.

'Your visa is valid for 30 days from next Monday, which is the 1st of July. It expires on the 30th July. You'll be in breach of your visa if you are in Germany after that date: do you understand?'

Henry nodded. He was hoping to be back in Switzerland long before then.

'You're only permitted to stay in Stuttgart. While in Germany you must not take part in any political activities; you are prohibited from meeting or consorting with Jews, criminals or other enemies of the state; you will register at a hotel within two hours of your arrival and are not permitted to stay anywhere else during your stay; you are not allowed to approach any military establishments or observe any movements of the armed forces; you are not permitted to take photographs. The only currency that you are allowed to use in Germany is Reichsmarks: upon your arrival you're to go to a bank and exchange your Swiss Francs for Reichsmarks. I should warn you that using the black market is regarded as a serious criminal activity. It should not be necessary for me to warn you that should anyone approach you and ask for your help, particularly in regard to bringing information or messages back to Switzerland, that is also regarded as a very serious criminal activity. You should immediately report any such approach to the authorities. Do you understand?'

Henry did.

'Good. I do hope you enjoy your visit to Germany, Herr Hesse.'

* * *

An hour later Henry Hunter entered a cobblers on an arcade on Kramgasse and explained to the bearded man just visible behind a mound of shoes on the counter he had caught the heel of one of his shoes in the tramline by the station. The cobbler nodded and lifted the counter top, beckoning for Henry to come through.

'Go up the stairs to the very top. He is waiting for you.'

The Hon Basil Remington-Barber greeted Henry warmly.

'Beauty of this place is I can get into it through the back of a café about five doors along. Now, tell me how you got on.'

Remington-Barber checked the passport and the visa. *All in order: good.* He was, he said, as certain as he could be the Germans suspected nothing. For the next hour he gave Henry a detailed briefing on the Stuttgart mission.

'You've got everything Henry. All clear?'

'Yes, though you say I'm going to be contacted by this Milo. I'm still not sure how I'll know it's him?'

'And I told you, don't worry. Milo will find you: you have memorised the codes so you will know. The less you know before you meet up, the safer it is.'

'In case I'm caught?'

'Exactly, in case you're caught. Remember, you do whatever Milo tells you, understand?'

Henry said he did.

'There are plenty of Swiss Francs in this envelope here: change them into Reichsmarks as soon as you arrive – don't risk hiding any on you. Go back now to the Schweizerhof and check out: there's a direct train to Geneva at 6.30. Before you leave the Schweizerhof, ask them to make you a reservation at the Hotel Victoria in Stuttgart, arriving on Tuesday the 16th, leaving on the Friday – the 19th. It looks better if you leave a couple of weeks between the visa being granted and you actually travelling there: makes it appear you're not rushing. Understand?'

Henry nodded.

'One other thing: be careful at night in Stuttgart. There's a curfew on and few places to eat, so you're to stay in the hotel. On the first night certainly you should order room service: in my experience that tends to draw less attention to yourself.'

'And how would you like me to get to Stuttgart?'

'On the Monday morning, you take the train from Geneva to Zürich: tell your mother you'll be there all week. Give her this address; we'll cover any contacts there. Stay overnight at the Central Plaza hotel by Oetenbachgasse, it's very near the station: a room has been booked for you there. On Tuesday morning there's a Swissair flight from Zürich to Stuttgart. It should only take 50 minutes, here's hoping the RAF doesn't shoot you down!'

* * *

Chapter 9: Salzburg Airport, July 1940

Early in the afternoon of the last Tuesday in July, at the height of summer, half a dozen men were doing their best to avoid each other in a stuffy room overlooking the runway at Salzburg Airport. The men were all dressed in uniforms denoting high rank in various branches of the German armed forces: two stood by the large window but well apart from each other; another appeared to be asleep; two others were leafing through their copies of the *Völkischer Beobachter* and another was pacing the room, drawing hard on a cigarette.

A short while after the clock struck two a nervous young Luftwaffe officer entered the room. *A delay: many apologies. The plane was delayed after refuelling in Munich. Departure will now be at three o'clock – four at the latest.*

Much muttering and shaking of heads around the room: the young Luftwaffe officer paused in the doorway just long enough to remember to give a hurried *Heil Hitler* salute, which was ignored by all the others.

The man who had appeared to be asleep stood up and carefully straightened his Kriegsmarine uniform before leaving the room. Outside was a small lawn with flowers planted neatly around its edges. He strolled up and down, and was soon joined by an army officer, one of the two men who had been by the window. The admiral and the general walked in step alongside each other in silence for a while. The general took his time lighting a large cigar before addressing his companion.

'I see we cannot even rely on the Luftwaffe to get us back to

Berlin on time! I imagine Jodl's plane wasn't delayed.'

'He flew back last night, I understand: soon after the briefing,' said the admiral, looking around as he spoke. 'He probably didn't want to hang around too long.'

'Indeed. I assume he wanted to avoid our questions,' said the general, speaking in a louder voice than his companion.

The admiral nodded and looked over each shoulder before he spoke. 'And how is your son?'

The Generalmajor paused, slightly surprised by the question. In the circles he moved in, in Berlin, asking questions about an acquaintance's family, especially about sons in the armed forces, was a form of code – a way of broaching the sensitive issue of what one really thought about the war. It was the same as discussing food shortages with people: questions only asked to people you could really trust.

'Karl is well thank you; he's an Oberleutnant now, based in Poland. And yours – you have two don't you?'

'One son, one daughter. Ernst joined the Kriegsmarine naturally, but unlike his father, uncles and grandfather, he seems to prefer to be under the water rather than on its surface. He's with the 7th U-boat flotilla based in Kiel.'

The two men paused to watch a Luftwaffe Junkers passenger plane pass low overhead from the south, neatly framed against Untersberg mountain. The plane banked to the left and began its noisy approach to the runway.

'That must be our plane; we could well be back in Berlin this evening after all. Tell me Ernst: what do you make of what Jodl had to say...?'

139

Generalmajor Ernst turned to face his companion, carefully studying his face. He wanted to be sure he was not being led into a trap.

'You mean about…?' It was clear he wanted the admiral to say it first.

'The invasion plans: what else were we there for?'

'He only wants us to *plan* for an invasion of the Soviet Union, Hans. That's probably prudent don't you think – to make contingency plans, in case…?'

'Come on Ernst: we've known each other for years! I was watching you yesterday during Jodl's briefing, you hardly looked enthusiastic. It's madness, you must know that better than me. Just imagine for a moment you were a British general rather than a German one and you'd found out the Fuhrer had ordered his high command to turn up in Bad Reichenhall yesterday to be instructed to plan for an invasion of the Soviet Union. You'd be delighted, wouldn't you?'

The Generalmajor shrugged. Behind them a plane was noisily taxiing in front of the building where they had been waiting. 'I think our flight will be ready soon, Hans.'

'Come on Ernst, answer my question. If you were a British general you'd be very pleased to hear Germany was planning to break its alliance with the Soviet Union and fight on two fronts, would you not?'

'I think that more than anything, Hans, I would be surprised. So surprised in fact that I'd struggle to believe it.'

* * *

Chapter 10: Stuttgart, July 1940

'I was only asking what business it is you have in Zürich, Henry. Surely I have a right to ask? One minute you're off to Basle, then Zürich... wherever next?'

Marlene Hesse had little choice but to accept her son's imminent and largely unexplained departure with her customary lack of grace. Henry had come to learn that, these days, all he needed to do was tell her what he was doing then leave it at that.

He arrived in Zürich on the Monday and spent the night in a hotel on Oetenbachgasse where his flight tickets were waiting for him. He left the hotel early the next morning and took the airport bus from Hauptbahnhof station at seven o'clock.

The flight left on time at 8.15, the Swissair DC-3 banking heavily to the east before climbing noisily through the cloud then appearing to float as they headed north and crossed the border. The plane landed at Stuttgart Echterdingen just after 9.30; a few minutes before they had begun their descent, the two stewardesses had come round and drawn all the curtains. Henry was in a single seat, but he heard a man across the aisle from him explain to his neighbour in French that they always did this: 'It's a military airport now. They don't want us to spy on the Luftwaffe!'

The captain welcomed them to Germany, with a noticeable lack of enthusiasm. 'Please respect all the special security rules in place at the airport. Please follow all instructions. Passengers for the onward flight to Berlin should remain in their seats. Passengers disembarking here in Stuttgart should ensure they have all their belongings with them. We hope you have enjoyed flying with

Swissair. We wish you a pleasant stay in Stuttgart.'

The plane taxied to a remote part of the airport: outside they could hear shouting and the noise of engines. The passengers were led down the steps to a bus with blacked-out windows that had drawn up alongside. Henry had no more than 30 seconds to glance around as they were led onto the bus: he could see very little, other than a ring of troops around the plane and a couple of oil tankers nearby.

There were few other passengers in the vast terminal building, although at the far end Henry could see groups of men in uniform hurrying along. At the other end of the terminal were the airline desks, most of which appeared to be abandoned. There were a few people waiting by one of the Deutsche Lufthansa desks but the only other airline desks that seemed to be operating were Swissair and Ala Littoria. While he waited, there were a few announcements made by a woman just managing to suppress her Swabian accent: 'Arriving passengers should wait until they are called; any passengers for the Swissair flight to Berlin are to proceed to the departure gate immediately; a further delay is announced on the Deutsche Lufthansa flight to Lisbon, Portugal.'

Henry was questioned by two men stood behind the desk; one in SS uniform, the other in a cheap suit with a swastika badge on each lapel. Behind them was a large clock with enormous swastika banners draped on either side.

They each checked the visa, silently. The man in civilian clothes left the desk at one stage with Henry's passport, but returned a minute later.

'How long are you intending to stay in Stuttgart, Herr Hesse?'

'Until Friday.'

'You have a return ticket?'

Henry handed it to them and they both studied it.

And the purpose of your visit? Where are you staying? With whom will you be meeting? Are you aware of the restrictions of your visa?

All questions that had already been asked at the embassy in Bern: Remington-Barber had warned him of this. *Routine: they'll just trying to catch you out: they'll be looking to compare your answers: nothing to worry about. Just play a straight bat. Don't smile too much. Don't get impatient.*

'We would like to know more about your business affairs in Stuttgart, Herr Hesse,' said the civilian.

An unnecessarily detailed and complicated account of his step-father's business affairs in Stuttgart followed. Henry told them how he suspected they had been mishandled by a man called Heinz Bermann – at the mention of which there was a knowing look between the two Germans – and how following his step-father's death, which was probably hastened by the activities of this Heinz Bermann, it was taking time to unravel everything but he felt it was his duty to come here and see what was going on… and so on. It had the desired effect of making the two officials look bored. Henry hoped to God that poor old Heinz Bermann had managed to get out of Stuttgart: he was a decent man and always very charming. It would be a shame if Henry had just added to his woes.

After ten minutes, Henry was taken through to a small side room where he and his bags were thoroughly searched by two policemen. His copy of that morning's *Neue Zürcher Zeitung* was removed from his briefcase and thrown away. Everything else was carefully examined. Nothing else aroused their suspicion, other than the Swiss Francs.

'Are you changing all of these here?' the official in charge of the search asked.

Henry nodded.

'Wait here while I count them.'

The official left the room, returning with the Francs five minutes later. Later, Henry would discover he'd helped himself to some of the money.

He emerged from the side room into the queue in front of yet another desk, but this was a much quicker process. His passport was stamped again and he was now in Germany.

'You are now permitted to cross the border, Herr Hesse. Please go the cashier's window over there and change all money into Reichsmarks. Welcome to Germany.'

Henry changed his money then joined a queue which had formed just outside the terminal for the bus into the city. It took half an hour. Again, the curtains were drawn and it was difficult to make out where they were, other than by occasional glimpses through the front window. Henry thought he recognised one or two familiar sights and, as far as he could tell, there were few signs of the war, other than a good deal of military traffic on the road. They passed through two road-blocks, and at the final one three policemen climbed on board and checked everyone's papers.

'Stuttgart-Mitte' announced the driver: The bus pulled into Fürstenstrasse, just off the enormous Schlossplatz.

It was no more than three or four minutes' walk to the hotel and Henry knew the area well, but somehow the city centre did not feel familiar. The buildings were the same and he recognised the street names and knew exactly where he was. But, for him, the city had always had a unique atmosphere, which was hard to describe but he knew it when he was there. Stuttgart today did not feel like somewhere he had been to before, it felt as though he'd only ever seen it on film. It now had an undoubted military edge; so many of the people on the streets seemed to be wearing a uniform of one type or another and there were anti-aircraft batteries on the Schlossplatz. Most of the buildings were draped in large red-and-black swastika flags.

By the time he reached the Hotel Victoria on the corner of Friedrichstrasse and Keplerstrasse and walked through its ornate entrance he had a better idea why Stuttgart felt so unfamiliar. It was the people and how they behaved; they were moving around in silence, avoiding eye contact and with hardly anyone speaking to anyone else. A city he had once found friendly now had a distinctly menacing air to it. Germans had always struck him as being smartly dressed but now, compared to the relative sophistication of the Swiss, they looked drab.

The man behind the reception desk did at least look him in the eye. 'Yes, we have a reservation for you Herr Hesse,' he said, holding up the telegram from the Schweizerhof in Bern. 'You're staying for three nights, correct?'

Henry said that he was and completed the various forms handed to him by the receptionist. He was then escorted to his room on the third floor by an elderly and evidently arthritic porter.

Once he had unpacked, he decided to go for a walk in the afternoon. As tempting as it was to remain in the relative safety of his room, he knew that would draw attention to himself and would not allow Milo the opportunity to approach him, though he was still none the wiser how that was going to happen. Back in Bern, Remington-Barber had been decidedly cryptic in that respect.

'You'll be approached by someone using the phrase "We usually have some rain in Stuttgart at this time of year,"' Remington-Barber had said. 'You are to reply, "That must be the case all over Europe." In response they'll say, "Surely there must be rain over the Alps." You'll reply, "There is always rain around the Alps even in summer," and when they say "How wonderful," then you'll know it's Milo and that it's safe.'

Remington-Barber had asked him to repeat it, many times.

'Good: you're to do precisely what Milo tells you. If they send you somewhere, you go.'

So Henry wandered around the centre of Stuttgart for the best part of an hour and a half and, as far as he could tell, he was not being followed. From Schlossplatz he walked down the Planie, which had now become Adolf Hitler Strasse and then into Charlottenplatz, which was now Danziger-Freiheit. *A different city.* He sat on benches, paused by shop windows – noticing there seemed to be far less in the shops than on previous visits. He crossed the road and back again, allowing anyone wanting to approach him plenty of opportunity to do so. He was beginning to get a sense of what a country at war felt like: it was as if the horizon was diminished and there was less air to breathe. Less colour, so much quieter and the ubiquitous slogans on buildings and flags hanging from them. From Danziger-Freiheit, he headed north to Neckarstrasse, where one of his step-father's property agents had their offices. He decided to go in, just in case he was being followed: it was good to be able to show the reasons he had given for visiting Stuttgart appeared to be genuine. Herr Langhoff took him into his office and was happy to talk for a while: times were very hard; many people had joined the military; Jewish property was being given away which meant less business for them; no, as Herr Hesse was surely aware, all of his step-father's properties had been disposed of.

He left the office after half an hour, satisfied that anyone watching would feel he had indeed been there to conduct business. A few doors along he found a small basement bar. The barmaid knew better than to ask too many questions, especially when she realised he was Swiss. From the bar he walked back across the Schlossplatz to the hotel, concerned at how and when Milo was going to approach him: he could hardly spend the next few days hanging around the hotel, going for the occasional walk and eating in his room.

He wandered around the lobby for a while then returned to his room. He closed the heavy curtains then ran a hot bath, rested, read a little before telephoning reception to order his evening meal. There were three dishes on the menu, only one of which was available: sausages and potatoes.

After his meal he left the tray, as instructed, in the corridor outside his room. It was only eight o'clock, but he began to think about settling down for the night. He was beginning to think this trip was no more than a test by British Intelligence to see how he coped – whether he could get in and out of Germany and no more than that. The more he thought about it, the more sense it made. After all, hadn't Edgar more or less told him his first mission would be something relatively straightforward? Whichever way you looked at it, he told himself, travelling into Germany and meeting with another agent was hardly straightforward. The British were unlikely to risk a novice agent's first assignment on anything too dangerous. Surely they would simply want to see whether he had the nerves to go there and return in one piece?

But what was it Viktor had told him at the weekend? *Don't think too much synok: they'll know what they are doing.*

There was an easy chair near a radiator by the window and he sat on it, kicking off his shoes and putting his feet on the small table. He began to recall another conversation with Edgar, when he had implied they may advance five hundred pounds of his aunt's money on successful completion of a mission. Would this count as a successful mission? Maybe he could now afford a car. He watched the patterns forming on the ceiling by the lampshade by the bed when a firm knock on the door disturbed his train of thought. He was annoyed, assuming they had come to collect his dinner tray when in fact he had left it in the corridor.

'The tray is out there for you,' he called out.

A female voice replied. 'Thank you, Herr Hesse. Please could I come in? We have managed to locate your missing case.'

'I think there must be some mistake, I...'

A car door slammed on Keplerstrasse below, followed by the sound of a lorry moving down the road.

'There's no need to worry sir, I am the duty manager: if you could open the door please?'

The woman who Henry let into his room was wearing the dark, formal uniform of the hotel staff. On her lapel was a badge: *Katharina Hoch, Night Manager*. She closed the door carefully behind her then looked him up and down, as if checking him out. 'It is good news we found your case, Herr Hesse.' She was carrying a small, leather bag.

'There's been a mistake, I'm afraid. I have my case here. I only brought the one with me.'

'Are you enjoying your stay at the Hotel Victoria?'

'I am, but...'

'And in Stuttgart: you are enjoying Stuttgart? We usually have some rain in Stuttgart at this time of year.'

Henry felt unsteady on his feet. *Milo?* 'I beg your pardon?'

She repeated the phrase in a pleasant, conversational manner. 'We usually have some rain in Stuttgart at this time of year.'

Henry sat down on the edge of the bed, aware he was shaking violently. He took a moment or two to remember his correct response.

'That must be the case all over Europe.'

Was it safe to have a conversation like this in a hotel room?

'Surely,' she said, checking behind the curtains then glimpsing into the bathroom, 'surely there must be rain over the Alps?'

'There is always rain around the Alps even in summer.'

'How wonderful,' she replied, as though she really meant it.

There was a long silence. Another car door slammed on Keplerstrasse; the sound of distant laughter. The woman smiled at him in what in other circumstances he'd have taken to quite a seductive manner. Her mouth was quite beautiful, without any trace of lipstick.

'So you are Milo?' He was speaking in barely more than a whisper.

'I am Milo, yes – don't look so shocked. Look, I am on duty, so I don't have too long and we have much to talk about.'

'Is it safe in here?'

'Do you mean are we being listened to? You don't need to be concerned. We provide the Gestapo with a list of all new guests and the ones they have some interest in we have to put in special rooms on the fifth floor, so you don't need to worry, not for now at least.'

She lifted the suitcase onto the bed and opened it. It was full of men's clothes, along with a hat and a pair of black shoes. 'Have you ever been to Essen, Herr Hesse?'

'Where?'

'Essen. In the Ruhr: north of Cologne.'

'No, I can't say I have.'

'Tomorrow will be your first visit then.'

'But… surely not. My visa doesn't permit me to travel outside of Stuttgart.'

'That's what all this is about.' She pointed to the suitcase on the bed. 'Henri Hesse will not be travelling to Essen. You will travel as Dieter Hoch.' She had removed a wallet from the suitcase and emptied its contents onto the bed.

'Dieter Hoch is my brother. Dieter is four years older than you but the photograph in his identity card here is not a good one and so we're confident your identity documents will pass a basic examination. It'll work as long as no-one has any reason to suspect you. You'll only wear these clothes here: they all belong to my brother. Everything you wear will be German-made. There must be nothing on you that could identify you as being Swiss. You will take this suitcase.'

'And your brother is in on this?'

'Of course: we both do what we can to help the British. We aren't Nazis, you may have gathered that. Dieter is a manager with the railway here in Stuttgart, which means he's able to travel more freely on trains. He's worked for the past seven days and finished this evening, so now he's off work until Friday morning. He'll remain at home until then and won't leave the house: he'll tell my parents he is unwell. That gives you two clear days to get to Essen, complete your mission and return here. We want you back in Stuttgart before the curfew on Thursday night.'

'But what about the hotel, won't people spot I'm not here?'

'I am the duty manager for the next two nights. I'll ensure all the paperwork is in order. I'll also come up during the night to ensure the room looks as though someone's slept in it. As I say, no-one suspects you. The Gestapo is kept busy enough with people it does suspect.'

'And what do I do in Essen?'

'Do you know anything about Essen?'

Henry shrugged. *Not really.*

'Essen is a major producer of steel and coal. The Krupps family own much of the industry in the town. The steel that's produced there is vital to the Nazi war effort. The British wish to destroy the factories, but their intelligence is poor. Some of the locations the

British are aware of are no longer in use, others have been opened. They're in the process of compiling a much more accurate map of Essen. That's your mission, to assist in that.'

'So I just wander around Essen drawing maps?'

Katharina Hoch looked irritated. 'I'll give you the details of how to make contact with someone in Essen. But this is going to be a dangerous mission: you'll be required to move around the town, memorise what you see then compile a grid of locations which you will then bring back to Stuttgart. Throughout Germany life is dangerous, but in Essen especially so.'

* * *

He was woken at five in the morning by Katharina Hoch; a gentle rap on the door so as not to disturb other guests. He washed and shaved then dressed in her brother's clothes and double-checked the minutiae of his new identity: address, date of birth – the details that could trip him up.

He left the room as quietly as possible and descended through the fire-exit stairs at the end of the corridor to the basement level, where Katharina was waiting for him.

She looked him over, like a parent checking a child was properly dressed for school. She asked him to empty his pockets to be sure he was carrying nothing incriminating: everything was in order.

'This is your ticket here for the rail journey: the train leaves at six o'clock, in 25 minutes. It's scheduled to arrive in Frankfurt at ten o'clock: Dieter says this train tends to run on time as it's carrying troops, so is less likely to be subject to delays. At Frankfurt you should purchase a ticket to Essen: there's a direct service that departs at a quarter to eleven and is due to arrive in Essen at a quarter past two or 14.15, that's how they like us to refer to it these days, presumably they think it makes everything sound more efficient. Dieter says he knows less about that part of the DR network, so you may encounter delays. Now you remember I told you last night about the purpose of your visit to Essen, in case anyone asks you?'

'Visiting an aunt?'

'Correct: Gertraud Traugott recently celebrated her 80th birthday and as you haven't seen her in a while this is a surprise visit. She lives in an apartment in the west of Essen, in Altendorf. This is her address, please copy it down now in your own handwriting and put the piece of paper in your wallet.'

She waited while Henry patiently copied down the address, folded the piece of paper and placed it in the wallet.

'But you aren't to go straight to that address. When you arrive at Essen station, you're to go to the lost-property office, which is located behind the main ticket office. You'll find it's well signposted. In the unlikely event that you arrive in Essen before two o'clock, don't go there any earlier. If you arrive after four o'clock, wait outside the office. You have a contact in Essen who's going to help you and he works in the lost-property office. His codename is Lido. He's always on his own there between two and four. Go into the office and ask if anyone's handed in a gentleman's umbrella, which you mislaid that morning. He'll ask you to describe it and you'll say it's black with a carved wooden handle engraved with the initials 'DH'. He'll then ask you to come into the back of the office to inspect the umbrellas. Once there and when it is safe, Lido will brief you on what's to happen during your stay in Essen.'

'And what if he isn't there?'

'If he isn't there or if something goes wrong, you should try and get out of Essen as soon as possible and head back to Stuttgart. Lido has very limited information about who you are or even where you're coming from, so your security shouldn't be compromised if he's arrested.'

Henry tried to take all this in: the detail was one thing but the sense of fear quite another. He was beginning to shiver, despite the warmth of the basement.

'It's nearly a quarter to six; you need to get a move on. Wear your hat; it'll help mask your identity. Carry the raincoat. The next thing I have to say is very important: in the event of you being arrested, your story will not stand a lot of scrutiny. It won't take the Gestapo long to find out you're not Dieter Hoch or that Gertraud Traugott is not your aunt. Hopefully, it won't come to that, but if you do find yourself being interrogated by the Gestapo you must do your best to hold out for 24 hours. That'll give us enough time to dismantle our cell here in Stuttgart and try to escape.'

Katharina put her arm around his shoulder and leaned close to him. Her mouth looked even more astonishing close-up. Her eyes did not blink as she stared straight into his.

'Twenty four hours, that's all that we ask. Tell them you're a Swiss citizen and your passport is here in the hotel to prove it. They probably won't kill you – the Germans can't afford to upset the Swiss. But if you keep your wits about you hopefully you won't arouse suspicion. You must leave now.'

'There is one final thing you should know,' she said. 'There's a pencil case in the suitcase, in a zipped compartment in the lid. Under no circumstances should you take it out of the case or open it. You're to give it Lido. That's very important. Do you understand?'

He nodded that he understood. Katharina led him up a steep flight of concrete steps to a door that led directly onto Keplerstrasse. She motioned for him to wait while she looked up and down the street, then waved him to come up. She pushed him along with a whispered 'Good luck'.

It was a quick five minutes' walk down Friedrichstrasse to the main station, which was reassuringly busy. Henry had just enough time to stop at a kiosk and buy a bread roll with a cold sausage and a copy of that morning's *Völkischer Beobachter*.

He spotted the Frankfurt train on platform six, with black-clad troops forming in lines to board it. Clouds of steam floated across the station, and the smell of engine oil and the sounds of metal and whistles and people calling out all felt oddly reassuring. He showed his ticket to the man at the barrier then a policeman asked to check his papers, but was quick to wave him through. Just as he was about to board the train, he felt a hand on his shoulder and when he turned round it was an officer in black uniform. He noticed the distinctive Death Head symbol: SS. He felt like laughing. He had not even managed to board the train to Frankfurt. It had all been a trap.

* * *

Chapter 11: Essen, July 1940

'Do you have a light?' The officer was holding an unlit cigarette and smiling. 'I seem to have found myself with a unit where no-one smokes. Imagine that!'

Henry apologised profusely. 'I don't smoke either.' *Perhaps I ought to take it up*, he thought as he climbed into his carriage.

* * *

He was both surprised and relieved when the train from Frankfurt pulled into Essen Main at 20 minutes past two that Wednesday afternoon. The journey could not have gone more smoothly; the Stuttgart train had arrived in Frankfurt at ten, allowing him ample time to buy his ticket for Essen and still be able to sit in a small café on one of the platforms, where he sipped a cup of bitter ersatz coffee and glanced at the *Völkischer Beobachter*. He was able to board the Essen train at 10.30 when the barrier opened, with the policeman on duty giving his identity card no more than a cursory look.

The train was packed all the way to Cologne, so he closed his eyes to avoid being drawn into conversation during the journey up the Ruhr. Inevitably, as he began to doze, Roza appeared before him: gentle at first, as always. Her fingers lightly touching his wrist and a shy smile as she tossed her hair back from her face. Then the fingers grasped his wrist so tightly he could feel the pain, and that was followed by her looking at him with more hate than he could imagine: 'You know what will happen to us now, don't you?'

He was about to explain when she began to fade away, asking one further question as she did so: 'Where are you going?' He sat up with a start, concerned he may have said something, but no-one in the carriage so much as looked at him. *Where am I going? Where indeed?*

As the train reached Essen, enormous factories loomed on either side of the track, with thick plumes of filthy smoke reaching far into the grey sky. The station was not nearly as large as the ones in Stuttgart or Frankfurt, and there seemed to be less security. There was a noticeable smell of coal and industrial fumes, and the large swastika flags draped above the platform were streaked with grime. He decided not to go to the lost-property office straight away; he needed to get a sense of his surroundings. He studied the timetable on the side of the ticket office. If he needed to leave Essen quickly there was a train to Dortmund in ten minutes and one to Cologne in 20. There was a café on the platform, but he felt too sick with nerves to even enter it.

He waited until 2.30 then entered the lost-property office. A man in DR uniform was behind a long, low counter, attending to an elderly lady.

'I can assure you I've looked very carefully and more than once, as you ask. There's no sign of your gloves. They may still be elsewhere in the station: I suggest you try again tomorrow. I'll keep a special eye out for them.'

Henry waited until she had left. The man behind the counter looked to be in his late fifties at least, his hair a steely white, and he moved in a slow and quite deliberate manner. He looked tired. His most noticeable feature was an impressive pair of eyebrows that seemed to join up above his nose and curve up at either end, lending him an owl-like air.

'Can I help you sir?'

Henry glanced around to ensure they were on their own.

'I appear to have lost my umbrella.'

No pause, no flicker of understanding, no sign of anticipation from the man behind the counter.

'And when did you lose it sir?'

'This morning. It's black with a carved wooden handle. My initials are engraved on the handle: "DH".'

The man behind the counter shook his head.

'I can't recall it, but perhaps you'd like to come behind the counter and have a look? We've quite a collection of umbrellas here, sir: I could open a shop!'

The man lifted up a section of the counter and slowly led Henry to a room at the back of the office. He closed the door and removed his cap, turning to face Henry.

'I'm Lido, by the way.'

'I gathered that: Dieter.'

Lido grasped Henry's hand and shook it warmly.

'There are some umbrellas over there, pretend to be looking through them. I'll look out the window in case anyone comes in, but it's very quiet at this time of the afternoon. It's quiet most of the time now. People don't seem to lose things in the war, apart from their lives.'

Lido spoke quickly and quietly, looking out of the little office window towards the counter as he did so.

'Just wait a moment.'

A woman with two young children had come in and Lido went over to the counter and after a very quick conversation she left. He came back to Henry.

'Every other person who comes in here thinks we are the left-luggage department. It says very clearly that we're lost property. Stuttgart explained that your cover for visiting Essen is to visit your aunt, yes? Let me tell you then that Gertraud Traugott is an elderly neighbour of mine. I live in an apartment block in Altendorf; her apartment is two doors down from me. However, Gertraud Traugott has not been in her apartment for three or four months now. She started to lose her mind a year ago, though she seemed capable enough of looking after herself. In November they took her into a sanatorium near Oberhausen. I went to visit her last month: she tells everyone there she is engaged to the Kaiser and she is waiting for him to come and take her away. I'm not sure how long she'll be there – one hears terrible rumours these days about what they are doing to people like her, but that is another story. Now, you need to listen very carefully and I'll tell you what you need to do.'

* * *

At ten to three Henry left the station by the north exit and headed into the centre of Essen. *I finish work at four*, Lido had said. *Wait for me by the Hindenburg Strasse exit: I will come out just after five past four. Follow me all the way to Altendorf – I'll make sure I take a route that takes you past as many factories as possible. Make sure you memorise everything. And don't forget to follow me at a safe distance, not too close, not too far. Can you remember all that?*

He could. He also remembered his training and the need to avoid wandering around a place without any apparent purpose. He decided to use the hour and a bit he was going to spend in the centre of Essen to purchase a gift for his aunt: he was there to celebrate her 80th birthday after all.

Lido had agreed that this was a good idea. *Go past the Handelshof Hotel and the Opera House and you'll reach Adolf Hitler Platz. The best places to go shopping are to the north and the west of that – around Verein Strasse and Logen Strasse. Any idea of what kind of gift you're going to buy?*

Perfume, they had agreed. *Any woman appreciates perfume; no-one is going to think that's an odd gift.*

He followed Lido's instructions: he had plenty of time, so he made sure he did not rush. Lido had said he thought there may be a perfume shop somewhere past Logen Strasse. It wasn't something he ever had occasion to shop for these days, he'd said. In an arcade off Limbecker Strasse he found exactly what he was looking for, a quaint *Parfümerie*: all wooden beams and leaded windows, reached by climbing down a couple of worn steps. There was a sign on the door to ring the bell and when he did so it was a minute or two before the elderly owner shuffled along to unlock the store.

'My apologies: when I'm preparing perfumes at the back I lock the door, I've had people stealing bottles in the past. Perhaps I should be more trusting these days. After all, it's not as if Jews come into the shop any more'. Henry noticed he was wearing the distinctive round Nazi Party membership badge on his lapel, a black swastika stark on a white background. The shop was tiny, with all the walls and counters covered in bottles of perfume in every imaginable size and colour. The smell was close to overpowering.

'Now, how can I help you?'

Henry explained he was looking for a perfume for his aunt, for her 80th birthday. The owner perused the shelves: 'Maybe something with lavender in it, which is always popular with older ladies – or perhaps bergamot? What kind of a lady is she?'

Henry explained he had not seen her in a while, this was a surprise visit.

'You don't sound as if you're from this area?'

'No, I'm from… the south.'

'I see: whereabouts in the south?'

'Stuttgart,' said Henry, regretting his answer straight away.

'You don't have that dreadful Swabian accent, thank God! You've travelled a long way to see your aunt. Where does she live in Essen?'

'Altendorf.'

'Altendorf? I know it well. I lived there myself for many years, before my wife died and my children left Essen. What's your aunt's name?'

Henry hesitated. There was something about the owner he found unsettling. It was not the Nazi Party badge, half the population of Germany seemed to wear one of those these days as far as he could tell and it was probably good for business. No, the questions seemed to be pointed and persistent rather than friendly. It was as if he distrusted Henry.

'Maybe I'll come back later. I need to do some more shopping.'

'Your aunt's name, you were going to tell me her name?'

'Gertraud. Gertraud Traugott.'

'Gertraud? But I know Gertraud, I know her very well! Tell me, how are you related to her?'

Henry momentarily considered leaving the shop, but had already revealed too much; Gertraud Traugott's name and Stuttgart. *Trapped.*

'I told you, she's my aunt.'

'But on which side?'

'My mother was her sister.'

The old man nodded as if he was satisfied with the answer. Henry felt a sense of relief. He had over-reacted.

'Ah, so you're Hannelore's son?'

'That's right, yes.' He managed a weak smile and felt faintly relieved. The old man leant against the counter, so close that Henry could smell the garlic on his breath.

'Gertraud has no sister. She had a brother but he was killed in the Great War and had no children. And she's not lived in Altendorf for months. You can't be her nephew. Who the hell are you?'

The old man's hand moved along the counter towards the telephone. Henry reacted quickly. He reached over the counter and pushed the man as hard as he could against the shelves behind him. His head struck one of the large glass bottles and he slumped to the floor. A few of the bottles fell on top of him, the glass shattering and the perfume spilling over the man, who was now groaning. Henry darted over to the door and locked it, turning the sign round so that it would show that the shop was closed.

Geschlossen.

He climbed over the counter and dragged the limp body into the small preparation room at the back of the shop and closed the door. The old man was bleeding from the head and soaked in perfume. Henry could hear someone trying to open the door, the handle turning against the lock and then a knock. The shopkeeper stirred, as if trying to call out. Henry held one hand firmly against his mouth then gripped his head with the other. He struggled, so Henry knelt on top of him, one knee pressed hard into his chest, until his eyes bulged and his face turned bright-red. The knocking stopped and it was quiet outside, but Henry continued to hold the man down. The struggle lasted for what seemed like an age. He could feel something hot and wet against his hand. Blood was trickling out of the man's nose.

Then it stopped. The body suddenly slumped, all resistance had flooded out of it and Henry knew he was dead. For a few minutes he sat on the floor, catching his breath and gathering his thoughts, watching the old man for any sign of life. The smells of citron, sandalwood and rose filled the room. He went back into the shop and drew the blinds on the door and windows. From the till, he removed all the notes and left it open. He turned off the shop lights and went back into the room, taking care to shut the internal door and lock it. He had already noticed there was another door from the room which he assumed would lead outside. He undid the bolts and carefully opened it just a few inches. Outside was a narrow, enclosed alleyway, the buildings opposite almost within touching distance. He went back inside the shop and removed the old man's wristwatch: this needed to look like a robbery. He was about to leave when he had another thought. From the old man's lapel, he removed the Nazi Party membership badge, checked that nothing was engraved on the back then put it on his own jacket. As he did, he noticed his raincoat, which had been on the floor alongside the man, had some bloodstains on the sleeve and reeked of perfume. He bundled it up, hoping to find somewhere nearby to dispose of it.

He carefully opened the door to the alleyway once more. It was dark and, as far as he could tell, deserted. He pulled his trilby low over his face and hurried down the alleyway, eventually emerging into Webster Strasse. Just before he did, he noticed a large bin that was nearly full. He looked around him then leant into the bin, pushing his coat as far inside as he could manage, covering it over as best he could with the other rubbish.

Lido was shocked to see him when he appeared in the Lost Property Office. It was five to four and he was preparing to close for the day. Fortunately, there was no-one else there. Lido gestured for him to come to the office at the back.

'What the hell are you doing here?' he hissed. 'I thought I told you to meet me in Hindenberg Strasse?'

Henry explained what had happened. Lido sat with his head in his hands.

'I'm sorry, but I had no alternative. For some reason, he suspected me. I should never have given him Gertraud Traugott's name of course, but how on earth was I to know he knew her... What're the chances of that? If I hadn't given a name it would have looked suspicious too. At least I did my best to make it look like a robbery.'

'That's the problem with this town, everyone knows everyone. Did anyone see you enter the shop?'

'Not as far as I know. It was very quiet.'

'At least you got rid of the coat. That could identify you too. Here, choose another one, there are a dozen or so on the rack over there. It was a dark-brown raincoat you were wearing, is that right?'

'Yes.'

'Choose one of the black ones then. And change your hat too. Choose something different from that trilby. You'd better give me the watch you took from him.'

Lido examined the watch with a professional interest.

'Shame, it's a good watch, but too distinctive. I'll lose it down a drain. My guess is it'll be a few hours at least before he's discovered. You're sure you locked the door?'

'Yes.'

'Let's hope so. We'd better go back to the original plan. You leave now and start following me once I emerge in Hindenburg Strasse.'

Lido called him back just as he was leaving the lost-property office.

'Did you remove everything from the pockets of your coat?'

'I didn't have anything in them, as far as I was aware.'

'Are you sure?'

Henry left the office without replying. If only he was sure.

* * *

Lido emerged from the station into Hindenburg Strasse at ten past four. Without pausing, changing his pace or looking around him, he walked on, turning left at the Krupps Hotel then left again into what, to all intents and purposes, looked like a factory. Towering above him on either side of the road were vast industrial buildings, whose sheer height shut out much of the daylight. He could feel the fumes fill his lungs, but the most overpowering sense was the noise: it was not simply the volume, that was to be expected, but the physical effect it had, sending tremors throughout his body. The buildings on the south side of the road seemed to be denser and every so often Lido would remove his hat and scratch his head for a moment or two before putting it back on. That was the signal for Henry to take special note, which may be the entrance of another factory, usually with a board outside. Most of the entrances had sentries outside them, their gaze following him as he walked past.

It soon became obvious to Henry that goods were moved around the factories and the town by rail: at frequent points on their journey the road was bisected by railway lines and bridges. They had to wait at one or two of these for trains to pass, which gave Henry a good opportunity to look around. He was making mental notes; of where different factories were in relation to one another, their names, where the railway lines went, where power plants were located.

After a while he noticed Lido had slowed down his pace and kept removing his cap, scratching his head. A factory to their left was more or less open to road and in it he could see half-built tanks and what appeared to be heavy artillery lined up in a yard. A bit further on they had to pause: a soldier was ordering pedestrians to stand back while a group of workers, all under close guard, were led past. There were about 30 gaunt men in the group, all dressed in a rough grey uniform. He heard them talking quietly as walked past him: he was sure they were speaking Polish.

Soon after that, they emerged from the complex of factories although the smell and the noise lingered on. They were now in the Altendorf district. Lido stopped to tie a shoelace, which was the signal for Henry to drop back further: they were nearing the apartment. Just after a school, Lido turned right into Rullich Strasse and at that point Henry slowed down even more to allow Lido to get out of his sight. He knew to turn from Rullich Strasse into Ehrenzeller Strasse then into the apartment block towards the end of the street. It was a large block; four storeys high with the apartments opening out onto an external corridor.

There are six apartments on each floor, all sharing the same corridor. I am in number 19 on the second floor. Gertraud Traugott's apartment is just along from mine, number 22.

Henry reckoned Lido had had the five minutes he said he needed to get inside his own apartment, so he climbed the steps to number 22. In common with all the other apartments in the block it was shabby with paint peeling from the door to reveal warped wood. He knocked, but there was no sign of life. He knocked again and waited. He knocked once more and the door of the apartment next door opened.

A woman in her forties came out. She was wearing a filthy apron with two equally filthy children huddled behind her.

'Who are you after?'

'Frau Traugott,' he replied.

'She's not here and with some luck she'll never come back. I had enough of her frightening the children. Who are you anyway?'

'A relation, from out of town: I'm in Essen on business and thought I'd pop in to see her.'

Lido had now emerged from his apartment and joined them. He nodded politely at the woman and asked if he could help. Henry explained his story again. Lido also informed him that Frau Traugott was not there.

Henry managed to look suitably disappointed. 'Oh, I counted on her being here,' he said. 'I was hoping to stay with her tonight. Do you know of a hotel nearby?'

'You'll have to head back into town,' the neighbour said, ushering her children back into their apartment. She was sensing she may be called upon to help out and her reluctance to do that marginally outweighed her innate nosiness.

'Manfred will help you. He's an old-fashioned gentleman!' With that she laughed and disappeared back inside, but not before hearing Lido ask him to join him in his apartment.

Number 19 was neat and cosy. Once Lido had locked the door and checked all the curtains were drawn he showed Henry into a small sitting room. There was a table, bookshelves, an easy chair and a sofa: he gestured for Henry to sit down.

'Let's wait ten minutes. If they were following us they'll come by then. If not, we can relax, if such a thing is possible these days. You can call me Manfred by the way. I don't need to know your real name, as far as I'm concerned, you are Dieter.'

After a silent ten minutes, Manfred removed his jacket and took Henry's then went into the kitchen, emerging a few minutes later with two steaming mugs.

'It's what we call coffee these days. Coffee was my passion. I'm assuming I'll never drink proper coffee again.' He sat there shaking his head, sipping at the drink and pulling a face as he tasted it. He removed a bottle of Asbach Uralt brandy from a shelf and poured some into their coffee cups, without asking Henry.

'You'll find it makes it more palatable,' he said. 'I'll make us something to eat soon. But now you must start making notes of what you saw. There's a false lining to your suitcase. When you've finished with the notes, we'll seal them in there. Before I forget, you have something for me?'

'Pardon?' said Henry.

'Stuttgart should have given you something for me... in a pencil case?'

'Oh yes, sorry. I forgot.' Henry opened the suitcase and removed the pencil case from the zipped compartment in the lid.

Manfred held it carefully with two hands and placed it on the table. He left the room and returned with a small towel, which he folded in half and placed next to the pencil case, which he slowly opened. From it, he extracted three brass, pen-like objects, one by one. He gingerly placed them on the towel and carefully wrapped them up. He left the room and returned a minute or so later. He handed the pencil case back to Henry.

'What were they?' he asked.

'Those? Oh, they're pencil detonators. For explosives, you understand. I'll pass them on quickly to the people who know what to do with them.'

'You mean I carried those detonators with me all the way from

Stuttgart?'

'Indeed you did. I'm most grateful.'

'But what if I'd been searched and they'd found them?'

'Then you probably wouldn't be here now, would you? We take such risks all the time.'

Henry sank back in the sofa.

'Are there any other surprises?'

'You are the man for surprises, Dieter, eh? You'd hardly been in Essen for two hours before you killed one of our citizens. With some luck, the police will assume it's one of the foreign labourers or a Jew. It's very handy they blame them for everything. It makes it easier for decent Aryans to commit crimes.'

They both laughed. Henry spent the next hour writing in pencil what he'd seen, then they sealed the paper into the lining of the suitcase. Manfred prepared an evening meal and they sat down at the table to eat: a hot stew with more potatoes than anything else.

'How long have you lived here, Manfred?'

'I moved to Essen in 1935. I was a teacher in Dortmund when the Nazis came to power and as I was a social democrat I lost my job. Soon after that my wife died and, as you can imagine, I was in despair: on my own and with no job and an apparent enemy of the state. However, my sister-in-law had a fairly senior position at the local authority in Dortmund and she was able to alter my records. My surname was Erhart and she changed it to the alternative spelling of Erhard. All my paperwork showed my Christian name as Hans, but she replaced it with my middle name, Manfred. So Hans Erhart became Manfred Erhard: very simple, but very effective. The thing about us Germans you see is that we can be too efficient, too methodical. Had I been Hans Erhart then the authorities would have tracked me down, but as all the paperwork is in order for Manfred Erhard, he has no problems. I moved to Essen, got this apartment and a job at the station. As far as people are concerned, I am what I appear to be, a rather lonely railway worker who lives on his own and bothers no-one.'

'So how did you get involved in this business?'

'By chance: a couple came to lost property who were clearly terrified. They were trying to get out of Essen but the Gestapo were after them. Without having time to think, I allowed them to hide in office overnight. The next morning they gave me the phone number of a contact of theirs and he arranged to collect them and managed to smuggle them out of town. A few days later that contact came to see me and asked if I'd like to stay involved, to help from time to time. I had no option of course, what could I do? I was already involved. Our main role now is to help gather intelligence for the British so they can bomb the Krupps factories. With some luck the intelligence we give them will be so good they hit Krupps rather than this apartment block. There are some mining engineers at the Krupps Maria mine in the north of Essen who are communist sympathisers: they can get hold of dynamite and, who knows, with the detonators you brought maybe we can do some damage to the factories ourselves, without having to rely on the RAF.'

'Maybe that'll be safer.'

'We're a small cell and it's very dangerous work, which goes without saying. So far we've been very lucky but that can't last. I'm 63 now, I have little to live for. Helping to resist the Nazis gives me some purpose, but I know I'll not survive long. I have a suicide pill: I just hope that when the Gestapo come for me I have time to take it.'

After Manfred had cleared the dinner plates he returned to the small room and checked the curtains once again.

'Are you ready for some entertainment?'

Henry nodded, uncertain what Manfred had in mind.

Manfred was by the bookcase, on top of which was a Bakelite cabinet.

'This is a *Volksempfange*: a triumph of German engineering. When the Nazis came to power they were so proud of their ability to communicate with us ordinary folk they had this radio receiver built. It was cheap, this one cost me something like 70 marks and it works well. It's important for them we catch all the speeches and fall for their propaganda. For me, I enjoyed listening to the jazz, but they soon banned that. Apparently they felt that it was all Negroes and Jews. So now they expect us to listen to their nonsense, but they failed to take into account this…'

Manfred was moving the dial to the left, stations momentarily bursting into life then fading away as he went through them. He settled on one station and turned the volume very low, beckoning Henry to join him crouched by the speaker.

'The BBC,' Manfred was pointing at the dial on the radio. 'We'll listen to their German-language service. It's excellent. If they catch you listening to a foreign radio station you can end up in prison. Goebbels clearly doesn't like his own propaganda to be contaminated, so now I spend part of my evenings knelt by the radio, with the volume so low I can only just hear it.'

Henry didn't sleep that night, wracked as his body was with exhaustion and fear. Every time he began to drop off, he saw the bulging eyes of the shop owner or would hear the resigned tone of Manfred, a man who knew his fate. It was another face that would now haunt him, along with Roza, who inevitably appeared before him in the very early hours, her fingers holding his wrist and slowly tightening over the course of what felt like many hours. There was a strong wind that night and the windows in the sitting room, where Henry was trying to sleep on the sofa, rattled viciously. Worse than that was the front door, which shook heavily when caught by the wind: each time it happened he imagined the Gestapo had come for them.

The next morning Manfred was up at 6.30 and they sat together eating black bread and jam, and drinking ersatz coffee.

'I start work at eight o'clock. You should aim to catch the quarter past nine train to Cologne. We're going to go on a more roundabout route to the station, but it's one that'll enable you to see much more of Essen. It's very busy at this time of the morning, so we should be alright, but who knows? Keep an eye on me and make sure you memorise well what you see – and, remember, if you see me remove my cap and put it in my pocket, we're in danger. If that happens, just ignore me and get away as soon as you can.'

Henry watched as Manfred packed his lunch neatly into a tin box, leaving space for the detonators wrapped in the towel. 'I'd better be careful I don't eat them!' Both men laughed nervously, grateful for the brief diversion of humour. They left the apartment just after seven and Henry followed Manfred to Altendorf station. They travelled north, allowing Henry ample opportunity to see yet more Krupps factories and the Maria and Amalie mines. At Altenessen, they changed trains and took one south: anyone following them would have been immediately suspicious that they were taking such a circuitous route when a more direct one existed, but it was busy and Henry was convinced no-one was watching them. Essen was like Stuttgart: people avoided eye contact with each other. The next stage of the journey had the added advantage of being painfully slow, as the train crawled down the track past yet more factories to the North Passenger and Goods station. It was now a quarter to eight and, as arranged, Manfred headed straight to the main station. Henry had more time and walked slowly, taking a slightly longer route so as to take in the power station and the electricity station around Viehofer Strasse.

As he headed towards the bahnhof, pleased with his morning's work and relieved to be beginning his journey back, he became aware of a commotion ahead of him. Too late he realised he was very near Limbecker Strasse, where the *Parfümerie* was. There were police everywhere, stopping all pedestrians and coralling them into different lines. He thought of turning around, but soon found himself being pointed to a queue. Ten minutes later he was at the front of it. A policeman directed him towards a man in a long trenchcoat, who beckoned him: *come here.* The man held out an oval metal warrant disc: there was the Nazi eagle on one side and the words *Geheime Staatpolizei* on the other. Gestapo.

'Papers.'

He handed over his identity card.

'Where are you heading?'

'The station.'

That seemed to satisfy the man, who did not press him.

'Open the suitcase.'

He rooted around in it for a moment or two but again was satisfied.

'Your watch.'

They'd be looking for the old man's watch. His was fine.

The Gestapo officer seemed satisfied.

'One last thing: let me see your wallet.'

Henry handed it over. He and Manfred had agreed it would be best to dispose of the Reichsmarks he had taken from the till. 'You never know,' Manfred had said, 'some shopkeepers mark their notes or there could be specks of blood on them.' Henry was certain there was nothing to worry about in the wallet, nothing that would arouse suspicion. He did have the slip of paper, with the name and address in Altendorf of his aunt, but that would appear as innocuous as all the other contents.

But it was as the Gestapo man handed the wallet back to him and told him he could go on his way that Henry had the most terrible thought. He remembered the slip of paper was not in the wallet: he had transferred it to his coat pocket just before he arrived in Essen the previous day. For some reason, he'd decided it would be safer there. And now it was in the blood-stained and perfume-soaked coat he'd abandoned and which there was every chance would be discovered. They would find the piece of paper and go to the apartment block in Ehrenzeller Strasse and start asking questions. The lady with the filthy apron in the next-door apartment would happily tell them about the man who had knocked on Gertraud Traugott's door and who had been taken in by Herr Erhard at number 19.

His legs were shaking as he hurried to the station. The large station clock had edged past 9.10 and he could see steam billowing from the Cologne train on platform three. There was a good chance they would find the coat any moment now – maybe they had already found it and had already spoken with the woman at the apartments. Maybe they were on their way to the station. He knew he should go to the lost-property office to warn Manfred, but he also knew if he did so then he'd almost certainly miss the train.

There was movement around platform three, the guard was about to close the gate. Henry ran along and managed to squeeze through in time. He hopped on board as the brakes were noisily released and the train began to ease along the platform.

Every time he closed his eyes on the journey back to Stuttgart he saw Manfred: he knew he could have warned him and given him a chance to escape, but that would have delayed his own departure from Essen and put himself at risk.

Poor Manfred, he thought: a decent enough man whose remaining ambition in life was that he could take his suicide pill before the Gestapo got to him.

I just hope he manages it.

* * *

Chapter 12: Lausanne and Bern, August 1940

Henry travelled to Lausanne on Monday 5th August, following the long weekend to celebrate Swiss National Day the previous Friday. He took the early morning paddle steamer from Geneva and, when the *Montreux* docked in Lausanne, a gleaming black Traction Avant was waiting for him.

On the 20-minute drive to Lutry, the Alps rose high to his left, the lake sweeping below him to the right. That summed it up, he thought: caught between two powerful forces. Not unlike serving two masters.

It took the Citroën a further ten minutes to climb the steep road out of Lutry to an isolated villa high above the town. Henry was led through to a magnificently appointed lounge, with large windows offering sensational views of the lake. The furniture was of the best quality, along with magnificent carpets and cabinets containing enough silver to fund a war slightly smaller than the current one.

As with all his meetings with Viktor, it began with an embrace. As Henry extricated himself, he turned round to admire the room.

'Bit luxurious isn't it Viktor?'

'The location is very discreet: that's what matters.'

'Do you lot own this?'

'We borrow it from a good friend, *synok*. We have very little time for questions; we need to get to work.'

Henry ignored him and walked around the room, genuinely admiring it. A pair of chairs on either side of the fireplace appeared to be genuine Louis XV: Viktor told him he wasn't permitted to sit on them. Someone brought in a tray of what smelled like proper coffee and he helped himself to a cup before sinking into a large armchair opposite Viktor, who had his brown leather notebook on his lap and was sharpening his pencil with a penknife, the shavings scattering on the precious carpet.

'You've not heard from your Mr Remington-Barber yet?'

Henry shook his head. So did the Russian.

'Strange. I'd have thought he'd have contacted you by now. As far as we can tell, you're not being watched. You certainly weren't followed today. He doesn't seem to be very suspicious, does he?'

'I've no idea, but maybe they're unhappy about what happened in Essen.'

Viktor raised his eyebrows momentarily and looked up. 'And what did happen in Essen, Henry?'

Henry took a deep breath. He had been dreading this moment. He wasn't sure who he feared telling most: Remington-Barber or Viktor. He closed his eyes and carefully recounted the details of his trip to Germany. He had decided to leave nothing out: the killing of the old man in the shop and the fact his carelessness had almost certainly compromised Manfred. Viktor allowed him to speak uninterrupted, carefully taking notes. When he finished, there was a long silence, broken only by the sound of Viktor sharpening his pencil. Henry leant forward in his seat, his elbows on his thighs, staring down.

'What's the matter *synok*: you look bothered about something?'

'He'll be dead now, won't he?'

'Who?'

'Manfred – Lido: do you think the Germans would have found

him?'

Viktor shrugged. 'I'd imagine so. Whatever we think of them, we can't accuse them of not being thorough, can we? I'd be most surprised if they didn't find the coat and that would have led to Manfred.'

Henry shook his head.

'You seem to be upset?' Viktor looked confused.

'Well, I am actually, yes. He was a decent chap and it was my mistake that probably did it for him.'

'He was a social democrat, Henry: their fate is to end up dead. And now he's a victim of war. How do you feel about killing the man in shop? Has that upset you as much?'

'Of course not: he was clearly a bad sort – a Nazi. I had no alternative.'

'Indeed. I imagine it was somewhat easier than with the boy in Interlaken, or the puppy. That's why we train you like that Henry, so you're used to killing. As far as your Mr Remington-Barber is concerned, it's your first.'

'You think I should tell him then?'

'Of course! It's always good to have an agent who's killed in the field. I'm not sure whether an English gentleman will approve or not, but he ought to be impressed with it. In any case, he may already be aware of it and it won't look good if you don't tell him.'

It was six o'clock now. Viktor checked back through his notebook, nodding his head at various points. He seemed pleased, though Henry knew better than to expect him to actually say he was. It was now Viktor's turn to speak, in his deliberate and concise manner.

Listen carefully Henry: this is what's expected of you.

We're satisfied so far Henry, but there are many difficult days ahead.

It's too risky for us to meet on a regular basis. We can keep an eye on you but we must keep these meetings to a minimum.

You must learn to operate on your own but to do exactly what we want you to.

It was a quarter to seven when Viktor finished.

'I think we can risk driving you back to Geneva, *synok*. We now need to wait until Remington-Barber contacts you: I imagine that'll be soon.'

Viktor stood up and embraced Henry once more. The two men who had brought Henry to the villa had come back into the room. *Time to go.*

'Before I go Viktor, there's something I need to get off my chest.'

Viktor raised his eyebrows and looked at his watch, clearly irritated. 'If you must: go on then.'

'I just wanted to say I'm risking my life now. I've told you what happened in Essen. I'm not playing games. I know what I let myself in for, I realise all that. But there is something that's made me very unhappy and I need to talk about it.'

Viktor shifted uncomfortably and looked at the two other men in the room. He nodded at them and they both left.

'Go on, but make it quick Henry.'

'I agreed to work with you – for you – because I believe in your cause: I see it as my cause too. You know that.'

Viktor nodded in agreement, unsure what was going to come next. Henry paused to compose himself.

'I agreed to work for you because I was ideologically committed.'

'We know that.'

'And I still am. But now I've started to lay my life on the line, I can't understand why we signed that bloody pact with them last year. I mean, they were meant to be our sworn enemy, they stood for everything we despise and now I have to get used to the fact they're our allies, our friends even. That seems wrong to me. Whose side am I meant to be on now?'

Viktor sank back into his chair and motioned for Henry to do the same. He leant forward, placed his enormous hands on Henry's knees, gripping them quite tightly.

'What you must understand *synok* is that they're not our friends. There is no question of that.'

'But our allies? That's bad enough… Perhaps even worse!'

'Hardly even that. It's a non-aggression pact Henry; that's all – a matter of expediency. I shouldn't quote Trotsky of course, but a couple of years ago he said "the end may justify the means as long as there is something that justifies the end." That end is the victory over fascism and the triumph of communism. The pact is to buy us time to achieve that. Our feelings about them haven't changed, but we need to be ready and this pact allows us to do that. It's not meant to make us feel comfortable; it's meant to protect us.'

'Well, I do feel uncomfortable Viktor.'

'And do you think you're the only one?' He gripped Henry's knee so hard he winced in pain. His raised voice meant one of the men who had been sent out of the room popped his head round the door to check all was in order. Viktor stood up and leant over Henry, his hot breath was moist and smelt of alcohol.

'We are not permitted the luxury of personal feelings or opinions: they are mere indulgences. Do you understand that?'

Henry edged back in his chair.

'We do as we are instructed, all of us. Maybe we permit you too many bourgeois indulgences, *synok*. Have you forgotten? Never question; never discuss; never hesitate. You would do well to remember that more often than you evidently do. Otherwise, *synok*, you'll be in a lot of trouble.'

* * *

Henry's journey from Essen to Stuttgart had been uneventful and when he arrived at the Hotel Victoria late on the Thursday afternoon Katharina Hoch had not yet come on duty. She came up to his room later that night to collect her brother's clothes and papers. She insisted he was not to tell her any details of the Essen trip. *I don't need to know anything else. Save that for Bern. They'll want to know everything.* He couldn't decide whether she had any inkling of what had gone on in Essen, but if she did she gave no hint of it.

He had removed the Nazi Party membership badge he had taken from the dead man in the perfume shop from his lapel before arriving at the hotel. *You never know*, he thought. He hid it in the lining of his washbag.

She was right – Bern would want to know everything, though he could not understand why it was taking quite so long. Before the mission, Remington-Barber had told him he was not to initiate any contact when he got back to Switzerland. 'Just wait, I'll be in touch. Be patient. Apparently it's a virtue.'

Henry had taken the Swissair flight from Stuttgart, which landed in Zürich just before 4.30 on the Friday afternoon, and had managed to catch a train straight back to Geneva. He was utterly exhausted. He had hardly slept for the past week: his plan now was to catch up on sleep that weekend. He assumed Remington-Barber would be in touch on the Monday, if not before.

But nothing: nothing on the Monday nor the following day. Nor the rest of that week nor, indeed, the following one. His visit to Viktor in the hills above Lausanne came and went, and it was the middle of August when he returned from his morning walk to be told by his mother that a messenger had come round from Credit Suisse. There was a letter.

'Whatever can be the problem, Henry?'

It was from Madame Ladnier. Henry tried to read it away from the prying eyes of his mother, who was trying to move behind him.

'I would like to meet with you today to review recent transactions. Two o'clock this afternoon, Quai des Bergues. Giselle Ladnier (Madame).'

At last. He felt relieved. His mother was looking at him anxiously, her eyebrows raised high.

'What's the problem Henry?'

'There's no problem mother, none at all. I have a meeting to review my account. It's just routine.'

Madame Ladnier was calm and businesslike. Henry had arrived at the branch in Quai des Bergues at five to two and as the clock struck the hour above the cashiers' counters Madame Ladnier emerged from a door and ushered Henry into a small office down a long corridor.

'How are you, Herr Hesse?'

'Very well, thank you.' *Do I ask about the delay, why I've not been contacted? Do I mention anything about Germany?*

'Good. Your account is in order. Please now take a few minutes to check your statements and initial each page to indicate you've read them.'

He scanned through the statements, initialling each page. There was no message for him on any of the pages as he thought there may be. He kept glancing up at Madame Ladnier, hoping for a smile or a nod or some acknowledgement of the situation, but she remained as impassive as one would expect of a Swiss bank official.

When he had finished, he returned the papers to her. She checked them and placed them neatly in a folder marked with his name.

'Thank you very much for coming in, Herr Hesse. I'm pleased your account is all in order. I'd also ask you to take this pamphlet with you: it explains the various options should you wish to invest any of your funds with Credit Suisse.'

She had stood up now, preparing to leave the room. As Henry rose, she came around to his side of the desk and bent to pick up a piece of paper from the floor.

'You appear to have dropped this paper, Herr Hesse.'

'I don't think so,' Henry replied.

She handed him the small piece of paper, her gaze making it

clear it was for him. It was a receipt from the cobblers in Bern where he had met Remington-Barber before the trip to Germany. Scrawled underneath the price of a shoe repair were the words: *'Collection Friday 16th August, 1pm.'*

Madame Ladnier held a long manicured finger over her mouth in case Henry was inclined to speak.

He left Geneva on the 9.30 train on the Friday morning and was in Bern in good time for his appointment on Kramgasse. There were no customers so he entered the leather emporium, where the cobbler glanced up and nodded, holding a few tacks between his lips and a hammer in his hand. He lifted the counter top and pointed the way up the stairs with the hammer. Basil Remington-Barber was standing by the window.

'Good trip?' He sounded as though he was enquiring after a holiday.

'Well, all things considered, yes.'

'All things considered?'

'Well, considering I was sent into Nazi Germany then into the heart of the Ruhr carrying detonators concealed in my baggage, yes it was fine thank you.'

'I'm not terribly sure what you were expecting old chap.'

'I was expecting that it'd be a bit more of a testing the water mission: you know, see how I got on...'

'... Which in a sense it was,' said Remington-Barber. 'Having said that, we're hardly going to go to the trouble of getting you into Germany and take the risk of exposing some of our very few remaining agents there just as part of a simple training exercise for you, are we, eh?'

'And the detonators?'

'One of the purposes of your trip, Henry. I'm told we British make first-class detonators. We managed to get a few into Stuttgart at the end of last year, but we needed to move some to the Ruhr, which is where you came in. Evidently Lido did manage to pass on the detonators to another member of the cell the morning you left, so that is rather good news: with a bit of luck we may be able to do some damage there. Aerial bombing tends to be a bit hit and miss, but if we can actually plant something inside a factory or a coal mine – well, who knows?'

'I think I ought to have been told a bit more about my mission before I was sent on it.'

'Not sure it works like that old chap. Not to put too fine a point on it, you do as you're told. You remember what Tennyson said? *Theirs not to reason why.* You're one of the "theirs", if you catch my drift.'

'Yes, but what worries me is what he said in the next line: *Theirs but to do and die.*'

'Let's hope it doesn't come to that. No reason why it should. Now then, old chap, care to tell me about it?'

'About what?'

Basil Remington-Barber stared at Henry for quite a long time, not in an altogether unfriendly manner, his eyebrows raised quizzically.

'About what led to Lido being arrested and killed: and be a good chap and leave nothing out, eh? It'd be safe for you to assume that you were – how shall I put it – observed while you were in

Essen. We have a good idea of what happened, even with that shopkeeper chap – but not all of it.'

Henry had already decided to explain what had happened, but confirmation that Manfred was dead caused Henry to swallow hard. When he regained his composure he began to recount the story in much the same way as he had with Viktor. Unlike the Russian, Remington-Barber interrupted him frequently, little questions to help him on his way or clarify a point. When he finished, he asked Remington-Barber what had happened to Lido.

'You left Essen on the Thursday. As we understand it, that evening he was pulled in by the Gestapo. Apparently they'd arrived at his apartment in the afternoon, turned the place upside down and were waiting for him when he got home. Thank heavens the detonators weren't there. He was then taken to the police headquarters in Virchow Strasse.'

'How do you know this?'

'One of his neighbours: most likely the one you met. Half the neighbourhood heard what happened from her and one of our chaps there overheard it. As far as the police are concerned, they've pulled in a number of retired detectives while the younger ones are in the army and another of our contacts heard all this at the bar that they frequent. Manfred was at Virchow Strasse right through the weekend: the Gestapo gave him their standard working over. Not pleasant stuff Henry: they're bloody barbarians. He was a bloody pulp when they took him to the Provincial Prison across the road on Zweigert Strasse. The Gestapo had another go at him on the Monday then, by all accounts, he died that night. Apparently they were due to give him another working over the next day. I

187

suppose in one sense they didn't kill him as such, but of course…'

'Of course.' Henry felt bereft. 'Do you think I should have warned him?'

'Well from what you say, you didn't have time, did you? If you'd done that then you'd have missed the Cologne train and you weren't to know how long it would take them to find the coat and the trail which would lead to Lido.'

'Good Lord… I don't know what to say.'

'Whatever they did to him, he didn't utter a word: gave nothing away. If he'd sung straight away, they may even have picked you up in Stuttgart – possibly even before you got there, but turns out he was a brave man. We always tell our chaps to hold out for 24 hours, though, to be frank, even that's pushing it with those animals. But he held out for far longer than that: remarkable how resilient people can be.'

'And brave.'

'Indeed.'

'And the shopkeeper?'

'What about him?'

'I'm sorry if that turned out to be rather… messy.'

Basil Remington-Barber looked confused. 'Messy? Not at all! You did absolutely the right thing. It would have been messy had you attempted to extricate yourself from the situation in any other way. No, we've all been rather impressed: it was desperately unlucky the shopkeeper knew Gertraud Traugott. Not your fault. Important thing is you acted decisively. Don't look so worried, Henry!'

'I rather thought that you'd be… I don't know… angry with me?'

'I'd have been angry had you not told me what happened. And, as I said, you were observed in Essen: what you told me tallies with what we already knew. And there's no harm whatsoever in having an agent who knows how to kill, not to put too fine a point on it, eh?'

Remington-Barber clapped his hands and ushered Henry over to a table by the window, on which a large map of Essen was spread out.

'You've brought your notes with you?'

Henry had.

'Good. What we need to do now is fill in all the information you picked up on the ground against this map. It'll be like doing a jigsaw: should be rather fun.'

Henry would not have described it as fun. They spent an hour going over the map, Henry doing his best to point out the location of factories and other key buildings. For all his bonhomie and apparent diffidence, Remington-Barber turned out to be highly adept at teasing information out of Henry. By 2.30 the map was much more detailed.

'RAF ought to be chuffed with this,' he announced, carefully rolling it up and slipping it into a metal tube. He then stood up and rubbed his hands, as if in excitement.

'Right then! If you hurry, you'll catch the six o'clock train to Geneva: saves us another hotel bill, eh? And talking of money, London are very pleased with the mission. Edgar says to tell you that 500 pounds will be put into your Credit Suisse account next week: says you'll know what all that's about. I hate anything to do with money.'

'And what happens now?'

'Go home and wait for us to contact you, which we'll do through Madame Ladnier.'

'And when might that be?'

'Good question Henry. The truth is, I've no idea. Could be next week, could be next year. The only thing I'd say is if London were so pleased with this mission, the next one could be a lot more interesting. Something to look forward to! So don't worry, I'm sure London will want to see you soon.'

Henry was alarmed. 'London! You want me to go to London?'

Remington-Barber frowned. 'Good heavens no! London will come to you.'

* * *

Chapter 13: Berlin, August 1940

Berlin in the first full summer of the war was a city of secrets and hushed conversations; a city at the centre of the conflict but a long way from the sounds or more obvious effects of it. The closer to the centre of power, the more secrets there were and the more hushed conversations became. Unless you knew someone well and were absolutely sure you could trust them, even a routine conversation was guarded and required a circuitous route to reach its point.

For Franz Hermann, such a cautious approach was by no means an alien one. As a lawyer he was used to being careful and non-committal; discretion came as second nature to him. But late in the afternoon of an extremely pleasant Tuesday in the middle of August he was mindful of the need to be even more careful than usual. Hermann was on his way to meet a very important client, a General in the Army High Command.

The lawyer had left his office in Friedrichstrasse to visit this client at his home in Moabit. Hermann headed west along the north bank of the River Spree and at Lehrter Station turned into Alt Moabit, past the Post Stadion. Four years earlier he had been there watching Norway unexpectedly beat Germany 2-0 to knock the hosts out of the Olympics football tournament. His initial disappointment at the defeat had been more than compensated for by the fact Hitler was at the game and was reported as being furious. He decided if Hitler was so upset by the result then maybe defeat wasn't so bad after all. *Your enemy's enemy...*

Halfway along Strom Strasse he reached his destination: a handsome apartment block, overlooking the Kleiner Tiergarten.

A maid, who looked as though she was still in her teens, let him into the apartment on the top floor of the building.

Generalmajor Werner Ernst was in his study, still wearing his uniform. He moved his large head slowly, as if he had a bad neck. His eyes were noticeablely small in comparison to the rest of his face. He smiled politely and pointed to one of two armchairs angled towards the window, a small coffee table between them. Behind him were enormous picture windows over the park. A breeze that had not been apparent on the street was causing the tops of the trees to sway gently from side to side.

'Please do sit down Herr Hermann: you'll have to excuse me, I've only just returned from work and I've not had time to change.'

They paused while the young maid came back into the room, carrying a tray that she placed on the coffee table. Hermann could smell real coffee, an increasingly rare sensation in Berlin.

'Thank you Anke, don't you worry, I'll pour the coffee. And Frau Ernst reminded me it's your night off. You may leave early if you wish.'

The Generalmajor busied himself pouring the coffee and offering freshly baked biscuits to his guest. He waited until he heard the front door of the apartment close before signalling to his lawyer he could proceed.

For the next half hour Franz Hermann went through various documents with his important client. *A signature here please; an explanation necessary there; another signature here thank you; just an initial here will suffice; let me explain this sheet; I have taken the liberty of having this form already witnessed; one more signature there; all is in order.*

'There we are sir. I think you'll find the business of finalising your mother's estate is now complete. I'd estimate the funds will be in your bank account within the month.'

'Thank you Herr Hermann. You've deal with this matter most efficiently. I realise it's taken some effort to sort everything out. I'm most grateful to you.'

'A pleasure sir.'

Hermann began to gather the papers and place them in his briefcase.

'Will you join me for a drink, Herr Hermann? My wife has gone to stay with her sister in Potsdam and it's a pleasure for me not to be ruled by the stopwatch at home for once.'

Without waiting for an answer, the Generalmajor produced a bottle of Armagnac and poured a large measure for himself and his guest. There was a long silence while he surveyed the drink before putting the glass to his lips and leaning back in his armchair, his tiny eyes first studying Franz Hermann carefully and then closing. It was a while before he opened them.

'Do you have children, Hermann?'

'No, sir.'

'I hope you don't think it's impertinent of me to ask, but it's something I've been thinking about recently. This may be a strange thing for an army officer to say, but I've noticed among my colleagues that the ones without children seem to have a very different attitude to the war than the ones with them, especially those with sons. My own son is based in Poland, Herr Hermann. He is an Oberleutnant and just 22 years old. As an army officer, I've never held any fears for my own safety. Of course, I've always done my best to avoid making rash judgements that could cause harm to men under my command. But now my own son is a soldier, I've found that's having an unexpected effect on my attitude to the war: I'm more cautious, I worry about the course of the war. It's had a much more profound effect on me than I'd imagined. I'd hoped my son would become an architect…'

The Generalmajor's voice tailed off; he seemed to be preoccupied with his own thoughts.

'Hopefully he won't need to remain in the army for too long sir: victory will be ours soon!'

The Generalmajor looked long and hard at the lawyer.

'You think so, Herr Herrmann? What makes you so sure of that?'

The lawyer shifted uncomfortably in his seat. 'One reads in the papers how well the war is going, that it's just a matter of time before Britain surrenders and…'

'And you believe everything you read in the papers, do you Herr Hermann? I'd thought lawyers were trained to question things, not to accept matters at face value.'

Hermann shrugged, unsure of what to say and wondering how he'd allowed himself to become drawn into a conversation like this.

'Tell me, Herr Hermann: are you a member of the Nazi Party?'

'I'm a lawyer sir. I'm not involved in politics.'

'Many lawyers are members of the Nazi Party.'

'I'm not one of them sir.'

Generalmajor Ernst stood up and unbuttoned his jacket then walked over to the window. The trees in the Kleiner Tiergarten had stopped swaying. The Generalmajor shut the window and turned around.

'Well if it makes you feel any better, Herr Hermann, nor am I.'

Hermann started to get up, relieved at the opportunity to finish the conversation at that juncture. The Generalmajor gestured for him to remain seated and sat down next to him, pulling up his chair alongside the lawyer's.

'You're a clever chap, Herr Hermann.'

'Thank you sir.'

'You're not just a very competent lawyer, but you're good at managing to appear to be what you are not.'

'I'm sorry, I'm not sure...'

'You do an excellent job of appearing to be a mild-mannered lawyer, with no interest in politics. You're quiet and you're discreet. You don't draw attention to yourself. But I also know that you have – now, how can I put this – that you have contacts.'

Hermann could feel his breathing tighten and the room become hotter. He did his best to sound relaxed.

'I suspect, sir, there must be a misunderstanding here. I am as you originally describe me: a lawyer with no interest in politics. But please be assured I am a loyal...'

'Please, please, Herr Hermann. I'm sure you're all of these things. But, you see, I know there's more to you than that and you'll find I'm not altogether unsympathetic. I know you have certain contacts and I wish to avail myself of them.'

Franz Hermann said nothing. The Generalmajor leaned towards him, so their faces were just inches apart. He could smell the brandy on Ernst's breath and see the tiny red lines in his eyes.

'Three weeks ago, on the 29th of July to be precise, I was in Bad Reichenhall. Have you heard of it?'

'Of course, a very pleasant spa town in Bavaria, not too far from Salzburg. My parents spent their honeymoon there.'

'Indeed. But I wasn't there to use the spa, I can assure you. Do you have a good memory, Franz?'

'Yes sir.'

'Werner. Please call me Werner. You'll make sure to memorise what I say now. Write nothing down.'

Hermann nodded.

'My area of expertise in the army is logistics. It's not a glamorous job, but few people in the high command know better than me how to move our troops around in an efficient manner and ensure they're well supplied. That's perhaps the most underestimated part of warfare. It is one thing to advance fast, especially against a weak enemy, but it is quite another to ensure the integrity of an advance is maintained by having good supplies of food, fuel and ammunition. That's what I excel at. But I'm not telling you all this to make me seem important. The reason I was in Bad Reichenhall was because the Chief of Staff, General Jodl, was holding a top-secret meeting there on the express instructions of the Fuhrer himself. You will have some more Armagnac, Franz? It's quite excellent, one of the more tangible benefits of our conquest of France.'

He poured two more large measures.

'Jodl is a busy man, he does not gather senior officers around him in pleasant Bavarian spa towns without very good reason. And the reason he gathered us last month was that, now that France has fallen, the Fuhrer has turned his attention to who we attack next. The common belief is that Operation Sea Lion is our priority and we'll soon launch an invasion of Great Britain. As you know, we started our aerial assault against them over a month ago. But the Kriegsmarine has serious doubts we'll ever be able to successfully invade the British Isles. Our hope is we win what they're calling the Battle of Britain, gain air supremacy and this leads to victory. But that doesn't appear likely. The RAF is proving to be a resolute opponent and Churchill shows no inclination whatsoever to surrender.'

With the window closed, the room had now become quite stuffy. The Generalmajor stood up to remove his jacket and loosen his collar.

'The Fuhrer has instructed Colonel General Jodl to explore other options, in the eventuality we do not invade Britain. The option we discussed in Bad Reichenhall was that of invading the Soviet Union.'

During the shocked silence that followed, Hermann heard the loud ticking of a clock from the hall. The treetops in the Kleiner Tiergarten had begun to sway again. The Generalmajor reached over to a side table and opened a box of cigars. He offered one to the lawyer, who declined, then slowly lit one for himself.

'Invade the Soviet Union? But surely that would be madness! We have a pact with them?'

'It's not as outrageous as you think it is, Franz. That pact was designed to keep our eastern borders quiet while we dealt with Western Europe. Now, I have no love for the Soviet Union but, for many of us Franz – those of us who approach matters from a professional military point of view as opposed to an ideological one – the prospect of invading the Soviet Union is a nightmare. To attempt to go in there would be to ignore the lessons of history. Bismarck himself said the secret of politics was to "make a good treaty with Russia", which is of course what we did. From a military point of view, invading the Soviet Union has all the potential to end in disaster. Even Field Marshall Keitel is trying to dissuade Hitler from the idea and he is well known for never disagreeing with the Fuhrer.'

'When will this invasion take place?'

'Too early to say, Franz. It may never happen. The purpose of Jodl gathering us in Bad Reichenhall was to get us thinking in theoretical terms about how we might prepare for such a plan. It's so sensitive and so secret, we can do little more than think about it. The final decision will rest with the Fuhrer. After the conquest of the Low Countries and France, he's convinced he's a military genius: he thinks we older Wehrmacht officers are too cautious, too conservative.'

The Generalmajor was now wreathed in cigar smoke, the colour of gun-metal. He leant back in his chair, staring up at the ceiling.

'However, Franz, even Hitler knows the timing of an invasion would need to be very precise if we aren't to be caught out in the Russian winter. If we've not achieved our objectives by the start of the winter then we're doomed. So we'd need to attack by mid-May at the latest. Then we have a chance of success, although not a very good one.'

'Why on earth are you telling me this?'

'Many of us believe that to invade the Soviet Union would be suicide for Germany. There are groups of us in the Bendlerblock who are of a like mind. We believe we're acting in the best interests of Germany. As you might be aware, the Abwehr has its headquarters in the Bendlerblock. A few days ago I was talking with an old friend who's a very senior officer in the Abwehr. His mother died a month ago and he asked if I could recommend a good lawyer to take care of everything. I told him about you and that was that. The next day he asked me to go for a walk with him along the banks of the Landwehr Canal. He confided in me that you have come to the attention of the Abwehr.'

'This is preposterous sir. It is simply untrue. I must insist that…'

'Franz, you must not worry.' He patted the lawyer on the arm in a reassuring manner. 'Just be very, very grateful it's the Abwehr and not the Gestapo. According to my friend, they're aware you're able to channel information to the Allies. They've permitted you to carry on doing this because they believed there may come a time when they wished to use this channel. That time has now come.'

Hermann held out his hands in a 'what can I say' gesture. 'I'm not a traitor sir. I consider myself to be a loyal German. I happen to believe that Germany should be a democratic country and that this war could ruin us.'

'No-one is saying you're a traitor. Nor am I, for that matter. We all have our different motives. Will you pass on this information, about the meeting at Bad Reichenhall and the possibility of an invasion of the Soviet Union?'

'Of course.'

When he left the apartment there was a cool evening breeze,

which was a welcome relief from the stuffiness of the apartment, but this had no calming effect on Hermann. He felt the huge trees closing in on him and imagined the people around him on the pavement were all looking at him. He would have to move fast, he could not afford to think about things.

* * *

When Franz Hermann was 16 or 17, it had been briefly fashionable among his group at school to root out ancient Chinese proverbs, which they would then quote to each other as if they had stumbled upon words of wisdom that unlocked the secrets of the universe. It was all rather pretentious and did not last long. A couple of their group had continued to grasp at various ancient beliefs long after they had left school and they were the ones who had become early members of the Nazi Party.

One of the sayings they had passed around sounded at first like a Chinese good-luck wish: 'may you live in interesting times.' The twist was it was actually a curse. He had never quite understood why hoping someone lived in interesting times was a curse. All his life he had wished his life had been more interesting: an obedient student; not fit for military service; a childless marriage and a worthy but dull career.

Now he was trapped between the gates of heaven and the banks of hell. A chance remark during an unguarded conversation at a dinner party a month after the start of the war was followed up by a clandestine meeting at the zoo a week later. He and the elegant woman with a Viennese accent who had had slipped him a note as he left the dinner party stood alongside the elephant enclosure watching the animals spray each other with water. *I noticed you made some remarks about the regime. You'd best be careful where and to whom you say such things.* He nodded, he realised he had been careless; his wife had told him as much in no uncertain terms on their way home. Too much good wine had been his excuse. *But you also said something about tensions in the Nazi Party leadership in Berlin? Where did you get that from?*

He had waited for two of the elephants to finish calling to each other. *From one of my colleagues*, he told her.

And what is his name?

He had hesitated before replying. The Viennese lady was evidently not quite what she seemed. Franz Hermann could have walked away at that point. He could have said he wanted to take matters no further and would appreciate it if they could both forget they had ever met. She was hardly likely to report him to the Gestapo. But there was something almost seductive about her manner. He found it impossible not to reply to her.

Alois Jäger: we work at the same law firm. He's some big shot in the leadership of the Nazi Party in Berlin. As far as he's concerned, I'm completely apolitical. I pick up a lot of his legal work while he's on Nazi Party business, so he has reason to be grateful to me. He can't help gossiping. I hear him talk about Goebbels: he can't stand him, they just don't get on. But, from what I gather, there's a feeling shared among a number of senior Nazis in Berlin that Goebbels can't be an effective Gauleiter of the city and Minister for Propaganda. They think he should concentrate on one or the other.

This is very interesting, she'd replied. *You're clearly in a position to pick up such information. I'd like to tell you how you can pass it on to people who need to know this kind of thing. Are you willing to do so?*

Hermann said he was. They walked round to the tiger enclosure then over to the aquarium. The lady had slipped her gloved arm through his as she explained in detail how he could make contact with the right people.

And then his position became even more precarious in December when Rosa had turned up on his doorstep. What could he do: turn her away? It made sense to lodge her and the children with his mother, and he was sure it would only be for a few weeks, but that was eight, nine months ago. Now he was a British spy and harbouring a Jewish family, and he understood why 'may you live in interesting times' was indeed a curse.

* * *

Franz Hermann would have preferred to walk and give himself some opportunity to compose himself, but time was against him so he took a tram from Alt Moabit into the Unter den Linden, getting off a stop earlier than he needed to at the junction with Friedrichstrasse.

Despite being so near, he decided against popping back into his office: had anyone been following him or spotted him in the street it would have looked normal for him to return to work, but he was in a hurry. He walked along the Unter den Linden for another two blocks before turning left into the Opernplatz.

Although he came to the pretty square at least twice a week and had done so for years, it nonetheless left him with an uneasy feeling. He could never forget what happened there seven years before, in May 1933, when the Nazis had burned tens of thousands of books. The smell had lingered for days, and for weeks afterwards people would come across tiny piles of ash throughout the area. Even months later it wasn't uncommon to come across scraps of paper that had somehow escaped the flames, floating around the city in a defiant manner, daring passers-by to steal a look at a word or two that may corrupt them.

His sense of apprehension increased as he entered St Hedwig's, the cathedral he'd worshipped at since he was a boy. Although they lived in Dahlem and there were plenty of Catholic churches near to where they lived, his mother was of the opinion their piety was increased by praying at the seat of the Archbishop.

Now, the cathedral served a very different purpose for him.

The mass was just coming to an end and most of the congregation were leaving the church. In the old days, people would gather in small groups and chat, but that was not the done thing now. You never knew who may be watching, or listening.

Hermann sat on his own towards the back of the cathedral, watching the small group of priests at the high altar as they began to disperse. Sure enough, the tall and slightly stooped figure of the young priest he was looking for emerged from the little group and walked in long strides towards the confession box that sat on its own to the side.

I always take confession after mass on Tuesday and Thursday afternoons. On those days I use the confession box that's on its own, the one near the high altar. Only come to me then. No-one can overhear us there. It is safer. Or at least, not as dangerous.

Franz Hermann left his seat and walked towards the altar, where he knelt and crossed himself before approaching the confession box the young priest has gone into. An old man with scruffy trousers had just entered, muttering silently to himself as he did so. The lawyer sat down next to an elegantly dressed lady with a blue silk scarf wrapped around her neck. She was clutching a photograph of what looked like a boy in Luftwaffe uniform and dabbing her eyes with a crisp, white handkerchief.

The old man shuffled out, still muttering to himself and the elegantly dressed lady replaced him, her high heels echoing sharply on the tiled floor. The confession box was in a perfect position: unlike the ones grouped together on the other side of the cathedral, this one was isolated in a quiet cloister and the chairs were some way from the box: it was impossible to overhear anything, not even the sound of voices, let alone the words.

A few minutes later the lady emerged, still dabbing her eyes. Hermann walked over to the box, crossed himself, closed the heavy velvet curtain and knelt down.

'Bless me Father for I have sinned. It has been two weeks since my last confession.'

He had not been sure if Father Josef was aware he was there, but he looked towards the grille and at the sound of his voice he saw the young priest sit up sharply. As Father Josef glanced towards him he caught sight of the priest's red nose, which always made him look as though he had just come in from the cold.

'Go on, my son.'

'I have sinned Father. I fear I've been treating our maid too harshly because I suspected she was stealing some small change left around the house, though I now think it was not her. And I've been guilty of the sin of envy: a friend has been able to find some best-quality cloth and had it made into fine suit – you must know how hard that is in these times and I find it's been the cause of feelings of jealousy in myself.'

'And any other sins, my son?'

'I'm afraid I took the Lord's name in vain: I used it in a disrespectful manner. I am sorry for these and all the sins of my past life.'

'And that's it?'

'That's it, Father.' The lawyer thought he had done quite well to muster three things he could pass off as sins.

The priest would be de-coding his message. The confession of treating the maid too harshly was for security: *all is well, I'm not being followed.* The sin of envy indicated he needed to meet his contact. Taking the Lord's name in vain meant it was urgent.

'I see.' The priest coughed, pausing to take everything in. Through the grill, Hermann could see the priest's head bob up and down, the red nose clearly visible in the gloom. 'Say three Hail Marys and pray for your sins. She will next be in on Thursday, my son. I will pass on your message. Meet her at the usual place at the usual time on the Friday. Can you manage that?'

'Yes Father.'

'If she cannot manage that or does not turn up, return here on Tuesday. You had better say an Act of Contrition, my son.'

'I am heartily sorry for having offended you my Lord and I detest all my sins, because I dread the loss of heaven and the pains of hell. I firmly resolve with the help of your grace, to confess my sins, to do penance and to amend my life. Amen.'

The priest replied with a prayer of forgiveness. 'Give thanks to the Lord for He is good.'

Hermann crossed himself and replied, 'For His mercy endures forever.'

He left the Confession Box: the waiting chairs had now filled. He paused in the main body of the cathedral and said his Hail Marys and a few other prayers then hurried out and headed home to Dahlem, his reply to the absolution repeating in his mind throughout the journey.

'*For His mercy endures forever.*'

He certainly hoped so.

* * *

The Military Attaché at the Portuguese Legation in Berlin was well aware his secretary attended Mass whenever she could. Although not as devout as he would like to be, the Colonel was rather impressed as he found religious observance in others somehow reassuring. At least it was a sign that his Dona Maria do Rosario, a reserved woman who shared little of herself, must be trustworthy. He sometimes liked to imagine what sins his secretary had to confess to. She led a pious life: she did not drink or speak out of turn; she was a hard worker and a loyal servant of the Portuguese Government, with a framed photograph of Salazar on her desk.

Berlin was, the Colonel was fond of reminding whoever would listen, not an easy posting and perhaps the most important of all of Portugal's overseas missions. A neutral country had to lean one way then the other, depending upon the wind of war. It required fleet of foot and the utmost discretion, and the Colonel in turn demanded that of his staff. So it was neither unusual nor even unexpected when Dona Maria do Rosario entered the Colonel's office with a neat pile of documents just after five o'clock on the afternoon of Thursday 15th August.

'These letters need to be signed sir; each one is appended to their relevant file; if you can sign them before you leave, I can ensure they're in the Diplomatic Bag on Friday evening. I'm leaving now to go to the cathedral, but I'm happy to return later if you require me, sir. Otherwise I'll be in first thing in the morning.'

'That's fine,' the Colonel told his secretary. 'I'll sign the papers and see you first thing. In truth, she arrived at work sometime before he did. She was invariably in the office by 7.30, when few other staff were around. He was unsure why she came in quite so early, but he had every reason to be most grateful to her for doing so. He would arrive at work between 8.30 and 9.00 to find all his papers in order and everything neatly set out on his desk, his day already organised for him. Of course, he was technically in breach of protocol by allowing her access to secret documents, but it made life so much easier and, of course, how could such a devout Catholic not be trustworthy?

Dona Maria do Rosario hurried out of the Legation at a quarter past five and arrived at St Hedwig's Cathedral in time for the early evening Mass. It was close to six o'clock when she finally entered the Confession Box, a slight early evening chill now around in the cloisters, causing her to pull her light jacket tight around her shoulders.

'In the name of the Father and of the Son and of the Holy Spirit. My last confession was one week ago.'

Father Josef looked at her, his face pressed tight against the grille to check it really was her.

'What are your sins?'

She gave the code: a sin of gluttony to indicate all was well and a sin of speaking ill of someone behind their back to ensure she had nothing to report. The priest spoke urgently.

'Hugo's been here: two days ago. He needs to see you as soon as possible. I told him it would be tomorrow, the usual place and the usual time. I hope you can make it?'

Dona Maria assured the priest she could. How are things, the priest asked her?

Very busy, she told him. 'So much material comes through the Colonel's office that I work late most nights and I'm starting earlier every morning just to find the most important papers. It's getting more and more risky though. I fear that sooner or later someone will suspect me.'

'Maybe moderate your hours. The material you're sending back is so good, I'm told, that you should not risk too much. Don't forget, you need to meet Hugo tomorrow and report back on what he tells you.'

'I know.'

'Do you want to pray? Shall I grant you absolution?'

Dona Maria do Rosario was already up and preparing to leave the confession box.

'No thank you Father.'

As she hurried out of the church she only just remembered to cross herself and pause for a very brief prayer.

* * *

The following day, the Friday, an unusual wind whipped around the centre of Berlin. It appeared to linger about four feet off the ground, creating the strange effect of leaves and small bits of litter fluttering around in mid-air. The wind was still at play when Franz Hermann hurried out of his office at one o'clock. He was going for a walk, he told his secretary, reassuring her he'd be back in time for his two o'clock meeting. He turned into Behrenstrasse then left into Wilhemstrasse. In between Wilhemstrasse and Hermann Goring Strasse was a small park, taking up no more than a block, where office workers and civil servants – but not too many of them – liked to take their lunch.

He entered and walked towards the north-west corner where a series of old benches surrounded an enormous tree. Perhaps because the benches appeared so uncomfortable or the size of the tree ensured that the spot was permanently in the shade, this area was deserted, apart from an olive-skinned woman in her late thirties poised demurely on the edge of one of the benches. Her jet-black hair was pulled back from a face that would have been prettier, but for the absence of make-up and the presence of a slightly disapproving look. She was eating an apple and an open book was resting on her lap. He sat on the next bench and removed his jacket, taking out a packet of cigarettes from the jacket as he did so. He offered one to the lady.

'No thank you sir. I don't smoke,' she replied in a foreign accent.

'Very sensible: my wife doesn't approve.'

'I can offer you an apple in return.'

And so the exchange continued. In the unlikely event of anyone overhearing the conversation it would have sounded like two strangers passing the time of day. But soon they had established each other was safe; they had not been followed and he had information to pass on.

Hermann shifted to the end of his park bench, so he was nearer to the one Dona Maria do Rosario was sitting on. She had opened her book and was giving the appearance of avidly reading from it. The lawyer was bent forward, busy smoking, his elbows resting on his lap. He was facing the ground, occasionally looking up to be sure no-one else was around. He spoke very quietly, but at a volume that ensured Dona Maria could hear everything.

'How quickly can you get a message to Lisbon?'

Without looking up from the book, she replied. 'It depends how long it is, but there's a bag going this evening. If I can type it up in time I could get it in.'

'You'll have to, it's urgent. This is what you need to tell them. Colonel General Jodl held a meeting at Bad Reichenhall on the 29th of July. My informant, a senior officer in the OKH, was present. I'm not giving his name, not at the moment. Apparently they're now entertaining the possibility that Britain may not capitulate after all and Hitler wants to have alternative plans in place. The purpose of Jodl's meeting was to get senior officers to start thinking about plans for the invasion of the Soviet Union.'

He looked up at Dona Maria. Her eyebrows had risen very

slightly and momentarily, as though she'd read something interesting in her book. She took a dainty bite from her apple.

'My informant says a lot of the professional army officers are against the idea of invasion as they think it'll end in failure. The thinking is that any invasion will have to start by the middle of May because it'd need to be over by the onset of winter. Have you got all that?'

Dona Maria said she had. Hermann noticed her face had relaxed now and she had even allowed herself a slight smile as she briefly turned towards him. He asked her to repeat what he had told her. Her repetition was impressively word-perfect. She would, she said, return now to the Legation and type it up in code in time for that evening's Diplomatic Bag. Was there anything else?

'I think that's enough!'

* * *

Chapter 14: Berlin, January 1941

'Oh, just one other matter, Herr Hermann.'

These days, Franz Hermann's secretary always seemed to have 'one other matter' that needed to be dealt with. Before the war, there had been enough work for the nine senior lawyers in the firm at 181 Friedrichstrasse to be kept busy and well-paid, but not so much that they were overstretched. That had all changed now: one of the senior lawyers had retired and not been replaced and two others had joined the armed forces, along with half of the junior lawyers. As if that was not bad enough, Alois Jäger now seemed to spend more than half of the time he was meant to be at work on Nazi Party business, which meant the remaining five seniors had to pick up more and more of Jäger's work. It was not as if they could complain; they just had to go along with it. As far as Hermann was concerned, as distasteful as it felt, at least it afforded the firm a degree of political protection.

'Do you remember Generalmajor Werner Ernst, Herr Hermann?'

He had heard nothing from the General since their meeting in August. He had hoped never to hear from him again. He did his best to look as if he was having a lot of trouble remembering who the General was.

'You'll have to remind me, Ilse. Was it something to do with a dispute with his bank?'

'No sir. That was another army officer. You were sorting out the affairs of Generalmajor Ernst's late mother. It was all tied up in August.'

'Yes, of course. I remember now. Doesn't he live near the Kleiner Tiergarten?'

'That's correct sir. He rang today while you were in a meeting. He says one or two issues have arisen regarding his mother's estate that he'd like to see you about.'

'You have my diary Ilse, please arrange the meeting.'

'He said it was urgent Herr Hermann.'

He knew Ilse would expect him to protest: matters arising from the estate of the General's mother all these months on could hardly be construed as urgent. But he also knew that if the General said he needed to see him urgently then it was urgent. He could feel himself getting hot again and became aware he was drumming his fingers loudly on the desk.

'Very well then Ilse. He can either come in here during the day tomorrow or I can go to his apartment after work.'

'He said you're to go to his apartment tonight sir.'

* * *

Franz Hermann waited impatiently for Ilse to leave work, spending the half hour before she did so optimistically trying to think of a possible genuine problem with the Generalmajor's mother's estate, which he knew was highly unlikely. Had there really been a problem it would have emerged some time ago. He feared that the Generalmajor was about to entrust him with another secret.

He allowed five minutes to pass after Ilse's departure then left, managing to find a rare taxi on the Unter den Linden to take him as far as Storm Strasse, from where he walked the short distance to Generalmajor Ernst's apartment block. The same teenage maid let him into the apartment, which was now in a state of chaos.

There were packing cases piled up in the hall, suitcases assembled by the door and furniture and paintings covered in dustsheets. A large lady who he took to be Frau Ernst briefly came out to check who the visitor was but went straight back into the kitchen, where Hermann could see at least one other maid busy scrubbing the sides. Generalmajor Werner Ernst came to meet him in the hall.

'Hermann: thank you for coming so soon. I have to go away very soon and need to sort out some annoying paperwork before doing so. Anke, please ensure we're not disturbed. Follow me Hermann.'

The study was in a similar state of upheaval to the rest of the apartment, but there were two uncovered armchairs towards the window, which Ernst led his lawyer over to.

'I'm sorry to hear there are problems with the estate sir. I'd assumed everything was concluded in a satisfactory manner back in August.'

The Generalmajor had been rooting around in a nearby packing case, from which he produced a bottle of Armagnac and two glasses. He poured a large measure for Hermann and a considerably larger one for himself. As he sat down, he shifted his heavy armchair close to Hermann's, so the two armrests were touching. When he spoke, it was in a quiet voice.

'Of course everything was satisfactory Hermann. You did an excellent job. However, I'm afraid for the sake of appearance, I've had to make a bit of a fuss: I told Frau Ernst you've been less than efficient and I wrote as much in a letter to my son. He has now been transferred to Norway and I assume the censors will be reading his post.'

The Generalmajor stood up and stretched himself then walked over to the curtains, pulling them together. Hermann noticed the Generalmajor looked more drawn than before, his tiny eyes slightly bloodshot. He appeared to have lost some weight and his face was more lined. He twisted a half-finished cigarette into an ashtray and took a cigar from a box on top of a packing case; he didn't bother to offer one to the lawyer.

'Things aren't good Hermann. The atmosphere in the Bendlerblock is terrible. The atmosphere in the whole of Berlin is terrible. Everyone suspects everyone else of conspiring against them: it's hard to know who to trust. The professional soldiers in the High Command and the leadership of the Abwehr are the most distrusted, I fear. Even if you join the Nazi Party it doesn't seem to make any difference these days. I felt obliged to join in November but I still think people are suspicious of me. The reason for all this upheaval in the apartment is that I'm being transferred to Warsaw. In my view, it's quite unnecessary; I can do my job just as well, if not better, from Berlin. But I think Hitler, Himmler and the rest of them want to dilute any possible sources of opposition to them. Maybe opposition is too strong a word; perhaps what I mean is disagreement.'

'Do you think they suspect you of having passed on information?'

The Generalmajor shook his head slowly, at the same time as lighting his cigar. He paused a while as he inhaled deeply.

'No, no, no! Look Hermann, if they did, I wouldn't be here –

and nor, I suspect, would you. I was very careful and I assume you have been too. The thing is, ever since the meeting at Bad Reichenhall at the end of July, a number of the senior officers like myself who were asked to think about the possibility of invasion have been advising caution. Not everyone, by any means. Too many people feel they have to say what the Fuhrer wants to hear, so they enthusiastically go along with it. A number of others, it should be said, actually agree with invading the Soviet Union. But for people like myself, well we've done nothing that could be construed as treason. In my case, I've been able to produce detailed papers about the difficulties in keeping our forces properly supplied. Tell me Hermann: do you know how far it is from our border in Poland to Moscow?'

The lawyer shook his head. *No idea.*

'Over 1,000 kilometres. To put that in perspective, from our western border, say near Saarbrücken, to Paris is around 340 kilometres: so an invasion of the Soviet Union would be three times that distance. And, let me tell you, the roads in France are considerably better. As well as the terrain, you also have to take into account other factors like the weather and you can see how risky an invasion becomes. That's what I've been saying in my reports: I am very careful to stick to the facts. But it's not done me any favours. They are keeping an eye on people like me. They don't completely trust me, hence my move to Warsaw.'

'So why are you packing up the apartment?'

'My wife doesn't want to remain here on her own. She and her sister in Potsdam are talking about moving to their family's old hunting lodge near Magdeburg. She says she'll feel safer there.

Look, Hermann, there's something else I need to tell you, one other piece of information for you to pass on through your contacts. This'll have to be the last information I give. It's too dangerous for us to meet again and, in any case, in a few days I'll be in Warsaw.' The lawyer nodded and leaned closer towards Ernst.

'I happen to know that a week before Christmas Hitler issued a detailed directive about the invasion of the Soviet Union. The Fuhrer is very sparing in the number of directives he issues, no more than one or two a month. And this one is so secret that I was only able to glance at it in the presence of others, certainly not allowed to take a copy away – which is perhaps another reason why I know I'm no longer trusted. I'm only vaguely aware of what's in this directive, though I do know it talks about the invasion taking place in the middle of May. You must pass this on: will you do that?'

'Yes, but they'll want to know more detail, surely?'

'I'm sure they will, they may even want to see a copy of the directive no doubt, but it is very, very restricted. From what I gather, there were only nine copies. If you only get across that the invasion is still on and scheduled for the middle of May, that's important. You'd better leave now, Hermann. I'm glad we've finally been able to sort out my mother's estate!'

As they left the study he placed his hand on the lawyer's shoulder.

'I doubt we'll meet again, Hermann. Maybe one day, if circumstances are very different. But who knows, eh? Good luck.'

As Franz Hermann headed home that evening he could not recall ever having felt more miserable, or so afraid.

* * *

'And that's the message? No more?'

Dona Maria do Rosario and Franz Hermann were walking around the enormous tree in the park between Wilhemstrasse and Hermann Goring Strasse, aware this was more exposed than sitting on the benches around the tree, but it had been raining and the benches were sodden: sitting on them would have looked suspicious.

'I know it's not long but it is very important. Remember, Hitler issued the directive a week before Christmas: they're still planning to invade the Soviet Union and they're talking about the middle of May. That's four months away.'

'Yes, I'd have hoped even the British would be able to work that one out, thank you.'

* * *

Franz Hermann had met Dona Maria do Rosario on Friday 17th of January. The following Tuesday, Ilse came into his office just before lunch. There had been a phone call.

'The man said he understood you specialised in sorting out estates, especially complicated ones. His uncle recently died in Bremen and he wanted to know if we had an office there. I said "no", and he said not to worry and that maybe he'd call back.'

'Bremen you say?'

'Yes Herr Hermann. I'm not sure why he'd think we had an

office in Bremen, but there you are. Now, these letters…'

This was only the second time that Father Josef had called him like this. Telephoning him at the office meant something was up. The Bremen reference meant it was extremely urgent. He was to attend confession that night.

* * *

'In the name of the Father and of the Son and of the Holy Spirit. My last confession was one week ago.'

Father Josef pressed his face against the grille separating the two men. 'We need to be quick. I have a message from her: she passed on your message and has been contacted urgently. Apparently you talked about a document. Don't tell me anything about it, but they're saying they need to see it. That's the message. Do you understand?'

'I understand Father, but I haven't got it. I'll see what I can do, but they need to understand my source has left Berlin. This is going to be very difficult.'

'I'm only passing on the message. She said you needed to know before you could meet at the usual rendezvous, in case you can get hold of it. Do your best, my son: I'm sure God will guide you. Do you want to take confession?'

Hermann shook his head.

'No thank you Father: I wouldn't know where to begin.'

* * *

In the 12 months since he had been reunited with his first wife and son, Gunter Reinhart had done his best to visit them at least once a week at the house in Dahlem. In one respect the arrangement had held up very well. Franz Hermann's mother could not have been better looked after and the talk of her having to move into a nursing home or even a hospital was long forgotten. Frau Hermann had no idea her excellent nurse was actually a doctor and certainly had no idea she was Jewish and had two children with her. Her hearing was so poor she never heard the footsteps on the floor above her or the subdued sound of the children's voices.

But in every other respect, their predicament was an increasingly hopeless one. The situation for Jews in Berlin worsened by the day: although it was still possible for some to emigrate, that was for those who had all the right paperwork and could afford the punitive taxes being charged. Even then, they needed to find somewhere that would take them. Most of Europe was occupied. There were rumours about Sweden, even Spain. The place most people aspired to go to was Switzerland, but those borders were sealed tight, on both sides.

Gunter, Rosa and Franz had come up with countless schemes to get the three of them out of the country, but all had too many risks and too many flaws. Gunter usually visited after work on a Wednesday. That was the day his wife took their children to their piano lessons in Reinickendorf and afterwards they stopped for tea at a favourite cafe on Holtzdamm. They rarely arrived home before 7.30, so Gunter found if he left work at five he could go down to Dahlem, spend an hour and a half there and be home in plenty of time.

He did his best to take some food and money with him, and Franz's wife Silke always tried to be there at the same time so she could sit with Frau Hermann while Rosa went upstairs to be with Gunter and the children. On the last Wednesday of January Gunter arrived at the house to find Franz Hermann sitting in the room upstairs that Rosa used as a lounge. Rosa followed him into the room.

'Where are the children? Is Alfred alright?' asked Gunter.

'They're fine. You'll see Alfred in a minute. I need to talk with you first.' Hermann was leaning forward on the low sofa, opposite Gunter and Rosa. His head was bowed low. As he talked, he continued to look down at the patterned carpet.

'I'm afraid I have some bad news Rosa.'

There was an audible intake of breath from her and she gripped Gunter's knee.

'Harald?'

'I'm afraid so.'

Rosa Stern lifted her head high and turned to the window, her head resting for a while against the thick curtains. When she turned round again her eyes had filled with tears. Gunter put his arm round her and pulled her close. She let her head fall on his shoulder.

'Tell me everything, Franz.'

'I'll tell you what I know, Rosa. As you're aware, we could hardly make a direct approach to Sachsenhausen: please can you tell us how Harald Stern is getting on? I had begun to hear that when people died at Sachsenhausen or any of the other camps they've taken Berliners to, the police turn up at the home of the next of kin. They bring their ashes with them – along with a bill for the cost of the urn.'

'Do we really need all this detail Franz?'

'No Gunter, don't be concerned on my part. I need to hear this.'

'Of course, you are Harald's next of kin, but fortunately the authorities don't know where you are. You remember a few months ago I managed to track down an address for his elder brother, Paul – in Spandau? I visited him and told him that, as far as I knew, you were in Paris. If he's questioned by the Gestapo, he can't tell them what he doesn't know. He'd heard nothing from Harald either but he did say he'd contact me if he did. I didn't give him any of my details; again, it's too risky. But I said I'd try and visit him every few weeks and, if he had any news, he'd be able to give it to me then. I visited him yesterday and he told me...'

Hermann paused to remove a handkerchief from his pocket and he blew his nose noisily. His voice was trembling when he next spoke. 'They brought the urn round last week. They say he died of a heart condition – natural causes. Apparently that's what they say with everyone. I'm so sorry Rosa.'

The ensuing silence lasted a lifetime and, as happens in such circumstances, even the quietest, least obtrusive sound reverberated around the room. Rosa cried solidly for the next ten minutes, then she stood up and walked around the room, deep in thought. When she spoke, her voice sounded resolute. 'I've made a decision Gunter. Do what you can to get Alfred out. It'll be easier if it's just him, no?'

Both men nodded: this is what they had been saying for months.

'We're all doomed. Alfred will be the easiest to smuggle out. Can you do it?'

Hermann nodded his head up and down and from side to side, weighing up the possibilities of success. *Maybe; there's a chance.* 'We can try Rosa, I promise you,' said Gunter. 'And then we'll get you and Sophia out too.'

It was seven o'clock before Gunter Reinhart left the house on the corner of Kaiser Wilhelm Strasse and Arno-Holz Strasse. Hermann said he would walk with him to the station while Silke looked after his mother, allowing Rosa to stay with the distraught children.

They walked in silence until they were on Königin-Luise-Strasse, each man wrapped in his own thoughts and overwhelmed by the enormity of the situation closing in on them.

'We must get Alfred out before it's too late,' said Gunter. 'But it's going to be so difficult, Franz, so dangerous. The boy has no papers. If there was any way I could get him to Switzerland then I've a good friend in Zürich who would take care of him, but how can I get him there?'

Franz Hermann said nothing for a while, but Gunter noticed he was shaking his head then nodding it, as if he was debating with himself. *Pros and cons.* Podbielski Allee station was in view by the time Hermann spoke, though only after he had carefully looked around to ensure no-one was within earshot: that was how people spoke in Berlin these days. 'This is about your son's life, Gunter, so I can absolutely trust you, yes?'

'That goes without saying.'

'Let me ask you a question first: how senior are you at the

Reichsbank?'

'Senior enough: I run a department.'

'And how close are you to Walther Funk?'

'We aren't friends as such, but I'm good at my job and he relies on me for certain matters: I handle our transactions with the Swiss. That's very important to him.'

'And the economies of countries we've occupied, do you get involved in them?'

'To an extent, certainly, if we need to move money and gold from those countries to Switzerland. Why are you asking?'

'I want to know how trusted you are at the Reichsbank. After all, you were married to a Jew.'

'That was many years ago, Franz. And, remember, I divorced her. It's no doubt on a file somewhere, but it's not an issue. I even made sure I joined the Nazi Party. In answer to your question, I'm trusted.'

'I have some… contacts, Gunter: people who may be able to help get Alfred out of Germany. But they'd want something in return, something you may be able to get your hands on.'

The two men had now moved to the side of the pavement, standing next to the railings and beneath a tree whose branches descended to just above their heads. Hermann paused and took a deep breath, about to take the plunge.

'Go on Hermann, what is it?'

'I'm going to ask you about something: if you've not heard of it, please forget I ever asked the question. Do you understand?'

He nodded. The two men waited while an elderly couple and their dog strolled past, nodding in reply to their greeting.

'Have you ever come across a document called Directive 21?'

Reinhart stared at Hermann long and hard, his eyes terrified. He looked more shocked than when he had met the lawyer in the bar and been told Rosa and the children were back in Berlin.

'Are you being serious?'

'Yes. Are you aware of it?'

'I am. But how on earth have you heard about it?'

'For heaven's sake, Gunter, keep your voice down. You don't need to know that. Have you actually seen it?'

'I have. Do you know how top-secret this is?'

'Tell me how you've had access to it?'

'There is one copy in the Reichsbank. It's kept in a safe in Funk's office, but I've been able to see it because he's concerned that if this… hang on, Hermann: you tell me what this Directive is about – you tell me that before I say anything else.'

'It's about plans to invade the Soviet Union.'

'Very well then: Funk and no doubt many of the others are nothing if not greedy. They're concerned that if – when – this invasion takes place we should have plans in place to get our hands on what assets we can and get them into our Swiss bank accounts. That's why I have access.'

'Presumably you can't take it out of Funk's office?'

'Yes and no: if I need to see it, I have to put a request in writing to his private secretary and if he approves it then I'm allowed to see it in a secure room next to Funk's office.'

'Are you alone in that room?'

'Funk's private secretary is meant to stay with me, but he's an impatient sort: he'll usually stay for five minutes and if it looks as though I'm going to be any longer, he'll go and sit at his desk, which is just outside the door.'

Very slowly the two men walked towards Podbielski Allee station, talking as they went. It was gone eight o'clock before Gunter Reinhart returned to his house in Charlottenburg and the inevitable wrath of his wife. He was, however, oblivious to it.

He had to make a plan.

* * *

Chapter 15: London and Lisbon, February 1941

On a blustery Tuesday afternoon at the beginning of February, Captain Edgar was summoned to Christopher Porter's office on the top floor of a building best described as functional. Edgar stood at the narrow window overlooking St James' Square, his back turned to his superior who appeared to be even more ill at ease in Edgar's presence than normal.

'I do wish you'd sit down Edgar.'

Edgar turned round, leaning against the window ledge.

'You said this was urgent, sir.' There was a pause before the 'sir'.

Porter cleared his throat and nervously straightened the fountain-pen holder on his desk. 'I have to tell you Edgar that I'm getting all kinds of flak from Downing Street. It's most trying.'

'I'm sorry to hear that sir: is this in connection with anything in particular?'

'In connection with our intelligence that Germany may be planning an invasion of the Soviet Union. You insisted on it being a complete secret, but now Downing Street has caught wind of it and they're not happy, to say the very least. Their view – and I'm informed it's very much the view of the Prime Minister – is that we should have shared our intelligence such plans existed more widely from the outset.'

'But we're not obliged to share every shred of unconfirmed intelligence, surely?'

'Indeed Edgar – but this is more than a "shred of unconfirmed intelligence", isn't it? We knew about the meeting in Bad Reichenhall last July and we know about this directive Hitler issued in December, don't we? The Prime Minister is of the view that this is the single most important area of intelligence at the moment and we must do everything we can to get our hands on it. It's been made very clear to me that our failure to share this intelligence is viewed most seriously: the one way in which we can redeem ourselves is by getting our hands on this wretched document. If...'

'... Get our hands on it! Are you joking? If that's seriously the view of Downing Street then one has to be most concerned at their grasp on reality. We've been told there are no more than nine copies of this Directive 21. The idea we can obtain one of them is ridiculous. How do your chums in Downing Street propose we go about this?'

Porter was now busying himself moving a large blotting pad around on his desk.

'You'll need to go out there, Edgar.'

'To Germany?'

'Not if we can avoid it. I was wondering about that chap Hunter?'

'Henry Hunter?' Edgar began to pace the room, turning once again to stare out of the window, deep in thought. 'That's not a bad idea sir, I'll grant you that. His trial run in Germany last year went well. He's still in Switzerland: he's got perfect cover to go into Germany.'

'The best bet would be for you to get to Switzerland through Portugal and Spain: can't see another way at the moment. Once you're safely there we can take a view.'

Edgar stared at Porter in disbelief as it dawned on him he was being serious.

'Any other country you'd like me to drop into while I'm over there? Italy perhaps? Poland? And how do you propose I get out there?'

Porter smiled as he unlocked a drawer in his desk and removed a small pile of envelopes.

'That, Edgar, is where I think I can surprise even you!'

'You are being serious then?'

'Indeed I am Edgar: not only serious but also resourceful. You may or may not be aware there is a scheduled daily air service from Bristol to Lisbon. You won't know how hard this has been, but I've managed to secure you a seat on the flight this Thursday.'

'This Thursday?' Edgar looked surprised. 'And when I get to Lisbon?'

'Well, Lisbon station is very much Sandy Morgan's show. He'll arrange for you to meet up with Telmo and the three of you can see where we are with regards to our lady in Berlin. After that Morgan will get you into Spain and over to Barcelona: there are scheduled Swissair flights from there into Switzerland. From Barcelona you're going to have to go into Switzerland with your American cover: no alternative, I'm afraid: the Swiss are terribly jumpy about us at the moment.'

* * *

Captain Edgar was acutely aware he appeared to have been cast as a character from one of those Agatha Christie crime novels of which his wife was so fond.

229

It was midday and he and the other characters were assembled in a draughty room at Whitchurch Airport, just outside Bristol. There were 15 passengers including a priest, two elderly women wrapped in furs, a woman accompanied by a young boy and two men speaking Portuguese. Edgar was half expecting to be joined by a Belgian detective with a waxed moustache.

It had been an hour since Edgar had checked in for the flight. For the purposes of the trip, he was travelling under a British diplomatic passport in the name of the Hon Anthony Davis. The 'Hon', Edgar assumed, was an example of Porter's public-school humour. The Hon Anthony Davis had various letters with him to the effect he would be spending an unspecified period of time at the British Embassy in Lisbon dealing with 'consular services'.

A few minutes after midday the passengers were led out of the room and across the apron to the DC-3 that would be flying them to Lisbon. Within minutes they were airborne, heading west along the Bristol Channel and out towards sea. When the southern tip of Ireland peeked out of the low cloud the plane changed course, at which point the captain spoke to the passengers:

'Welcome aboard this BOAC flight from Bristol to Lisbon, where we expect to arrive just after four pm local time. Due to wartime flying regulations we will be flying at a maximum altitude of three thousand feet.'

Edgar closed his eyes and tried to rest as the captain continued to speak. He recalled being told the pilots on these flights were all Dutch: they had managed to fly most of the KLM fleet to Britain just before the German invasion of the Netherlands, and they and their planes now serviced the few remaining BOAC flights.

To his surprise, Edgar must have fallen asleep straight away because he was woken by a stern-looking stewardess shaking him by the elbow. They were beginning their descent into Portela Airport.

The plane was flying low, hugging the Portuguese coast, the sky cloudless and the remains of the sun lighting up the land to their left. Edgar glanced to his right: across the aisle the priest was fervently praying, the rosary gripped tightly in his hands. The plane banked sharply over the city, buildings rushing by underneath them. Within a minute, Portela Airport appeared below them. The pilot made one pass of the airport, turned 180 degrees then began the final approach.

* * *

At the British Embassy just off the Rua de São Domingos, Sandy Morgan greeted Edgar like the old friend that he was. He hurried out from behind his desk in a crumpled white suit and after grasping him by the hand and warmly shaking it, removed a large bottle of Bells from a cabinet by the window. Two glasses were on his desk, one of which he pushed towards Edgar.

'Now then old chap, bet you can do with one of these?'

Edgar smiled.

'Good flight, I hope? Beats me how we can get away with it: can't understand how they just don't take a shot at our planes. Mind you, I suppose we'd do the same to theirs, eh? Handy though, can't tell you how much useful stuff we pick up at the airport. We have people watching it the whole time. Germans do as well, so I suppose we cancel each other out. Even pick up their newspapers, which London is rather keen on. Anyway, cheers!'

Morgan downed his whisky, which had clearly not been his first of the afternoon, in one go and quickly refilled his glass from a new bottle he produced from behind his desk. Edgar held his hand over his glass and shook his head.

'Now then, quick run through the plan. Idea is you stay at my place, which is in an annexe of the embassy, so no need for you to be seen out and about. We'll sort you accreditation with the Ministry of Foreign Affairs tomorrow. Correct me if I'm wrong, but the story is you're here to check our consular system?'

'Something like that.'

'Funnily enough, they could do with sorting out but I can't imagine you're interested in that. That gives you the cover you need: the PVDE keep a careful eye on us, but it's not too difficult to fool them. Idea is that after a couple of days you'll come down with something nasty which'll keep you in bed for a couple of weeks. The doctor we use is a rather helpful chap; he'll back up any story. That'll give us enough time to get you to Barcelona and Switzerland then back again, and home without the PVDE spotting it. Sound reasonable?'

Edgar nodded, slightly unsure. Sandy Morgan, despite his manner, was a good operator. He was one of the few station chiefs whom he trusted.

'We'll meet with Telmo on either Saturday or Sunday: it's quieter then, easier all round. I'll only know for sure late tomorrow. Assuming that goes well, you'll head off to Spain on Monday. Madrid station will look after you and get you over to Barcelona and a flight from there to Switzerland. You'll be using an American cover, I understand?'

* * *

Sunday was warm; it almost felt spring-like. Edgar and Morgan sat on the balcony of Morgan's small apartment in the Embassy annexe, sipping fresh coffee. Edgar had been aware Morgan had left the apartment very early in the morning, before six as far as he could tell.

'I wouldn't say that Telmo has got cold feet but he's nervous, Edgar. Things aren't quite right in this city. Portugal is meant to be our oldest ally, but Salazar trusts no-one: not us, not the Germans and certainly not Spain. He seems to have got it into his mind that Spain has plans to invade this place. Upshot is that everyone is very twitchy. The PVDE are watching everyone and Telmo is worried they're watching him. He tried to cry off on Friday night and then again last night, which is why I had to sneak out this morning. He's agreed to meet you Edgar, but be gentle with him. He's one of us, after all.'

'When and where?'

'This afternoon: hope you like football.'

Morgan and Edgar left the Embassy later that morning, half an hour apart, and met as arranged at a bar on the Rossio an hour later. They then travelled by tram, taxi, foot and tram again. By the time they had finished their second tram journey they were part of a crowd heading in one direction. They were, Morgan announced, in Lumiar.

'We're in the north of the city, not far from the airport.'

Twenty minutes later Edgar was inside a football ground for the first time in his life.

'Quick briefing Edgar: you're now in the Campo do Lumiar which is the home of Sporting Clube de Portugal, who are always called Sporting. They're one of the top clubs in the country; some would say *the* top club, though I daresay Benfica and Porto might disagree. Their opponents this afternoon are Barreirense, so it's something of a local derby.'

They were walking down the stand now, Morgan looking carefully along the rows.

'Just so you don't appear too ignorant, Sporting play in green, Barreirense in red.'

'And who do we want to win, Sandy?'

'Doesn't matter, does it? Personally I have a soft spot for Benfica, so I don't mind. Barreirense are quite a good side this year so it could be a close game. Perhaps best if you don't shout too much anyway. Clap in the right places. Ah… good, there's Telmo; so he turned up after all. Now remember to be nice to him – make him feel wanted. We don't want him turning cold on us, do we?'

At the very end of a row Telmo Rocha Martins was standing up, waving casually at them. *Here I am.* He was short – about five foot five, bald, with a neat moustache and round, black glasses. A large crowd had already formed in the Campo do Lumiar and Telmo, wrapped in a large, slightly shabby jacket, was just one of them.

It was the first time Edgar had actually met Telmo Rocha Martins, one of the most important British agents in Portugal. Telmo was a middle-ranking civil servant in the Portuguese

Ministry of Foreign Affairs – not regarded highly enough nor ranked so senior as to be considered a diplomat, but the kind of civil servant who ensures everything runs smoothly while other people grab the glory. This had been a source of increasing resentment to Telmo, one that had led him to approach the British when the war started with an offer to pass on the kind of information for which money changed hands.

Now, his status and his low profile suited him perfectly. No-one suspected this diminutive, bespectacled man for a moment. The quality of intelligence he passed on to the British improved all the time. He had been given a miniature camera and at first it was copies of Ministry briefing papers and some telegrams from overseas embassies that were passed on. Then, in early 1940, Telmo asked Morgan at one of their regular meetings whether he would be interested, by any chance, in more material from Berlin?

Rather had been Morgan's response, careful to show he was not too desperate. London had been crying out for *anything* from Berlin, such was their paucity of sources in the city. *And we mean anything: even bloody bus tickets!*

What Telmo came up with was much better than 'bloody bus tickets'. There were briefings from the German foreign ministry, minutes of meetings with German officials, assessments of the strengths and weaknesses of the armed forces, telegrams: half the contents of the diplomatic bag, as far as Morgan could work out. And from what London was telling him, it was all first-class stuff. *Well done. Plenty more of that will do nicely thank you!*

But Morgan was a cautious chap. He was well aware this intelligence coming out of Berlin could turn out to be too good to be true and, if that were the case, he did not fancy getting the blame for it. So one Saturday afternoon he took Telmo out for a drive to Cascais and they went for a long walk along the seafront.

London want to know how come you're getting such good material out of Berlin?

They had walked for quite a while with Telmo saying nothing, evidently weighing up whether or not to come clean.

'I've been considering raising this with you. If there's ever a problem, will you promise you'll ensure you can get me to England, maybe on one of your convoys?'

'I'd do my very best Telmo: what kind of problem were you thinking of, though?'

'If they ever suspected me, that kind of thing. I'd like to go to England. I'd like to have a house in London. Maybe near to Buckingham Palace.'

'I'd certainly see what we can do. Not sure how near to the Palace, but there are some other lovely parts of London.'

'And if my source in Berlin was to accompany me, would that be a problem?'

'No! Not at all. I'd need to know who this person is, of course…'

'Even if we weren't married?'

Which was how Telmo Rocha Martins came to tell Sandy Morgan all about Dona Maria do Rosario. He told him how Dona Maria had been a secretary to his head of department in the Ministry of Foreign Affairs; how they had become close and eventually became lovers; how it would be impossible for him to leave his wife and remain in his job and stay in Portugal. He told Morgan about how Dona Maria had become proficient in German and had been transferred to the Legation in Berlin, but not before he had confided in her and she had agreed to supply information. In her case, the motivation was personal and political. Her fiancée had been imprisoned during the 1926 coup and had died soon after. Following this she had left Porto and moved to Lisbon, working her way through the various Government ministries around the Praça do Comercio.

Telmo had chosen a good spot. They were at the end of the front row of their block, so there was no-one sitting in front of them or to the right. Morgan sat between Telmo and Edgar, acting as interpreter.

'We're very grateful to you Telmo,' said Edgar quietly, pausing while Morgan translated. 'Very, very grateful. I want you to know how much we appreciate your help. I can assure you if there's ever a… problem here in Portugal, we'll do our very best to get you to London.'

Telmo smiled and nodded his head, not taking his eyes off the pitch. 'I'm very grateful. But can you promise me this assurance will also apply to Dona Maria?'

'Of course.'

They paused as the crowd rose around them: a Sporting player was fouled on the edge of the penalty area. They continued to stand while the free kick was taken then sat down after it soared over the bar.

'I need to ask you about Dona Maria. She's sending a lot of material. How is she able to do this? Is she not suspected at all?'

'I assure you she is careful. Because of my job, I'm in a position to see the diplomatic bag soon after it arrives at the Ministry, before anyone else other than a clerk has seen it. I'm then able to take the material, which is all in code. It's not possible for other people to spot it. No-one suspects us. But I have something important to tell you.'

There was another delay as a Barreirense winger beat a succession of Sporting defenders then shot wide. 'Our defence is too slow today, far too slow,' Telmo said thoughtfully. 'Listen carefully, please: Dona Maria passed on your message to Hugo, about getting hold of this document. A message came through on Friday. Hugo wants you to know he may be able to get hold of the document: it seems he has a source who has access to it. But there's a price to pay.'

'How much?'

Sporting scored and the crowd leapt up. Everyone around them were patting their companions on the back, as if they'd played a part in the goal. Telmo looked delighted.

'Fortunately our attack is much better than our defence,' he said. 'It's not money. It's a lot more complicated. You'd better listen carefully.'

Edgar did listen carefully. It was complicated. He would need to get to Switzerland as soon as possible.

He was only shaken out of his thoughts by Sporting's second goal.

The game finished 2-0. If only everything in life was so clear cut Edgar thought as they left the ground and Telmo melted into the crowd.

* * *

Chapter 16: London, February 1941

By noon on Wednesday 12th February, Christopher Porter had been kept waiting in a narrow corridor in a draughty and heavily guarded basement under the Admiralty building in Whitehall for well over an hour past the time of his appointment. When he was finally called in to the office outside which he'd been waiting, there was neither apology nor explanation, just a mildly exasperated look from Sir Roland Pearson.

'How can I help you, Porter?' Sir Roland had once been a colleague, but now worked in Downing Street and currently had the ear of the Prime Minister on all matters to do with intelligence. He gave the impression he was now far too important for his time to be wasted.

'As you know, Sir Roland, we met on the 3rd when you made clear the Prime Minister's feelings regarding our intelligence from Berlin and the directive regarding a possible invasion of the Soviet Union. I subsequently dispatched Edgar to Lisbon, where he met our source Telmo on Sunday.'

'Telmo: remind me?'

'Telmo Rocha Martins: he works in the Portuguese Ministry of Foreign Affairs in Lisbon and has proven to be an extremely useful source of information for us. His main informant is Dona Maria do Rosario, who is secretary to the Military Attaché in the Portuguese Legation in Berlin. As well as passing on information through Telmo, she also serves as a contact for Hugo – Franz Hermann, the Berlin lawyer who is working for us. Any information he has, or messages we have for him, comes through Dona Maria

Alex Gerlis

in the Portuguese diplomatic bag.'

Porter had now opened a notebook and put on a pair of reading glasses.

'When Edgar met Telmo on Sunday he passed on the latest from Hugo. We were aware Hugo has been sheltering a Jewish family, which we thought an unnecessary risk and therefore did not wholly approve of. However, it transpires this family may be critical in terms of our obtaining a copy of the directive. The family Hugo is sheltering is comprised of Rosa Stern and her two children: an 11-year-old boy called Alfred and a five-year-old girl called Sophia. Rosa's husband is a businessman called Harald Stern, who was arrested by the Nazis sometime in late 1939 and subsequently died – or was killed – in one of their prison camps. Stern was the father of Sophia but not of Alfred. Alfred's father is one Gunter Reinhart, Rosa's first husband. Reinhart is not Jewish: he and Rosa divorced in 1935 after Hitler's law that prohibits marriages between Jews and non-Jews.'

'I hope this family saga is leading somewhere important, Porter.'

'It is, sir. From what we understand, Reinhart and Rosa Stern remained on good terms and he did what he could to help them. Rosa and the children had moved to Paris, but returned to Berlin when Harald was arrested – it seems he may have remained there to try to sort out some business matters. Now they're being hidden in the home of a relative of Hugo's. However, Reinhart works for the Reichsbank, where he occupies a fairly senior position. Part of his job is helping to move money out of countries occupied by the Germans. In this respect, it appears he has access to a copy of this

240

Directive 21.'

'Good heavens.'

'Good heavens indeed. You see why I needed to give you the background.'

'And this Reinhart – he can supply us with Directive 21?'

'Yes, but…'

'… He wants money, I imagine: how much?'

'I only wish it were that simple. His condition is that we smuggle his son Alfred out of Berlin. Reinhart has a friend in Zürich: once Alfred has been safely delivered to that friend, he'll release a copy of Directive 21 to Hugo.'

Sir Roland had leaned back in his chair and was staring at the ceiling, as if the solution may be hidden in the cobwebs he had spotted above the coving.

'So how do we get Alfred to Zürich?'

'Even as we speak Sir Roland, Edgar is on his way to Switzerland. We have an agent there called Henry Hunter. Hunter also has a genuine Swiss identity and is able to travel into Germany with it. A year ago we sent him there on a test mission of sorts, which went well. I've said to Edgar that he and Basil Remington-Barber must come up with a plan to get Hunter to Berlin and out again with Alfred.'

'Which won't be straightforward.'

'Indeed, Sir Roland. But we have to get Alfred out – the prize is too great not to attempt it.'

Sir Roland stood up, walked away from the table and over to his desk, from which he picked up a silver box and lit a cigarette he selected from it. He offered the box to Porter, who refused, then removed his jacket and hung it over the back of his chair. On the wall behind him was a map of Europe and for a while he studied it, reacquainting himself with the various locations. With his forefinger he traced an angled line south from Berlin to Zürich.

'And once this Alfred is safely delivered to this friend in Zürich, we get the report?'

'Once the friend has confirmed it.'

'And I presume Hugo then hands the report over to Dona Maria whatshername and she pops it into the diplomatic bag, and we pick up the report in Lisbon?'

Porter closed his notebook and folded up his reading glasses. Twice he started to speak, but hesitated. He was clenching then unclenching his fists and clearly finding difficulty in knowing where to start.

'Can I be most frank and most honest with you, Sir Roland?'

'I'd rather hoped that'd been the case up to now anyway, Porter.'

Porter's hands were now clasped as if in prayer. He inhaled deeply before speaking.

'The most obvious route to bring the directive out of Berlin would indeed be through the Portuguese diplomatic bag, I quite agree. But if there's an overriding purpose to us obtaining this document, it's to help prove to the Russians their supposed allies are not what they seem and in fact have plans to invade them. Correct?'

Sir Roland nodded.

'Up to now, the Russians have chosen to ignore all these warnings, especially the ones that can be attributed to us. Frankly, they don't believe what we tell them. They're convinced our motives are to stir up trouble between them and the Germans. They choose to believe whatever intelligence we're passing to them is false. Our concern is that if we – the British – show them the directive or tell them about its contents, they'll similarly ignore them, as they have all the other warnings. All the considerable effort of obtaining the directive will have been wasted.'

'What do you suggest then Porter?'

'This is where I have to be very frank. Henry Hunter, our agent in Switzerland, is not quite what he seems. I think I'll have that cigarette after all, Sir Roland.'

Sir Roland rejoined Porter at the table and slid the silver cigarette box across it, followed by a box of matches. He noticed Porter shook slightly as he lit his cigarette.

'We had our eyes on Hunter for some time. He's ideal in many ways: very good Swiss identity, speaks all the relevant languages. Even the Swiss believe he is Swiss, if you get what I mean. We picked him up here just before the start of the war: he was trying to smuggle out some money he'd inherited and we gave him the choice of working for us or spending a few years breaking rocks or whatever we make people do in prisons these days. He chose to work for us.'

'Good.'

'However, what he didn't know – and still doesn't – is we know something else about him, which is that he'd already been recruited as an agent: by the Russians.'

Sir Roland had been moving his cigarette towards his mouth. Now he stopped, holding it is mid-air. He leaned towards Porter.

'Really? When did this happen?'

'We think it was around 1930 or 1931, Sir Roland – a couple of years after he moved to Geneva from Zürich with his mother and step-father. Basil Remington-Barber had an informant in the Geneva branch of the Communist Party of Switzerland. He thought we'd be interested because Hunter had dual British and Swiss nationalities. He'd seen Hunter at one or two meetings, then he disappeared from view. Normally, we wouldn't have attached a good deal of importance to that: plenty of young chaps go to these type of meetings then lose interest. But Remington-Barber's informant thought he'd seen Hunter chatting to a French chap rumoured to have links with the Comintern; and we know it's a well-established recruitment tactic of the Soviet intelligence agencies for them to keep an eye open for likely recruits who've joined or try to join their local communist parties. What happens is they spot someone then persuade them the best way to serve the cause is not to be a party member but to work for them. They leave the party, all records are destroyed and they display no outward affiliation with or interest in communism – often the opposite, in fact. We assume this is what happened with Hunter.'

'And how and when did you get to know he was a Soviet agent?'

'Not until early '39. We think he must've been told to lay low until they needed him and, certainly the way he was living in Geneva, no-one would have had any reason whatsoever to suspect him We became very interested in a Soviet spy master, chap called Viktor Krasotkin. Very bright chap: based in Paris but moves around Western Europe as if he owns the place. Quite brilliant actually, but our people in Paris were aware of him and for a while had someone quite close to him. This person tipped us off about an

English chap with Swiss nationality who was one of Viktor's agents. Once we knew this, we tried to recruit him and he rather fell into our hands.'

'But what has this to do with the directive?'

'Once Henry delivers the boy Alfred to Zürich and Reinhart gets the green light, Henry can return to Berlin and bring the document back to Switzerland.'

'The point of that being…?'

'He'll be made well aware quite how important the document is – top secret, et cetera. We know as soon as he gets back to Switzerland, he's bound to show it to Viktor Krasotkin, even before he hands it over to Edgar. That way, the Russians will know it's genuine. It'll have come straight from the horse's mouth, so to speak. They'll have to believe it then, won't they?'

* * *

Chapter 17: Zürich, February 1941

Under the identity of Patrick T O'Connor Jr, a US citizen, Edgar left Muntadas airport in Barcelona just before ten in the morning on Swissair flight 1087. The flight landed on time in Locarno at a quarter past one. Five hours later he was in a small apartment above a hardware shop on Basteiplatz. He was let in by a pleasant-looking Austrian who introduced himself as Rolf.

'No need to worry about Rolf,' Remington-Barber had assured him. 'Completely trustworthy: he's an Austrian social democrat. Whitlock recruited him in Vienna sometime around '36. Nazis rolled into Vienna in March 1938 and Rolf rolled out soon after that: hates the Germans more than we do, if that's possible. His fiancée's a prisoner of theirs. When Whitlock had to leave Vienna and he found out Rolf was here in Switzerland, he recommended him to me.'

* * *

Basil Remington-Barber and Henry Hunter arrived in Zürich late on the Thursday afternoon and checked into the same hotel on Oetenbachgasse where Henry had stayed the previous February, the night before he travelled to Stuttgart. The next morning Remington-Barber left Henry in his room to rest and met Edgar as arranged on Bahnhofquai. Together they watched a noisy barge make its way up the Limmat.

'Hunter alright, is he?'

'After a fashion, yes. Picked him up yesterday morning in

Geneva during his morning walk and told him to pack his bags, bid his farewells and we're off to Zürich. It's a year since he was in Germany and I rather think he assumed we'd forgotten about him. Not very happy I haven't told him what's going on, but then I hardly know myself, do I?'

'And did you give him an opportunity to make contact?'

'Naturally. I told him we'd catch the one o'clock train to Zürich and I'd meet him by the platform with his ticket at a quarter to one. That gave him ample opportunity to get a message to his other people that something may be on. Good to dangle bait of some kind in front of them.'

'Good, well done Basil. Sorry to be elusive, but I need to track someone down. Come along to the apartment later this afternoon with Hunter.'

* * *

All things considered, it had not been a good day and a half for Henry Hunter, and it showed no signs of improving. On the Thursday, he had been whisked away from Geneva by Basil Remington-Barber, with little by way of an explanation other than 'We're going to Zürich: pack for a few days. Don't forget your passport.' The subsequent train journey had passed mostly in silence, Remington-Barber declining to answer any of Henry's questions.

Then Remington-Barber had ordered him to remain in his stuffy little hotel room for most of Friday morning. He had no idea what was going on or what was going to happen, so he was feeling increasingly anxious. There was a small part of him – a very small part, admittedly – which was relieved that, after a year of hearing nothing from the British, at last they now seemed to have plans for him. An even smaller part of him was excited at the prospect of what those plans may involve. He had spent the past year reflecting on the fact the trip to Stuttgart and Essen had been fraught with danger, but the excitement of having completed the mission so successfully had surprised him. The months since had been a mixture of boredom and nervous anticipation: added to this was the pressure of serving two masters. The 100 pounds paid into his Credit Suisse account each month was some consolation.

Now Remington-Barber had sent a friendly Austrian called Rolf to bring him to a small apartment above a hardware shop on Basteiplatz. It was 3.30 in the afternoon and they had been waiting in the sparsely furnished lounge for the best part of an hour. Henry was sitting on an uncomfortable sofa while Remington-Barber nervously paced the room, darting over to the window overlooking Basteiplatz every time he heard footsteps below. The diplomat had said very little since they had arrived there. *Sit over there Henry; yes, we're waiting for someone; please be patient.*

Eventually, a bell rang and Remington-Barber sent Rolf downstairs to open the door. Henry heard two pairs of footsteps ascending the stairs. At first he didn't recognise the tall figure wearing a trilby hat who had to stoop as he entered the door. But then he removed the trilby and said 'Henry' – no more than that, just 'Henry' – before taking off his raincoat and slinging it over a chair, then angling the single armchair so it was directly facing the sofa.

'Sit down Basil, you're making me nervous. No need to keep looking out of the window: no-one has followed me; I can assure you of that. Make yourself useful – pass me that ashtray then go and sit next to Henry. Either of you chaps fancy a cigarette?'

Edgar lounged back in the armchair, stretching out his long legs so they almost touched the feet of the two men opposite him. Not bothering to stifle a series of yawns he closed his eyes momentarily and it looked for a while as if he was about to fall asleep. Then he sat up straight, slapped his thighs and rubbed his hands.

'Right – down to business. Henry, you look rather shocked to see me: understandable I suppose. I imagine you rather hoped you'd never see me again, eh?'

Henry said nothing.

'And are you keeping well Henry?'

'I'm well thank you. And you?'

'Basil tells me your little trip to Germany last year went well.'

Henry was about to reply but Edgar raised a hand to stop him.

'And the money's going in to your account every month as promised, I presume? Along with the 500 you received after your trip.'

Henry replied that it was.

'Which in a sense is why I'm here: time for you to do something more to earn that money. How about if I were to tell you you're going back to Germany?'

Henry drummed his fingers on his knees and very slowly nodded his head. 'To Essen?'

'Good heavens no. We can hardly have the murderer returning

to the scene of his crime, can we?' Edgar laughed heartily and Remington-Barber joined in nervously.

'We thought Berlin would make a nice change.'

Henry gazed quizzically at Edgar, as if he was trying to work out whether the man opposite him was being serious.

'Berlin?'

'Yes, Henry, Berlin. Capital of the Third Reich.'

'Really?'

'Yes, really. Look, I could tell you all about it now, but I'd just end up repeating myself later on. We have a chap coming to see us in an hour or so and we'll put all of our cards on the table then. Talking of tables, Basil, how about some tea, eh?'

Basil Remington-Barber headed over to the small kitchen, pausing in its doorway.

'You certain this chap is going to turn up, Edgar?'

'Don't worry Basil. I'm certain of it. He really has no alternative.'

* * *

Captain Edgar had finally approached the man at lunchtime that Friday. It felt, to him, as if he'd spent half of his life following people, waiting for hours in the shadows of doorways for them to appear, calculating when they would emerge and what would then be the best time and place to approach them. He had learnt through years of experience that most people tended to be unpredictable in their habits, but he could have guessed that if anyone would be a man of precise routine it would be a Swiss banker. And Michael Hedinger did not disappoint him.

According to the message that Hugo sent through Lisbon, Gunter Reinhart's friend in Zürich was a man called Michael Hedinger who worked for Bank Leu. Hedinger was apparently aware 'in principle', whatever that meant, that his friend Gunter in Berlin wanted him to help look after his son, but he would have no idea he was about to be approached.

Edgar had watched the bank over the past couple of days. It had been founded in 1755 and some of the employees he watched coming in and out looked as though they had been there that long. Now it was one of the 'Big Seven' Swiss banks: not one of the largest, but still big enough to have its snout in the German trough, along with all the others. With the help of a porter at the bank who had been paid generously in return for doing no more than giving a signal when Michael Hedinger entered the building, Edgar had been able to spot his quarry.

Hedinger left the head office of Bank Leu on Paradeplatz at precisely one o'clock, presumably on his way to lunch. He turned into Bahnhofstrasse and Edgar decided now was the time he had to make his move.

'Herr Hedinger, may I have a word with you?' Edgar spoke in German.

He had approached the banker from behind, having got as close to him as possible and making sure he placed himself between the man and the road. It was a well-practised technique, as was the friendly but firm hand on the man's elbow and the enforced shaking of his hand. *Hold one arm, shake the other arm: take control.* That way, anyone watching would assume it was a chance encounter between two acquaintances.

'I beg your pardon?' Hedinger replied, sounding surprised rather than annoyed. This was encouraging but Edgar could not assume this would last for long.

'I need to talk to you about a rather important matter, Herr Hedinger. Is there somewhere quiet perhaps we could go?'

'I don't know who you are. What's this about?' Now Hedinger was beginning to sound annoyed, and a man and woman turned to look at them as they passed by. People were not accustomed to raised voices on the streets of Zürich.

Edgar edged even closer to Hedinger. 'It's in connection with Gunter Reinhart in Berlin, Herr Hedinger.'

Edgar was not prepared for the reaction that followed. He had hoped that at the mention of Reinhart, Hedinger would relax and want to know more: quite possibly he had expected to be contacted and may even be relieved. What he had not expected was to see the look of sheer panic and fear that spread across Hedinger's face. Edgar could not be sure, but it looked as if his eyes had filled with tears. The banker appeared unsteady on his feet.

'Come with me.'

Michael Hedinger meekly allowed Edgar to shepherd him across Bahnhofstrasse and then onto Kappelergasse where they settled on a bench overlooking the river. Edgar could see the man next to him was terrified. Edgar took his time lighting a cigarette and held the packet in front of the other man. Hedinger shook his head. 'No, I don't smoke.'

'What's your name, what's this about? Please tell me!'

Edgar ignored the first question. 'I told you: it's in connection with Gunter Reinhart. You know Herr Reinhart – from the Reichsbank in Berlin?'

'I'm not sure. Why do you ask?'

'It's a very straightforward question, Herr Hedinger. Either you know him or you don't?'

'We are acquaintances, in a professional capacity.'

Edgar had prepared his next line: *Herr Reinhart has asked for help in bringing his son Alfred out of Berlin and he tells us you are prepared to look after him in Zürich.* But before he had an opportunity to speak, Hedinger gripped his forearm and turned to face Edgar. He was a man of medium height, but with the kind of shrunken appearance reserved for those of especially nervous disposition. With his unhealthily pale complexion, watery blue eyes with scarcely a trace of eyebrow above them and his few remaining wisps of hair dancing in the wind, he reminded Edgar of an English country clergyman, the type sent to only the most undemanding of parishes. Now he looked like a clergyman who had been caught in a compromising situation and was about to be defrocked. He was utterly terrified. Edgar could smell it on his breath.

'I've always feared this moment and had resolved that if – when – it came about, I'd immediately be honest.' Hedinger's voice trembled as he spoke. 'It's all been a terrible misunderstanding... a most unfortunate misunderstanding. Herr Reinhart wanted to divert some of the funds from Germany into a private account in his name and, in a moment of weakness, I agreed. And in a moment of even greater weakness I accepted some money from Herr Reinhart for myself... for my efforts. I regretted it immediately.

My money is held in a separate account. I can arrange to have it paid back to you within a matter of days. I can see to it this afternoon in fact.'

Edgar loosened the grip Hedinger had on his arm and stood up to face the river. In a world of surprises, it was very rare for one to shock him, but this one had. By the sounds of it, Hedinger and Reinhart were involved in a scheme to smuggle German state funds out of Germany into their own private accounts here in Zürich. Hedinger must have assumed Edgar was a German official. He turned around: Hedinger was trembling, his feet tapping on the ground.

'I have a young family and I'm a good man: I go to church every week. Please understand I didn't intend to keep your money. I'm sure I can have it all returned to you this afternoon – along with the money in Herr Reinhart's private account.'

'Are these accounts with Bank Leu?'

'Naturally.'

'Do you have the account numbers please?'

Hedinger obediently removed a slim black notebook from his jacket pocket and turned the pages with trembling fingers that had the appearance of having been manicured. From what Edgar could see, the notebook was full of numbers, figures, initials and dates. Edgar opened his own notebook and, turning to a blank page, wrote 'Reinhart' then 'Hedinger'.

'Write the account numbers underneath each name please. Don't forget to put down how much money is in each account. I'm sure we can resolve this matter in a satisfactory manner. If you co-operate, Herr Hedinger, there should be no need for us to take further action.'

Hedinger grasped the bait like a hungry fish, eagerly copying down the account numbers. When he had finished he handed the notebook with its incriminating lists of bank accounts back to Edgar.

'Can I ask you sir, are you from the Gestapo?'

Edgar laughed: the outcome to the encounter with Michael Hedinger had been far better than he could have hoped.

'Well, that's where I think I'm going to surprise you, Herr Hedinger.'

* * *

'How can you be so sure he'll turn up Edgar?'

'Because it's not in his interests not to turn up.'

Basil Remington-Barber shook his head and moved away from his spot by the window overlooking Basteiplatz, which he had occupied on and off throughout the afternoon.

'Well, I wish I were able to share your confidence. In my experience, things don't always turn out quite as planned.'

'Basil, do stop pacing around and sit down quietly, as Henry's doing. It's now five o'clock. At this moment, our visitor will be leaving his office on Paradeplatz and commencing his short walk here. It will take him six minutes; I timed it myself earlier this afternoon. In fact, I walked the route three times and it takes six minutes and 20 seconds, but I wouldn't want you to think I'm a pedant. He'll be with us by 5.10 at the very latest, mark my words. What is it they say about the Swiss and clockwork? And just one warning: he may tell us things we're already aware of – like the boy, Alfred. Pretend it's the first time we've heard it, eh?

At seven minutes past five a knowing smile crossed Edgar's face as the bell rang. He gave Remington-Barber a 'told you' look and went downstairs to let their visitor in. Two minutes later Michael Hedinger had joined the three Englishmen in the apartment.

For a moment the four of them sat in an uncomfortable silence. The newcomer was in a state of considerable nervousness. He had declined offers to remove his coat and had only reluctantly taken off his gloves and hat. He was clutching a brown briefcase to his chest and was clearly edgy, jumping at the sound of a car engine backfiring and at a door slamming in an apartment above. Edgar had placed himself at the head of the table: Hedinger was sitting to his left, opposite the other two men.

When Edgar began to speak it was initially to Henry and Remington-Barber.

'Henry, Basil – this is Michael Hedinger. I will speak in German by the way: Herr Hedinger's English is very limited. Herr Hedinger works for Bank Leu, of which more in due course. Perhaps I should explain that when Herr Hedinger and I first met, some four hours ago, there was something of a misunderstanding. It was perhaps a fortunate misunderstanding from my point of view, less so from Herr Hedinger's. Is that not correct?'

The banker looked up in an absent-minded manner, with a 'what me?' expression. He nodded meekly in reply to Edgar's question.

'Not to put too fine a point on it, it turns out Herr Hedinger here in Zürich and Herr Reinhart in Berlin have been operating a… how can one put it… a scheme whereby a proportion of the funds transferred from the Reichsbank to the safekeeping of Bank Leu have been diverted into private numbered accounts: one belonging to Herr Reinhart, the other to Herr Hedinger. Is that correct, Herr Hedinger?'

Hedinger began to speak but was stopped by Edgar. 'You'll have ample opportunity to talk in due course, Herr Hedinger. It's a very risky but lucrative scheme. Herr Hedinger tells me that of the millions of Reichsmarks transferred through Herr Reinhart's operation at the Reichsbank to Bank Leu, some 25,000 have ended up in the private accounts – that's around 2,000 pounds sterling. Is that not correct, Herr Hedinger?'

He nodded, avoiding eye contact with anyone around the table.

'And the money is split equally, is it not?' Again, Hedinger nodded.

'Now this is where Herr Hedinger must be kicking himself. When I approached him earlier today, I knew nothing of this scheme. However, the private enterprise with Herr Reinhart has obviously been on Herr Hedinger's conscience and he assumed I was an official – a *German* official, would you please – investigating the matter. Before I'd even had an opportunity to explain what I'd approached him about, he confessed. Have I accurately summed up what happened, Herr Hedinger?'

The Swiss coughed and spoke in a soft voice. 'I never intended to keep the money, but Gunter – Herr Reinhart – is a very persuasive man: he insisted that with the amounts being transferred and the fact some of it was obtained from private accounts by the

Reichsbank, well... he said it'd be impossible for our accounts to be traced. He may well have been correct, but I've been terrified I'd be caught and I'd lose my job and my house – so much so that I've been a nervous wreck in recent weeks. I felt it was just a matter of time before someone came for me. When you approached me on Bahnhofstrasse I assumed I'd been caught: I was almost relieved, hence my rather too hasty confession.'

He shrugged his shoulders and spread his hands out in a 'so there we are' manner.

So there we are.

'As I told you earlier, Herr Hedinger, I couldn't care less about the money. Keep it. As far as we're concerned, it's better it's in your account and that of Herr Reinhart than in one belonging to the Reichsbank. The money isn't our concern. Neither Bank Leu nor the Reichsbank need find out about it: you will keep your job and your fine house. But a happy outcome of that misunderstanding is our knowledge of it has ensured your complete co-operation, Herr Hedinger, am I correct?'

'Indeed.'

'So now we come to our main business, of which we spoke briefly and of which Henry here is unaware. Herr Hedinger, for the sake of my colleagues here, please tell me again about your relationship with Herr Reinhart.'

The Swiss cleared his throat and paused for a while, clearly giving careful consideration to what he was about to say. His soft voice and the careful way in which he spoke reminded Edgar even more of a country vicar, someone more suited to talking to elderly ladies than spies.

'Gunter and I have known each other for some five years. As you're aware, Gunter occupies a senior position in the foreign department of the Reichsbank. He's been involved with the transfer of funds from the Reichsbank to foreign banks, and Bank Leu is, in this respect, one of their main clients. I've been working in the international division of Bank Leu for a number of years and I'm currently its deputy head. You should be aware there is a very close relationship between Germany and the Swiss banks: they're an important client for us and we're very important to them: an efficient and discreet way of moving funds in and out of the country. Not all their funds, it has to be acknowledged, have been obtained in entirely legal ways. As part of my job, I oversee our relationship with the Reichsbank, so over the years I have visited Berlin on a regular basis and I think it's reasonable to say Gunter and I have become good friends. We found we have much in common; it took us a couple of years to really trust each other but, once we did, we found we could confide in each other. We've been able to talk frankly about our private lives and our worries. About a year ago, when I was in Berlin, he took me into his confidence and told me a secret that he said if it came out, would cost him his job and quite possibly his freedom. What I'm about to say will stay within these walls?'

Edgar laughed. 'We're hardly likely to inform the Gestapo, are we?'

'I realise that, but I'm divulging something told to me in complete confidence. What Gunter told me was this: he had married a woman called Rosa in 1924, when he was 29. Rosa, I think, was two or three years younger than him. He describes Rosa as the love of his life. She happened to be Jewish but was not practising and Gunter said their differences of religion were simply not an issue, or at least not for them. Their son Alfred was born in 1929, so he's now 11 or 12. Gunter absolutely dotes on Alfred. He described their life together as idyllic, but that began to change when the Nazis came to power in 1933. Until then, not many people knew Rosa was Jewish, but life became increasingly uncomfortable. Then the Nazis started to bring in all these anti-Jewish laws and one of them, in 1935 I think it was, banned marriages between Jews and non-Jews. So they had a choice, either leave the country or get divorced. May I trouble you for a drink please?'

There was a pause while Remington-Barber disappeared into the kitchen, emerging a few minutes later with a tray of tea, a jug of water with glasses and a bottle of whisky. Hedinger poured himself a glass of water.

'Gunter told me their original plan was to emigrate: they'd have had to leave everything behind, pay a hefty tax then find somewhere that'd give them an entry visa. Nonetheless, they were prepared to do that. But then it was made very clear to Gunter that unless he divorced Rosa immediately, he'd lose his job at the Reichsbank. From what I understand, they both still loved each other and saw the divorce as a temporary measure: Rosa and Alfred would try to go to England or France then Gunter would join them there and they'd remarry. But for reasons of which I'm unclear, Rosa delayed leaving Germany: I think it may have been she really wanted to go to England but she couldn't get an entry visa. Gunter, meanwhile, was finding life difficult. He met a woman called Gudrun and they married – I think he felt that, until he remarried, there'd always be suspicion about him. He remained in contact with Rosa, but it was difficult and in 1936 she remarried – a Jewish man called Harald Stern. They soon had a daughter, Sophia. My understanding is all this was done with Gunter's blessing, because Harald's plan was for them all to move to France, and Gunter just wanted Rosa and Alfred to be safe. Gunter even helped them financially and tried to obtain the right papers.'

'Could he not have had custody of Alfred himself?' asked Basil Remington-Barber.

'A good question: Gunter told me he could have done and if he had contested custody he'd almost certainly have won, though Alfred's status would be a difficult one. The Nazis say that anyone who has three or more Jewish grandparents is a Jew. Someone like Alfred, who has two Jewish grandparents, is what the Nazis call a *mischlinge*, which means a 'crossbreed' – like a dog. Nonetheless, Gunter felt he could have taken Alfred in and dealt with that – there are ways, you know. But Gudrun, his second wife, would have none of it. As far as she was – and is – concerned, he's to have no contact whatsoever with his first family.

'Now what I am about to say is complicated and highly sensitive: forgive me if I'm unclear as to the exact dates. Essentially, what I believe happened is that soon after war was declared, Rosa did go to Paris with the two children and Harald was meant to follow them. But he was arrested and taken to a camp for Jews and political prisoners, called Sachsenhausen. For some foolish reason, in an act of utter madness, Rosa retuned to Berlin with the children in an effort to get Harald freed. She failed and had to go into hiding, and a few months later she heard Harald was dead.'

'And has Gunter been in touch with them?'

'Yes, since January or February 1940. There's a Berlin lawyer called Franz Hermann who's an old friend of Rosa's. He's hiding Rosa and the children in his mother's house in the city and Gunter is able to visit them. They're trapped there though. Hermann is the connection between Gunter and Rosa and the children.'

'And you say that Gunter told you all this last year?'

'Yes.'

'Do you remember when last year?'

'Maybe March… possibly April. In fact, that was when he started diverting the money into our private accounts – he said the reason he was doing this was that he needed the money was to help Rosa and Alfred. I was last in Berlin at the very end of January, just a couple of weeks ago. It was a very short visit and I only saw Gunter on his own very briefly. He said to me that if he were able to arrange for Alfred to be brought out of Germany, would I promise to look after him in Switzerland? I said yes… What else could I say? That's why he told me about the lawyer, Hermann. He also said he may even need my assistance to help get Alfred out. That was the last I heard – until we met today.'

Michael Hedinger looked less nervous now, as if he was pleased to have got things off his chest. His pale head was wet with perspiration, the strands of hair now plastered to it. Edgar was nodding his head, taking everything in and thinking, while Henry looked bemused, unsure of what his role in all this was meant to be. It was Edgar who spoke next.

'How often do you go to Berlin?'

'Perhaps every other month.'

'And other Bank Leu officials, how often do they go?'

'Hard to say exactly, but on a very regular basis. Look, the Reichsbank is one of our most important clients, but it's a very sensitive relationship. The money they're placing with us comes from sources that require utmost discretion on our part.'

'What do you mean by that?'

'The Nazis have confiscated millions of Reichsmarks from Jews and plundered money from the countries they've occupied. They need to move that money around; so much of it comes to banks like ours to be converted into Swiss Francs, which is probably the safest currency in the world at the moment. They're also sending us a lot of gold, not just us – all the Swiss banks. The business we get from Germany is extremely profitable, so we prefer to deal with the Reichsbank in person. We ask very few questions and we leave nothing to chance.'

'Do you send couriers to Germany?'

'Of course. Every week, if not more frequently. Documents need to be signed, letters need to be delivered. Couriers are a very important part of our relationship with them.'

'And these couriers are…?'

'Employees of Bank Leu or people who do this on a regular basis – people we know and trust.'

Edgar was thinking and looking around the table. His eyes fell on Henry, and he smiled while addressing the Swiss. 'Tell me Herr Hedinger, do you have the authority to decide who can be a courier on your behalf?'

'Yes, in fact only in November I used my own brother-in-law.'

'I see.' Edgar was still looking directly at Henry as he spoke. Henry was beginning to feel uncomfortable. 'So Henry here could become one of your couriers?'

'I'm not sure, maybe he…'

'You don't need to worry. Herr Hesse is a Swiss citizen and a regular visitor to Germany himself. I have no doubt he'd be a most capable courier on behalf of Bank Leu.'

* * *

Michael Hedinger left the apartment at 6.30. Before he went, Edgar pressed him on how soon he could arrange Henry's accreditation.

'It's now Friday evening, so obviously I can't do anything before Monday. It'll take me a few days from then. We have a procedure at the bank, you see. Fortunately I'm in a position to organise my own couriers, but the paperwork has to be done properly, otherwise we'll arouse suspicion. If Herr Hesse can give me his passport now, that'll speed things up. Also, remember I'll need to sort out paperwork for Alfred. That won't be easy.'

Edgar nodded at Henry, who looked as shocked as he had done when he first heard about the plans for his trip to Berlin. He removed his passport from his jacket pocket and handed it over to Hedinger.

'How soon then?'

'By the end of next week. I'm sure I can have it sorted by then.'

'End of the week! I thought it could be done in a day or two.'

The Swiss shook his head vigorously. 'No, no, no – I told you, we have our procedures. I need to fill in the form, send it to the correct department, they need to process it, then the form has to be counter-signed by a director. Once that's all done, I need to arrange Herr Hesse's registration as an official courier of Bank Leu with the German consulate here in Zürich. I can assure you it'll take a week. Hopefully by next Friday morning it'll be sorted.'

They agreed they would meet again at the apartment the following Friday lunchtime. As well as Henry's accreditation, Hedinger would bring along documents for him to take to Bank Leu's clients in Berlin. They waited for Michael Hedinger to leave the apartment and all three of them stood at the window watching him cross Basteiplatz.

'I thought that went rather well Edgar. Good work.'

'Thank you Basil. This scheme of his and Reinhart really is most helpful. I was able to tell him that unless he fully co-operated with us, we may be obliged to inform the Swiss authorities. It means that we have him over a barrel. So, Henry, you're going to Berlin. Looking forward to it I hope?'

Henry had poured himself a glass of whisky that he drank in one go. 'It's madness: you seriously want me to go to Berlin pretending to be a courier for a Swiss Bank then return accompanied by an 11-year-old half-Jewish boy? It'll never work.'

'Why shouldn't it? Your Swiss identity is perfectly genuine and your visit to Stuttgart last year would've been in order as far as the Germans are concerned. After all, they've no idea you went to Essen. If you get questioned, you simply say you now have a job as a courier for a bank.'

'And the boy?'

'We'll see what paperwork Hedinger comes up with, but it's in his interests for it to be good.'

'It'll have to be more than good, Edgar. I'm not sure whether you're aware of it, but the Swiss are doing their level best to stop Jews crossing the border from Germany. They'll be looking out for the likes of him.'

'Yes, I'm aware of that, thank you Henry. But they'll not be looking out for the likes of you, will they? And the fact he's with you, in whatever capacity… well that ought to ensure a safe passage. Anyway, that's only half of the story.'

'What do you mean?'

'Obviously we didn't want to say too much in front of Herr Hedinger, but going to Berlin and coming back with the boy is only half your mission. Once the boy is safely in Zürich, Herr Hedinger will send a coded message to Gunter Reinhart. Herr Reinhart has an extremely important document that he'll hand over to us once he knows his son is safe. It's a document that could determine the future course of the war, so it's vital it's brought out of Germany as soon as possible.'

'How's it going to be brought out, Edgar?'

'By you, Henry!'

* * *

Chapter 18: Switzerland, February 1941

After the meeting in the apartment on the Basteiplatz, Henry was instructed to return to Geneva for a few days while Michael Hedinger sorted out all the paperwork.

'Basil will come and collect you on the Thursday. Just act normally until then,' had been Edgar's advice.

As soon as Henry arrived at Gare Cornavin on the Saturday he walked to a phone booth in a quiet area at the back of the station. The call was brief and, as a result of it, he found himself on the Monday evening in the private room at the back of the Armenian restaurant in Grand-Lancy where Viktor had first taken him in 1931.

'So, Edgar himself was in Zürich, was he *synok*?' Viktor sounded incredulous, so much so he had poured himself another glass of something that to Henry tasted like liquorice-flavoured acid. 'I don't suppose he told you how he got to Switzerland?'

Henry shook his head. 'I presume he came on some roundabout route.'

'I'm not interested in presumptions, *synok*. I'm interested in facts. It's quite a feat to travel from England to Switzerland these days, so it was obviously by a roundabout route: he was hardly going to fly direct, was he? I'd be curious to know what that route is. You know, it would be a pleasure to meet your Captain Edgar. I think we'd have much in common, despite everything. Tell me Henry, this must be important if Edgar himself has come to Switzerland.'

'I have to go to Berlin next week. I'll be using my own identity and acting as a courier for Bank Leu. I've to bring a boy back from Berlin, a Jew, or a half-Jew to be precise. Once I deliver the boy to Zürich I'm supposed to return to Berlin, where I'll be given a document to bring back to Switzerland.'

'That's it?'

Henry laughed. 'That's it? Surely, smuggling a Jew out of Germany then returning to collect a document is enough isn't it?'

'What I meant was whether you can tell me any more.'

'Edgar said the document is so important it could decide the future course of the war. I asked him what he meant and he was reluctant to tell me at first, but I told him if I was going to put my life on the line by going into Berlin twice then I had a right to know. So he told me it's a document from the very top of the Reich – those were his words – about a proposed German invasion of the Soviet Union.'

Viktor had removed a pencil from his top pocket and had been in the process of sharpening it when Henry said this. He stopped, the knife poised in mid-air, pointing towards Henry.

'Say that again.'

'The document is to do with a proposed German invasion of the Soviet Union.'

Henry could have sworn the deep lines on the Russian's face grew as he took in what he'd just been told.

'Edgar told you this?'

'Yes: he seemed to regret having told me as soon as he'd done so, but I was quite persuasive, don't you think?'

'When you return from Berlin the second time – with the document, that is – did he say where you go?'

'Zürich, because that's where I'm supposed to be based: it would look suspicious to Germans if I went elsewhere in Switzerland. However, once I get to Zürich, I'm to hand the routine bank papers over to the contact at Bank Leu then head straight to Bern to give the document to Edgar.'

Viktor looked worried, lowering his head in thought then looking up to the ceiling for inspiration.

'Plans for a German invasion of the Soviet Union, you say?'

Henry nodded.

'You don't know what day you will be back in Zürich with the document, do you *synok*?'

'No. Edgar said that all being well I go on the first trip to Berlin a week today, which I think is the 24th. Depending on how things go, I'll probably be back there the following Monday, which would be 3rd March, I suppose. So I guess I'll be back in Zürich sometime that week. Maybe the Wednesday: the sooner the better.'

'We'll be waiting in Zürich for you: don't head to Bern until we've made contact with you. Do you understand?'

'Of course. But how will you know when I'm there? Edgar says I'm not to hang around in Zürich: I'm to go from the station to Bank Leu, hand over the bank's papers then go straight back to the station and travel to Bern.'

Viktor removed his heavy coat and paced around the room. From an inside jacket pocket he took out a small notebook and leafed through it. When he found what he was looked for he wrote on a piece of paper, which he then handed to Henry.

'Here, memorise this number. When you arrive back in Zürich, ring it and say Peter is coming round for dinner: that is all. Peter is coming round for dinner. They'll reply by asking if you're bringing wine with you. If you say yes, we'll know you have the document. We'll meet you at Zürich Hauptbahnhof exactly one hour after the phone call, you understand?'

* * *

The journey to Berlin began in Zürich, in the borrowed apartment above the hardware shop on Basteiplatz. Michael Hedinger arrived a shade after a quarter past one on the Friday, breathless and busily explaining how he had been waiting on one extra document.

'I have to be back at my office by two o'clock for a meeting. I have everything here.'

From his brown leather briefcase Hedinger removed a number of items, which he placed neatly in front of him on the table. He took Henri Hesse's Swiss passport from the top of the pile and handed it to him.

'All is in order, Herr Hesse. Thanks to our excellent relationship with the German consulate here in Zürich your passport now allows you to travel freely between Switzerland and Germany a maximum of six times over the next six months – until 20th August to be precise. That is a routine arrangement for our couriers.'

Edgar and Remington-Barber both studied the visa, emblazoned with a swastika and a rampant eagle, and made approving noises.

'And here are the documents you're carrying from Bank Leu to the Reichsbank in Berlin, for the attention of Herr Reinhart: they are, of course, the purpose of your trip as far as the German authorities are concerned. You'll see they're all in sealed envelopes. I'd ask that they remain that way until they're handed over. In this envelope…' he passed a long white envelope with the bank's crest to Henry, 'is your letter of accreditation from the bank and here are your rail tickets from Zürich to Berlin: you change at Stuttgart. It's a long journey, but you'll travel first-class which is very tolerable. I've taken the liberty of booking you on the train that departs Zürich at six o'clock on Monday morning. You should be in Berlin by six o'clock that evening.'

Another envelope was handed to Henry.

'In Berlin you'll stay at the Kaiserhof: our couriers either stay there or at the Excelsior on Askanischer Platz, but the Kaiserhof is rather charming and is slightly closer to the centre. It's certainly more discreet than the Adlon: everyone stays at the Adlon, it is not private enough I think – too many journalists and possibly spies. Here's the letter of confirmation from the Kaiserhof. The bill will be settled directly by the bank, you don't need to worry about that. Your room will be en-suite.'

Henry checked the contents of the envelope.

'Very efficient, Herr Hedinger,' said Edgar. 'I trust you've addressed the somewhat more complicated issue of young Alfred?'

Hedinger nodded. 'I'm proposing he travels under the identity of my own son, Andreas.'

The banker pulled a large white handkerchief from a pocket and used it to wipe his forehead. He hesitated a while before he spoke again. 'I have to be honest with you, this has been most difficult. I've had sleepless nights over it. I've never met Alfred but Gunter has shown me photographs of him. Alfred is 11 or 12. My own son, Andreas, is ten, but is tall for his age. I wouldn't say Andreas and Alfred look alike, but I think with a bit of imagination, you could ensure that at the very least they don't look too different, if you see what I mean. Here's his passport.'

The three men studied the passport photo of Andreas Hedinger. His black hair was straight and had a distinctive parting low down on the left side. He wore a pair of round, wire-framed glasses.

'Here are the very glasses Andreas is wearing in that picture.' Hedinger brought a pair of spectacles out of his briefcase. 'We bought him a brand-new pair yesterday. I think if you make sure Alfred's hair is like Andreas's and he wears these glasses, then you have a chance.'

'Have you told your wife about this?'

'I had to. If this works, we'll need to keep Andreas off school until Alfred arrives in Zürich. Also, I've had to tell her about Alfred: he'll be coming to stay with us, after all.'

'What does she think of it?'

'Fortunately, Helga is braver than me. She's a very devout woman and believes this is her Christian duty. As long as there's no danger to Andreas, then she'll go along with it.'

'That's all very well, but why on earth would Andreas be in Berlin – and with me?' Henry was holding the boy's passport. 'What am I to say when I'm asked what I'm doing in Berlin with the son of my boss at Bank Leu? And what about how he got there – won't they spot he didn't come into Germany with me?' Henry sounded annoyed.

'Turn to the third page of the passport please,' said Hedinger. 'This is where my relationship with the passport clerk at the

German consulate paid off. I asked him to stamp the passport showing that Andreas entered Germany this coming Monday – the 24th. I explained this was a treat for Andreas. As ever, he was most obliging: given the way the bank looks after him, he ought to be. In this envelope is the train ticket for Alfred to use from Berlin to Zürich. It's a return, showing the outward part of the journey – from Zürich to Berlin – was on Monday 24th February. There's no reason why the German border guards should question this and the Swiss ought not to be difficult about allowing a Swiss boy to re-enter his country.'

'And the story, Herr Hedinger?' asked Remington-Barber. 'We always need to have a very good story.'

'A reward! Andreas has done so well at school I promised him a visit to Berlin. I was planning to take him myself but have been unable to arrange it because I'm so busy, so I asked one of my couriers to do so. Andreas is fascinated by everything he sees about Germany, the marching – everything. He is so excited.'

Henry sat very still with his head in his hands. Edgar raised his eyebrows high and looked at Remington-Barber who shook his head.

'Henry: any better ideas?'

'None I can think of at the moment.'

'Basil?'

Remington-Barber shook his head. 'It's a bit thin, to be honest, but then very few cover stories are quite as watertight as we'd like them to be. We have to rely on no-one probing too deeply. I suppose it does at least have the merit of being relatively simple. As long as no-one pushes too hard on why a mere courier would be entrusted with taking his boss's son to Berlin. Perhaps we could say Henry's also a close family friend of yours: maybe your wife could write a letter thanking him for putting himself out and all that?'

'That's a good idea, Basil,' said Edgar.

'Herr Hedinger, you'll need to give Henry some important information: your address, what Andreas likes and doesn't like, all about his school, sports – that kind of thing,' said Remington-Barber. 'Alfred will have to learn all that in case he's questioned.'

Edgar sighed loudly, stood up and paced around the room, a trail of cigarette smoke following in his wake.

'Let's be frank. If the Gestapo pull in Alfred and interrogate him, the whole thing will fall apart. We have to hope, as Basil says, we don't get to that point; that no-one probes too deep. If none of us can come up with a better tale, I suppose that's it. Herr Hedinger, you'd better get back to the bank. Can I suggest you invite Henry round to your house at the weekend? That way he can familiarise himself with Andreas and your family. Basil, I think you ought to go too.'

* * *

Chapter 19: Berlin, February 1941

Henry Hunter arrived at the Kaiserhof hotel on Wilhelmstrasse a few minutes after six o'clock on the evening of Monday 24th February. It was only his second-ever visit to Germany's capital, the first being in 1934 or 1935 – he couldn't remember for sure – when he had accompanied his mother as a late replacement for his step-father, who had pulled out 'because of business.' He remembered his mother being charmed by Berlin, in a rather naïve way. Utterly oblivious to the politics, she was much taken with what she saw as people's enthusiasm and the enormous swastikas draped from the buildings. She admired the dramatic colours and the way they swayed very gently, even in the absence of a breeze. For Henry, the visit was simply an affirmation of what he believed in: he could not wait to get out of the city, vowing never to return.

But now he had returned. The hotel made a fuss of him, assuring him that Bank Leu were most valued clients and would he like to make a reservation for dinner? There were numerous forms and cards to fill in, which he did with the utmost care. He had spent the weekend going through the trip in detail with Remington-Barber and Edgar, and he had been warned about the hotel cards. They were destined for the Gestapo, which had a special office in Berlin where every night the cards of newly arrived foreigners would be carefully examined against the Gestapo's meticulous records.

Remington-Barber had been quite candid. 'If they've got anything against you from last year's Stuttgart trip, then alarm bells will go off. They'll either haul you out of bed that night or first thing in the morning. That's the bad news, Henry. Good news is that if they've nothing adverse on your file – and there's no reason why they should – then you're in the clear: should make the rest of the trip that much easier, relatively speaking.'

Henry ate little for dinner that night and slept badly, alert to every sound on the corridor as he waited for the Gestapo to come and arrest him for the murder of the owner of the perfume shop in Essen. At four in the morning he was convinced he could hear footsteps in the corridor and finally decided to unlock the door and have a look, but the long passageway was deserted, apart from neat pairs of shoes outside a number of the doors.

He felt a bit more relaxed and drifted asleep, only to be visited by the familiar face of Roza – her image far more in focus and its presence remaining for longer than usual. She spent much of the night asking questions, but each time he tried to reply he found he couldn't form the words. When he woke on the Tuesday morning, he was exhausted, but as he lay in bed his mood lifted. It was a quarter to eight and in the corridor he could hear the chambermaids gathering. At least, he decided, he'd passed the scrutiny of whichever Gestapo clerk had been scrutinising the hotel registration cards overnight.

This upbeat mood continued as he went down to breakfast, despite having to walk down corridors and stairs adorned with a gallery's worth of framed photographs commemorating Hitler's various visits to the hotel, of which there appeared to be many.

He knew he was likely to be in Berlin until Friday. According to Hedinger, it was not unusual for the bank's couriers to have to wait a few days to collect the return documents, and Edgar and

Remington-Barber were clear that a few days would be essential for Alfred to prepare for the journey to Switzerland.

'If all goes to plan,' said Remington-Barber, 'you and Alfred will come out on Friday morning. After that it depends on your journey: with a very fair wind you could be in Zürich late Friday, but more likely Saturday. Make sure you send Hedinger a telegram from Stuttgart when you know what train you're going to be on.'

He was due at the Reichsbank at ten o'clock and his instructions were to go by taxi: it was not done to walk the streets carrying important papers. Henri Hesse from Bank Leu entered the bank through the enormous doors on Französischestrasse. It was ten o'clock and he had been warned to expect delays. He was not to be disappointed. First he was searched, then he had to report to reception, which was a tall, polished-oak desk behind which a row of serious-looking receptionists peered down. After that he was given a form and sent over to another desk to fill it in. When he returned to the main reception desk, the form was carefully checked and only then did the receptionist deign to telephone Gunter Reinhart's office. *Herr Reinhart will be with you in due course. Please wait over there.*

'Over there' was a small waiting area where half a dozen other people were sitting quietly. The man opposite was clutching a Swiss passport and a padlocked briefcase. He told Henry he was a courier, from the Basler Handelsbank. He was surprised not to have seen Henry there before, he said: sometimes there could be as many as half a dozen couriers at the Reichsbank from the different Swiss banks.

The man got up and sat next to Henry. He was no more than

Alex Gerlis

five feet tall and was wearing a dark, formal suit that seemed to be a size too large for him. He stretched up to whisper in Henry's ear.

'I don't know who needs the other more – us or the Germans. I used to work for the SBC in Basle: I can't tell you how much work they were getting from this side of the border. Basler Handelsbank has recruited five of us in the past couple of months. From what I understand, it's been even busier for you lot in Zürich, is that right?'

'Indeed.' Henry shifted to his left, away from the man, whose breath reeked of stale tobacco.

'I don't want to know where the Germans are getting all this gold and cash from – but what I do know is that if it wasn't for us they'd be stuck with it. We're doing them a big favour – and we're making a lot of money in the process. How are things with Bank Leu?'

'Yes... very good, thank you.'

'So, where are you staying? Maybe tonight...'

At that point a secretary appeared in front of them, a gold swastika the only touch of colour on her dark suit.

'Bank Leu?'

Henry stood up.

'Come with me.'

Five minutes later Henry was in the small, deeply carpeted office of Gunter Reinhart. Reinhart had assured his secretary they would not be needing coffee and yes, thank you, he had all the papers he needed. *That would be all, thank you.*

It was silent in the office apart from the ticking of a clock that Henry couldn't see. He and Gunter Reinhart eyed each other carefully. Reinhart waited a moment then walked over to close the door his secretary had left ajar. He gestured for Henry to sit and held up his hand – *wait*. A minute later he walked softly over to the door, opened it, looked around, closed it again and came to sit at his desk.

'My secretary is – how can I put it tactfully – very efficient but nosey. She's the kind of person who likes to know everything. That's bad enough, but in these times – that can be quite a problem. Recently she joined the Nazi Party and she's forever telling me about how her husband has become some kind of party representative in the street where they live. That means they spy on their neighbours, so naturally I assume she spies on me. I'm very careful with her.'

Gunter had relaxed a bit now and his manner had now become noticeably friendlier. He reached across the desk and held out his hand to shake Henry's. 'I'm Gunter Reinhart, by the way, as you've no doubt gathered. I'm pleased to meet you. You have the documents? It's important they're here and in order. We don't want people questioning why you came!'

Henry handed over the envelopes containing the Bank Leu documents. Reinhart opened them carefully with a dagger-like letter opener. He glanced over the documents then put them to the side of his desk.

'I'll deal with them when we've finished. The documents for you to take back to Zürich won't be ready until late Thursday, you realise that?'

'So I understand.'

'It's not unusual for a courier to hang around Berlin for a few days.' He had left his desk now and come to sit next to Henry, speaking more quietly.

'Most couriers seem end up at the zoo, I've no idea why – I suppose they get bored. It's not as if they can go to a library, not now we've burned most of the books worth reading! As far as you're concerned, you won't get bored: we've plenty to keep you busy.' Reinhart paused and coughed. He hesitated before he resumed speaking, this time in an even lower voice. He gestured for Henry to lean closer.

'I can't tell you how grateful I am…' Reinhart looked as though he was overcome by emotion. 'My family situation… has been a source of great stress. It's been explained to you, I take it?'

'Yes.'

'I should never have divorced Rosa. We thought it was for the best. We assumed it would be a short-term measure and that maybe the Nazis would change their minds or go away. How could we have been so stupid as to think that? Once we realised that was never going to happen, our plan was for Rosa and Alfred to move to another country and I'd join them in due course, but it didn't turn out like that. We both remarried. At least I believed they'd be safe once they moved to Paris, but to find they'd returned to Berlin… Madness: it was a terrible shock. Now they're trapped here and I've been desperate to find a way of getting them out. For a while Rosa wanted the three of them to remain together, but once she found out about Harald's death, she agreed with me that, at the very least, we must get Alfred out. Once he's in Switzerland then I can see what can be done with Rosa and of course Sophia, too. But for now, getting Alfred out of Germany is the priority.

That's what I pray for.'

'Does Alfred know about the plan?'

'Not yet. You're going to meet him this afternoon. You'll obviously need to spend some time with him. Rosa knows there's a plan and she knows something will happen this week, but she doesn't know the details – for that matter, neither do I. Tell me briefly what the plan is: if you stay too long then my secretary will become suspicious.'

Henry took Andreas Hedinger's passport out of his jacket pocket and carefully placed it on the blotter pad on Reinhart's desk.

'The plan is for Alfred to accompany me back to Zürich using this identity – Andreas is Michael Hedinger's son.'

Reinhart nodded. *I know.*

'This passport is two years old, so anyone looking at it wouldn't be surprised the person in the photograph has changed. Also, I have with me the very spectacles Andreas is wearing in the photo. You can see Andreas has quite a distinctive hairstyle…'

Reinhart picked up the passport and put on his own glasses. He turned on his desk lamp and studied the document carefully, his face impassive.

'Andreas's hair is much darker than Alfred's. As far as his hair is concerned, Alfred inherited my Aryan genes rather than his mother's. I'd always thought that'd be an advantage.'

'We've thought of how to deal with the question of his hair colour. I've brought some black dye with me: it's back in the hotel. If we can use it on Alfred then style his hair to look like Andreas, it may work: especially with the glasses.'

'It's certainly feasible; there's no doubt about that. But how come you'll be accompanied back to Zürich by the boy?'

Henry breathed in deeply, anxious not to betray any of his own scepticism. 'The story will depend on us not being questioned too much but, in a nutshell, as well as acting as a courier for Bank Leu, I am also posing as a family friend of the Hedinger's. It's because of that I brought Andreas with me to Berlin as a treat.'

Reinhart said nothing but stared at Henry for a good few minutes.

'That's it?'

Henry shrugged his shoulders. *Yes, I know… don't tell me.*

'You think it'll work?'

'Hopefully. On the positive side, the passport is a genuine Swiss one. As long as they're not suspicious, they probably won't push Alfred too hard.'

Reinhart snapped the passport shut, handed it back to Henry, turned off his desk lamp and walked over to the window. He looked out over the Spreekanal then turned to face Henry.

'The alternative is to smuggle Alfred out and that's too dangerous. This plan will have to work. And you know about the document that'll be released only once I know Alfred is safe in Zürich?'

Henry nodded.

'Good. You're to meet Franz Hermann at one o'clock. He will escort you to the house where they're all hiding. Let me give you your instructions: you'll need to listen carefully. Incidentally, Herr Hesse, are you fond of flowers?'

* * *

Henry went from the Reichsbank back to the Kaiserhof, where he sought out the concierge. 'I have an unexpectedly free afternoon. I wonder if you could suggest anything I might do?'

The concierge smiled obligingly. *Please could he have his guest's details?*

Henry recalled what Gunter Reinhart had told him that morning. 'Anything you discuss with them could be reported back to the Gestapo, they like to keep tabs on foreigners – so your plans will need to appear plausible: use them to create an alibi.'

'And what would you be interested in doing, sir?' the concierge asked. 'The cinema maybe, or shopping?'

Henry shook his head.

'I've been spending so much time indoors that I wouldn't mind some fresh air.'

'The zoo perhaps? It's within the Tiergarten so you could combine the two.'

Henry shook his head. 'To be honest, I'm not very keen on animals. They make me nervous.'

'I quite understand, sir. Do you want to stay in the city?'

'I think so, it'll be dark soon.'

'That's true. I was going to suggest a visit to Potsdam, but perhaps that's for another day. Are you by any chance interested in plants and gardens?'

'Yes, I am actually.' He managed to sound just the right side of enthusiastic.

'Well, we have an excellent Botanischer Garten down in

Dahlem. It's a quite wonderful haven of peace and quiet in the city, and the gardens are most beautiful.'

Henry managed to look as if he was having second thoughts. 'In Dahlem you say: isn't that far away?'

'Not at all sir' said the concierge, 'it's no more than six or seven stops on the S-Bahn from Anhalter. The gardens are just a few minutes' walk from Botanischer Garten station. Here, let me show you how to get there.'

* * *

Every minute of your visit will be laced with danger, but no moment will be more dangerous than the one in which you drop your guard.

Edgar's parting words had been menacing enough, but they hardly began to describe what Henry encountered at Anhalter. The station was busy, but unnaturally quiet apart from the noise of dogs barking in the distance. A number of the people were exiting the station as he entered it, looking over their shoulders and apparently relieved to be in the open air. He noticed there were a large number of troops milling around, dressed in the black uniform of the SS rather than the grey of the Wehrmacht. He purchased a return ticket to Botanischer Garten, making sure to ask the clerk behind the tiny window if he knew how long it would take for him to walk to the gardens from the station.

Continuing to feel pleased with how things had gone, he headed for the platform, which was when he saw them. His first impression was it was a lot of people waiting for one train, especially at lunchtime. *Maybe an outing.* They were two platforms away, crowded together and hemmed in by the SS men in their black uniforms. Some of the SS had Alsatians with them, and though they held them on a short leash they allowed them to rear up at the people on the platform. All the while there was non-stop barking, which every so often orchestrated with the sound of a train's whistle or a station announcement.

Henry moved along his platform, trying to get a better view. The crowd was mixed: men, women and children; old and young. They seemed to be quite well-dressed and all the were either carrying suitcases or clutching bundles. From what he could see, the SS men were checking what the people had with them and a few of the bundles ended up being strewn on the platform, with some clothing spilling over onto the track.

He was still trying to make some sense of it when his train pulled into the platform and there was a scramble to board. Henry positioned himself by a window looking out onto the crowded platform. The window was dirty and it was hard to make out much detail through the screen of soot and grease. With his sleeve, he tried to clean his side of the glass and as he did so he caught the eye of the woman who had sat down opposite him. She followed his gaze across the track then looked down, intently studying the rail ticket she was clutching in her gloved hands. He leaned forward to get a better view, but then the doors of the train slammed, a guard called out and the train lurched forward. Within seconds the crowd of people on the opposite platform became a blur and soon they were out of Anhalter.

'Do you know who they were?' he asked the lady.

She looked around her before answering. 'You don't know?'

He shook his head.

'Jews: they've started to take them away,' she said in a matter-of-fact tone.

'Where to?'

A ticket inspector had appeared next to them and they both silently handed him their tickets. She glanced up at him. *Keep quiet.* Over the crackly speaker the driver announced the next station: 'Grossgorsenstrasse.'

The lady stood up, smoothing her coat as she did so. Before moving into the aisle she bent down and, barely pausing, whispered into Henry's ear. 'Wherever it is they take them to, they don't come back.'

He got off the train at Botanischer Garten, crossed the Unter den Eichen and entered the gardens. He did his best to appear every bit the interested visitor and made leisurely progress to the Italian Garden, which was actually quite beautiful and in other circumstances would have been an ideal place to relax.

If you're not approached by him within ten minutes of entering the Italian Garden, walk back to the station and travel back to Anhalter then to the hotel. Just act normally. Just because he doesn't turn up doesn't necessarily mean something is wrong.

He had been in the Italian Gardens approaching ten minutes when a smartly dressed man with a broad-brimmed hat came up to him and spoke in an educated Berlin accent.

'Excuse me sir; could you point me in the direction of the greenhouses?'

'I'm sorry, but I'm not very familiar with the gardens. I can tell you the lake is in that direction though,' said Henry, sticking carefully to his script.

The man held out his hand and shook Henry's. 'I'm Franz. I'm pleased to meet you. Everything appears to be in order. We'll spend another few minutes separately in these gardens then I'll head out. Follow me at a safe distance. We'll exit through Königin-Luise-Strasse. If, at any stage, I remove my hat then that's a signal something is wrong. In that case, keep on walking and make your way back to the station, for which you'll need to take a circuitous route. Assuming everything is in order, you'll see me enter a house – no more than five minutes from here. Allow two minutes from when I enter before you approach. There's a small window above the front door. Only approach the house if the curtains in that window are open. If they're closed, head back to the hotel. Have you got all that?'

Henry nodded.

'Good. Now point me in a northerly direction. I'm sure no-one's watching us, but just in case they are, they'll see you directing me.'

For the next few minutes they strolled apart around the Italian garden. Henry did his best to appear fascinated by the plants. A group of young Luftwaffe officers were also walking around and he wondered if their presence might cause a delay, but then he noticed the lawyer head out of the gardens. He followed him until he entered the white house on the corner of Arno-Holz Strasse.

Allow two minutes from when I enter before you approach.

He had slowed his pace right down and allowed himself one quick glance behind him. The area appeared to be deserted. In a house across the street a maid had come out to put something in a bin and was looking at him. He bent down to tie his shoelaces and a glance at his watch told him a minute and a half had elapsed since Hermann had entered the house. He would head over now.

The curtains in the small window above the porch were open and as he walked down the path the front door opened. Hermann was in the hall, gesturing for him to go upstairs. The landing was dark; he could only just make out two doorways in a corridor. One of them opened and at first the woman in the doorway was only in silhouette, with the light flooding in behind her. She gestured for him to come into the room. It was a small lounge with two sofas and a table in the corner: a boy and a girl were sitting on the sofa. By now, Franz Hermann had joined him and made the introductions. 'Alfred and Sophia.' The boy and the girl both stood up and shook his hand, the girl only after being prompted to do so by her brother. 'Herr Hesse is a friend of the family from Switzerland, from Zürich,' said Hermann.

Alfred looked younger than his 12 years: he had a pleasant face that showed signs of beginning to turn handsome and the fair hair his father had described. He was thin and slightly gaunt-looking, with a pale, unhealthy complexion that no doubt owed much to having been confined indoors for so long. He had a natural smile, but it did reveal a set of yellow teeth.

Henry was unable to gauge whether Alfred's sister looked older or younger than five, but Sophia did share her brother's unhealthily pale complexion. She held her head down and stared up at whoever she was looking at with enormous, dark eyes that managed to appear both innocent and knowing at the same time. She had a head of thick, dark hair that fell over her thin shoulders and was a clutching a dirty toy rabbit close to her.

And this is Rosa.

Rosa.

Roza.

With long, dark hair that flowed over her slim shoulders and dark eyes that sparkled, this Rosa looked too much like her Russian namesake. In a lesser light she could easily be mistaken for her. And though it was ten years since Henry had last seen Roza in the flesh, in truth he'd seen her image most nights since then, far too stark and too lifelike to have allowed her to fade from his memory. This Rosa was as he imagined Roza would have grown up to be: the face slightly more lined, the small breasts now fuller under the blouse and cardigan, the eyes having lived that much longer and experienced that much more. He fully expected her to gently touch his wrist and then, as she was wont to do in the dreams, grip him tightly and admonish him. 'You were the one person I thought understood me, you were someone I trusted,' she'd said then, certain in the knowledge of the fate that awaited her.

Roza.

Rosa smiled and shook his hand then asked the children to leave the room.

'Go upstairs. I'll call you down later. And remember, be quiet!'

The children silently shuffled out of the room. When Rosa spoke again Henry noticed she did so in such a soft voice it was barely above a whisper.

'This is the house of Franz's mother. She is elderly and infirm, and I look after her. I'm a doctor, but as far as she's concerned, I'm a nurse. She has no idea I'm Jewish and nor does she have any inkling the children are here, which is why we have to be so quiet. Her hearing is very bad, but we're careful nonetheless. The children never go downstairs. We have been here for well over a year and life is barely tolerable. The children have to live in silence: we can't risk putting the lights on when it gets dark. We're so grateful to Franz, but life is difficult: we have limited food, despite Franz's generosity. Gunter helps too, but he has to be careful as his wife knows nothing. We live in constant fear that someone will find out about us. Gunter feels that at least we should try to get Alfred out, he's insistent about that and I've come round to accepting it, even though it breaks my heart. I understand you've come to help; I'm so grateful. Please tell us everything.'

Over the following hour Henry went through the plan in detail. Rosa was impassive, perched on the edge of the sofa, straight-backed and occasionally asking him to repeat himself. Once, Rosa placed her hand on his, allowing her long, thin fingers to brush his wrist. Henry must have showed his emotions because Franz Hermann leant forward.

'Are you alright, Henri?'

'Pardon?' He felt as if though he'd just woken up, momentarily unsure of exactly where he was.

'Are you alright? You look worried.'

'No, no… I'm fine. I was just thinking about what we have to do. There's so much detail to think about.'

They both agreed that if Alfred's hair could be dyed and styled like that of Andreas, then, along with the glasses, he would have a reasonable resemblance to the Swiss boy, especially given that the passport photograph was taken two years previously. Even the most rigorous person inspecting it would have to acknowledge Andreas had aged.

'Alfred is an intelligent boy,' said Rosa. 'I know that most mothers would say that, but he is. I'm sure he'll be able to remember the details of the cover story, but how he'll act under pressure is a different matter: we simply don't know, do we? He's well aware of how much danger we're in. He'll know he may never see us again.'

Henry only realised Rosa was crying when he saw Franz had moved closer to her and had a comforting arm around her shoulder. Henry looked first at the floor then at the window, awkward and unsure of what to say. At first he slid along the sofa towards Rosa, thinking it was his place to comfort her too, but then he checked himself. It would not do to appear too familiar. How could he begin to explain himself?

'In many respects, we're well-prepared,' said Franz. 'You have the passport and the rail ticket, and you said something about the Swiss side of the border being potentially the hardest part of the journey. From what I've also heard, that's correct: the Swiss are very strict about who they let in: one of their own citizens ought not to be a problem. The Germans will be more concerned with someone who has a German passport trying to leave the country. The priority now is to start work with Alfred.'

Rosa stood up and walked over to the window, drawing the curtain.

'I'd better go and check on your mother, Franz. Then let me have some time alone with Alfred. I'd like to tell him myself. How long can you stay, Herr Hesse?'

'I suppose I have a few hours?'

'No, no,' said Hermann. 'It'll look suspicious if you arrive back too late at the Kaiserhof. There's no question they'll be keeping a note on your movements, which happens with all foreign visitors. You can have one hour with Alfred then come back tomorrow, when you'll have all day.'

* * *

It was the Friday, the last day of February, and as the train pulled out of Potsdam station Henry noticed that Alfred, who he could now only think of as Andreas Hedinger, was crying.

It was a very private cry, the silent type where a few tears trickle down the cheek and any sobs are suppressed by a cough and biting the lip. Andreas had shifted in his seat so he was looking directly out of the window and neither of the other passengers in the carriage could possibly see his face. Henry caught glimpses of him in profile, along with the reflection of his face on the window.

Alfred had held himself together so far that morning and over the previous two days. Ten minutes previously, he'd passed his first major test. Security at the station had been lighter than they'd expected, with the main check being to ensure the tickets were in order. But Henry knew that sooner or later they would be questioned, and that had happened during the wait at Potsdam station when a Gestapo officer had entered their compartment, with two Wehrmacht soldiers waiting in corridor outside.

Tickets. Identity documents. Quick.

The Gestapo officer's eyes darted from Henry to Andreas and

back again, then to the other two men. Both appeared to be travelling on business: one to Jena and the other to Würzburg. The Gestapo officer seemed satisfied with their papers. Then it was Henry's turn.

'Your ticket is to Stuttgart.'

'Yes: then we're travelling to Zürich.'

'Let me see those tickets.'

He studied them then said to Alfred, 'You are travelling together?'

'Yes.'

'You are related?'

'No, Andreas is the son of a friend and colleague. He's been in Berlin visiting while I was on business in the city. His parents asked me to look after him.'

'What is your business?'

'I work for a bank: Bank Leu. Here's my letter of accreditation.'

The Gestapo man read every word then turned to Alfred. 'You: your papers.'

Alfred handed over the passport.

Say as little as possible and, when you do, don't speak too clearly: the Germans will obviously expect a Swiss person to have an accent.

'What's your date of birth?'

That was no problem. They'd been working very hard over the past couple of days.

Two more questions and I'll begin to worry.

'And where did you visit in Berlin?'

Henry did begin to worry. Surely the Gestapo man would spot Alfred was speaking with a Berlin accent, certainly not a Swiss one.

'Pardon?'

'I said, where did you visit in Berlin?'

The carriage door opened and one of the Wehrmacht soldiers came in.

'Otto wants your help in the front: there's a problem.'

Too easy. Every minute of your visit will be laced with danger.

But that was that. Henry wanted to tell Alfred how well he had done, but all he was able to do was smile.

* * *

Alfred had been a model student, carefully writing down the details he needed to remember to pass as Andreas Hedinger from Zürich and memorising the story about how he had come to be in Berlin with Herr Hesse, who was such a good friend of his parents. He was so good to have agreed to take him to Berlin with him.

My father is so busy, I hardly see him these days! He kept promising to take me to Berlin and was always cancelling. Herr Hesse has been so very kind!

That was the agreed line they would take if anyone questioned why he was in Berlin with Henry. In an effort to persuade Alfred to believe in the story, they all kept up the pretence of how plausible it was. The adults knew the first line of their defence lay in the paperwork: if that in any way failed to convince, then the story would be probed and Henry knew it would not stand up to a lot of scrutiny. Their displays of confidence in the story must have worked: by the time they got on the train in Berlin, Henry had even come to believe it himself.

Henry had gone to the Reichsbank first thing on the Wednesday morning – the briefest of trips, just enough to be able to show the hotel where he was going. From there, he travelled down to Dahlem and spent the whole day with Alfred. Gunter Reinhart had joined them for an hour in the afternoon: when he left, it was to say farewell to Alfred. He followed the same pattern on the Thursday. Franz brought Alfred to the station on the Friday morning. His hair had been cut and dyed, and along with the wire-framed spectacles, the passage of time and the relatively poor quality of the photograph, he presented more than a passing resemblance to Andreas Hedinger. Alfred stood on the platform clutching his small knapsack with a few clothes and one or two other innocuous items in it. In the pocket of his jacket was the Swiss passport, his lifeline. Franz shook hands briefly with both of them and disappeared into the crowd.

* * *

After Potsdam, there had been a long wait in Leipzig and when the train finally left the city it moved very slowly through Saxony, meaning they were more than two hours behind schedule when they arrived in Jena. Henry spent the long hours alternating between staring out of the window and closing his eyes but, when he did so, Roza was staring at him as always.

Henry knew their chances of getting into Switzerland that night were remote. By the time the train crossed over from Thuringia into Bavaria, the rain that had accompanied them since Jena had become incessant. Alfred sat quietly in one position: he had eaten very little apart from a sausage and milk Henry had bought on the platform at Leipzig. Since Potsdam he had appeared composed.

There was another long wait in Würzburg and they were joined in their carriage by three new passengers: a woman with a pinched face accompanied by a pretty teenage daughter and a Waffen SS Obersturmführer who was one small glass of something short of being drunk. Henry saw the boy tense as the SS officer stumbled into the carriage. At the sight of the girl, who could have been no more than 17, the Obersturmführer's eyes lit up. For the next half hour he did his best to impress her, while the girl tried to ignore him, helped by the clear disapproval of her mother.

Then he turned his attention to the boy. *Where are you from? Switzerland? I LOVE Switzerland! The Swiss are our friends! YOU are my friend. Where have you been in Germany? Tell me what you saw in Berlin.*

Henry struggled hard to conceal his amazement as Alfred confidently enthused about everything he'd seen in Berlin, not least the soldiers – he loved seeing the soldiers and the marching, and it was so exciting, far more exciting than anything we have in Zürich or indeed anywhere in Switzerland. He'd love to return to Germany, maybe when he was older he could even…

Fortunately the SS man seemed to be oblivious to Alfred's apparent lack of a Swiss accent, helped no doubt by the contents of the flask he'd finished since joining the train. Within minutes he had insisted on being called Karl and was showing Alfred his Mauser automatic and describing how he had captured Paris single-handed. *When you're old enough to meet girls, Andreas, the first*

*place you go is Paris! Which football team do you support Andreas? FC
Zürich? Ah, Grasshoppers! A good team.*

Just outside the city, still in the blanket darkness of the
countryside, the train pulled to a noisy halt. It was seven o'clock.
Silence for a few minutes, then shouting and the sound of dogs
barking. It took an eternity for the commotion to work its way
down the train. When it reached them, a Gestapo officer who
seemed to be wider than he was tall squeezed into their
compartment, breathless and with sweat dripping from his brow.
He was wearing a leather raincoat that was so tight it remained
unbuttoned. He looked around then shouted at Alfred.

'You: get up... now!'

Henry clutched the seat to stop himself swaying. The boy was
so terrified he did not move a muscle, but all the blood drained
from his face.

'Did you not hear me? Come with me now.'

The SS Obersturmführer rose slowly and slightly unsteadily,
standing directly in front of the Gestapo officer and very close to
him. He was at least a foot taller than the other man and used
every inch of that to ensure he looked down on him with the
maximum effect.

'What's the problem?'

'We've had reports that some Jewish boys got on the train at
Würzburg. The police discovered some of the vermin hiding in a
cellar and had been chasing the gang: they last saw them in the
vicinity of the station. We're checking all youths on the train.'

'Well, Andreas is my friend and it's impossible he's Jewish.'

He was shouting at the Gestapo officer, flecks of spit spraying onto the other man's reddening face. When the Gestapo officer replied, it was in a much more uncertain voice.

'And how do you know that?'

'Because he's Swiss!'

The big man wiped his face with his sleeve, clearly puzzled by the Obersturmführer's logic.

'I still need to check his papers and question him though…' He held his arm out towards Alfred, beckoning him to join him. The Obersturmführer grabbed hold of the Gestapo man's arm and pushed it down.

'You won't need to be doing that.'

'How come?'

'Because I got on the train at Würzburg and Andreas was already on it, so stop wasting your time.'

The Gestapo officer appeared reluctant to argue. By now a pair of Alsatians were barking outside the open door of the compartment. 'Let me have a look at your passport,' he said to the boy.

Andreas passed it to him. Henry noticed the Gestapo man's hands were trembling as he quickly flicked through the passport, before handing it back.

'That's all in order.'

'Next time, try and serve the Reich in more useful ways,' the Obersturmführer spat at him as he left the compartment, defeated.

It was nine o'clock by the time the train arrived in Stuttgart. Henry knew he could have gone to the nearby Hotel Victoria, where he imagined that Katharina Hoch was still the night manager, but it would be too risky. He decided instead they would stay overnight in the station, where there was a large air-raid shelter. The first train to Zürich was at 8.20 in the morning, which meant he would also have an opportunity to send a telegram to Hedinger.

The air-raid shelter where they slept was crowded. The boy was still in a state of anxiety and stress from the events of the day, and Henry had to whisper to him how well he had done; how proud his parents would be of him. *We're nearly there now, you'll be safe.* They found a corner of a wide bench at the back of the shelter into which they wedged themselves. Henry put his arm round the boy and gradually felt him relax, and within a few minutes he was fast asleep, on what he both hoped and feared would be his last night in his homeland.

* * *

Chapter 20: Stuttgart, Zürich and Berlin, March 1941

For the first few hours in the air-raid shelter in Stuttgart, Henry hardly slept. The spot they had found turned out to have a noisy pipe running directly above it and every time he dropped off he was soon woken by the sound of clanging hissing air. Then, when he did sleep, Roza would appear: her admonishing eyes fixed on him, telling him what he knew all too well. For a full hour she haunted him: she was there if he shut his eyes tight and still there when he opened them wide and there when he held his head tight in his hands.

But then the strangest thing happened: Roza stared at him in her familiar fashion, her eyes full of sadness and hatred. But then her face began to dissolve and when it came back into focus the dark brown eyes were there as was the dark hair flowing over slim shoulders, but now the features belonged to Rosa and, with that, an unexpected calm came over Henry. Rosa was no less sad, but there was the faintest of smiles on her face and a look of pleading in her eyes. And as the very beginnings of an idea began to emerge in Henry's mind, a calm he was quite unused to came over him and the few hours of sleep between then and when he woke up were the deepest he'd experienced for years.

People began to leave the shelter from six in the morning and by half six it was almost deserted. Henry had hoped to stay until nearer to eight o'clock, but when they ventured up onto the main station concourse they spotted a café was open and they were able to remain there for the next hour and a half. At eight, the telegram booth in the station opened and Henry sent a message to Michael

Hedinger, who he knew would have gone into the bank that morning as arranged.

Departing Stuttgart 8.20 stop Arriving Zürich 2.40 stop Papers all in order stop

Papers all in order: Alfred is with me, a successful mission… so far.

The train left Stuttgart at 8.30 but then was held at a red light on the outskirts of the city to allow a military train to pass, its open trucks carrying dozens of tanks. By lunchtime it had made its steady progress through Swabia towards the border town of Singen, the last stop in Germany before Switzerland. They were held at an isolated platform, where they were told by a loudspeaker announcement that any passengers wishing to travel on into Switzerland should remain in their compartments: all other passengers should leave the train forthwith.

For half an hour there was no sign of anything. There was just one other passenger in their compartment, an immaculately dressed German man with the long elegant hands of a pianist and the complexion of someone who rarely ventured outdoors. He had spent most of the journey reading sheet music and attending to his nails, occasionally removing a watch from his jacket with a flourish, studying it with some fascination, tutting then returning it to his pocket. Eventually, the delay in Singen was too much for him. He was going to see what was going on, he told Henry, and left the compartment. Henry leaned over to Alfred, who he had noticed looked considerably more relaxed than yesterday. 'Don't forget, this is the most dangerous part of the journey. The Swiss border police will be watching for anyone trying to get into Switzerland who shouldn't. Don't make any mistakes. Soon you'll be able to relax. You have done very well, my boy. But be careful now…'

Alfred looked worried and Henry wasn't sure he'd said the right thing. *Maybe I should have just kept quiet.*

Their fellow passenger returned to the carriage. 'They've got to wait for the Swiss police to arrive,' he told them. 'I thought the Swiss were meant to be efficient. Ridiculous.'

Ten minutes later the Swiss border police arrived on the platform, where they and the German officers greeted each other like old friends. Working in pairs – one Swiss, one German – they went through the train compartment by compartment.

The Swiss officer who eventually arrived looked no more than 20. He checked the passport of the pianist, asked to see his return ticket then handed them to the German policeman. Both appeared to be satisfied.

The officer then turned to Henry. *Passport.* It was only when he saw the Swiss passport and said 'grüezi' that a fatal flaw in their plan they had overlooked until now hit Henry hard in the face.

The Swiss border policeman had used the traditional Swiss-German greeting. If he was going to speak in Swiss-German, the boy would not understand. He and his story would unravel very quickly.

'Where have you travelled from in Germany?' he asked, still speaking in Swiss-German.

'I've been in Berlin, on business for Bank Leu. Here's my letter of accreditation.' Henry made a point of replying in standard German.

The young policeman took it and read it carefully. 'So how long have you been in Germany for?' Still in Swiss-German.

'Since Monday.' Standard German. It had become like a surreal game.

'The boy: is he with you?'

'Andreas is the son of friends. He's been visiting Berlin.' Henry had tried to avoid looking at the boy, but caught a glimpse of his worried face as he mentioned him.

'And you stayed where in Berlin?'

'Jan, I keep telling you! Speak proper German; don't confuse me!' It was the German policeman, standing in the doorway of the carriage and clearly impatient.

His Swiss counterpart shrugged and took the passport of Andreas Hedinger. He checked the visa, looked up at Alfred and back again at the photo, repeating this three or four times, his bright-blue eyes darting up and down.

'How old are you?' He spoke in standard German. Alfred gave Andreas' age and date of birth.

'Did you enjoy Berlin?'

'Yes sir, thank you. But I'm looking forward to going home.'

* * *

He was in Zürich for less than 40 hours.

They arrived in the city at three o'clock on the Saturday afternoon and were met at the station by Herr and Frau Hedinger. Alfred had shown no signs of relief as they crossed the border into Switzerland and by the time they arrived at the station he was in a state of shock, totally overwhelmed by what was happening to him. The fact he was free and safe did not seem to occur to him as he was warmly greeted by the Hedingers. Frau Hedinger led Alfred over to the station café for a hot chocolate while Michael Hedinger and Henry found a quiet bench. Henry handed over the papers.

'Everything was in order?'

'Yes, thank you. Your arrangements were very good; faultless in fact.'

A tall man in a trilby was strolling purposefully towards them: it seemed he had appeared from nowhere. He removed his leather gloves and shook Henry's hand.

'So that's Alfred, eh?'

'I wondered when you might show up, Edgar.'

'You didn't imagine I'd miss this, did you? I trust there were no problems?'

'No. It was nerve-wracking, but we've arrived in one piece.'

'As I can see. Hedinger, have you sorted your wretched documents out?'

Hedinger took the sealed envelopes from Henry and handed him a few more in return. 'You're returning to Berlin on Monday,' he said as he stood up. 'Edgar will tell you all about it. He has your tickets.'

'You're going to be alright with the boy?'

Hedinger nodded.

'And you'll send the telegram to Reinhart?'

'First thing Monday morning, as we arranged.'

'Won't Reinhart want to know sooner that Alfred's arrived safely?'

'I'm sure he would, but this all has to look proper,' said Edgar.

'It'd be odd for an official of the Reichsbank to receive a telegram from Bank Leu on a Saturday acknowledging safe receipts of papers. It'll have to wait until Monday. By the time you see Reinhart on Tuesday morning, he'll know Alfred arrived safely and he can hand the other document over to you. Go on Hedinger, you'd better take Alfred off. Henry, perhaps you want to go and say goodbye?'

Alfred had relaxed by the time Henry approached him and Frau Hedinger in the station café. He had been drinking a hot chocolate and was devouring an enormous cream pastry. He had a big grin on his face.

'Alfred was telling me he loves dogs but has never had one. He's so looking forward to meeting Mitzi! And guess what, Herr Hesse? She's expecting puppies! I've told Alfred he can choose one of them to be his very own pet.'

Henry embraced Alfred and promised he'd come and visit him. He mustn't worry; everything would be fine. When he released the boy from his embrace he noticed Alfred's eyes were moist. He kept saying 'thank you' and as he disappeared out of the station he turned round and gave Henry a nervous little wave.

* * *

Henry and Edgar spent what remained of the weekend in the apartment above the hardware shop on Basteiplatz. When they arrived there, Basil Remington-Barber was making up a camp bed in the lounge. The three of them sat around the table.

'You're booked on the six o'clock train on Monday morning.

That got you into Berlin that evening, didn't it?'

'Yes: I was fortunate with the connection in Stuttgart. Coming back yesterday was a different matter. True, we left Berlin a bit later, but whether it was bomb damage or something else, it was a much slower journey: hence the reason we had to stay over in Stuttgart.'

'I trust that you didn't go anywhere near the Victoria?' asked Remington-Barber.

'No, we stayed overnight in the station – in an air-raid shelter.'

'Let's get down to business. Here's your ticket for Monday. We want to get you and the document back here as quickly as possible, so the plan is that you go to the Reichsbank first thing on the Tuesday morning, hand Bank Leu's envelopes to Reinhart and he'll give you the ones to be brought back here. One of the sealed envelopes will contain the document – he'll let you know which one. According to Hedinger, neither the German nor the Swiss police have ever tried to open a sealed envelope from any of the banks. I imagine that'd be bad for business. I can see no reason why you shouldn't be able to leave Berlin by lunchtime. I know the couriers often hang around for a few days, but we need to get you back here so we'll risk it. You won't make it into Switzerland that night, but go to Stuttgart then take the first train out on Wednesday morning. Does that all make sense?'

'Yes… but shouldn't the document be concealed?'

'We thought of that,' said Remington-Barber, 'but if they decide to search you then they'll probably find it anyway. As Edgar says, they don't touch bank envelopes. You're booked in the Kaiserhof there – here's the telegram confirming it. You still have the letter of accreditation from the bank? Good. And of course your passport has the correct visas. Tell me Henry, what's Gunter Reinhart like?'

Henry shrugged. 'He's a German banker, which seems to be rather like a Swiss banker and I daresay British bankers: efficient enough, but what do you want me to say? I'll doubt we'll become close friends, if that's what you mean. He's very tall, too, for what it's worth.'

'What I think we mean,' said Remington-Barber, 'is what kind of a chap do you think he is? Is he trustworthy? After all, we've used one of our few agents able to travel in and out of Germany to help his son escape. How do we know this document he's promising us is genuine, or is it a trick. Has he just been leading us along as a ruse to get Alfred out?'

'I've really no idea,' said Henry. 'He seems genuine enough. I suppose if the document turns out to be either a fake or not exist at all then he runs the risk of upsetting us and that could have implications for his own safety – and that of Rosa and Sophia.'

Edgar and Remington-Barber looked at each other, partially reassured.

'You see, he still wants to help Rosa escape and obviously that means little Sophia too.'

'I can see why Reinhart wanted to get his son out, but why his ex-wife?'

'He obviously cares very much for her and, to be frank with you, I can see why. She really is the most marvellous woman, you know. She's been holed up in that house for well over a year now. Poor little Sophia can barely speak; she's so terrified of making a noise. It would be marvellous if we could do something to help them.'

'I beg your pardon?' Edgar was staring at Henry as if he had completely misheard him.

'I was just saying I thought it'd be marvellous if we could help Alfred's mother and sister.'

Edgar sat there open-mouthed. It was Remington-Barber who spoke next.

'Help in what way, Henry?'

'Possibly help them to leave Germany?'

'Has Reinhart asked you raise this?'

'No.'

'So it's not a condition of his handing over the document?'

'No.'

'So why on earth are you raising the matter then?'

'Don't forget I've just come back from Berlin, Edgar. It's like a bloody prison camp, uniforms everywhere. It can only be a matter of time before they're caught. If there was any way we could help get them out before that happens then we'd be doing the decent thing.'

Edgar slammed the table with his hand. 'Are you stark raving mad? Who the hell do you think we are – the Red bloody Cross?'

'I was only thinking…'

'Well don't. What's got into you? Have you fallen in love with this woman or something?'

Henry hesitated as he realised that was exactly what he had done. He could feel his face reddening. 'No, not at all. I just feel awfully sorry for them.'

'Well don't,' said Edgar, who was no longer shouting. 'In our profession, we simply can't afford to have those kinds of feelings. Do you understand?'

Until they saw him off at the station early on the Monday morning, Henry was never alone. Either Edgar or Remington-Barber was always near him. When he got up in the early hours of the Sunday morning to go to the bathroom, Edgar was awake in the lounge, sitting in an armchair he had angled to face the open lounge door. Henry wondered whether talking about Rosa had caused them to distrust him. He had learnt his lesson.

He was woken at four o'clock on the Monday morning for his final briefing. 'When you get back here on Wednesday go straight to Bank Leu on Paradeplatz; hand the envelopes over to Hedinger, apart from the one for us. Understood?'

Yes.

'Use the telephone in Hedinger's office to call this number. Both Edgar and I will be in Bern. One of us will answer. Tell us what train you're catching from Zürich and I'll meet you at Bern station. You'll be back home in Geneva that evening.'

'Assuming everything goes well,' said Edgar, 'we'll put a further 500 pounds into your Credit Suisse account. Two trips in and out of Germany, you'll have deserved it.'

Henry told them how grateful he was. 'Just one thing though,' he said. 'It seems to be the most enormous effort to go to Berlin, bring the boy out and go back again to collect this document.'

'Only way of doing it Henry: Gunter will only release the document once he's sure his son is safe in Switzerland. We've already told you that.'

'Must be a damn important document then.'

'That, Henry, is for us to decide. Oh… and one other thing,' said Edgar as they prepared to leave the apartment. 'That Rosa woman: don't be tempted to go anywhere near her. Forget about her. Understand?'

Henry assured them he understood.

* * *

Gunter Reinhart had left home just after seven o'clock on the Monday morning and, as luck would have it, the U-Bahn and the trams were all running so smoothly he was concerned he would arrive at work too early. It would not do to be noticed. So he got off the tram early on the Unter den Linden and walked the rest of the way. By the time he turned onto Französischestrasse it was 7.40, which was still early but hopefully not so early he would draw attention to himself. He tried to appear as casual as possible as he entered the Reichsbank on Werderscher Markt, but as he found himself alone in the corridors leading to his office his pace quickened.

He waited until five past eight, then he picked up the telephone he had been staring at since he had arrived in his office and dialled an internal number.

Yes, Herr Reinhart: a telegram has indeed arrived for you. I beg your pardon? Yes, from Zürich. From Bank Leu. Our messenger starts at half past eight. I'll ensure he brings it straight to you.

Gunter Reinhart could not bear to wait even for half an hour, so even though it was unusual for him to do so, he went down himself to the telegram bureau in the basement. He did manage to restrain himself from opening the telegram until he was back in his office.

Documentation all in order stop Courier with you again Tuesday stop All well stop Hedinger stop.

He read the telegram twice before folding it up carefully, slipping it into an envelope and placing it in the bottom of his briefcase. He felt he a wave of emotion overwhelm him for a minute or so. Alfred was safe in Switzerland. Now he had to keep his side of the bargain.

He telephoned Funk's private secretary at a quarter past nine.

'Why do you need to see it, Reinhart?'

Funk's private secretary was an unpleasant man who had a habit of following his master around like a dog, his hands held in apparent supplication before him, an admiring smile on his face. He took considerable pleasure in controlling people's access to the Minister and generally making life more difficult in an effort to make himself seem somehow important.

'Because Herr Funk has asked I prepare a paper on dealing with assets that may come under our control should certain events happen and to complete that paper to the Minister's satisfaction I need to see the document once more.'

'When?'

'This morning.'

'This morning! Impossible: I need to accompany Herr Funk to the Reichstag. In any case, Reinhart, you know you need to put your request in writing.'

'Very well. Perhaps you would inform the Minister I will not be able to let him have that paper by the end of today.'

There was a long pause, during which Gunter could hear the Private Secretary's worried breathing at the other end of the line.

'Very well, you can come up now if you promise to be quick.'

He waited in the secure room behind Funk's office while the private secretary fussed around; making sure the document was in order and signed for. He stood behind Reinhart as he opened the document on the table in front of him. There was a distinct smell of mothballs from the secretary's three-piece suit, which had a Nazi Party badge on one lapel and a swastika on the other.

'How long will you be?'

'Maybe half an hour, possibly a bit longer.'

'I'm meant to remain with you,' the private secretary said impatiently, 'but I have to prepare for this meeting at the Reichstag. I'll come back in 20 minutes. Remember; don't write on the document!'

Reinhart had practised in his locked study at home over the weekend and he reckoned he could photograph the whole of Directive 21 in ten minutes. He waited for five then walked over to the door, which the private secretary had left ajar. Through the gap he could see the man busy at his desk at the other end of the outer office. He waited another minute then pushed the door a bit more, so it was still open, but only just.

The camera Franz Hermann had given him was tiny and he had been warned it was very sensitive, so he had to concentrate on remaining as still as possible as he photographed each page twice. He had placed himself with his back to the door, which would give him a second or two to react but the danger of being caught was still acute.

It took 12 minutes to complete the task and he allowed a further five minutes to check the document was in order, that he had made some notes and to compose himself. When the private secretary returned he was able to announce he was ready.

'Would you like to check my notes?'

The secretary glanced at them then checked the Directive carefully. He seemed to be slightly disappointed everything was in order.

* * *

Henry Hunter arrived in Berlin slightly later than he had the previous Monday and the staff at the Kaiserhof seemed to be pleased to see him again. The concierge enquired whether he required advice on any trips during his stay, but Henry assured him this was a much shorter visit: he expected to leave Berlin the next day. He noticed the concierge making a discreet note as he walked away from his desk.

He was in Gunter Reinhart's office by 10.10 on the Tuesday morning. Reinhart carefully opened the sealed envelopes from Bank Leu and signed a receipt for each one, making a note in a ledger on his desk as he did so.

'Please sit down, Herr Hesse. You're making me nervous standing there; this will take a few minutes more.'

Reinhart quietly walked over to his office door and opened it, checking no-one was outside. When he came back in, he silently slipped a lock down. He gestured for Henry to move his chair nearer the desk.

'Everything is in order,' he was speaking quietly. 'I received the telegram from Herr Hedinger this morning: he told me the package arrived safely. Thank you: tell me, how was the journey?'

Henry told him the journey was fine. So was the package.

'It goes without saying that I'm indebted to you, but I'm now about to repay that debt in full. There are four envelopes here,' he pointed to a pile of bulky envelopes on the desk in front of him, 'for you to take to Bank Leu. You'll sign for these in a moment. This one...' Reinhart pointed to the third envelope in the pile, 'is the one that's to go elsewhere. You understand – I don't need to be more explicit, do I?'

Reinhart held up the package, which as far as Henry could see was identical to the other three. 'You'll see there's a tiny tear on the flap of the envelope here, can you see? And, on the front, this corner of the label has come slightly loose. There's one final way of distinguishing this envelope: the others have a full-stop after the word 'Reichsbank' – before our address. On this one, there's a comma. In all other respects, it's identical to the other three. Tell them I had to photograph it: obviously I couldn't possibly take the original. The document is on film in here.'

* * *

It was a quarter to eleven when he left the Reichsbank: he would need to be at the station by 2.30, giving him a shade under four hours to do what he had planned. He was cutting it very fine; he would need to hurry.

He walked, neither too fast nor too slowly, down by the canal as far as the Spittelmarkt U-Bahn station. He passed one or two shops on the way, but he didn't want to go into one until he was further away from Werderscher Markt. The journey to Gleisdreieck took 12 minutes; it was now a quarter past eleven. He changed lines, heading west to Wittenberg Platz where he changed onto another U-Bahn line, now heading south. By the time he arrived at Podbielski Allee it was a quarter to twelve. The last leg of the journey had taken him much longer than he had expected. It would take at least another ten minutes to get there and he needed to find a shop first.

He came across a parade of three shops: one with a collection of ladies dresses hanging forlornly behind a dusty window, another appeared to be some kind of bookshop with more pictures of Hitler than books and the third was a grocers. He was annoyed to see a queue of a dozen or so people waiting outside the shop: he wasn't sure he had the time to wait.

'How long will I have to queue for?' he asked the man at the front of the queue. The man was wearing a suit and a smart overcoat, but his posture was stooped and he had a sallow expression. He looked as if he had not understood the question: Henry repeated it. The man said nothing but pointed to a handwritten sign stuck to the inside of the shop's glass door.

Jews may only shop here between four and five o'clock.

Taped beneath it was a cartoon cut out from a newspaper showing a Jewish man with a long nose stealing food from angelic-looking children.

'I'm sure you can go in now,' said the man. 'It's us who have to wait.'

The shopkeeper had tiny eyes and an enormous belly that appeared to rest on the counter-top. His face was heavily pockmarked and there was a growing layer of perspiration on his forehead.

'I feel like having a bath every time those rats come in here,' he said, gesturing at the queue outside the window. 'Some of them start queuing first thing in the morning, you know? There's not much they can buy these days: not even white bread or vegetables! Good thing too. I'm happy to take their money though, better that I have it than some others: I joined the party before '33, so I reckon I'm entitled to it. Now, how can I help you sir?'

'I need to buy some food, but I'm afraid I have no ration book.'

'No ration book?' The man's tiny eyes narrowed. *A problem.*

'I'm from Switzerland, you see. I'm visiting friends for lunch and would like to take them some food as a gift. I'd be happy to pay in Swiss Francs, if that helps.'

The shopkeeper's little eyes lit up. *No longer a problem.*

He indicated for Henry to move to the back of the shop, where it was darker and further away from the prying eyes of the people queuing outside.

'Of course,' he whispered. 'You understand it's hard to charge you the exact rate, because of difficulties, you understand?'

Henry understood. He would be very generous, he assured the shopkeeper.

Five minutes later he left the shop, unable to look at the people waiting until four before they could enter. The queue seemed to have grown since he had gone in.

Within ten minutes he was knocking gently at the door of the white house on the corner of Arno-Holz Strasse. The interior of the house was dark and he could not hear a sound. He waited a minute and then knocked again. A lady being pulled along by two yapping dogs watched him carefully as she passed by. Still no reply. He knocked once more. It was now past midday and he was beginning to worry. He became aware of a slight movement to his right, where the curtains were drawn on the window of the front room. A few seconds later, he heard Rosa's worried voice from behind the door.

'Who is it please?'

'It's me, Henri!' The door opened quickly and a hand poked out, gesturing for him to enter. *Quickly.*

Since he'd begun to formulate this plan, he had imagined that Rosa would be overwhelmed with gratitude to see him. She would be relieved. Instead, she looked horrified.

'It's me Rosa: Henri.'

'I know it's you. You must keep your voice down. What on earth are you doing here? What's the matter? What's happened to Alfred?'

Her dark brown eyes were just like Roza's, but now they were red around the lids, as though she had been crying.

'Everything's alright Rosa. I came to visit you and Sophia. I've brought food.'

'But what about Alfred? Please tell me.'

'Alfred's safe, Rosa,' Henry moved closer as he spoke, placing a hand on her shoulders. She backed away. 'He's in Zürich. I managed to get him there safely. You don't need to worry.'

'You shouldn't have come here. It's so dangerous. Go upstairs quickly. You can't stay long. I have to give Frau Hermann her lunch. Go upstairs and let me settle her. I'll be a few minutes.'

In the small lounge upstairs there was no sign of Sophia. When she finally came upstairs, Henry asked Rosa where she was.

'In bed: she's been there almost all the time since Alfred left. She misses him so much that it's making her ill. He was wonderful to her, her only companion. I don't think she's uttered more than half a dozen sentences since he left.'

'Well perhaps these'll cheer her up.' Henry triumphantly emptied the content of his bag on the rug and placed a packet of sweets and some chocolate to one side, then handed Rosa a large cheese, a long sausage, a bag of fruit and another of vegetables. Rosa looked embarrassed.

'I don't know what to say.' Tears were streaming down her face. She knelt down beside him and gently touched his wrist with her fingers, holding them there for a few seconds before busying herself sorting the food. 'Of course, I'm very grateful, but you coming here is so dangerous.'

Henry raised his eyebrows.

'I'm serious, Henri. Our only hope is to stay here with no-one finding out. Franz does his best to ensure we get as few visitors as possible, but neighbours spy on each other and watch out for comings and goings.'

'Come with me Rosa: you and Sophia, come with me.'

She looked at him as if she had misheard what he had said.

'Come where?'

'Back to Switzerland.'

She burst out laughing. 'Henri – do you think we haven't thought about how we can escape ever since we got here? It's impossible: we've no papers other than our own and they are useless because I'm wanted by the Gestapo. I know you're trying to be kind but...' She held up her hands in a gesture of helplessness.

'But you can't stay here, Rosa. What if something happens to the old lady? And what about food? People say it's becoming scarcer. Then there's the neighbours... someone could inform on you. I could help you. I could get papers.'

Rosa was looking at him as if she had misheard him again.

'How can you do that?'

At that moment there was a weak shout from downstairs.

'I must go Henri: Frau Hermann wants her lunch.'

Henry grabbed her by the arm and moved towards her. 'I'll get papers Rosa, I'll be back. Trust me.'

As she stood up, Henry did too, positioning himself immediately in front of her.

'Henri, please: I have to go to her. You must leave now. In any case, sometimes an old friend comes to see her on Tuesdays. Please let me get through.'

He hesitated for a moment, wondering whether it would be wrong to embrace her. He had expected her to be more grateful. She pushed past him and headed downstairs, beckoning for him to follow her, a finger pressed to her lips for him to keep quiet.

* * *

He eventually left Berlin on a train for Nuremberg just before three, only a few minutes late, and the journey was much quicker than the one to Stuttgart a few days earlier. He arrived in Nuremberg at seven o'clock and it felt like a garrison town, troops everywhere. The concourse of the station was a seething mass of grey uniform, with a sprinkling of black. He could see few other civilians.

He joined a long queue of soldiers at the ticket office and had enough time to observe that most of them belonged to the Seventeenth Infantry Division: a gift for Edgar. When he reached the window he discovered the first train to Stuttgart was at 8.20 the next morning. 'All being well,' added the ticket clerk as he carefully stamped then initialled Henry's ticket.

Henry calculated he could be in Stuttgart sometime late morning and Zürich by mid-afternoon. *All being well.*

The clerk told him he would find the hotels if he turned left out of the station and walked over to the next block. There he found a selection of grey buildings, each reflecting the ubiquitous uniforms milling around on the street. He went into the first three hotels, each more miserable than the previous one and settled on the fourth only because it was now pouring with rain and he was exhausted.

As the manager laboriously completed the paperwork that would allow him the privilege of being a guest there for one night, Henry had an opportunity to have a look into what the manager called the dining room. If pushed, Henry would have described it as a workhouse, a memory from Dickensian novels read out loud at the end of dark autumn afternoons at school in England.

'You'd better go and eat now, the dining room closes in 20 minutes,' the manager said in what Henry thought could be an Austrian accent.

'I'm alright, thank you,' said Henry, the smell of grease and tobacco settling already at the back of his throat. 'I think I'll eat elsewhere.'

'You'll be lucky: there is no "elsewhere" these days. Leave your case here and go in and eat.'

He reluctantly went in to the dining room, having passed up the offer of leaving his case with the manager. There were two long tables inside and each had six or seven men – only men – hunched around it, all eyeing each other suspiciously and spooning black stew into their mouths in apparent unison.

Henry found a small space at the end of one table and the man next to him reluctantly moved along no more than an inch or two. No sooner had he sat down than a filthy hand deposited a bowl in front of him. The thumb and one finger were dipped in the stew. Henry moved his gaze up the hand and the frayed sleeve just above it: both belonged to a hunched body and pale face flecked with red sores, a woman in her fifties who looked as if she were about to collapse.

A plate of black bread was pushed in front of him, along with a glass of watery beer. No-one was speaking to anyone else around the table and Henry was grateful for that.

His night was not any more comfortable: the room had bare floorboards and just one small threadbare rug by the bed. There was a basin with a stained sink by a window that had a crack in the glass and Henry doubted the sheets had been changed since the last guest but one. As there was no functioning lock on the door, he wedged the single chair in the room against it and lay on the bed fully clothed, his briefcase containing the sealed envelopes under a pillow that smelt of sweat. In the distance he could hear the muffled sound of explosions: he could not tell whether it was bombs or anti-aircraft fire, but when he went over to the window and peeled back the blackout curtain he could see flashes far to the north.

He left the hotel at seven in the morning, the manager and the woman from the dining room confused as to why he declined their offer of breakfast ('but you've paid for it sir!').

For the next hour the station café provided a welcome refuge from the all-pervading odour of the hotel. The Stuttgart train left on time and the connection from there to Zürich was good and he arrived at 2.10. He was under pressure now. There was a train to Bern at 5.10, which was the one he would need to catch if Edgar and Remington-Barber were not to be too suspicious about his late arrival. It ought to give him enough time, but only just.

He needed to get to Bank Leu as soon as possible, but only after he had made the phone call. There was a bank of phone booths on the main station concourse, but they felt too public so he left the station and walked across to the Bahnhofquai, where he found a café with phone booth at the rear, well away from the few customers. He rang the number Viktor had given him.

'Yes?'

'Peter is coming round for dinner.'

A pause and a muffled noise at the other end of the line, which sounded as if the person had placed their hand over the receiver and was talking to someone else in the room.

'And will you be bringing wine with you?'

'Yes.'

With that, the line went dead. He checked his watch: it was 2.25: according to Viktor's instructions he was to be at the station exactly one hour after the phone call. That would leave him just over an hour and a half to catch his train: he would need to hurry. He left the café by the back door and took a taxi to Bank Leu's head office on Paradeplatz.

Michael Hedinger was apparently in a hurry. He came down to the reception and took Henry up to his office on the top floor. He checked the three envelopes from the Reichsbank for Bank Leu.

'And the fourth envelope is for your friends?'

'Yes.'

'When do you see them?'

'I'm going to Bern now. May I use your phone to tell them what time I'm likely to be there?'

Hedinger gestured at the phone: *be my guest*.

Edgar answered: 'Welcome home. What kept you?'

'I'm catching the train at ten past five: I ought to be in Bern by eight at the latest. Where shall I meet you?'

'Don't worry old chap, we'll meet you.'

That was that: it was now a quarter to three, he had plenty of time. He could even afford to stroll back to the station along Bahnhofstrasse, which would at least give him time to compose himself.

'And all went well?' asked Hedinger.

'Yes… yes, thank you.'

'And I presume you wish to ask me a question?'

Henry had no idea what the Swiss was on about.

'I'm sorry?'

'Alfred! Don't you want to know how he is?'

'Of course, of course! How is Alfred?'

'My wife and the children and the dog make such a fuss of him: it's as if he has been released from prison. He's such a sweet boy and very considerate. We'll take good care of him. He's obviously sad though. At night we can hear him sobbing in his room. He must miss his mother.'

* * *

Arriving too early for a rendezvous is as dangerous as being late for one.

He had arrived outside the Hauptbahnhof at a quarter past three, ten minutes early. Without thinking, he had continued into the station, assuming he would find a bar then go out onto the concourse ten minutes later. This is what he did, but no sooner had he stepped out onto the concourse than he was aware of two men either side of him, marching him out of a side exit. One of them was Viktor, his face impassive but his voice not disguising his fury.

'We said be at the station one hour after the phone call, not 50 minutes. What do you think you are up to *synok*?'

Henry shook himself from Viktor and the other man, who had now stepped back into the shadows.

'Learn to do as you are told, Henry, you understand? Now, follow me – stay behind me. I will go into a shop and through to the back. You are to do likewise. Sergei will be behind you.'

The shop was a narrow tobacconist in a warren of alleys behind the station. The counter top was already open when Henry arrived. Viktor was in a room at the back, along with a shrivelled-looking man half the size of the Russian. He was dressed in a faded pinstripe suit and peered up at Henry through thick glasses that sat unsteadily on the bridge of his nose.

'Have you spoken with Edgar?' Viktor sounded impatient.

'Yes.'

'Where is he?'

'In Bern: they're expecting me to be on the train that leaves here at ten past five. I've no excuse for not being on that one.'

'Don't worry, you will be. You have it?' Viktor looked anxious.

Henry took the sealed Reichsbank envelope out of his briefcase, but held on to it while he spoke.

'I do Viktor, but it's sealed. How are you going to open it without Edgar and Remington-Barber realising?'

Viktor took the envelope and passed it over to the man, addressing him in German.

'Arndt, what do you reckon?'

The man took the envelope and held it under the light, turning it very slowly one way and the other, moving it close to his eyes then running his fingers along its every surface. He nodded and replied into a squeaky, high-pitched voice.

'This shouldn't be a problem. Give me an hour, but I want everyone out of here.'

'Apart from me,' said Viktor.

'Of course, apart from you, Viktor,' Arndt said obediently, halfbowing as he spoke.

As Henry left the room he could see the man arranging a large camera, a lamp and various tools on a bench. He was about to operate. Henry spent the next 15 minutes standing silently in the alley behind the tobacconist with Sergei. When Viktor called Henry back in, he was clearly finding it hard to contain his excitement. Little Arndt was packing away his equipment, the surgery over. The envelope was handed to him. 'Examine it, please. See how perfect it is.'

Henry looked at it carefully. It was impossible to see how it could have been opened. With a huge arm around his shoulder, Viktor shepherded Henry to a corner of the room and whispered into his ear.

'We have made a copy: you have no idea how important it is, *synok*. We will transmit the entire text to Moscow tonight. You have 40 minutes before your train, so tell me everything you can about this man who supplied the document. It's so important that Moscow will ask me many questions about it: I need to have the answers.'

'Before I do that Viktor, I need to ask a favour of you.'

Viktor looked at him puzzled: a favour? *Henry did not ask favours of them. They asked favours of him.*

'What is it?' he asked, hardly managing to hide his irritation.

He looked at the Russian, wishing he was more sympathetic at times. Even some gratitude wouldn't have gone amiss.

'I don't want to sound like I'm going soft or anything, and I've coped very well in Germany so far, but I have this worry they'll send me back there, and sooner or later, I...'

'Why, have they said anything about that, *synok?*'

'No, but I get the impression they don't exactly have a team of agents queuing up at the border waiting to be sent into Germany. I feel exposed when I'm in Berlin and I was wondering: do you have anyone I could contact there – in an emergency?'

Henry shrugged, eager Viktor should not think the request an unusual one. *What I am I to do – tell him I'm determined to go back there anyway?*

Viktor looked at Henry, suspicious at first but then more understanding.

'Let me see what I can do, Henry. There's the embassy, but I don't trust anyone there. I do have some people, I'll let you know. Now, tell me how you got this document.'

* * *

Chapter 21: London, March 1941

Edgar arrived at Whitchurch Airport just after 12.30 on Monday 10th March on BOAC flight 777 from Lisbon. A black Humber Imperial with military plates was parked close to the base of the aircraft steps and three hours later it deposited an exhausted Edgar outside the building overlooking St James's Square where Christopher Porter was waiting for him in his office on the top floor.

Edgar handed over the film of Directive 21 to Porter, who promptly left the room, returning five minutes later.

'We'll have that developed straight away and sent off to the analysts tonight. They've been told to deal with it as a matter of priority. We'll meet here tomorrow afternoon to hear what they make of it. But well done Edgar: something of a coup to get our hands on that. How's our chap Hunter?'

Edgar leaned back in his chair, barely stifling a yawn. 'Turns out to be rather good at his job actually. Not someone you'd automatically think of as spy material, but I suppose that's the whole point, isn't it? I remember that classics don who trained him saying he looks for people who're slightly apart from the crowd but not so much that people would notice them. He said he'd never come across someone who fitted that bill quite so well as Hunter. He's survived three missions into Nazi Germany now: if he looked or acted like a spy he wouldn't have lasted more than an hour or two.'

'And his other masters... Would they have seen the Directive?'

'I certainly hope so. We allowed him enough time in Zürich.

One of Basil's men spotted him leaving the station with Viktor, so I think we can assume they have the document. There is one concern, though…'

'With Hunter?'

'No, with our Portuguese friends actually. When I came back through Lisbon Sandy was in a bit of a flap about Telmo. He's been rather elusive and Sandy's worried he may be getting cold feet. Telmo seems to think the PVDE may be on to him, though there doesn't seem to be any evidence for that. Personally, I think he's just getting twitchy; agents get like that from time to time, as you know. There is a well-founded concern about Dona Maria though.'

'The lady in Berlin?'

'Correct.'

'Telmo says she's been transferred within the Portuguese Legation there: she's no longer working for the Military Attaché, she's now with the First Secretary.'

'A demotion?'

'Not as such, but it gives her less access to the kind of intelligence we're interested in and also to the Diplomatic bag. Apparently the First Secretary is quite high up the hierarchy at the Legation, but his role is more ceremonial. She's worried they may be watching her: she's certain her desk was searched recently and she thinks she's been tailed on a few occasions'

'By whom?'

'Not the Germans; security people from the Legation. Also, her home leave has been brought forward to 24th March: which is two weeks on Monday. She's worried that once she returns to

Lisbon she won't be allowed back again. Telmo is demanding an absolute promise from us that the minute Dona Maria arrives in Portugal, we put both of them in hiding and bring them to Britain as soon as possible.'

'And you said?'

'Yes, of course. I told Sandy to agree to whatever he asks for. I told him to say that once they get to England they'll be given money, a house and new identities. I hope that's in order?'

'Oh, I'm sure the Service will be happy to find them some love-nest somewhere or other.'

* * *

The following afternoon, Edgar and Christopher Porter were in a large map-room in the basement of the St James's Square office, along with a number of colleagues from the Service and a few men in uniform. Copies of Directive 21 were handed round by a lanky Brigadier from Army Intelligence who cut a colourful figure with his florid face and a large black-and-grey striped moustache. When he spoke it was with a Welsh accent.

'These are English translations, as you'll see. The document itself is astonishing, quite astonishing. Let me quote: "The German Armed Forces must be prepared, even before the conclusion of the war against England, to crush Soviet Russia in a rapid campaign." That last bit – crushing the Soviet Union – is underlined. The Directive says preparations for the invasion "... will be concluded by 15th May 1941".'

There was murmuring around the room, and people looked at

each other with raised eyebrows and barely concealed surprise.

'They even have a code name: Operation Barbarossa. However, we must be cautious. The most important question we have to address is whether the document is genuine because there's no point in us acting upon it if we feel that, on balance, it's not what it purports to be. We've had all types of experts studying this ever since we got our hands on it.'

The Brigadier removed a pair of reading glasses from a case in front of him and glanced at some handwritten notes.

'First of all, we've had the Directive subjected to something called text analysis by a German expert. What he does is compare one text with others, to see if they're from the same source. He believes it's very similar to other ones released by Hitler. I quote from his report: "It feels identical in terms of tone, syntax and vocabulary to other documents released by Hitler. The mixture of rhetoric and military detail, the constant reference to himself in terms of orders being given and decisions being made – all that is very familiar."

'Then there's the question of how feasible it is that Germany would consider breaking its pact with the Soviet Union. The consensus is this is perfectly likely. The Nazis hate Communists and Russians and Slavs almost as much as they hate the Jews. In fact, they tend to see them as one and the same thing: when they think of a Russian, they see a Jewish communist. So the pact was a surprise in one respect, but not in another – Hitler was being shrewd. He was buying time, ensuring his Eastern Front remained quiet while he conquered Western Europe and attempted an invasion of the British Isles. So, breaking the pact would not be a surprise, it was only ever a short-term ruse.'

The Brigadier walked over to a large map on the wall behind him.

'So if we accept this document is genuine, then we need to analyse its feasibility from a military point of view. It's an extremely ambitious plan: one which depends on co-operation from the Finns in the north and the Romanians in the south, which may be a problem as they're unlikely to be as committed to an invasion of the Soviet Union as the Germans are. It also depends on two other critical factors: a significant element of secrecy and surprise, and the Red Army being utterly ill-prepared for this. We do know the Red Army isn't in a good state, but even so...'

The Brigadier was looking at the map then at the directive. He peered closely at the map and pointed to a spot around the Polish-Russian border.

'Hitler seems to be talking about concentrating the main German thrust here, around the Pripet Marshes. He talks about having two Army Groups operating north of the Marshes and one Army Group south of it. The key object of the southern group looks like the Ukraine, with all its agriculture and industry. The aims of the northern groups, it says here, are Leningrad and Moscow. This is what he says about Moscow: "The capture of this city would represent a decisive political and economic success, and would also bring about the capture of the most important railway junctions."'

A colonel wearing the insignia of a Guards regiment walked noisily over to the map, his boots echoing on the floor. After studying it for a while he turned around and spoke unnecessarily loudly, each syllable carefully enunciated. 'Personally, I can't see the Germans attempting this with less than 100 divisions – talk about putting all your eggs in one basket. If Hitler thinks he's going to get as far as Moscow the only advice I can give him is that he'd better get a move on. Once that Russian winter starts even the greatest army in the world doesn't stand a chance. From a logistics point of view this would appear to be almost impossible.'

For the next two hours the men crowded into the map-room weighed up the pros and cons of Directive 21. All the participants took it in turn to play devil's advocate at every opportunity, but the discussion kept coming back to a point of agreement: on the balance of probabilities, the document was a genuine one.

It was ten o'clock that evening when Porter and Edgar went up to the office on the top floor. Porter pulled back the blackout blinds and turned off his desk lamp, allowing the light from the full moon to fill the room. For a while they sat in silence, picking at the plate of stale sandwiches on the desk between them.

'And what happens now?'

'Number Ten will be informed first thing in the morning,' said Porter. 'I'm told the Prime Minister and Eden discussed the matter this morning once they knew the directive had arrived. They agreed that if this meeting concluded the directive is genuine we'd not waste any time. We'd get a copy of it over to Moscow as soon as possible and Cripps himself will take it to the Kremlin. So, well done Edgar – you've done an excellent job. The Soviets can hardly ignore Directive 21 now, can they? It corroborates the copy Hunter showed Viktor.'

The two men left the office together and walked as far as Pall

Mall.

'You look exhausted Edgar.'

'I've booked two weeks leave sir.'

'Splendid. I expect your family will be pleased to see you. Heading down to Dorset are you?'

Edgar carried on walking in silence, apparently oblivious to what Porter had been saying. They had now reached Waterloo Place, from where each would be going in different directions.

'Probably not sir: as far as my family are concerned, I'm in the Far East: it's easier that way. I shall probably sleep for a week then go walking on my own in Scotland.'

Porter slapped Edgar on the back. 'Understood: Five have an interesting case on at the moment and have been asking for your help, but first have a good rest. Remember, I don't want to see you for a fortnight, that's an order.'

* * *

Edgar had gone straight to his small apartment in a mansion block behind Victoria Street and slept most of the next day and a good deal of the day after that. By the Thursday, he felt rested and even slightly bored. He visited the dentist, had his hair cut and began to suspect that two weeks off may be a week too long. He decided to wait until after the weekend before deciding whether to go to Scotland, stay in London or even go back to work. The decision was made for him by a ring on his doorbell early on the Monday morning. It was a driver he recognised from the offices in St James.

Very sorry to bother you sir: Mr Porter would like to see you sir. Now sir, if you don't mind coming with me. There's a car waiting outside sir.

Christopher Porter was pacing up and down his office, managing to look both angry and embarrassed. He told Edgar to shut the door and sit down.

'I thought I was under orders not to see you for a fortnight?'

'You were Edgar, but those were my orders and I consider I'm allowed to break them. I'm not going to beat about the bush: there's been a change of heart. It's all Winston's fault – and the bloody Foreign Office. Wouldn't be surprised if Five haven't tried to queer our pitch too.'

'I'm not sure I'm following you sir.'

'Let me lay the cards on the table then. As you know, we agreed the copy of the Operation Barbarossa directive Hunter brought back from Berlin is genuine. It was sent in code to Moscow and Stafford Cripps took it to the Kremlin and handed it to Molotov personally on Thursday. Cripps said that Molotov appeared to be angry, but he couldn't tell whether he was angry with him or the Germans, or more likely it was just his usual demeanour. Then last night I was summoned to Downing Street. Apparently they've been having second thoughts.'

'Second thoughts about what?'

'About what we should be telling the Soviets after all. Their thinking – and one has to acknowledge it does have a certain logic to it – is that the whole business could rebound on us. As things stand at the moment, Hitler's priority is still to invade Great Britain, even though we seem to be doing a rather decent job of defending ourselves. If this Operation Barbarossa turns out to be true, it'll take an enormous pressure off us. Hitler will be diluting his forces by fighting on two fronts and it makes the chances of even an attempted German invasion of these shores – let alone a successful one – very remote indeed. I can hear the tinkle of teacups approaching Edgar; shall we pause for a moment?'

Five minutes later, fortified by surprisingly strong cups of tea, Porter resumed. 'If the Soviets finally choose to believe the Barbarossa Directive and other intelligence, and accept the Germans do have hostile intentions towards them, they'll stop trusting the Germans, shore up their defences and reinforce the border. That would make a German invasion of the Soviet Union significantly less likely. The question that Number Ten have been asking themselves is this: would such an outcome be in our best interests?'

Edgar leant back in his chair and removed a cigarette from his silver case. He was halfway through smoking it when he replied. 'So you're saying there's now a feeling it's actually in our interests for Germany and the Soviet Union to go to war?'

'Absolutely: if they go to war with each other then the chances of an invasion of Britain significantly diminish and at the same time Germany risks a dangerous war in the east that they could well lose.'

'So when you say that there's been a change of heart...'

'What I mean by that is they now want us to play down the fact Germany has plans to invade the Soviet Union. They think we should switch from doing the decent thing and telling the Soviets about the German plans to actually misleading them, telling them quite the opposite.'

'Bit bloody late for that isn't it, for Christ's sake! I'm sorry sir, but it's been one of the intelligence coups of the war thus far to get hold of that directive and make sure the Soviets see it, and now you're saying it's all been a bloody waste of time. Jesus!'

'Don't shout Edgar, please. Remember I'm only the messenger. I...'

'... And you said something about them now wanting "us" to play down reports of German intentions and even mislead them. How on earth are we going to do that?'

'I'm afraid it means we now need to provide the Soviets with another report courtesy of your man Hunter, one which reflects serious German concerns about Operation Barbarossa and talks of its postponement at least, possibly even its cancellation. I have to say it's not entirely unfeasible: you yourself said Hugo's General admitted there were serious concerns in the army high command about invading the Soviet Union. This report would simply reflect those.'

'And how do "we" get hold of such a document?'

'Please don't be so sarcastic. Naval Intelligence are apparently rather good at this kind of thing. This morning I've asked our people to talk to their people and see what they can come up with. I've told them I want it to be ready by the end of the week.'

'And how do we then get it to the Russians?'

Porter heaped another spoonful of sugar into his tea, sipped it then stood up and walked over to the window, looking out of it as he spoke.

'You said that Dona Maria do Rosario has to leave Berlin on 24th March, which is a week on Monday – correct? This report needs to be taken to Lisbon, where Telmo is to get it into the diplomatic bag to Berlin. In her final act of service for us in Berlin, Dona Maria will pass the report on to Hugo. Hunter can then go back to Berlin to collect it so he can let the Soviets see it when he returns to Switzerland – as before. I grant you it's a complicated route by which to get it to the Soviets, but hopefully it's one they regard as plausible.'

'By the sounds of it Porter, the Hon Anthony Davis is about to return to Lisbon.'

'Correct, Edgar: and thereafter to Switzerland.'

* * *

Late on the afternoon of Sunday 16th March, Edgar was back in Christopher Porter's office. Edgar noticed Porter was looking uncharacteristically confident. He had a broad grin on his face. On the desk between them was a black, leather-bound book, with an ornate cross on the padded front cover.

'Contemplating the priesthood are you sir?'

'Now, now Edgar. You may remember that when we met last Monday I said we'd need to concoct a report purporting to show the Germans were now having second thoughts about invading the Soviet Union?'

Edgar nodded. 'And you want this report to fall into Soviet hands?'

Porter rubbed his hands and tenderly picked up the leather-bound book. He passed it over to Edgar. The words 'A Bíblia Sagrada' were etched onto the cover in gold leaf. Edgar gently picked it up and turned it round in his hands.

'Careful, Edgar. The team that put this together want us to know how much trouble they went to to get hold of a bible in Portuguese. They've done a pretty impressive job though. Here, pass it to me.' Porter took the bible and opened it at the inside back cover. The thick paper was loose and Porter carefully peeled it away to reveal a gap, folded into which was a document that he carefully removed and opened: three pages on brown paper, typed in German with some scrawled handwritten notes.

'This is the Rostock Report: it's a note on a meeting supposedly held a couple of weeks ago in Rostock, on the 3rd and 4th March. If you look here, it lists the various participants…' Porter turned the page. 'And on this page it describes the purpose of the meeting: "To review plans for proposed campaign against the Soviet Union (Operation Barbarossa)." The next section is essentially a summary of what was in Directive Number 21.'

Porter was checking the document against a typed sheet in English. 'It makes the case for the invasion of the Soviet Union and repeats pretty much what was in Directive 21. Then we have a rather clever link from the Hitler directive to the fake report. We already know that at the end of the first one, Hitler said "I await submission of the plans of Commanders-in-Chief on the basis of this directive. The preparations made by all branches of the armed forces, together with timetables, are to be reported to me through the High Command of the Armed Forces." What follows is in effect the Commanders-in-Chief doing just that.'

Again Porter was consulting his typed sheet, the English translation. 'There's a rather long section detailing the submissions of all the different services, I don't propose to go into detail. But then there's a paragraph concluding thus: "It is the unanimous view of the OKW, OKH, OKL, OKM" – those being the High Commands of the Armed Forces, the Army, the Air Force and the Navy – "that for the reasons summarised below, Operation Barbarossa should be postponed until the spring of 1942 at the earliest." It then goes on to give those reasons: are you happy for me to read them out to you?'

Edgar nodded. He was leaning back in his chair, his eyes half shut as if to fully absorb what was being read to him.

'"Number One – we are of the opinion that our intelligence services may have seriously underestimated both the size and the strength of the Soviet forces. The ability of Stalin to motivate the Red Army is significant.

'"Number Two – we consider that our own planners may have overestimated our ability to supply our forces adequately if the advance through Soviet territory is as rapid as it will need to be. There is a serious danger that our forces could be dangerously exposed by shortages of ammunition, fuel and food.

'"Number Three – Operation Barbarossa depends on the co-operation of Finnish and Romanian forces. We are of the opinion this co-operation cannot be taken for granted and could leave the northern and southern sections of our front vulnerable.

'"Number Four – the Russian winter presents a very severe risk to our forces. To achieve our objective of capturing Moscow before the onset of the winter, we would recommend that Operation Barbarossa is launched by early May. At present, factors such as the Yugoslavia campaign mean that this is highly unlikely. The risk of maintaining an offensive during the winter is unacceptable.

'"Number Five – Great Britain is proving to be far more resolute that we had expected. We had been of the opinion either they would have surrendered by now or would have been weakened to the extent that an invasion could be launched. That is not the case and therefore we have to take into account the fact that we would be fighting on two fronts."

'There's a bit more about future meetings and such like, but that's the gist of it. What do you think?'

Edgar said nothing but asked to look at the report. As he read through it he nodded approvingly, once or twice allowing a knowing smile to cross his face.

'It's good enough to make the Soviets pause at least. Depends on what mood Stalin is in: that line about his ability to motivate the Red Army is a clever touch – does no harm to appeal to the man's ego. My feeling is that at the very least it'll confuse the Soviets.'

'And at the very best?'

Edgar glanced again at the report and turned it round in his hands, as if checking its weight. 'At the very best, they'll believe it: it's good.'

'Provided we can make sure they see the damn thing,' said Porter. 'The plan is we seal the report in the bible – I've even been supplied with special glue for that purpose – and you take it to Lisbon: you have a seat on tomorrow's flight from Bristol. Telmo will have to get the bible in the diplomatic bag to Dona Maria and she'll pass it on to Hugo. All being well, that'll happen on Thursday or Friday. Meanwhile, Basil Remington-Barber has been told to make sure we get Hunter out to Berlin for a week on Monday, where he'll collect the report and bring it back to Zürich. Naturally we're counting on him showing the report to Viktor first.'

Edgar nodded approvingly. Porter picked up some other papers on the desk.

'These are for Sandy to show to Telmo. They're the carrot we're dangling in front of him and Dona Maria. This photograph here…' he handed over a picture of a pretty thatched cottage, with a broad expanse of wisteria across its front. 'This is the place we can tell Telmo we've rented for him and Dona Maria to live in once they get here. And this is a statement from Barclays Bank in the Strand confirming that accounts have been opened in each of their names to the tune of five hundred pounds each. Then there are various other bits and pieces, all amounting to what we hope is a demonstration of our positive intent towards them.'

* * *

Chapter 22: Portugal, Switzerland and Berlin, March 1941

'And what if Telmo refuses? He's so nervous at the moment, he's hardly communicating with me at the moment. To persuade him to send this on to Berlin is going to be extremly difficult, Edgar.'

It was late in the afternoon on Monday 17th March and Sandy Morgan was far from his convivial self. In front of him was the black, leather-bound bible.

'Tell him it's an order.'

'Yes, yes – I understand that Edgar: you don't need to keep repeating it. All I can say is we're pushing our luck. Remember, he's under no obligation to obey our orders.'

'Look, Sandy, you have to make him realise this is in his best interests. Show him the picture of the cottage the Service has sorted out for him and show him the bank statements and all the rest of it. In short, promise him the earth, anything to make sure he sends the bible over to Dona Maria and gets her to hand it over to Hugo. If he says he wants to play cricket for England at Lord's, tell him it's no problem. If he wants tea with the King and Queen at Buckingham bloody Palace, ask him how many sugars he takes. Promise him the minute Dona Maria arrives back in Lisbon, you'll spirit both of them into a safe house – tell him that Sandy, he needs to hear it.'

'And what if he's still difficult?'

'Tell him that unless he co-operates you'll go straight to the Rua Victor Cordon and tell the PVDE all about him and Dona Maria. And make sure he knows we mean it.'

* * *

On the Wednesday morning the telephone rang twice in the space of five minutes in the apartment Henry shared with his mother just off Quai du Mont Blanc. On the first occasion his mother answered and after a minute said 'pas de problème' in a somewhat resentful manner, as if her being disturbed was indeed a problem. *Wrong number.*

When the phone rang a few minutes later, Henry answered. A lady spoke very quickly in French.

'Monsieur Hesse, this is Madame Ladnier at Credit Suisse. I need to see you urgently here at the bank: two o'clock this afternoon. Now, please respond to this call as if I have called the wrong number again. Two o'clock.'

'No, it's not,' replied Henry, aware he was sounding rather aggressive. 'You have the wrong number. Please don't disturb us again.'

At two o'clock he was ushered from the reception in the Quai des Bergues branch of Credit Suisse by Madame Ladnier, taken through a warren of corridors at the back of the bank and up a staircase to the first floor. She unlocked the door to a small office then opened an interconnecting door. Lounging on a leather sofa on the other side of the room was Basil Remington-Barber.

'When you've finished, ring me on this telephone. I'm on extension 18,' said Madame Ladnier.

'Henry, Henry – how nice to see you. Do come in, sit down. Sorry I can't offer you a drink but it seems Swiss banks aren't very good on that score. Apologies, too, for all the subterfuge: I needed to contact you urgently and had to rather prevail upon Madame Ladnier to make the calls. All's well that ends well, eh?'

Henry sat down on a more formal chair opposite Remington-Barber.

'Look, Henry – little bit awkward this: I know we promised you a nice long rest but something urgent has cropped up.' Remington-Barber stood up and paced around the room, at one stage slapping Henry jovially on the shoulders.

'Rather annoying really, but I'm afraid we need to send you back to Berlin somewhat sooner than we'd envisaged. We thought there was an outside chance of that but we didn't imagine it'd be quite so soon.'

Basil Remington-Barber had returned to the sofa and seemed a bit less hesitant now he had passed on the message.

'When would this be?' Henry sounded casual, even rather keen.

'Monday, I'm afraid. Hedinger is sorting things out from the Zürich end, and Edgar wants to see you there on Saturday. I have to return to Bern this afternoon but I'll travel over with you on Saturday morning. Apparently some of the Swiss banks have started to fly their couriers in and out – seems less risky if they're carrying important documents – and he thinks he can find some top-level papers for you to take in. Plan is for you to fly in via Stuttgart on Monday morning and out the next day by the same route – means you should be back in Zürich early Tuesday evening: hand over the bank papers to Hedinger then hop on the last train to Geneva, where I'll meet you. With any luck you'll be in your own bed by midnight.'

Henry did his best to affect a tone of mild annoyance. 'And what is it that's so important now?'

'Another document, nothing to do with Reinhart this time: this one is even more important than the last one. Hermann will pass it on to you and you bring it back to us.'

* * *

Henry arrived at the luxury villa high above Lutry at Friday lunchtime . He waited for 20 minutes in the magnificent lounge, watching the ferry that had brought him to Lausanne that morning heading along the lake towards Montreux and another ferry steaming in the opposite direction towards Geneva. It was a clear day and he had a good view of Évian-les-Bains on the French side of the lake.

Outside there was a slamming of car doors followed by the sound of men speaking Russian in the hallway. Viktor did not so much walk into the room as storm into it, slamming the door as he did so. He was wearing a long, black coat, gloves and a black Homburg hat. 'Get me a coffee,' Viktor shouted at whoever was outside the room.

'This is urgent, is it *synok*?'

'Of course, otherwise I wouldn't have contacted you.'

'I was in Vienna,' Viktor said, as if being in Vienna was a reason why he should not have been contacted. The door opened again and one of Viktor's men came in with a tray of coffee and sandwiches. Still wearing his coat and hat, but having removed the gloves, Viktor sat down and began to devour the food in front of him. He indicated to Henry he should join him. Viktor ate most of the sandwiches and finished two cups of coffee before he removed his hat, tossing it onto a chaise longue on the other side of the room. He was still wearing his overcoat and from one of its inside pockets he removed a leather notebook. A knife emerged from another pocket and the Russian began to sharpen his pencil in an aggressive manner.

'Moscow is very satisfied with the material you brought back two weeks ago by the way. Very satisfied indeed.'

'Good: I think I may have more.'

Viktor stopped sharpening the pencil and blew the shavings from it off his coat onto the floor.

'Really? From the same source?'

'I'm not too sure, it sounds like it's from the lawyer this time, rather than the Reichsbank. But Remington-Barber did say "this one is even more important than the last one".'

'He told you that?'

'Yes, two days ago.'

'They tell you a lot, Henry.'

'Maybe they trust me.'

'Maybe they do, maybe that's how the British operate. We tend not to be so forthcoming. What are the travel arrangements this time?'

'They want me in Zürich on Saturday – apparently Edgar's going to be there – then I'm to fly to Berlin on Monday, via Stuttgart. Back the same way on Tuesday. I still have to deliver bank documents over to Hedinger, that's my cover after all, then catch the late train from Zürich to Geneva, where I give the document to Remington-Barber.'

'Alright Henry: we make the same arrangement as before. When you return to Zürich on Tuesday you go straight to Bank Leu then to the station. From there we'll meet you and we'll go to have the document copied. Are you sure they weren't suspicious last time?'

'I'm sure: they seemed very pleased with how things had gone.'

Viktor stood up, slowly hauling himself out of the chair and walking over to the window before turning to face Henry. His enormous frame appeared as a silhouette, with the sun behind him.

'Let me tell you *synok*, it's possible to be pleased and suspicious at the same time. But I think if Edgar is here again, it must mean the document is at least as important as the last one. I still find it odd, though, that they don't meet you in Zürich to collect the document.'

'The British don't like Zürich, I keep telling you. Everyone speaks German there, or their version of it. They feel safer on this side of Switzerland.'

'Alright Henry, you go back to Geneva now and we'll see you in Zürich on Tuesday.'

'There is one thing…'

'What's that Henry? You want to ask me again if I'm still a believer?'

'In Zürich I asked a favour – if you could give me the details of any comrades I could contact in Berlin, in an emergency.'

Viktor nodded his head: yes, *I remember*. The Russian sat back in the chair opposite Henry.

'I used to run networks in Berlin, Henry. To be honest, it was a surprisingly easy city for us to operate in: even after Hitler came to power in '33. I'm convinced there were still more communists in the city than Nazis – and many committed ones at that, very ideological and very disciplined. That's what I realised about Germans, they like to have an ideology, whether it's Communism or Socialism or Nazism or Catholicism.'

Viktor paused and thought for a moment. 'It's a few years now since I operated in Berlin and most of my networks have either been arrested, switched over to the Nazis, left Germany, or have been taken over by the NKVD or the GRU boys at the embassy. But I have kept a couple: I'm going to tell you how to contact one of them, listen carefully.'

Henry leaned forward in his seat; he was just inches from the Russian and could smell coffee on his breath.

'There's an agent called Kato, who I've no reason to believe has left Berlin. Kato was my prize agent; I was never going to give them up. Do you know Wedding?'

'I've heard of it, but never been there.'

'Just north of Charlottenburg, not far from the centre. The important thing about Wedding is that it was always a communist stronghold and even now I understand it's a more amenable part of the city for us, which doesn't mean it's safe. Catch the U-Bahn line that goes north through Friederichstrasse and Oranienburg, and get off at Leopold Platz. From there, walk north along Müllerstrasse and turn into Wannitz Strasse. If you come to Amsterdamer Strasse you've gone too far. Have you got all that so far?'

Henry nodded.

'On Wannitz Strasse you'll see a row of five or six shops under a large apartment block. One of those shops sells items for the kitchen – pots, pans, plates; that kind of thing. Go in there and ask if you can leave something for a Frau Schreiner in apartment 12. Tell the person you've come from Dresden to deliver it. The reply you should expect is that they'll say their sister lives in Dresden. You'll know then you're dealing with Kato: hand them the envelope. In it will be a message from me: I will write it now. Once they read it, they'll give you their full co-operation. You don't need to worry about the message, by the way, there'll be nothing incriminating in it: it will look like a shopping list.'

'And how will I know the man in the shop is Kato?'

'You will, don't worry. In any case, Kato is a woman.'

* * *

That same day, at the Portuguese Legation in Berlin, Dona Maria do Rosario had to wait until the First Secretary left the office at five before she could open the bible which had arrived in that day's diplomatic bag.

Telmo's message the previous day had told her exactly where to look and how urgent everything was. She carefully removed the Rostock Report from the book and placed it inside an envelope, which she slipped into her handbag. After that, she stuffed some blank paper into the gap where the document had been and glued the card back in place before placing the bible in one of the drawers.

She delayed leaving the Legation until 5.30, timing her departure to coincide with that of a number of the other secretaries. She walked with them for a while then quietly peeled away from the little group and headed for Opernplatz and the vast sanctity of St Hedwig's.

She knew Father Josef was not due to be taking confession that night, but he would be assisting at the Mass. She would sit towards the front and wear her red scarf: he would know then she needed to see him urgently.

Father Josef was one of a number of priests on the altar during Mass and not once did Dona Maria notice him looking at her. When it was time to take Communion, Dona Maria chose to join the small queue in front him. He bent down as she received the wafer and whispered in her ear: 'Go to the undercroft; wait for me there.'

The undercroft was deserted and she sat quietly on a narrow wooden bench set back in the shadows. After a few minutes she heard gentle footsteps echoing towards her. Without acknowledging her but looking all around him Father Josef walked to the furthest chapel and beckoned her to follow.

'Are we safe here?' she asked him when they were alone.

'For a few minutes, with any luck. I rarely see people down here after evening Mass. What's the problem?'

'I have something urgent for Hugo.'

'Very well: I'll send a message for him to come to confession tomorrow: then you can meet him on Friday.'

'No Father! I can't wait that long, it may be too dangerous. I'm returning to Portugal on Monday and I fear for my safety. After today, I can't do anything else.'

'So what do you want me to do?' Father Josef looked terrified. *A messenger, I'll be no more than a messenger.* That's what he had said in the beginning.

Dona Maria removed the envelope from her handbag and pushed it into the priest's hands.

'Here, please give this to Hugo, Father.'

'No, I can't do that.'

'You have to Father.' At that moment, they both heard the sound of heavy footsteps walking towards them. The priest started to say something then slipped the envelope into the folds of his cassock and sunk to his knees in prayer. By the time he had finished, Dona Maria had slipped away.

* * *

Chapter 23: Berlin, March 1941

Henry Hunter arrived in Zürich on the Saturday afternoon and all through the weekend was briefed by Edgar and Remington-Barber on what was expected of him in Berlin. If all went well, he was assured, he would be in the city for little more than 24 hours.

Henry tried hard not to show he was pleased he was to be returning to Berlin. He felt more relaxed than he had for more than ten years: he was going on his own mission, as well as theirs.

He left Zürich airport on the first leg of the journey early on the Monday morning and by the time he landed in Stuttgart it was a clear day. It was a year and a month since he had last been at the airport and this time the plane taxied to an even more remote section, well away from any buildings and the few Luftwaffe planes he could make out in the distance. When all the passengers had disembarked, they were counted on the tarmac then divided into two groups. Those remaining in Stuttgart were to board a bus that would take them to the terminal building; those flying on to Berlin were to transfer to the waiting Junkers Ju-52 plane.

The flight for Berlin took off half an hour after they had landed in Stuttgart and two hours and 20 minutes later they had landed at Tempelhof: getting through security took almost as long. For the first hour after he landed he was kept in a small room with the three other non-German passengers. One by one, they were taken into a room to be questioned and he was the third to go in. He was in there for just under an hour, during which time he was searched, as was his case, then he was thoroughly questioned. *How many times have you been to Berlin?; what do you do when you're here?;*

where do you eat?; do you meet anyone not connected with your work?; why have you flown into Berlin on this occasion?; what views do you have on the policies of our government?; have you met any Jews while in Germany?; or communists?; please tell me again, how many times have you been to Berlin?; what do you do when you're here…?

Then another wait, this time on his own at the end of an overlit corridor, followed by a few more questions and finally he was able to leave the airport. On Edgar's advice, he walked over to Flughafen station, from where he took the U-Bahn north for three stops as far as Koch Strasse. From there it was a short walk across Wilhelm Strasse to the Excelsior on Askanischer Platz, where a room had been reserved for him. It was an enormous hotel, with well over 500 rooms and, as far as Henry could tell, eight or nine restaurants. Both Edgar and Remington-Barber felt the anonymity of the hotel would be more suitable for this visit.

It was 2.30 by the time he checked into his narrow room on the third floor, overlooking Saarland Strasse. The room was overheated, but when he opened the window the noise of the city flooded in and he found himself unable to think properly.

'Stay there until the next morning,' Edgar had told him, which was all very well but that left no time for anything. Tuesday was going to be very tight as it was: meeting Hugo at nine o'clock to collect the document then to the Reichsbank to exchange papers with Gunter Reinhart. After that, he was supposed to go to Tempelhof in good time to catch the 12.30 flight to Stuttgart.

Maybe.

He managed to stay in the hotel room for 20 minutes, pacing up and down, still not fully decided on his course of action. There were too many flaws to his plan; it depended too much on chance and it meant ignoring everything he had been trained to do over the past ten years. He was truly caught between a rock and a hard place.

His mind still unresolved, he left the hotel through a side entrance and from Stadt Mitte caught the U-Bahn north as far as Leopold Platz. He was in Wedding and he was about to use the favour he had asked of Viktor. Depending on how that went would help make up his mind.

Carefully following Viktor's instructions he turned into Wannitz Strasse and spotted the small parade of shops with the hardware shop in the middle. He walked past it from the opposite side of the road and, when he noticed a woman leaving, crossed the road and entered.

The shop was empty: behind the counter was a well-built woman, in her late thirties or possibly older. She had an untidy nest of hair that was turning grey and a face noticeable mainly for the thick mascara around her bright-green eyes and the dark lipstick, which was closer to black than red. On the wall behind her was a small framed photograph of Hitler, next to a shelf-full of white candles. They smiled at each other and he spent a minute or two showing undue interest in a copper saucepan. He checked the inside pocket of his jacket: Viktor's note was there, in an envelope from the hotel. *You don't need to worry about the message by the way, there'll be nothing incriminating in it: it will look like a shopping list.*

'Can I help you?' The woman had come out from behind the counter and was alongside him. She pointed to the copper saucepan he was holding. 'This is best quality: a company in Magdeburg manufactures them.'

'I've come from Dresden,' said Henry, aware his voice sounded uncertain. He was trying to speak quietly. 'I've something for Frau Schreiner in apartment 12: please could I leave it here?'

The woman glanced anxiously towards the door then edged slowly back towards the counter. 'Of course: my sister is from Dresden.'

Kato.

The woman casually walked back behind the counter, smiling at Henry, who smiled back at her. There was silence as she looked at him, waiting for him to speak.

'You have something for me, maybe?'

'I'm sorry, yes, I forgot.' He handed the envelope to her.

She removed the note from the envelope and momentarily gasped as she began to read it. The hand holding the note was shaking, while her other steadied herself on the counter. He heard her quietly say, 'Viktor'. When she had finished reading, she indicated for him to wait and went to a room behind the counter. There was a brief smell of burning. She back came out with two lit cigarettes, and handed one to Henry.

'No thank you. I don't smoke.'

'Smoke it please: in case anyone comes in. It's better to disguise the smell. So, you are a comrade?'

Henry nodded. *A comrade.*

'I never thought I'd hear from Viktor again, never. I know I'm not supposed to ask any questions, but just tell me this – is he well?' Her eyes were moist and the hand holding the cigarette was shaking, so much so she used her other hand to steady it.

She loved him. She still does.

'Yes.'

She looked at him quizzically, hoping he would say more, but he just smiled and nodded his head.

'He says you're to be trusted and I'm to help you,' said Kato. 'I've heard nothing from anyone for over a year. There were five of us, all loyal to Viktor. He told us not to trust anyone at the embassy. Two comrades managed to escape to Sweden, another was arrested and died at Sachsenhausen and one disappeared: she's a Jew and I suspect she's gone underground. I'm fortunate none of our cell went over to the Nazis: that happened with a number of comrades. What do you need – somewhere to stay, some money?'

'Is it safe to talk here?'

'Of course! Do you think I'd be doing it if it wasn't? There's no-one in the back and I can see whoever comes in. Take the saucepan from the stand, and one or two others – we can make it look as if you can't decide which one to buy: men never can anyway. Tell me what you need.' Her hands still shook as she inhaled deeply on the cigarette, and her green eyes danced with a mixture of fear and excitement.

When he had finished telling Kato what he needed, he expected her to say it was impossible, but she acted no more surprised than if he had ordered a new dining set.

'You want this for tomorrow morning you say?'

'Yes please.'

'What time?'

'Around 11 o'clock, possibly a bit later, but certainly by noon. From here?'

'No, most certainly not. When you leave here, we'll never see each other again. You should avoid Wedding anyway, the Gestapo have too many people around here. What you want will be ready from 11 o'clock. Will you be around the centre of Berlin?'

'Yes.'

'Do you know Ku'damm?'

He shook his head.

'It is actually called Kurfürstendamm, but everyone knows it as Ku'damm. It's a very well-known street in the south of Charlottenburg: before the war it was very fashionable. Now, nowhere is fashionable. Go to Uhland Strasse U-Bahn and come out on the Kurfürstendamm exit, then cross the road and head west for two or three blocks – not far. On the corner of Kurfürstendamm and Bleibtreustrasse, you'll see a kiosk set back in the wall; it sells newspapers, cigarettes, that kind of thing. Don't be put off by the swastikas and the pictures of Hitler. Tell the old lady in the kiosk you've come to collect Magda's cigarettes: she'll hand you a pack of Juno. What you need will be inside the packet, but put it straight in your pocket, buy a newspaper and leave. Carry on up Bleibtreustrasse and take the second left, Niebuhr Strasse. Open the packet when you get into Niebuhr Strasse, there'll be a note there telling you where to go. Now, I need to check you've remembered all that.'

* * *

At six o'clock on the morning of Tuesday 25th March, Henry finally gave up trying to force himself back to sleep, as he had been attempting to do for most of the night. They had all come to visit him during his brief spells of sleep: Roza, of course, but also her brother and the man in the perfume shop in Essen. Even Foxi the dog. They'd all been shouting at him. Rosa had appeared and for a brief moment she sat on the end of the bed alongside Roza.

Henry had a bath then sat on the floor, with maps spread out before him. He had been absorbed in these since returning to the Excelsior late the previous afternoon. He could see the routes; there was no doubt about that. He wandered over to the window. Down on Saarland Strasse a group of Waffen SS were happily chatting away and slapping each other on the back. Not for the first time since he arrived in Berlin, he felt real fear. His chest tightened and the maps shook as his hands trembled.

I don't have to do this. I'm not committed to anything. If I abandon my plans now, no-one will know.

Back to the maps: during his training by the British he had been told he was a natural map reader: he could study a map and its contents would come to life; he was immediately able to picture the area as if he were observing it from above and could envisage different routes and all the options available to him.

First of all there was the map of Berlin, then that of Germany. It appeared straightforward; he knew where he had to be and how to get there, but he could not foresee the hazards and he knew there would be plenty of those.

He checked out of the Excelsior at 8.30 that morning, assuring one of the over-attentive managers on duty he had indeed enjoyed his stay, everything had indeed been to his satisfaction and he would most certainly consider staying at the Excelsior when he returned to Berlin.

There was a light drizzle as he walked to the Opernplatz, where the expanse of St Hedwig's Cathedral rose before him. He reminded himself of Edgar's instructions.

Don't enter the cathedral before five to nine.

He paused at the entrance to Opernplatz. It was 8.50 and, realising it was too early, he found a stone bench to sit on, despite the rain. He waited, steeling himself to go in. He had a passionate dislike of churches, buoyed by a fear he had first encountered in his childhood, that churches were the one place where secrets weren't safe; even the statues and gargoyles seemed to know all about him.

Five to nine.

Enter the cathedral through the main entrance.

A few people were coming down the steps after the eight o'clock Mass.

And don't forget to cross yourself.

Find a seat about halfway along, between the entrance and main altar.

The cathedral was enormous and there must have been no more than two dozen people dotted around it, sitting alone or in pairs, all in silent prayer.

If he's seen all is clear, Hugo will appear on the same row as you and sit two or three seats away. Don't expect to see him before 9.10. But if he hasn't appeared by 9.20, leave the church and walk back to Unter den Linden. Don't look around for him.

Ten past nine. The cathedral was much emptier now as the last Mass worshippers had left and made their way to work. He tried hard to close his eyes and hope some spiritual feeling would come to him, something to reassure him and tell him everything would turn out right. Nothing, but at least the ghost of Roza did not appear. He became aware of a scrape of chairs alongside him as someone moved down his row.

Don't look directly at him, but do look in his direction so you can be sure it's him.

It was Hugo, dressed in a long black coat, and clutching a hat and briefcase.

If he places his briefcase on a chair either side of him that's a sign of danger. Leave immediately. If the briefcase remains on the floor, all is well.

The briefcase was on the floor. He saw Hugo remove a bible from the small wooden receptacle on the back of the chair in front of him and slip something into it.

Remain where you are until Hugo has finished and left. Then you'll know how to retrieve the document.

After five minutes Hugo finished praying. He returned the bible to where he had taken it from, stood up and left.

The document will be folded in the middle of the bible. Remove it as soon as you can.

He stood up and straightened his coat, and when he sat down again it was in the seat next to the one Hugo had previously occupied. He picked up the bible Hugo had left and opened it: the document was indeed in the centre, folded as if ready to be inserted into a narrow envelope. He glanced around, but no-one was close to him or looking in his direction, apart from a reproachful medieval saint or two. Within seconds, the document was inside his jacket pocket.

Once you've retrieved the document remain in your seat for another five minutes. Remember to pray.

He thumbed through the bible and stopped randomly. It was a psalm, 130: 'Waiting for the Redemption of the Lord'. 'Out of the depths I have cried to you O Lord. Lord hear my voice!' A shiver ran down his spine and he looked up to see if anyone was watching him now. He looked back at the psalm. 'For with the Lord there is mercy, And with Him is abundant redemption'.

He found himself shaking and becoming so hot the sweat from his hands was staining the page. He glanced up and saw a stone angel on a pillar near him looked like Roza. He had never been a religious man; it was alien to his ideology. But he was quite clear now. What he had just read decided him. He was certain. He had to concentrate very hard now to remember Edgar's instructions.

Put the bible back behind the seat and leave the cathedral. Don't forget to kneel and cross yourself. There's a chapel just before the porch from where you leave the cathedral. Hugo will be in there: if he gets up to leave as you go past and his coat is folded across his arm, you'll know all is well. He'll follow you but don't look round. Leave through Opernplatz then walk down Oberwallstrasse: if Hugo is certain you're not being followed he'll approach you before you go into the Reichsbank to check everything is in order.

As he walked past the chapel he glimpsed Hugo beginning to follow him out, his coat folded across his arm. He walked through Opernplatz back into Unter den Linden and, after a block, turned right into Oberwallstrasse, which was a long, narrow street leading down to Französischestrasse and the Reichsbank. About halfway along the road was filled with rubble from what appeared to be a bombed building. He paused to look up at it, allowing Hugo to catch up with him.

'Everything appears to be alright. I'll walk with you as far as the Reichsbank. You have the document safe?'

'It's here in my pocket,' said Henry.

'Good. Make sure you get a proper envelope from Reinhart to put it in, along with some other Reichsbank papers – and don't forget to get him to seal it. It's essential it looks like a normal letter from the Reichsbank to Bank Leu, I'm sure you realise that. Then go straight to Tempelhof.'

'Franz!'

A smartly dressed man was striding towards them. 'Oh no,' Hugo muttered, then under his breath said, 'Give me a minute; I need to get rid of him. I'm giving you directions to the Reichsbank, remember that.'

'What are you doing down here Franz? You should be in the office. I'm on the way there myself.'

Henry had a feeling he knew the man, but could not place him. He was wearing a formal suit and spoke with a Berlin accent. He had begun to stare at Henry, as if he recognised him too.

'Yes Alois, I'm on my way to the office too. I'd been at Mass and this gentleman asked me to direct him to the Reichsbank.'

'I think we may have met.' The man Hermann had called Alois had now turned to face Henry, positioning himself uncomfortably close. Henry was convinced they had met, but had no idea when or where.

'Are you from Switzerland, by any chance?'

Henry replied that he was. He could now remember the man. Franz Hermann was standing behind him and looking worried.

'Alois – I do need to get to the office. Perhaps you'll join me? I'm sure our friend now knows his way to the Reichsbank.'

Alois ignored Hermann. 'I remember now! Bern, last June – we met at the Schweizerhof. My name is Alois Jäger: I said you should contact me if you were ever in Berlin. Do you recall our meeting?'

Henry noticed the Nazi Party badge on Jäger's lapel. 'Yes…' he said hesitantly, appearing to recollect their meeting from the back of his memory. 'I do remember. Of course I do.'

'You name is Henri, correct?'

Henry nodded.

'And what brings you to Berlin?'

'I'm here on business.'

'For whom, may I ask?'

'Bank Leu – I work for Bank Leu in Zürich. I have business on their behalf at the Reichsbank.'

'Ah – a Swiss banker! I'm most impressed. I have some good friends at the Reichsbank. Perhaps you know Herr…'

'I should explain, Herr Jäger – I'm just a courier. My dealings with the Reichsbank are limited to delivering and collecting documents, I'm afraid.'

'Don't worry my friend. It's all very important. I'm told the support we're getting from the Swiss banks is proving to be a lifeline for Germany: such discretion – we're so grateful. And you're from Zürich, a most charming city, so… proper.'

Jäger paused for a moment. 'But I'm confused Herr Hesse,' he said. 'When we met in Bern you said you were from Geneva? You were travelling to Stuttgart, I think, on business. I recall that because I remember wondering why such a good German speaker was from Geneva.'

Henry could see Hermann's eyes shine with fear. 'Geneva, you say? Ah yes! For a while I did live there, but now I live in Zürich and work for Bank Leu.'

'So you're no longer in business?'

'No, no longer.'

'I see,' said Jäger, sounding unsure. 'And what a remarkable coincidence that not only should I encounter you today in Berlin, but you should also be talking with my good friend and colleague Herr Hermann. You looked as though you knew each other – it shows what a hospitable city Berlin has become under the Führer. Perhaps we could have dinner tonight – the three of us?'

Henry explained he was leaving Berlin that day. 'In fact, I have a flight from Tempelhof at 12.30.'

'Well, I want you to promise the next time you are in Berlin, you'll contact me? We shall have a meal together. What do you think Franz?'

All three men agreed this was a most agreeable idea as they walked together to the end of Oberwallstrasse, where they enthusiastically shook hands: Alois Jäger and Franz Hermann then turned right towards their office in Friederichstrasse, Henry left towards Werderscher Markt.

Henry was shocked. Jäger was clearly suspicious and the fact he was wearing a Nazi Party badge and Hugo looked so horrified was a worry. He would have had even more cause for concern had he looked around just before he entered the Reichsbank and noticed the formal figure of Alois Jäger watching him from the other side of the road.

* * *

When Henri Hesse presented himself at the Reichsbank reception his heart was racing, his chest felt tight, he was perspiring heavily and beginning to feel quite unwell. It was 10.30. His options were still open: he could exchange documents with Reinhart, go to Tempelhof, return to Switzerland and please both his masters. But the chance reading of the psalm in the cathedral had made up his mind: he would take a much harder option, but one he knew would bring him peace.

Gunter Reinhart appeared to have aged ten years in the short time since Henry had last seen him and, other than thanking him once again for taking Alfred to Switzerland, said very little. He took the envelope from Bank Leu, signed for it and handed over the sealed envelope for him to take back to Switzerland.

'I need you to give me another envelope, perhaps with another document in it?' said Henry. 'I'd then like to put something in myself and ask you to re-seal it.'

The German looked uncomfortable.

'I said to Hedinger, this has to be the last time. I can't risk this anymore. You took Alfred to Switzerland, for which I'm eternally grateful, and in return I supplied the directive. Now I've done you this one more favour. Life is getting too dangerous: if I give any more cause to suspect me, then not only will I be in danger but so will Rosa and Sophia, not to mention my wife and children, of course. You must promise me this, don't ask me to help again. Don't come back to Berlin, you understand? It's too dangerous, far too dangerous.'

He took another envelope from a drawer, found a few sheets from a tray on his desk and slipped them in. Henry carefully inserted the papers he had taken from the bible between the sheets and handed the envelope back to Reinhart to seal it.

Henry promised Reinhart they would never meet again, which was not difficult as he had every intention of keeping it. It was unusual for him to make a promise he intended to keep.

After leaving Werderscher Markt, he travelled by U-Bahn to Uhland Strasse. Kato's instructions had been clear enough. He came out on the Kurfürstendamm exit, crossed the road then headed west as far as the corner with Bleibtreustrasse.

Sure enough, there was a kiosk set back in the wall, with narrow swastika banners hanging down from either side of a large advertising sign: 'Berlin Raucht Juno'; Berlin smokes Juno. Lucky Berlin.

The old lady in the kiosk appeared to be wearing two coats and had a scarf wrapped round her head with a woollen hat on top it. Behind her was a large picture of Hitler at a slightly jaunty angle and in front of her a small queue of people in a hurry. He courteously allowed a woman in a fur coat to go first so, by the time it was his turn to be served, there was no-one else waiting.

'I have come to collect Magda's cigarettes.'

The old lady glanced up at him and held eye contact for a moment before she scanned the street behind him. He wondered whether he was meant to say anything else: had he forgotten something? He added 'Please' and smiled.

She bent down and, from under the counter, produced a white packet of Juno cigarettes, which she pressed into his hands. As he slipped the packet into his pocket, he could tell there was something heavier inside than cigarettes. By now he had been joined at the front of the kiosk by two Waffen SS officers. He picked up a copy of the *Völkischer Beobachter* and placed two Reichsmarks into the old lady's mittened hands. By the time she had pocketed the money she had already turned her attention to the SS men.

Niebuhr Strasse was a quiet street, in marked contrast to the bustle of the Ku'damm. He stood in the doorway of a dress shop and removed the packet of Juno from his pocket. There were only four or five cigarettes in it and he placed one straight into mouth and lit it – it would have looked too suspicious to do otherwise. Tucked into the packet was a car key attached to a small metal disk with the word 'Opel' engraved on it. There was also a folded slip of paper, which he unwrapped: UTM 142.

He looked down the street. There were few cars parked on it but he could not see the one he was looking for. He walked down the block and the last car on the corner before Schlüterstrasse was an Opel Super 6 sedan: UTM 142. It was a handsome car; four doors, dark green, white wall tyres and neither too clean nor too dirty that it might stand out.

He unlocked the door and settled into the driver's seat. The car had a musty smell to it, a mixture of damp and old leather. 'I'll do my best to get hold of the papers you need, but it won't be easy,' Kato had told him the previous afternoon. 'Whatever I can get will be in the glove box, inside the log book.'

He reached across to the glove box in front of the passenger seat and removed the black-leather log book, with the word 'Opel' in faded silver on the cover. The back cover of the book formed a sleeve and within that was what he had asked for: identity cards and a form showing that the owner of UTM 142 was entitled to buy petrol. Tucked behind the log book was something hard wrapped in a thick grey cloth.

'The car has been hidden in Weissensee since before the war began,' Kato had told him. 'A mechanic who's a secret Party member has been looking after it. He now works in an SS garage, so he's been able to obtain the correct documentation. I've kept the paperwork up to date. I was keeping it for an emergency, but if Viktor says… The identity cards won't be easy, not with so little time. It's possible to purchase these things though; the black market is very active at the moment. Do you have money I can use, by any chance?'

He had handed her a substantial sum of Swiss Francs and her eyes lit up. 'That should make it much easier,' she said. 'I'll do what I can.'

A policeman had walked past the car and now, in his rear-view mirror, Henry could see him turning around and heading slowly back in his direction. He needed to move, but first he removed from his pocket a tightly wrapped piece of paper, from which he produced the Nazi Party membership badge he had taken from the perfume shop owner in Essen. He pinned it carefully to his lapel and checked in the mirror it was at a proper angle. The car started first time, if rather noisily and lurched forward as he selected the gears. He drove slowly down the side streets to get a feel of the car before turning into Kurfürstendamm.

Create a commentary: decide your route, write it down then memorise that route in the spoken form. When you're driving along, keep reciting the commentary, it means you can avoid using a map and drawing attention to yourself.

East along Kurfürstendamm, then right into Joachimstaler Strasse, which becomes Kaiser Allee. There was surprisingly little traffic on the road, though he had to be careful of the trams. The Opel was heavy but powerful, and he had to concentrate hard to keep his speed under control.

Through Wilmersdorf and Friedenau. Kaiser Allee leads into Rein Strasse. At the end of Rein Strasse you will see the Botanischer Garten signposted. Turn right into Grunewald Strasse: you will know where you are from there.

It was 11.20. The journey had been quicker than he imagined and the Opel now handled beautifully: he had little doubt that once it got out on the open road it would perform well, assuming they got that far. In Kaiser Wilhelm Strasse he eased the car slowly to a halt in a position where he could see the house on the corner of Arno-Holz Strasse.

At various stages since he had arrived in Berlin he had been telling himself he did not need to do this, that he could pull out now. No-one would know if he did, with the possible exception of Kato. He could drive on towards Tempelhof, abandon the car and still have time to catch the 12.30 flight to Berlin – there was just about enough time – and for a brief moment he hesitated.

Then the image of Roza appeared again, smiling this time and the sense of calm that he had first encountered in the air-raid shelter in Stuttgart station returned.

He left the car and walked over to the house, knowing there was no going back.

* * *

Chapter 24: leaving Berlin, March 1941

Henry Hunter's career as a secret agent ceased the moment he knocked on the door of the house where Rosa Stern was hiding. He had been a Soviet spy since 1930 and a British one for a year and half. Serving first one then two masters had required him to be constantly on his guard, and to be in control and exercise caution all the time. Despite sometimes affecting an air of detachment and possibly coming across as a bit too questioning, Henry knew he had survived because he had actually always done what he was told.

Now, he was doing the opposite. From this moment on he was turning his back on the obedience that had dictated his life for previous ten years. He would be exploiting his training for his own interests.

When Rosa opened the door she looked as though she'd seen a ghost.

'What on earth are you doing here? I told you it was too dangerous to return: you have to leave now! Oh my God Henri this is so dangerous. Please go. Please!'

'Let me in Rosa. I need to explain. You'll understand when I tell you why I'm here. You know it's dangerous for me to stand here. Please.'

So she let him in and hurried him upstairs while she settled Frau Hermann. When she came up to the small lounge on the first floor she look flustered and stood by the closed door, arms folded.

'What is it Henri – and how come you're still in Berlin? My

God – what's that?' She was pointing at the Nazi Party membership badge on his lapel. 'You're not…'

'Don't worry Rosa; it's to stop me looking suspicious.'

She laughed sarcastically. 'A Swiss citizen walking round Berlin wearing a Nazi Party badge: you think that doesn't look suspicious?'

'Listen to me Rosa. You're in danger, you and Sophia.'

'Thanks for telling me that Henri. Don't you think I'm already very well aware of that?'

'No, no… What I mean is you're in immediate danger. You have to leave the house now!'

She gasped and moved away from the door, moving to the sofa opposite Henry.

'What do you mean?'

'I saw Franz this morning. He told me he's heard through a contact that the Gestapo have been informed you're hiding in this area: they've been told you're in a house in one of the roads just north of the Botanischer Garten. They're planning to search every house. The search could begin at any time.'

'But Franz was here yesterday, he never said a word about this. I'd have known if something was wrong, surely?'

'I saw him early this morning: he'd only just heard.'

'Are you sure?'

'Of course I'm sure. Why else do you think I'm here?'

'But Franz had a plan we'd use if we're ever in danger: he'd telephone and use a code word, then Sophia and I would go to Pankow, where a friend of his has a shop and we'd be able to hide in the attic. He…'

'There's no time Rosa. I'm sure Franz made all these plans but maybe he panicked. I told you, they could start the house-to-house search at any time. We have to leave now.'

'We?'

'Yes. I've got a car. I'm going to take you and Sophia, but we need to leave now.'

'This is madness Henri. We have no proper papers and what about Frau Hermann? I can't just abandon her.'

'I have papers Rosa, here – look.'

He handed her the identity cards Kato had left for him in the car, hers in the name of Dagmar Keufer, Sophia's in the name of Gisela Keufer. Rosa studied them carefully.

'The photographs Henri – they're not even of us!'

'No, of course not – there was no time. But they *could* be of you: they ought to be good enough for a basic check, they're not too bad and I have a card in the name of Erich Keufer, so we'll be able to pretend to be a family. You see our address is in Frankfurt: we can say we're driving there.'

'To Frankfurt – are you mad? We'll be lucky to get out of Berlin. And what do we do when we get to Frankfurt – buy a house, join the Nazi Party?'

'We're not going to Frankfurt, Rosa. We're going to Switzerland. I've got Swiss papers for you and Sophia, too, I had them prepared only last week. They're very good, but I think we can only risk using them when we're much closer to the border.'

Rosa was pacing around the room in a circle, shaking her head and running her hand through her hair. 'I'm sorry Henri but this doesn't make sense to me. You seem to have got hold of these papers very quickly – I thought you said it was only this morning that Franz told you he heard we were in danger?'

'Can be honest with you Rosa? When I first visited you here it was apparent your situation was too dangerous. I thought something like this would happen, but I didn't want to voice my fears to Franz as he's been so good to you. I was so worried I had these identity cards prepared: just in case.'

Rosa sank back in the sofa, looking overwhelmed and confused. She clearly thought Henry's plan was crazy, but then so was remaining in the house if there really was a chance it was about to be searched by the Gestapo. Henry was sure she was far from convinced but he was counting on her not risking her life and that of her daughter by ignoring him.

'And Frau Hermann?'

'Make her comfortable and tell her you'll be back later. Franz will come round after work. Rosa, we need to move fast – you need to get Sophia ready. Pack a few things, but nothing that identifies you or Sophia. We also need to take food and blankets; we might not be able to stop.'

Rosa was back by the door now, her hand on the handle. She peered at Henry sceptically.

'Perhaps I should contact Franz? We've got an agreed system to use in an emergency – I telephone him pretending to be a secretary from another law firm.'

'No Rosa! Under no circumstances! Franz said he thinks they'll be listening in to all telephone calls in this area – maybe that's why he hasn't contacted you himself. If you phone him at his office it could reveal your location and bring him under suspicion. You must do nothing that would draw attention to this house, do you understand?'

Once Rosa decided she had no alternative but to go along with Henry, she moved fast and decisively. She gave Frau Hermann her lunch early and told her she would be back later. She packed a small suitcase for her and Sophia, telling the little girl they were going on a long journey and if she was a very good girl and did everything she was asked to, and told anyone who asked her name was Gisela, she would see Alfred. *But only if you're good. And only if you remember your name is Gisela.*

Henry decided to bring the car right outside the house rather than risk Rosa and Sophia being seen crossing the road with a suitcase.

* * *

Always see a car journey in the same way as one on foot – as a series of short journeys: a car trip from London to Edinburgh, for example, should be broken down into a series of shorter stages – London to Northampton, Northampton to Nottingham, Nottingham to Sheffield, et cetera. These are much easier to explain if stopped, as long as you have a feasible story ready to explain that journey.

This aspect of his British training and more was racing around in Henry's mind as they left the house in Arno-Holz Strasse at noon. They were just ahead of the schedule he had in his mind when they pulled into a layby just outside Potsdam 40 minutes later. He turned off the engine and took out a road map from beside his seat.

'Here, let me show you our route.'

'Where to?'

'To Switzerland, I told you.'

'You're serious, aren't you? How are we going to get that far?'

'Let me show you, I have it all planned.'

Henry opened out the map, allowing it to rest on the dashboard and their laps. He moved towards Rosa as they looked at it. As he got closer he caught the scent of a delicate perfume. She flicked her hair out of her eyes, looking carefully at the map as he pointed at the Swiss border.

'I know where Switzerland is.'

'There are two possible routes, Rosa. This one here – I've called that the east route. It's more direct. We'd go south-west in more or less a straight line: Leipzig; Bayreuth; Nuremberg; Ulm. The plan would be to cross the border around Lake Konstanz…'

'Attempt to cross the border, Henri.'

'Attempt to cross the border then. I understand the Lake Konstanz part of the frontier can be a bit less dangerous than some other crossings. But that'd take us through Bavaria and close to the border with the Protectorate, where I'm told security is especially strong'.

Henry leant over Rosa to unfold more of the map. Her hair brushed his face.

'This is what I call the west route: it's much more circuitous. We'd drive to Brunswick then down towards Stuttgart before crossing the border around Singen, with an option to go over the mountains. It has the advantage of taking us close to Frankfurt, which is where our identity cards say we are from.'

Rosa studied the map for a while. She frowned.

'I suppose your west route is the lesser of two evils. Do you know how long it'll take us?'

'From here to Brunswick is just over 110 miles, but I'm planning to come off the main roads and stick to the side roads as much as I can. If anyone asks why, just say you get car sick on main roads. I think we'll get south of Brunswick – maybe as far as Göttingen – before it gets dark. We can then look for a wood to drive into and hide for the night. We'll be 200 miles from Stuttgart: we can be there by Wednesday night and drive to Switzerland on the Thursday.'

Rosa said nothing, but shrugged as if in reluctant agreement. Henry restarted the Opel and they pulled out into the road.

'You must drive slower, please – and not so close to the centre of the road. You had this all planned, didn't you?'

'What do you mean?'

'You're too near the kerb now, just slow down a bit,' said Rosa. 'Are you seriously telling me you saw Franz this morning and since then you've sorted all this out, including working out how long it's going to take?'

'Yes and no. I told you Rosa, since I first met you I'd been so concerned at the danger you were in that I'd given some consideration to this. And when Franz told me this morning I had to move fast.'

To the surprise of both of them, the journey to Brunswick was uneventful. Where they could, they dropped off the main road: the Lower Saxony countryside was ideal for this kind of driving, with plenty of small narrow roads leading off the larger ones. On the occasions they passed police or military vehicles no interest was paid to them: a husband and wife and their daughter out for a drive. A few miles to the north of Göttingen, with the light beginning to fail, they came across a wood with a track leading into it from the road. Henry stopped the car and managed to open a creaky wooden gate, then drove as deep into the wood as possible. When he walked back to shut the gate it was impossible to see the Opel from the road. It was when he returned to the car, feeling pleased with himself and almost relaxed, that Sophia started crying. It was a soft cry at first, almost a series of sobs, but then it became louder.

'What is it darling?'

When Sophia replied she spoke so quietly her mother had to lean across the front seat to hear her.

'I can't hear you darling; you'll need to speak up.'

'But I can't, Mama,' she whispered. 'You told me to whisper. You said people mustn't hear me speak.'

Rosa turned around and stroked her daughter's face.

'It's alright now darling. You don't need to whisper here in the car: only if there are other people around. Now, what were you going to say?'

'I'm frightened.' Each word punctuated by a noisy sob.

'What are you frightened of?'

'The goblins! There are always goblins in a forest.'

'There are no such thing as goblins,' said Henry impatiently. 'And, in any case, this is not a forest, it's a wood.'

This only seemed to make things worse and Sophia's cry turned into a wail. Rosa left the front seat and went to sit next to Sophia in the back. After a long cuddle, the little girl calmed down.

'Where are we going?'

'You should rest now darling.'

'But where are we going?' Sophia sounded as if was pleading with her mother.

'Somewhere safe darling. Now, please rest.'

'If we're going somewhere safe, does it mean we'll see Alfred there?'

'Yes darling, I told you we would, especially if you're a good girl. You should rest now.'

'Will we also see papa in the safe place? Why don't you tell me?'

Rosa didn't reply. Henry glanced back at her, her head had dropped and she was tapping her teeth with her knuckles as her eyes filled with tears. Sophia was sitting with her legs hunched up to her face, her enormous dark eyes unblinking as they looked up at him from behind her kneecaps. In the gloom her pale skin now appeared chalky-white. She gave him the beginnings of a smile and waved one of the paws of the dirty, white, one-eared rabbit she was clutching at Henry, who waved back awkwardly.

'If you're quiet, Sophia, and behave very, very well,' said Henry, 'then I promise that when we get to the safe place you'll get a present. But you have to be quiet.'

'What kind of present?'

Henry shrugged. 'Chocolates.'

The little girl said nothing but pulled a face.

'What about a new rabbit? That one looks very old – it's only got one ear.'

'But I love Mr Rabbit! You can't take him away!'

The little girl started crying again. Rosa pulled her close.

'No-one is going to take Mr Rabbit away darling. Henri meant we'll buy you a friend for Mr Rabbit.'

During the long silence that followed the light dimmed quickly and when Sophia spoke again it was almost dark.

'It'll be nice for Mr Rabbit to have a friend, won't it Mama?'

'Yes darling. You try to rest now.'

'Because we don't have friends anymore, do we?'

'What do you mean darling?'

'Alfred told me that. He said the reason we had to be so quiet in the house and not go near the window is because no-one is our friend. Is that true?'

Rosa said nothing, but busied herself arranging a blanket around Sophia, allowing the rabbit's head to poke out of the top.

'Here are some biscuits darling. Eat those then try to get to sleep.'

She munched at the biscuits, her eyes looking around the car, unblinking.

'Why is no-one our friend, Mama?'

'Don't keep asking questions, darling. Where we're going, everyone will be our friend.'

'Is Henri our friend?'

In the rear-view mirror Henry caught Rosa's face as she hesitated briefly before replying.

'Yes, darling. Sleep now.'

Henry watched through the mirror, waiting for Sophia to fall asleep. When she finally did, he cleared his throat and turned around to talk. Now was the time, he had decided, to be honest with Rosa. Maybe then she would see him in a better light.

But when he turned, Rosa was fast asleep too and the moment had passed.

* * *

On the Tuesday morning, before the Opel had even left Berlin, Franz Hermann was becoming increasingly worried. He had been unnerved by the encounter with Alois Jäger in Oberwallstrasse and even more so by the way his colleague had been since then. First of all Jäger had only walked with him part of the way to the office, then had suddenly stopped and said he needed to go back and check something. Back at the office he had come in to see him.

'If you had not told me otherwise, Franz, then I'd have thought you and that Swiss man knew each other. You looked like you were acquaintances, rather than one stranger giving directions to another.'

He assured Jäger he was mistaken: he had been to morning Mass and, as he'd left the cathedral, the man had asked him for directions. He had even gone somewhat out of his way to make sure the man went the right way.

'And fancy the coincidence of me having met him in Bern last year!'

Franz agreed with Jäger it was indeed a coincidence. *It's a small world, as they say.*

'But so strange. When I was in Bern, he was about to travel to Stuttgart on business – I even helped him with his visa at our

Embassy there. He was staying at the Schweizerhof, which, I tell you, Franz, is a very expensive hotel. And now look – he's a mere courier.'

'Perhaps he fell on hard times, Alois.'

'Perhaps.'

Both men continued to be uneasy about the encounter. As was the custom on Tuesdays, the senior lawyers at the practice lunched together and the two men eyed each other throughout the meal. Hermann was worried Jäger did not believe him and Jäger was convinced Hermann was nervous. When they went back into their respective offices, each man closed his door and made a phone call. Jäger made his first, telephoning a good friend of his who was in charge of the Gestapo office in Treptow. 'Tell me Lothar,' he said after a brief exchange of pleasantries, 'you must have good contacts with your colleagues at Tempelhof, no? You're practically neighbours... Good, I thought as much. Do me a favour will you, Lothar? I'm sure it's nothing, perhaps just me being suspicious, but could you discreetly check whether a Swiss citizen called Henri Hesse travelled on a flight from Tempelhof to Stuttgart at around 12.30 today?'

Lothar asked one or two questions. *We are very thorough in the Gestapo, you know Alois!* Both men laughed. Lothar checked the exact spelling of the man's name. *And could you describe him?*

'Perhaps mid-thirties; average height, slightly overweight. Pale complexion, darkish hair as far as I could tell, but he was wearing a trilby hat.'

'I'll see what I can do Alois.'

At the same time in his office one floor below Jäger's, Franz

Hermann was pacing up and down. Something was not right, but he had no idea what he could do about it. He picked up the telephone and dialled his mother's number in Dahlem. At least he could be reassured all was well there.

* * *

Captain Edgar and Basil Remington-Barber had travelled to Geneva after spending the weekend with Henry in Zürich. They based themselves at a perfectly decent if somewhat anonymous hotel within sight of Cornavin railway station, where they hoped to meet Henry late on the Tuesday night.

The hotel had been chosen carefully: as well as their proximity to the station, they had been able to book two rooms on the top floor, set apart from the others on the corridor. Each room had a telephone and they made sure, from the moment they arrived, one of them would always be beside it. They did not expect to hear anything until 4.30 on Tuesday afternoon at the earliest, when Hunter's flight from Stuttgart was scheduled to land at Zürich. Rolf would be waiting at the airport to see Henry arrive and check he travelled onto Zürich; one of Rolf's men would then be at the station to watch Henry meeting with the Russians and catch the train to Geneva. Edgar and Remington-Barber ensured they were both waiting by the phone in Geneva from four o'clock on the Tuesday afternoon. At a quarter past, Remington-Barber observed Henry's flight ought to be landing and they should be hearing from Rolf at any moment.

'It's a tight schedule we've allowed him, Edgar. He has to go to

Bank Leu, then meet up with his Russian chap, allow them to copy the document and still make that last train to Geneva.'

'He'll be fine Basil. Why don't you sit down and relax? Hedinger will stay on as late as he needs to and the last train to Geneva leaves at a quarter to eight. Please stop worrying. You can pour us another drink if you think that'll help.'

By five o'clock Edgar, if pressed, would have described himself as concerned. Five minutes after that the phone rang and both men jumped. Remington-Barber answered it. *Yes, Hello Rolf... I see... Yes... No... Are you sure?... And you've checked there?... Do it again please Rolf... Yes... Probably... Call us back in ten minutes.* As he replaced the phone his hands were shaking.

'Well?' asked Edgar.

'Henry wasn't on the flight.'

'Are you sure?' Edgar's face was just inches from his colleague's.

'You heard what I said, Edgar. Rolf Eder is no fool, he's one of the best men I've ever had in the field, doesn't miss a thing. He said there were 12 passengers who came off the Swissair flight and Hunter wasn't one of them.'

'Maybe he missed the connection at Stuttgart? After all, there was only a 20-minute gap between the Berlin flight landing and the Zürich flight taking off...'

'Yes, but they're connecting flights. If the Berlin flight is late they hold the Zürich one. It's possible he missed the flight from Berlin, but it's unlikely: he had ample time to meet Hugo, go to the Reichsbank then get to Tempelhof.'

When Rolf called back ten minutes later he said he'd been able to check the flight's manifest with a Swissair contact: though a

Henri Hesse had been booked in, he had not been on the connecting flight from Berlin. Edgar snatched the phone from Remington-Barber.

'Rolf? It's me, Edgar. Look, your best bet is to get to the station in Zürich as soon as possible and join your man there. See if you can spot Viktor and his chaps. If Henry's not going to show up they'll probably get worried at some stage and break cover. Just see what they're up to. If we see them looking for him, then at least that tells us something.'

'Jesus Christ!' said Edgar, slamming the phone down and pacing the room. 'Basil… You telephone Hedinger and ask if his courier has arrived from Berlin. I can't imagine he will have done, but there's a distant possibility he may have heard from him or Reinhart. In fact, ask him to send a telegram to Reinhart asking if all went well with the courier, then tell Hedinger to stay on until at least seven. Jesus Christ.'

By eight o'clock they knew little more. Michael Hedinger told them he had neither heard from nor seen his courier and promised to send a telegram to Reinhart that night. Rolf reported he had managed to get to the station by six o'clock, where he was joined by three of his men. At seven they spotted Viktor prowling around, looking anxious. There was no sign of Hunter boarding the last train to Geneva or any of the ones before it. Viktor had been waiting by the ticket barrier, his face creased in anger as the train departed.

'At least he's let them down too.'

'What do we do Edgar?'

Edgar continued to pace the room angrily, cursing under his

breath. 'It's that bloody woman, I'm sure it is. Jesus Christ. We'd better get on the first train to Zürich in the morning.'

* * *

The mood in a dingy rented apartment between the railway tracks and the river in Zürich was scarcely any better. Each of the four men who had been with him at the station were brought in one by one and questioned by Viktor, but, as he had been there himself, there was little point in it. Henry had not come anywhere near the station.

'He seems to have disappeared,' said Viktor.

'When we met him last week, he said something about having asked you for the details of any comrades he could contact in Berlin, in an emergency,' said one of Viktor's men.

'So…?'

'So I was thinking that if you did give him details of any comrades in Berlin, then they might know what's happened to him.'

Viktor said nothing for a while, thinking how little he could trust even those closest to him.

'You're mistaken. I've no comrades left in my network in Berlin: they've all gone – either escaped, disappeared, dead or become Nazis. I told him to contact the Embassy.'

'Really? I thought you didn't trust anyone there?'

'I don't,' said Viktor 'I don't trust anyone.'

* * *

Back in Berlin that Tuesday evening Alois Jäger finally heard back from his friend in the Gestapo. It was 6.30 and Jäger had remained behind in his office awaiting the call.

'You say his name is Henri Hesse and he's a Swiss citizen?'

'Yes,' said Jäger.

'Well, I not only contacted Heinrich at Tempelhof but I actually went over there to his office myself, so I was able to look at all the paperwork. There were three Swiss nationals on the Deutsche Luft Hansa flight that left for Stuttgart at 12.30, but none of them had that name. The officer in charge of checking the papers as the passengers boarded the plane said, as far as he could recall, one of the Swiss was a woman and the other two were men in either their fifties or sixties.'

'He wasn't on that flight then, obviously.'

'However,' said Lothar, 'he was *booked* onto that flight, he just didn't turn up for it. And furthermore, there's a record of him having arrived at Tempelhof yesterday, on the flight from Stuttgart. What is it that concerns you about this man, Alois?'

Jäger thought long and hard.

'I'm not sure, Lothar. Something about him doesn't quite add up. And now missing his flight like that...'

Very odd, they both agreed – so much so they decided to meet up the next day to discuss the matter.

* * *

Franz Hermann had telephoned his mother's house five times on the Tuesday afternoon and each time the call went unanswered his anxiety increased. By 4.55 he decided he had to go down to Dahlem to check, but he was wary of Alois Jäger; he decided it would be unwise to leave the office before him. Normally his colleague was so preoccupied with Nazi Party meetings in the evening he invariably departed the office no later than five o'clock, but that day it was 6.30 before he left.

As soon as he did, Franz Hermann made his exit too. It was nearly quarter past seven before he arrived at his mother's house on Arno-Holz Strasse. He knocked on the door but there was no answer, so he used his own key to let himself in. The house felt empty and there was no reply when he called out. The lights were on downstairs but the upper floors were dark. Certain he was walking into a trap he headed for the room at the back overlooking the garden, where his mother spent her days.

He found her propped up in her armchair, swathed in blankets with a tray next to her and her eyes red from crying.

'I've been calling her for hours Franz!' she said in a hoarse voice. 'She said something about going out but that you'd be here later. What does she think she's up to? I've been on my own all this time. I'm desperate to go to the toilet and I haven't had my evening meal yet. The telephone was ringing but I couldn't reach it!'

Setting aside his fear, Franz Hermann acted swiftly. He helped his mother to the toilet then settled her before going upstairs. There was no sign of Rosa and Sophia, and within half an hour he had gathered up any items belonging to them or that could even be associated with them. He bundled everything into old laundry bags and carried them into the attic, where he locked them in an old trunk, which he then covered with old tennis rackets, a cello case and other reminders of when life was more normal.

When he came downstairs he telephoned Gunter Reinhart at his home. He knew it was a big risk, but he had no alternative.

'Did your courier visit today?'

'Yes – why?'

'And was he acting normally?'

'I think so, hard to tell really. Is there a problem?'

'No, no, no – of course not. I was just checking what time he left you?'

'I'm not too sure, I would say by 10.30. Something like that.'

'Perhaps we'll meet tomorrow for a chat?' said the lawyer, hoping the other man would recognise the urgency in his voice.

'Yes, perhaps that would be a good idea.'

After that Hermann telephoned his wife and told her he would stay at his mother's house tonight as the nurse had been called away. He telephoned his sister with the sad news that the nurse who cared so well for their mother had been called back to Bremerhaven because her husband had been killed at sea. *It was terrible*, they both agreed. The poor nurse had no idea how long she would be there, but in the meantime they needed to sort out their mother. Hermann's sister paused for a while then said if he could look after her until Thursday, she would come over and bring her back to Brandenburg. She can stay with us for a week or so: *I imagine the nurse will be back by then.*

'I'm sure she will,' replied Franz.

* * *

It was some time after dawn on the Wednesday before enough light to wake them penetrated the woodland just to the north of Göttingen. Sophia was upset again when she woke up. The tall trees frightened her and she wanted to know if there was no such thing as goblins, what about witches? Hardly reassured by her mother's promise that they were quite safe, she then wanted to know when she was going to see Alfred.

'Soon, darling.'

'When is soon, Mama?'

Henry had been out of the car for a few minutes and had just returned.

'The sooner we can leave this place, the better,' he said.

'Give us a few minutes, Henri,' said Rosa. 'Sophia, eat these biscuits and drink the milk, then we can be on our way.'

'To see Alfred and Papa?'

'Maybe not today, but hopefully soon. And remember, darling, if anyone asks, your name is Gisela: Gisela Keufer. We'll all play that game until we meet Alfred, do you understand?'

Henry checked the map and tried to show the route to Rosa, but she wasn't interested.

'It's amazing we've got this far, Henry. Our luck can't hold out much longer.' She spoke quietly so Sophia could not hear, but there was no disguising the annoyance and fear in her voice.

'I don't see why not, especially if we keep to the back roads.'

'What if they're looking for us?'

'How would anyone know? Franz is unlikely to report us, is he?'

They waited until seven o'clock before starting off, first heading south through Göttingen then keeping to the patchwork of smaller roads until they reached Würzburg at lunchtime. They needed to stop for petrol, which was risky, but Würzburg was just 70 miles west of Frankfurt, their supposed home town. They drove slowly through the town centre, looking out for a petrol station. The first one they found had a police van waiting at one of the two pumps, so they drove on. Then just before the river they came to a garage with a solitary pump and an elderly owner sitting outside on a bench with a large dog sitting next to him and less than an inch of a lit cigarette protruding from his lips. He asked to see the documents entitling them to petrol.

'If I was minded to be difficult,' he said in a gruff Bavarian accent, 'then I'd say you're only entitled to half a tank.' He smiled, revealing a mouth filled with near-black teeth. The cigarette stub seemed to be stuck to his lower lip. The man's eyes focussed on the Nazi Party badge on Henry's lapel and swiftly his mood became less hostile. 'But, fortunately for you sir, I'm not minded to be difficult. I had a delivery yesterday – the first for over a week. I'll fill you up but you don't need to tell anyone that. Come inside. It takes longer these days to do the paperwork than it does to repair a car… Maybe even longer than it takes to build one.' The man's throaty laugh echoed around the workshop before breaking into a violent cough.

They went over to a counter at the side of the garage. The owner checked the paperwork painfully slowly: he looked at the identity card in the name of Erich Keufer and the documents showing that the Opel Super 6 sedan, registration number UTM 142, was entitled to petrol every ten days. Henry glanced out of the garage and saw Rosa looking worried: this was taking a long time. The owner wrote slowly in a large ledger.

'So tell me, are you returning to Frankfurt?'

'No, we're just on our way from there. We're visiting my wife's family in Nuremberg.'

'You sound like you may not be from Frankfurt?'

'Well spotted my friend: I've lived all over Germany, which explains my accent!'

The owner nodded and handed back the paperwork, which was now covered in grey grease marks. 'Odd that your petrol entitlement document was last stamped in Berlin.'

When he returned to the car Sophia was asleep on the back seat and Rosa looked pale and tense.

'Why did it take so long?'

'Paperwork,' he said.

* * *

The garage owner, Jürgen Neumann, was a worried man as he watched the Opel Super 6 pull away awkwardly from the forecourt of his garage. He was not a political man by any means and nor was he any good at keeping his mouth shut, and that was his problem. In recent months he had rather too openly complained to his decreasing number of customers, about the infrequency of his deliveries, the cost of food and the lack of business. This had led to a series of visits, firstly from a Würzburg police officer who happened to be a friend of his, and culminated in a visit from the deputy head of the local Gestapo, who was no friend at all.

This complaining has to stop. If you're out to make trouble then be

*assured we can make plenty of trouble for you. It's about time you were
more co-operative with us.*

And that had been followed by a noticeable drop in business
and in the delivery of fuel. So now Jürgen Neumann had decided
enough was enough. Unless he went out of his way to ingratiate
himself with the powers that be he would have to close down his
business. He picked up the telephone and dialled the number of
the deputy head of the local Gestapo, the man who had recently
given him his warning.

'It's probably nothing, sir, but I did promise to contact you with
any information.'

He explained about the car that had come from Frankfurt but
whose petrol entitlement document was last stamped in Berlin,
and whose driver said they were heading for Nuremberg but had
driven off in the other direction. It all seemed rather... odd.

Do I have the registration number sir? Of course I do.

* * *

Three hours before the garage owner in Würzburg contacted the
Gestapo office, a lady in Berlin rang her local police station and
began in a similar manner.

'It's probably of little consequence and I was unsure whether to
trouble you, but I thought I'd pass on this information in case you
were interested.'

The officer who took the call at Dahlem police station was well
used to this. These days he seemed to spend half his time taking
calls from people eager to inform on neighbours, work colleagues,

friends and even family. This one sounded little different and he took down the details. The lady, a Frau Werner, said she lived in Arno-Holz Strasse and although she was minding her own business and was certainly not the kind of person to spy on her neighbours she couldn't help but notice something unusual the previous morning – *yes, Tuesday.*

'There's an elderly person who lives opposite me: a Frau Hermann. I hardly ever see her these days, she's virtually housebound. She has a nurse, I understand, who also hardly ever leaves the house. But yesterday, it must have been around noon, I happened to notice a man leave the house and walk over to a car parked just across the road. He then parked immediately outside Frau Hermann's house. Within two or three minutes, no more than that, I saw the man come out of the house along with Frau Hermann's nurse and with them was a young girl. They all seemed to be rather nervous, looking around. I've never seen a child going in or out of that house before: never. How old do you say? Four or five, I'm not sure. They were in a hurry. Do I think they saw me? No: I don't want you to think bad of me, sir, but I was kneeling down on the floor, peering through a gap in the net curtains… As it happens, sir, yes I did. Are you ready? It was an Opel – I'm not sure what model, but it was dark green and the registration number was… Do you have a pen ready? UTM 142.'

Up until a couple of weeks previously, the policeman would have annoyed by this call, as it would have meant hours of work just to satisfy the whim of a nosey neighbour. But recently the rules had changed. After one or two unfortunate incidents, the Gestapo had realised criminals and others they were interested in were finding it too easy to move around the Reich by car. As these people drove from one town or district to another, there was no proper system of keeping track of them. So the Gestapo brought in a new one: the details of any cars the Gestapo or other sections of the police were interested in would be passed on to a central control in Berlin.

Suits me fine: more work for them, less for me, thought the officer. He filled in the form and took it upstairs to the Gestapo liaison office in the station. Still, he thought, they will be pleased enough with this one.

It's not often we get a registration number.

* * *

Chapter 25: the Black Forest, March 1941

Franz Hermann woke early on Wednesday morning, checked on his mother then walked around the house he had grown up in, preoccupied with thoughts that had played around in his head all night. He needed to move fast.

Once his mother was settled, he left the house through the back gate, from where it was a swift ten-minute walk to his own home. He explained his plans to his wife. Before leaving the house, he telephoned his sister then the office, telling them he would be slightly late as he needed to see a client on his way in.

He rarely used his car these days but the Daimler started at the third attempt and within two minutes he was back at his mother's house, parked by the back gate he had departed through barely half an hour previously. He told his mother she would be coming to his house for a day or two, then his sister would collect her and she would go and stay with her in Brandenburg for a week or so. Hopefully after that the nurse would return and everything would be back to normal. His mother was confused but there was no time to argue.

Once she was settled at his house, he left for work, but not before stopping once again at his mother's, where he spent an hour checking again there were no signs anyone had been there for at least a day or two.

He made a point of leaving the house though the front door and boldly walking over to the house opposite, from where the lady carefully observed all the comings and goings in the street. As he approached her door he noticed the net curtains in the front window twitch; a moment later the door opened, a split second before he had knocked.

'Frau Werner, I thought I'd let you know in case anyone asks that there'll be no-one at my mother's house for a few days. In fact, she's not been there since Sunday – she's staying with my wife and me. Her nurse has had to return to Bremerhaven suddenly: a death, I'm afraid. Her husband was in the navy, he died in the cause of the Reich.'

The woman was very grateful to be told. She told Franz she had wondered about Frau Hermann because only the previous day she had seen the nurse leave the house with a man… and a young girl. They had been carrying a case and some other things they had put in the boot of a car parked outside the house then driven off.

'Oh really?' He was trying his best to sound confused rather than shocked. 'Could you describe the man?'

With unerring accuracy she described Henri Hesse. Franz Hermann did his best to look none the wiser. 'As I say, Frau Werner, my mother has been staying with us since Sunday. I've no idea about this man; it's possible he was taking her to Bremerhaven.'

'And what about the girl?'

'As far as I'm aware no child has been in the house for a very long time. How old would you say she was?'

'Perhaps four or five, hard to say. I didn't get a perfect view, you understand. She was such a slight thing.'

'And you're certain they came from my mother's house? Maybe they were just passers-by.'

She was certain. She just happened to be cleaning the windows at the time – by coincidence.

'I don't suppose you saw what car it was, by any chance?'

'I do, Herr Hermann: it was an Opel, a dark-green one. And not only that: I even wrote down the registration number. But don't worry; I've given all the details to the police.'

* * *

When they left Würzburg, Henry announced they would head south-west, into the Black Forest.

'The Black Forest?'

'Yes, Rosa, the Black Forest.'

'You're crazy! Do you still read fairy tales?'

Sophia started to cry in the back seat. She didn't want to go into a forest. She was afraid of witches. Henry turned round and snapped at the little girl.

'I told you! There's no such thing as witches, or goblins. Or fairies, for that matter.'

Sophia's crying became louder.

'Don't shout at her: she's a little girl. She's frightened and she's not the only one.'

'Trust me Rosa, the Black Forest stretches down to the Swiss border: it almost goes as far as Basle!'

'I'm aware of that, but do you really think we can just stroll over the border? Maybe the SS or whoever's guarding it will help carry our cases!'

'Listen to me, Rosa: our Swiss papers are very good, far superior to the German ones. I'm using my own papers and I managed to get ones that show you're my wife and she's our daughter. They're hidden in the boot. When we get near the border we can use them, but we'll need to abandon the car first.'

They stuck to the side roads and, at 4.30, emerged from a long lane onto the main road at Heilbronn, before taking the road to Pforzheim and from there into the Black Forest.

* * *

Edgar and Remington-Barber arrived in Zürich on Wednesday afternoon and were met at the station by Rolf, who took them to another of their safe houses, an apartment above a bar on Predigerplatz. On the way up, he collected a bottle of whisky.

'I think it's a bit early for that,' Edgar said once they were in the small apartment.

'Not when you hear what I'm about to tell you,' said the Austrian. 'I went to see Hedinger this morning, he'd just heard from Reinhart. Apparently Henri did come to Reinhart's office at the Reichsbank yesterday morning to collect the documents. Last night Hugo called Reinhart to ask whether Henri had been to his office and they arranged to meet up today, which they did at lunchtime. It seems that rather than heading for Tempelhof, Henri headed for Hugo's mother's house in Dahlem.'

In the shocked silence that followed Remington-Barber looked confused, as if he had not heard properly what Rolf had said. Edgar had heard clearly enough and looked furious.

'No!'

'Yes, I'm afraid so. Hugo knows this because he was telephoning his mother's house all Tuesday afternoon and when there was no reply he went round there after work. His mother was all alone; there was no sign of Rosa or her daughter. This morning he spoke to a neighbour who'd seen Rosa leave the house with a young girl and a man who seems to match Henry's description. They drove off in a green Opel.'

Edgar leaned over to the whisky bottle and poured himself a measure that in other circumstances would be described as excessive. He drank most of it, repeating 'Jesus Christ' several times.

'How on earth has he managed to get hold of a car?'

'Your guess is as good as mine, Basil: the fool probably stole it. Carry on Rolf.'

'Reinhart is in a terrible state, according to Hedinger. He thinks the Gestapo are about to knock on his door and, of course, Hugo is worried sick too – not least because when he was with Henry on Tuesday morning they bumped into a colleague of his who is not only an active Nazi but also claims he'd met Henry in Bern a year ago.'

Remington-Barber was watching Edgar very carefully, expecting him to explode at any moment, but he remained calm. Edgar drank the whisky remaining in his glass, removed his jacket, loosened his tie and walked over to the window. 'Thank you Rolf. By the sounds of it, Henry decided that rather than return to Switzerland as instructed, he'd turn his return journey into some kind of rescue mission.' Edgar was speaking very calmly, as if everything he said had a perfect logic to it.

'But he's carrying the Rostock Report, Edgar. It's meant to be falling into the hands of our Soviet friends!'

Edgar turned from the window. 'Thank you Basil, I'd realised that.'

* * *

By March 1941 few people in Germany would have been foolish enough to accuse the Gestapo of inefficiency. When the deputy head of the Gestapo in Würzburg was informed by the garage owner about the 'odd' dark-green Opel Super 6, he simply followed procedure. He sent a telex giving the details of the car to his regional headquarters, where in turn the duty officer followed procedure and passed on the details of the car to the new central control room in Berlin. Around three o'clock that Wednesday afternoon an officer at the control room in the Gestapo headquarters in Prinz-Albrecht-Strasse was reviewing the 'alerts' received since his lunch break. When he spotted that a dark-green Opel, registration number UTM 142, had been added to the watch list he thought there was something familiar about it, so he checked that morning's alerts. Sure enough, the Gestapo liaison office at Dahlem police station had passed on details of the same car: a woman who lived in Arno-Holz Strasse had observed a man, woman and young girl leaving a neighbour's house and getting into the car. They seemed, according to the neighbour, 'nervous'.

The officer wrote up his notes: the car was seen in Berlin at noon on the Tuesday and just over 24 hours later it was in Würzburg. It would certainly be worth putting this one out for national alert: he should have been less sceptical about this new system, maybe it was working after all. And thank heavens for frightened business owners and nosey neighbours, what would the Gestapo do without them?

At four o'clock that Wednesday afternoon officer Reinhard Goetz left the police station in Pforzheim for a routine patrol, briefed – among other things – to keep an eye out for the dark-green Opel. 'Berlin is interested and it was last seen in Würzburg,' he had been told. 'It was heading south – so you never know. It's the Gestapo who're interested, so keep your eyes peeled.'

The traffic policeman headed east on his BMW motorbike and after a while changed direction: south into the Black Forest. At five o'clock he decided he had earned his first cigarette break, so just before the small town of Tiefenbronn he pulled into a clearing in an area where the forest was starting to become dense. He would be able to enjoy his cigarette in peace. But as he turned into the clearing he noticed a car was already there. A dark-green Opel Super 6. He parked his motorbike so it blocked the path back to the road and walked over to check the registration number of the car.

Henry was on his own in the car when Goetz pulled into the clearing, Rosa having taken Sophia into the trees to go to the toilet. He watched as the officer parked his bike and headed towards the car. Henry glanced to his left, but there was no sign of Rosa and Sophia. Watching the policeman all the time, he leaned over to the glove box and removed the bundle of grey cloth from behind the log book. The policeman smiled at him from a distance and Henry smiled back as the policeman moved in a wide arc to the front of the car. Henry held the bundle below the steering wheel and slowly unwrapped it. By now, the officer was in front, peering down at the registration plate. He looked up at Henry and made a motion with his fingers to unwind the window.

Officer Goetz bent down by the window, his face inches from Henry's.

'Is this your car?'

'Yes.'

'Where have you come from today?'

'Frankfurt.'

'And where are you going?'

'We're just out for a drive – to see the forest.'

'We?'

'My wife and daughter – they've gone to the toilet down there.'

'Have you been in Berlin in the past day or so?'

'Berlin? No, of course not!'

'Or Würzburg today?'

Henry hesitated for too long. He had no idea how to respond. 'Maybe… We stopped at a town for petrol. I don't know what it was called.'

'Right: get out of the car now, I want to check your papers.'

He noticed the policeman's right hand moving towards the holster on his hip and knew he had just seconds to act. The policeman stepped back as Henry opened the car door and at that moment both heard the voices of Rosa and Sophia emerging from the trees. As the policeman glanced in their direction Henry pushed the revolver into his stomach and fired. It was a muffled shot and the man staggered back before collapsing to the ground. He was still conscious and trying to remove his own pistol from its holster. Behind him, Henry could hear Rosa and Sophia screaming.

He stepped towards the prone body of the policeman. A pool of blood was forming beneath him as he tried to lift his own revolver, but he didn't have the strength. Henry held his gun no more than a few inches from the man's head and pulled the trigger. In the ensuing seconds, his world slipped into slow motion.

He was aware of a chunk of the man's head flying away, of gore splattering around him, of the sound of the shot bouncing off every tree in the forest and what appeared to be thousands of birds swarming in every direction. Then there were Rosa and Sophia standing in front of him, their mouths wide open in silent screams. By now he had sunk to his knees, the gun still in his hand, staring at the body of the third person he had killed.

For a time he could not hear anything other than the ringing of gunfire in his ears. When his hearing began to return Rosa was shouting at him.

'What on earth have you done? You've killed a policeman!'

'Calm down and get Sophia into the car. We need to sort things out.'

Rosa bundled her daughter into the back of the Opel and came back over to him.

'He was looking for us. He checked the numberplate then asked whether we'd been in Berlin or in Würzburg today. He told me to get out of the car and I could see he was reaching for his gun. He was distracted when he heard you so I knew I had to do something. We need to move him and his bike – quickly.'

It took the two of them ten minutes to carry the man's body as deep into the forest as they could manage, covering it with undergrowth. While Henry wheeled the motorbike far amongst the trees in another direction, Rosa did her best to clean up the ground where the man had been shot.

'What do we do now?' They were both standing by the car, breathless and filthy.

'We need to get away from here as quickly as possible.'

'Even I could have worked that out. Which direction do we head in? Towards the Swiss border?'

'No, not now – it's too late and he'll be reported missing soon. We don't want to be stuck in the forest or even near the border when that happens.'

'So where do we go then?'

'We'll go to Stuttgart and ditch the car.'

Rosa sniffed. 'And what do you propose we do then – check into the best hotel in town?'

'Something like that – yes.'

* * *

Chapter 26: Munich and Stuttgart, March and April, 1941

'Basil, without in any way wishing to appear rude, may I suggest you pause, take a deep breath then start again?'

It was the evening of Friday 28th March, and Edgar and Basil Remington-Barber had been stuck in the apartment above the bar in Zürich since Wednesday. They had heard nothing further about Henry since Hedinger's report that he had last been seen in Berlin on Tuesday. The circumstantial evidence he had possibly left Berlin with Rosa and her daughter was bad enough; the fact he had the Rostock Report with him rather than it being in Soviet hands was disastrous.

Now Basil had received a phone call from the embassy in Bern: *some news.*

'I'm sorry Edgar; the tension does rather get to one at times. They're in Stuttgart.'

'Who?'

'Henry, Rosa and her daughter.'

'Jesus Christ: I knew it. What on earth does he imagine he's up to? Is he safe?'

'For the time being, yes, though I'd say considering their circumstances, safe is a very relative word. '

'And how do we know this?'

'You remember Milo, the Night Manager at the Hotel Victoria? Well, we've heard from her. She contacts us in code by telex to a travel agent in Bern, one with which we have an understanding. It's a safe form of communication – a hotel confirming bookings with a travel agent, terribly routine stuff – if a bit cumbersome. It rather relies on the travel agent passing the messages on to us quickly. And though Milo sent the telex on Thursday night, the travel agent didn't see it until this morning and, for reasons that aren't entirely apparent, waited until this afternoon before informing my office at the embassy. They in turn seem to have taken their time before thinking of letting me know. I shall be having harsh words with them about this, I can assure you.'

'So how does Milo know about them?'

'Because they're in her hotel Edgar.'

* * *

By the time they left the Black Forest, it was 5.30 on the Wednesday evening and it took them another two and a quarter hours to reach Stuttgart. It was a quarter to eight when Henry parked at the northern end of the Schlossplatz, as near as he dared to the railway station. As they parked, a squadron of Heinkel fighters flew low overhead.

'You're sure this is going to work?' asked Rosa, not for the first time since he'd explained his plan.

'No, Rosa, I'm not sure. But it's our best hope. They're bound to find the car and I just hope they'll assume we must have caught a train, so with any luck they'll look for people leaving Stuttgart rather than staying in it. And when we walk away from the car, we'll look like travellers who've just arrived by train.'

It took them five minutes to walk from the Schlossplatz to the Hotel Victoria, Rosa carrying an exhausted Sophia. Instead of going to the main entrance on Friedrichstrasse they walked into Keplerstrasse at the side of the hotel. It was quiet, the night was drawing in and there was no movement in the street. In a room above them, possibly the restaurant, they could hear people laughing and glasses clinking. Henry moved Rosa and Sophia into a concealed doorway.

'Wait here and keep an eye on me. If I can get the door open, watch out for my signal then hurry along but don't run.'

'And if you can't?'

Henry hesitated. 'Don't worry: I'll think of something.'

Keeping as close to the wall as possible Henry edged towards the door that led to the basement of the hotel. He had last been there with Milo on the morning of his journey to Essen the previous year. He had no idea whether Milo was still working at the hotel. For all he knew, she could have been arrested, but it was the only plan he could think of.

The door to the basement was stiff, but started to give after a few pushes and when he used his shoulder it sprung open. He descended the steep concrete steps: the basement was warm and dimly lit, beyond the machinery he could make out a laundry area. After that was a door he seemed to remember led to the stairs into the main part of the hotel. There was no sign of anyone down there.

He climbed back up the stairs and gestured for Rosa and Sophia to join him. Once they were safely in, he shut the door and whispered to Rosa.

'We'll find somewhere in here to hide and after midnight I'll go up to the hotel and see if she's there.'

'You say this woman is on duty at night?'

'Most nights, but not every night. But I have to tell you, Rosa, it's nearly a year since I saw her, I can't even be sure she's still here.'

They found a corner of the basement that was dark and warm, and huddled together. They gave what little food they had left to Sophia and soon she fell asleep in her mother's arms. At midnight, Henry decided to go up into the hotel.

'How do I look?'

'Terrible! Here, let me see what I can do.' Tenderly, Rosa wiped his face and brushed his clothes down. She took a brush from her handbag to tidy his hair.

'That's better. You have your Swiss papers with you?'

Henry patted his jacket pocket. A few minutes later he was on the ground floor of the hotel and walking across the deserted foyer to the reception desk, where a young night porter was on his own.

'Can I help you sir?'

'Yes, I had some dealings before with a most helpful manager. I wondered if she was on duty tonight? Her name was Katharina Hoch, I seem to recall.'

'Fraulein Hoch: indeed she is sir. May I ask your name?'

'Herr Hesse – from Switzerland.'

'Thank you sir. And which room are you in?'

'I beg your pardon?'

'Which room shall I tell her you're staying in?'

Before he could think what to say, Katharina Hoch emerged from the office behind the reception desk. It was a good job the night porter had his back to her because her eyes widened in fear as she saw Henry. She steadied herself against the doorframe and wiped her brow before regaining her composure.

'Herr Hesse! How good to have such an honoured guest back with us. Please do come through to my office.'

She took Henry down a corridor at the back of the reception and into another office.

'What the hell are you doing here?' she said after making sure no-one had followed them.

'Hiding.'

She stared at him for a minute, slowly shaking her head.

'Well you can't. It's too dangerous. Everything is so dangerous now that we do nothing other than pass the odd bit of information on to Bern. As for helping agents and hiding people, that's a thing of the past. You've no idea how much of a risk it is for you to be here. You must leave.'

'I can't.'

'You have to, please. Since you were last here, the situation has got so much worse. Everyone informs on everyone else as a matter of course.'

'But I can't leave.'

'You have to, I told you. I can give you some money and something to eat, then you go. How did you get in here?'

'Through the basement, you remember you took me there the morning I went to Essen?'

'You must leave that way then.'

'I can't, I'm not on my own. And I killed a policeman today.'

* * *

411

Katharina Hoch said nothing as Henry told his story. By the time he had finished she was running her fingers through her hair. He noticed she was now wearing a bright-red lipstick, which managed to make her lips look less sensuous than before.

'I was foolish enough to imagine we may be safe,' she said.

'What do you mean?'

'My brother Dieter – you remember you used his identity when you travelled to Essen – he even joined the Nazi Party after you left, the situation has become that bad. We thought that may help us if there was any suspicion. Now what happens? You kill a policeman and turn up here with two Jews. What do you expect us to do?'

'Help us get to Switzerland. I was hoping to drive to the border, but I can't use the car now. It's too risky. They're obviously looking for it.'

'And how do you propose to get to the border? They'll be searching for you: hide in the basement tonight, but no longer than that please. I'll have to send a message to Bern, but I'll wait until tomorrow night, I must to talk to Dieter first.'

'Why are you sending a message to Bern?'

'At least we can let Basil know you're here. He may have an idea.'

* * *

'Is the only way we can communicate with Milo through this travel agent?'

Edgar was chain-smoking now and sitting close to Basil

Remington-Barber, as if he were interrogating him.

'It's not the only way, Edgar, but it's by far the safest way. The problem is it's now Friday evening and the travel agent doesn't reopen until Monday morning. In the meantime, we could send a telex direct to the hotel, but that's not without risks. At least we know Milo's on duty tonight and over the weekend so the chances are she'll be the only person to see it.'

Edgar stood up and walked slowly around the room, a trail of cigarette smoke following in his wake.

'The first time I met Henry was in August 1939, at Croydon Airport. I had to remind myself that appearances can be deceptive, that he may have looked and even acted as something of a nonentity, but there was clearly more to him than that. I recall saying he was actually rather impressive. No hint whatsoever who he was really working for and there was a danger we could underestimate him. God knows what we're to make of him now.'

Remington-Barber started to speak but Edgar held up his hand. *I'm thinking.*

'What telex machine would you use from this end?'

'One of Rolf's contacts works in a hotel here in Zürich. We can get a message out through her tonight. It's open I'm afraid, but needs must.'

Another pause while Edgar paced the room, deep in thought.

'You ready to write this down Basil? Tell Milo to let Henry know he's to leave Stuttgart and get back to Switzerland as soon as possible. He's to come on his own. Under no circumstances should he attempt to bring that woman and her daughter out with him. He's already been told we're not the Red Cross. That last bit isn't part of the message.'

* * *

Katharina Hoch went down to the basement in the early hours of the Thursday morning. It was not only for reasons of humanity she realised she could not turn the three of them out onto the street. It was likely they would be arrested within minutes and one of them was bound to say something about the hotel. She realised she would have to hide them until at least she had spoken with Dieter.

At the back of the basement was a narrow corridor, no more than five feet high. It led to a room behind the main boilers, which had been used to store equipment. Now it was empty and seldom-visited. She led the three of them in. The room had no lights, a rancid smell and the scuttling sound of mice. Its saving grace was that it was warm and safe, for the time being. Once they were inside, she brought down blankets and some food, and told them to remain there until her next visit: she would come down when it was safe.

It was 3.30 on the Saturday morning before they next saw her, holding a torch and carrying a bag with some food in it. She asked Henry to come out with her.

'I can't stay long, there's a problem with the plumbing on one of the floors and I really need to be around to supervise things.'

They were at the end of the corridor, back in the main part of the basement.

'We've heard from Bern. You're under orders to return to Switzerland.'

'Good! I told you that's where we want to go.'

'Just you: the message is very clear. You're to go back on your own.'

'What – and leave them? Of course not, they're coming with me. What did your brother have to say?'

'According to him, the police at the railway station are searching for you. They have your names, but no photographs, which I suppose is something. They found the car, naturally, and the fact it was so close to the station means they think you may not be in the city, but that isn't the point: as soon as you leave the hotel you'll be at risk. The only chance you have is for Dieter to drive you south on Sunday, which is his day off. He may be able to get hold of a van from the railways, so that ought to be safe. He'll try to get you as close to the border as possible. You stand a chance if you try and cross at night: alone.'

'But I told you, I'm not going anywhere without Rosa and Sophia.'

* * *

The next time Edgar and Remington-Barber heard from Stuttgart was on the morning of Monday 31st March. Milo had sent a telex overnight to the travel agents in Bern and this time the message was passed on promptly.

'According to Milo,' said Remington-Barber, following Edgar as he paced around the room. 'Henry absolutely refuses to leave the basement of the hotel without the others. Dieter turned up on Sunday with his van, but Henry wouldn't budge. Milo and her brother are at their wits' end. They know they can't turf them out of the basement because the three of them together are bound to be caught within minutes. But she's convinced it's only a matter of time before someone finds them. If the Gestapo haven't caught them elsewhere they'll assume they must still be in Stuttgart and she's worried they'll search the hotel.'

'Tell her to hold on then. Keep them in the basement and we'll sort something out. Do you still have that cache of German identities?'

'Yes, but I'm down to three, possibly four, which I'd say I can totally trust.'

'Where are they?'

'In the safe in Bern.'

'Better get them sent here as soon as possible. What about good Swiss identities, do you have many of those?'

'A couple that are watertight, Edgar. I'll get them to send those.'

'How much do you trust Rolf, Basil?'

'I've told you, he's one of our best, no question about it: type of chap you'd want to open the batting with.'

That's Basil's world, thought Edgar. *Judging people on whether you trust them enough to open the batting with you.*

'And on the train you mentioned something about him having been across the border before – into Germany, I mean.'

'Yes, late '39 it must have been. We needed to get some cash to an agent I was running in Freiburg. We sent Rolf in over the mountains and he came back the same way.'

'You'd better get him up here.'

When Rolf joined them, Edgar gestured for him to sit down.

Rolf was only slightly shorter than Edgar. He was slim and sprightly looking, the kind of person who was always moving, but in an energetic rather than nervous manner. And, with his blond hair and blue eyes, he was far closer to the Aryan ideal than his fellow Austrian, Adolf Hitler. Rolf's undoubted good looks were marred by one characteristic though: large, protruding ears that gave him a slightly comical appearance. He invariably had a pleasant smile on his face, as he did now.

'I understand you're familiar with Germany, Rolf?'

'I've been many times, though of course not recently.'

'And excuse me asking, but do you sound like an Austrian when you're there?'

'A good question: I can sound like a Swiss when I'm in Switzerland, an Austrian in Austria and a German when I'm in Germany. I suppress my Viennese accent in Germany, it's too distinctive. Why do you ask?'

'Because you and I are going to Germany.'

To Edgar's surprise, Rolf's smile was wider than before.

* * *

They crossed the border late on the morning of Tuesday 1st April. The German identity papers had arrived from Bern late on Monday afternoon and another of Rolf's contacts had worked through the night to turn Edgar and Rolf into impeccable German citizens. Rolf Eder had become Ludwig Kühn, an engineer from Landshut, just north of Munich. Edgar became Karl Albrecht, a businessman from Hanover, a city he was not only familiar with after having spent a year at university there, but for which he could also manage the correct accent.

'I hope this chap of yours is reliable,' said Edgar as they drove towards Lake Konstanz from Zürich. Both Rolf and Basil Remington-Barber looked at each other, unsure of who should answer.

'All I can say is he hasn't let us down so far,' said Remington-Barber.

'And how many times have you used him?'

A long pause.

'Once.'

Edgar said nothing but slowly shook his head.

'At short notice he's our only option,' said Rolf. 'We're paying him a lot of money and he's running an enormous risk.'

They pulled off the main road between the small towns of Rorschach and Arbon, and after a while the track they were on petered to a dead end and they found themselves surrounded by trees, with the lake just visible through them. They waited for five minutes and once Remington-Barber was certain they had not been followed nor were being watched, they set off through the small wood. When they emerged they found themselves at a small jetty, with the black water of the lake lapping high against it and the shorelines of both Germany and Austria clearly visible. Rolf removed a pair of binoculars from his jacket and scanned the lake. He handed the binoculars to Edgar and pointed to a tiny shape in the middle of the water.

'That's her. She'll be with us in maybe 15 minutes. We'll wait in the trees until she arrives.'

Twenty minutes later the fishing boat had pulled up alongside the jetty and the three men were scrambling across it. The skipper, who had a deeply tanned face and a heavy moustache, snatched the thick envelope Remington-Barber handed to him. He gestured for Rolf and Edgar to go below deck, where despite the noise of the idling engine they could hear the conversation going on above them.

'Don't worry Paul, it's all here: Swiss Francs and Reichsmarks.'

'And those two – they're not going to cause trouble are they?'

'Of course not.'

'And you promise me they're not Jews.'

'Are you crazy Paul? What Jews would want to escape from Switzerland to Germany?'

'Ones who've money hidden there. They still control many businesses, you know.'

'No Paul, I promise you they're not Jews. You'd better get a move on. Your brother knows what to do? Don't forget that's why we're paying you so much. It's for the whole journey.'

'Don't worry, he knows what to do. You're getting us on the cheap. I'm thinking of putting my price up.'

As the boat pulled away from the jetty and accelerated into the main body of the lake Edgar realised they had not properly said goodbye to Remington-Barber, which was probably just as well. Sending agents into enemy territory was always the worst part of the job, not so different from pronouncing a death sentence.

They remained in the hold throughout the crossing. They briefly caught sight of the two other crew members, a boy who looked as if he should be in school and a giant of a man who had a permanent grin and seemed to communicate through sign language.

'We've been lucky so far today,' said the skipper when he came down into the hold for a minute. 'The Swiss and German patrol boats are all near Konstanz at the other end of the lake – there's been some row there about fishing rights. The Austrians are lazy: they're just putting out one patrol boat a day at the moment and they seem to prefer to stay around Bregenz. There's a small landing just outside Nonnenhorn – Johannes will be waiting there with his truck. If it's all clear, we'll pull in there. If not, we'll continue into port and we'll get you off the boat later on, when it is quiet.'

On the first pass there must have been a signal all was well, because the boat suddenly cut its speed and turned sharply to the shore. Once the boat was tied up, they were called up to the deck, where the skipper had been joined by a man who looked like his identical twin. *Johannes.* After a quick shaking of hands, they were hurried along to a narrow road and into the back of a van waiting there. There was just enough room for the two of them between the crates of fish. Once he was in the driving seat, Johannes turned around. 'I can't pretend this will be anything other than a very uncomfortable journey, but I'll get you to Munich in good time, don't worry. And we should be fine if we're stopped: all my papers are in order. You're staying at the Hotel Bayerischer Hof, yes?'

'I am,' said Edgar. 'My friend is staying at a smaller one by the station.'

* * *

They arrived in Munich just before five o'clock and during the journey Edgar and Rolf talked through their plans. They would have no contact with each other while they were in Munich or on the journey to Stuttgart, so if one was caught there was a chance the other would make it.

'I'm not terribly sure why we're taking this route to Stuttgart: it's hardly the most direct way,' said Rolf.

'True, but when we arrive in Stuttgart it'll be as travellers from Munich. That should make us far less suspicious.'

Johannes dropped both Rolf and Edgar off in a side street by Munich Hauptbahnhof. It was only around the corner from the station hotel where the Austrian would be staying and for Edgar the ten-minute walk to the Bayerischer Hof on Promenadeplatz not only meant he would not be seen getting out of a van delivering fish at the hotel, but also gave him the opportunity for a bit of fresh air and the chance for the smell of the van to evaporate.

On the Wednesday morning both men were on eight o'clock train from Munich to Stuttgart. They had stood close to each other on the concourse at the Hauptbahnhof, as arranged, but did not exchange a word nor make eye contact. Both were carrying a small suitcase in their left hand and holding their hats in their right, the signal all was well. They purchased seats at opposite ends of the same carriage so they could spot if there were any problems, but the journey was straightforward. Their papers were checked as they boarded the train and once during the journey after the stop at Augsburg, but each time the guards seemed more bothered their tickets were in order.

Both men had bought copies of that day's edition of the

Münchner Neueste Nachrichten and they made sure they were prominent as they arrived in Stuttgart, where security was far more noticeable. Their papers were checked but neither man was pulled out of the queue for their bags to be searched. They took different routes to the Hotel Victoria, Edgar arriving 15 minutes after Rolf.

Milo had reserved rooms for the two men close to each other on the second floor and just across the corridor from the back stairs that led down to the hotel basement. Hidden in an envelope taped to the underside of the wardrobe in Rolf's room was a key to the basement and a note as to where to find Henry, Rosa and Sophia. It was 1.30 in the afternoon when Edgar reckoned it would be safe to knock on Rolf's door. The two men stood in the tiny bathroom, the tap running to mask their voices.

'You have the key?'

Rolf dangled it in front of Edgar. 'She says they're hiding in a room at the rear of the basement – here, she's drawn a map.' Rolf handed the piece of paper to Edgar.

'I don't like the fact she took such a risk, putting it down on paper like that.'

'What else was she meant to do? You need to decide, when do we go down and do we go together?'

'Just let me have another look at that note.' Edgar read it carefully, nodding his head, formulating a plan. 'She says she comes on duty at 11 o'clock tonight and we're to wait in our rooms. She'll come up to us between 11.30 and midnight, apparently. I don't think we can risk waiting until then, they've been here almost a week already. You have Henry's new identity papers?'

Rolf gestured towards his small suitcase.

'Good. Let me tell you the plan then you go down and bring Hunter up here.'

Rolf was impressed with Edgar's plan; it was not without considerable risk and would require nerves of steel, but it was clever. He then left the room and went down the back stairs that led down to the basement. It took him ten minutes to check it was clear then navigate his way through to the room hidden behind the boiler. When Rosa heard him she cried out in fear.

'It's me Henry: Rolf. You remember me from Zürich?'

Henry clasped Rolf by the arms.

'It's alright Rosa – don't cry Sophia. Rolf's a friend. He's come to rescue us. Are you here on your own, Rolf... When can we leave?'

Rosa had lit a candle in the room and Rolf glanced around in the dim light. It was cramped, with rusty equipment against the walls, and blankets and an old mattress on the floor. The heat was oppressive and there was a foul smell.

'Yes, we've a plan, don't worry. First you need to come with me Henry, just for few minutes – don't worry Rosa, he won't be long.'

* * *

There was only enough space for the three men to stand more or less shoulder to shoulder in Rolf's bathroom, which meant Edgar and Henry were facing each other. When Edgar finally spoke, after a minute of looking Henry up and down with the makings of a sneer on his face, his voice could only just be heard above the noise of the tap.

'As much as I'm a reasonable man Henry and I'm prepared to give you the benefit of the doubt, I struggle to see how you can possibly manage to come up with a satisfactory explanation for all this.'

'For all what, Edgar?'

Edgar inched closer to Henry, clenching and unclenching his fists.

'For what? You were supposed to fly from Berlin to Zürich last Tuesday morning then meet myself and Basil and in Geneva. What happened?'

An embarrassed smile on Henry's face and a shrug of the shoulders. *What can I say?*

'I bent the rules a little bit and decided to rescue Rosa and Sophia at the same time. I thought if I did so then Gunter Reinhart would be better disposed towards us and provide us with more intelligence.'

'Oh really, Henry? I've never regarded myself as particularly naïve, but I'd be bordering on the certifiable if I were to believe a word of what you're saying. You've set yourself up as some knight in shining armour, rescuing a damsel in distress…'

'I thought there'd be no harm…' Henry shifted uncomfortably, his face now flushed red.

'No harm?' Edgar's voice was raised for a split second before Rolf nudged him. 'You've seriously jeopardised this mission, the purpose of which – in case you've forgotten – was to collect a document from Hugo and bring it back to Switzerland. Do you have that document?'

Henry coughed and stepped away as far as he was able from Edgar.

'I'm afraid not. I know this is going to sound dreadful, Edgar, but after we left Berlin it dawned on me there was a possibility we could be caught. I thought the worst thing that could then happen from a British point of view was for the documents would fall into German hands, so I burnt them.'

'Where?'

'In some woods where we were hiding on the Tuesday night. I'm so sorry, I know I failed in my mission, but I felt the alternative would be far worse.'

Edgar turned around, facing the frosted window. 'Jesus Christ,' was all he could say.

'We need to get you back to Switzerland as soon as possible. We can't risk you being caught by the Germans, as tempting as that may be in some respects. Heaven knows what you'd say to the Gestapo...'

'Now, look here Edgar...'

'No, you look here, Hunter. Rolf and I are putting our lives at risk by attempting to rescue you. The very least you can do is co-operate, you understand?'

'I will, but I'm not leaving without Rosa and Sophia. I'm adamant about that.'

'So I'm told and we understand that. We'll get them out, too, don't worry, we have it all worked out. We've very good German identity papers for you: your photo and everything. We also have new Swiss papers, as you can hardly re-enter as Henri Hesse, not after all the fuss you've caused.'

'But what about Rosa and Sophia?'

'We've papers for them too, but you can't leave together as they'll be looking for the three of you. If you travel separately it'll be less conspicuous. You'll leave first with Rolf and take the train to Switzerland: your documentation is good enough to risk that kind of journey. We can't risk Rosa and Sophia being stopped and questioned, so I'll drive them to the border myself.'

Henry stared at Edgar, his face full of scepticism.

'Really, you're sure this'll work?'

'It's the best way, Henry, believe me. Dieter is sorting out the car: we'll be able to hide Sophia under the rear seat, and Rosa and I will look like a married couple.'

'But how can I be sure you'll follow on?'

'I'm hardly likely to stay on in Stuttgart, am I?'

'You promise me this Edgar – on your life: that you'll bring Rosa and Sophia out with you?'

'I promise you, Henry. You can trust me. Now we need to move fast. You and Rolf must leave this afternoon. Dieter will bring the car tonight so I'll follow with Rosa and Sophia in the morning. All being well, we'll meet up in Zürich either tomorrow or Friday.'

Rolf accompanied Henry back to the basement, where he explained the situation to Rosa. He could tell Henry was uneasy, he had his head in his hands and kept shaking it. When Rolf had explained everything, Henry turned to Rosa.

'What do you think?'

'I'm not sure what you mean?'

'Should we go along with this, do as they ask?'

'What else can we possibly do? They're right: the three of us will never make it anywhere near the border on our own, let alone cross it. Nor can we stay here: it's only a matter of time before we get caught. We have to do as your friends suggest.'

There was a brief goodbye, hurried along by Rolf. A few minutes later he and Henry were back in Rolf's bedroom.

'It's a quarter to three,' said Edgar. 'There's a train from Stuttgart leaving at 3.30, the last one to cross the border tonight. You and Rolf will catch it, but first you need to have a shave and a bath, and get changed: you look a mess and smell like you haven't had a proper wash for days. You'd better get undressed in here while Rolf runs the bath for you.'

As soon as Henry went into the bathroom Edgar whispered urgently to Rolf. The Austrian positioned himself by the bathroom door while Edgar frantically searched Henry's clothes and case. It took him five minutes before he found what he was looking for. He then meticulously replaced everything as he had found it and beckoned Rolf over. Through the bathroom door they could hear the sound of splashing. Edgar was holding three sheets of brown paper with German type on them.

'The Rostock Report!' he announced, waving it triumphantly at Rolf. 'For some reason he's taken it out of the envelope.'

'Are you sure?' Rolf whispered.

'Of course I'm sure: I saw it in London,' replied Edgar.

'Where was it?'

Edgar was holding a pair of thick, dark trousers. 'Inside the lining, look – that's why I made him get undressed in here, so I could check his clothes.'

'But how come you knew he had it? He told us he'd burnt it.'

'Keep your voice down, Rolf. When I was talking with Basil the other day I told him how one could very easily underestimate Henry. I simply didn't believe what he told us and my instinct was correct: he may have embarked on this mad mission to rescue Rosa and Sophia but, despite everything, he couldn't risk upsetting his Soviet masters by not delivering this report back to them. All the more reason to get him back to Zürich as soon as possible.'

Through the bathroom door came the sloshing noise of Henry getting out of the bath.

'Are you going to be long?' Edgar asked, as he carefully replaced the envelope.

'Five minutes, no more I promise.'

'And what do I do with him when we get to Zürich?' Rolf whispered.

'Check him into a hotel, one of the smaller ones around the station. Tell him to stay there while you make contact with Basil. Then leave him, make sure he thinks he's on his own for a while. Have one your boys keep a watch, but it's vital he's left alone.'

'Not long now – mind if I use both towels?'

Edgar assured him he could use as many towels as he wished.

* * *

Chapter 27: Stuttgart, April 1941

From the window of his room Edgar had watched Rolf and Henry as they left the hotel, both seemingly relaxed and chatting away. They gave the appearance of amicable colleagues: a small group of men in the black uniform of the Waffen SS walked towards them, but there was no hesitation in the step of either agent, and the SS men politely parted to allow the two men to walk on through. Edgar continued to watch as the pair walked down Friedrichstrasse towards the station, eventually disappearing as dots into the distance.

He would have to remain in the hotel that evening. Rolf – Ludwig Kühn – had explained to the receptionist he had been called back to Landshut. *So inconvenient, I'm so sorry. I insist on paying for my room.*

Edgar had been discreetly watching this as he scanned a nearby notice board. The receptionist had insisted this wasn't necessary ('these things happen, Herr Kühn'), but Edgar knew if two guests checked out within hours of their arrival it could arouse suspicion. In any event, he needed to see Milo. He would stay the night and slip away in the morning: ahead of the hounds, with any luck.

Edgar ate early in the hotel's ornate but largely deserted dining room and retired to his room. He would wait until Milo came on duty at 11 o'clock.

* * *

Because he had been in his room on the second floor since eight o'clock Edgar was unaware of what was happening below him.

The police had turned up at nine: the manager was asked to gather all the staff together in an office. They wanted to know if a family of three – a man and woman in their mid- to late-thirties and a girl, perhaps four or five years old – had been staying at the hotel. Unfortunately, the police told them, they had no photographs, but they had names and descriptions. *Please think carefully; remember they'll probably have used different names. The man is Swiss; the woman and child are Jews. It's possible they may have split up.*

They passed around the sheets with the names and descriptions on them. No-one recognised them. But at the back of the room was the young night porter, who had just come on duty. He stared at the sheet; gripping it tight in the hope no-one would notice his hands shaking. He looked up and around the room, then back again at the sheet of paper, hoping he had misread the name on it the first time he had looked at it. It was still there: 'Henri Hesse, Switzerland.' And then the description: unmistakably that of the man who had turned up the week before asking to see Katharina Hoch.

Even though he had said nothing about it at the time, the porter had thought there was something odd about the situation. When Fraulein Hoch had taken the man to an office well away from reception he had checked the register. There was no-one staying at the hotel called Hesse. It was not his place to say anything to Fraulein Hoch and he had thought no more of it, until now.

'You're all certain you've not come across these people, these criminals?' The police officer in charge looked as though he were in a hurry. 'We need to move on, you're not the only hotel in

Stuttgart, you know. Look once more, but remember: withholding information from the authorities is a serious crime.'

At the end of the month the porter was leaving the hotel, the time had come for him to join the army. What had his father told him even the before the war started? *Keep your head down. Don't get involved. Don't express an opinion, never volunteer and do as you're told.*

That was his instinct, to keep his head down and say nothing. But then what would happen if they caught this man and they found out he had spoken to him that night and had failed to mention it? *A serious crime.*

The police decided they were going to get no help from the staff at the Victoria and told them to go back to work. One of the officers brushed past him as he left the room.

'Please could I have a word with you sir?'

'Is it in connection with this matter?'

'I think it may be, yes.'

The officer called one of his colleagues over and the two policemen shepherded the night porter to a quiet corner. 'Tell us.'

'I'm not sure how relevant this is, sir, but a week ago I was on duty at reception. Sometime after midnight a gentleman appeared at reception and asked if Katharina Hoch was on duty.'

'Who's she?'

'She's the Night Manager.'

'He said his name was Hesse, from Switzerland. I asked him which room he was staying in but, before he had a chance to tell me, Fraulein Hoch appeared from her office behind me and greeted the man, who she appeared to know. She then took him down a private corridor to an office well away from reception.'

'Which day was this?'

'Wednesday, so really it was in the early hours of Thursday morning.'

'You've seen the description of the man; does it match that of the man you saw?'

'It does sir, very much so.'

'And what happened after that?'

'He must have been with Fraulein Hoch for a while – I didn't see him again.'

'And is he still staying here?'

'Well that's the odd thing, sir. I checked his name on the register and there was no record of him staying here that night.'

The officer signalled to the other policemen with him to wait. He spoke kindly to the young porter, who looked terrified. 'We're not the Gestapo, you know!'

'And Fraulein Hoch – when is she next on duty?'

The porter glanced at his watch, the one his grandparents had bought him for his last birthday. 'In just over an hour, sir – at 11 o'clock.'

* * *

Edgar spent the evening in his room, alternating between resting on the bed and almost relaxing to getting up and pacing around, peeking out into the street through the thick curtains or pausing by the door in case anyone may be approaching.

He became aware of a lot of activity below his window, cars

pulling up and people entering the hotel, and a fair amount of talking. It was, he decided, what one might expect from a busy city-centre hotel and, in any case, he was not minded to look out of the window and draw attention to himself. He would wait in his room until Milo came up, as she had promised. He waited patiently, even when 11.30 had gone, with midnight soon after. *Who knows how busy she may be? Another half-hour.*

There was no sign of her by half past midnight, when he allowed himself to open his door as quietly as possible and glance up and down the corridor. It was empty and there was no note on the floor. An hour late was worrying, there was no denying that. Edgar stood with his back to the door, surveying the room. He tried to imagine how it would look to someone coming in to question him. It looked ordinary enough but he was more concerned about his false identity. The papers for Karl Albrecht from Hanover were good enough, but he was not sure how long he could sustain his story if anyone suspected him.

By one o'clock he decided to go down to reception. He would ask if they had any aspirin for a headache. *For some reason I was unable to get through on the telephone!*

He took the main stairs down to the reception. He opened the glass doors onto the landing before the final flight of stairs swept down to the entrance lobby, only to be pushed aside by a uniformed policeman running past him. Edgar paused then edged slowly towards the staircase, just able to see into the lobby while still hidden in the shadows of the landing. The area was crowded with police and Gestapo, and in the middle of them was a young woman. She towered above a man in an ill-fitting suit, who was standing in front of her.

'Fraulein Hoch, you have spent two hours refusing to give a satisfactory explanation as to why this Herr Hesse came to see you.'

'Look, I keep telling you, why do you not believe me?' She sounded annoyed – exactly as Edgar would expect her to do in such circumstances. *Don't come across as defensive: the more aggressive you are the more they may believe you.* 'I know nothing about him. He was a guest who had stayed here last year. He asked to see me because he was staying at the Marquardt on Schlossplatz and wanted to see if he could transfer here, but he didn't want to make a fuss about it.'

'At midnight?' The short man in the ill-fitting suit looked confused, unsure whether to believe her. Edgar took a step back into the shadows. He could now hardly see what was going on, but he could still hear clearly.

'Very well,' said the man. 'Remain in your office Fraulein Hoch. Oberg, seal the hotel; make sure there are guards on every floor. No-one comes in or out. First thing in the morning, we shall thoroughly search this place.'

* * *

Edgar crept back to his room on the second floor. They clearly knew Hunter had been at the hotel, but he had no idea how. Had Henry and Rolf been arrested before they reached the border? If that was the case, it was possible Hunter would not only have told them about being in the Hotel Victoria in Stuttgart but would also have said something about him – but then, if that was the case, they would be looking for him now rather than waiting for the morning.

Edgar went into the bathroom, undressed and washed his face in cold water. Speculating on what may have happened merely served to stop him thinking about more important matters: what to do now. He changed into his pyjamas and pulled back the sheets and blankets on the bed: if they did come to his room it must look as if he had been asleep.

There was no question now of his going down to the basement, even to warn Rosa. What would be the point? Unless Rosa had heard the commotion and decided to escape they would be found in the morning.

Edgar dozed off in a series of 15- to 20-minute spells during the night. Each time he woke he lay still in bed, listening for any hint of a sound. Then he would roll slowly out of the bed and crawl along the floor to the door. By lying flat he was able to look through the inch-high gap at the bottom, but not once could he see anyone near his room.

At six o'clock he decided he could not risk dozing off again. Seven o'clock, he decided, was the earliest he could leave the hotel without it looking suspiciously early. He checked his small case. There was nothing in it to give him away, other than his Swiss papers, and they were so skilfully concealed in the lining they would pass any routine search. At seven o'clock he did a final check of the room, emptied all his pockets, looked over his papers for what felt like the hundredth time and left the room.

The lobby was beginning to fill with police and Gestapo: it was obvious the search had begun. All around was the sound of doors slamming and boots moving heavily across corridors and rooms.

'Can I help you sir?' It was a manager, his face pale and drawn, his fingers nervously intertwining with each other. Next to him was another man, his arms folded, looking Edgar up and down.

'Yes,' said Edgar, placing his room key on the desk in front of the manager. 'I wish to check out, please. If I may settle my account?'

'Most certainly sir,' said the manager, scanning the hotel register. 'Your name, please?'

'Karl Albrecht.'

'From Hanover, I see.'

'Are you returning to Hanover now?' It was the other man. As he spoke he stepped forward, holding out his Gestapo identity badge. 'Your papers, please.'

Edgar handed over the papers for Karl Albrecht. The Gestapo man looked at them carefully. 'Please can you confirm your address?' Edgar recited it, hoping he was not overplaying his Hanoverian accent. The other man looked over to the register, which the manager was still holding. 'Just a short visit then?'

'Indeed. Thankfully my business here went well.' *He's now going to ask me about this business.* Edgar glanced at his watch.

'Are you in a hurry Herr Albrecht?'

'Well, there's a train to Frankfurt at 7.30 which I'd like to catch if at all possible; it has a good connection to Hanover.'

'Indeed. Come over here and I'll examine your case.'

Edgar moved over to a table by the side of the reception desk. As he placed his case on the table there was a noise to his right. It was just a shout at first, followed by the commotion of people running and then more shouting.

'Quick, we've found them!' It was a policeman, running past reception. The Gestapo man who was about to search Edgar looked up and around, clearly eager to join in. He ruffled through Edgar's suitcase, looking up in the direction the noise was coming from for most of the time.

'Empty your pockets, quickly.'

Edgar placed the contents of his pockets on the table. The man shuffled them around, finding it hard to disguise his haste. The noise was getting closer now. Edgar turned around, in time to see a woman and young girl being manhandled across the reception area; they were both blinking and looked terrified. *Rosa and Sophia.* The policemen and Gestapo who had found them brought them to a halt in front of the reception. They were just yards from Edgar. He turned around and looked at the Gestapo man.

'Can I leave now?'

The other man was already moving from around the table. 'Yes, yes. Go.'

The senior officer and the short man in the ill-fitting suit moved over to Rosa and her daughter.

'We found them hiding in a room at the back of the basement, sir.'

'What about the man?'

'It was just them, sir.'

'You're certain?'

'Yes, but we're continuing to search the basement.'

'We must search every inch of this wretched hotel. What's your name?'

Rosa clutched Sophia, but a man dragged the child away. As he did so, a toy rabbit the little girl had been holding fell to the floor. A policeman kicked it out of the way.

'Dagmar Keufer, from Frankfurt. I have papers. This is my daughter, Gisela.'

The Gestapo officer held his hand out for the papers. He looked them over and snorted, passing them to a colleague.

'A joke! Not even good forgeries – the photographs look nothing like you! You, little girl. What's your name? Come on!'

He had bent down in front of Sophia, hands resting on his knees. Sophia's eyes were wide with fear as she tried to look at her mother.

'Go on, your name!'

'I don't know.' Tears were streaming down her face.

'You don't know! What girl doesn't know her own name, eh? It's Sophia, isn't it? Sophia Stern?'

'Yes,' she said, sounding relieved. Edgar took his time in picking up everything he had removed from his pockets and putting them back. They were still searching for Henry: he must have got away after all.

'So,' said the Gestapo man, standing directly in front of Rosa. As he shouted, his spit covered her face. 'If this is Sophia Stern, you must be Rosa Stern. I'm pleased to meet you.' Rosa said nothing.

'Where's the Swiss man?'

'I don't know.'

'He was here with you?'

She nodded. 'Yes, but he left.'

'When?'

'Yesterday.'

'Where did he go.'

'I don't know.'

'Was he on his own?'

There was a long pause before Rosa replied.

'Yes.'

The Gestapo officer hit Rosa so hard that Edgar heard the crack of bone. *Leave now, go*, a policeman was indicating. *Go. None of your business.*

'I'm not going to tell you anything.' Rosa's voice was defiant, even confident.

'I think you may now!'

Edgar straightened his coat and moved towards the door. He turned around to see the Gestapo man holding a revolver against Sophia's head, the barrel buried in the girl's thick hair. One officer stepped back and another held out a hand, as if to restrain the man with the gun.

'You tell me exactly where he is and who's helping you!'

'But I don't know.' Rosa sounded panicked, no longer defiant.

Because he was holding the revolver directly against Sophia's head, neither the sound of the gun nor its echo were nearly as loud as Edgar would have expected, especially in a relatively confined space. Then there was the silence. Edgar stepped closer to the hotel exit, not certain he could avoid being sick. He noticed a horrified look on the face of a policeman and broad grins on the faces of others. Then the scream came. It was restrained at first, like someone calling from a distance. By the time Edgar reached the hotel entrance it had turned into a wail, so loud people in the street stopped to see what it was.

He turned into Friedrichstrasse, pausing to compose himself before quickening his stride towards the station. With every step that took him away from the hotel, the scream became louder. He turned into a small alley, crouched behind a large dustbin and vomited. The noise drowned out the scream, but for no more than a second or two. He waited a minute then hurried to the station.

During the short walk, something died inside Edgar. He felt tears welling in his eyes and he pulled his hat down low to hide them. He had never experienced anything quite as dreadful as this and was quite unprepared for its impact. He continued to hear the scream long after he entered the station, the noise of the trains unable to muffle it. The scream was still ringing in his ears as he asked the clerk for a ticket; he heard it above the sound of the train that took him south.

It was the last sound he heard as he slipped out of Germany that night and the first sound he heard as he entered Switzerland.

* * *

Chapter 28: Zürich, April 1941

Edgar arrived back in Zürich on the morning of Friday, 4th April.

He had started out from Stuttgart the previous morning well aware of how perilous the journey could be, but throughout it he was accompanied a sense of almost surreal detachment, brought about by the shock of what he had seen at the hotel and the consequences of his own failure to do anything. Had it been a routine search of the hotel or had they been tipped off? If it was the latter, who could have told them?

He had been forced to deceive Henry: he knew that promising him he'd help Rosa and Sophia escape was the only way to ensure he would leave the hotel with Rolf. Trying to bring Rosa and Sophia with him back to Switzerland was always a risk he simply couldn't contemplate; they would never have stood a chance. Even going into the basement to warn them would have been too dangerous.

But the sight of little Sophia being shot in cold blood had utterly overwhelmed him. For a few hours, his defences were down and his normally pin-sharp judgement was blunted. When he looked back on that day in the months and years that followed, he realised that for much of it he hardly cared what happened to him. It was not just Sophia: he did not want to contemplate what fate awaited Rosa, and he doubted Milo and her brother would survive either. For all he knew, Rolf and Henry may even have been caught after all. It had been an utter disaster and what would displease London most was the possibility that the Russians would not even get to see the Rostock Report. But, for a few hours that day, it did not bother him at all.

Edgar's trance-like state continued as he broke all the rules by not taking the first train out of Stuttgart. Instead, after buying his ticket, he sat in a corner of the draughty station buffet, nibbling a sausage and sipping at an ersatz coffee he'd allowed to get cold. By 8.30, a sense of reality slowly began to return to him as the initial shock thawed and he began to think more clearly. Rolf and Henry would have tried to cross the border after Singen and he decided to try a different route, just in case. He chose to wait for a train that would give him other options and caught one heading south at 9.30. The train was crowded, with a large number of soldiers on board. About ten minutes out of Stuttgart a woman brushed past him as she pushed her way down the carriage. Even from behind there was something familiar about her and, as she turned to open the door at the other end of the carriage, Edgar caught a glimpse of her face: had he not thought that at that moment she was in the hands of the Gestapo he would have sworn it was Katarina Hoch.

He did not spot the woman again and left the train at Tuttlingen. It was 11.45 and according to the timetable on the wall of the deserted forecourt there was a train to Waldshut-Tiengen leaving at 2.20. Waldshut-Tiengen sat on northern bank of the Rhine, with Switzerland on the other side: it would be a safer place to cross the border.

The ticket office was closed, so Edgar walked into the town and came across an inn. The innkeeper was leaning against the bar, seemingly intent on avoiding serving anyone. Edgar had to position himself directly in front of the man and cough loudly to attract his attention. When he did deign to look at his new customer it was with a pair of eyes that never stopped blinking.

'Yes?'

'I'm looking for a room please, just for a couple of hours.'

The eyes blinked faster then narrowed. 'A couple of hours? What kind of a place do you think we are?'

'I am sorry, there's a misunderstanding. I've been travelling for a long while and I'm just looking for somewhere to have a bath and change my clothes before I return home to Geneva. I'm catching a train in a couple of hours.'

The innkeeper leaned closer to Edgar. 'But the journey from here to Switzerland will take you just two hours.'

'I realise that, but then I have to travel on to Montreux, which means I'll arrive home late. Look, I'm happy to pay the full daily rate for the room if that helps.'

Edgar peeled a generous amount of Reichsmarks from his wallet and slipped them into the innkeeper's hand, whose eyes stopped blinking for a moment. He smiled briefly, allowing Edgar a glimpse of dirty yellow teeth.

'No problem, sir, use room four. Here's the key. Can I send some food up?'

Edgar said that would not be necessary, he would eat later. Once in the room he locked the door, jammed a chair against it and placed his small suitcase on the bed. It took him ten minutes to carefully unthread the lining just far enough to extract his Swiss papers. He was now Marc Rassier from Montreux. What remained of Karl Albrecht was torn up into little pieces then burnt in an ashtray, the charred scraps flushed down the toilet. Once he had washed and changed, Edgar went back to the bar and ordered lunch, leaving the inn as soon as he felt it was reasonable to do so.

The 2.20 train arrived on time to take Marc Rassier to Waldshut-Tiengen, arriving at the station in the north of the town at half past four. An elderly policeman checked his Swiss papers as he left the station.

'Are you taking the bus across the border?'

He had saved him from asking the question. 'Yes. When does it leave?'

'An hour: you'll need to register for it though. They have to check everyone who gets on. Wait over there – those ladies are going too.'

Edgar waited with two Swiss-German women, who were thankfully as reserved as he would have expected them to be, especially when they realised he was French-speaking. At 5.30 a noisy blue bus pulled up in front of the station, by which time another four people were in the waiting area. A police car arrived and a young officer, wearing a smart raincoat and leather gloves, checked everyone's paperwork.

'What's been the purpose of your visit to Germany, Herr Rassier? I need to know where you've visited in the Reich.'

Edgar affected broken German. *I am sorry; my German is poor. Do you speak French perhaps?*

He didn't. One of the Swiss-German ladies explained to the officer this was typical. 'They make no effort: they expect us to speak French but you never hear them speak German!'

She spoke to Edgar in slow French. 'He wants to know where you've been in Germany.'

Edgar launched into a lengthy travelogue, covering as much of

Germany as he could manage and speaking quickly. The Swiss-German lady clearly did not understand too much of what he said.

'I'm not terribly sure, sir,' she told the police officer. 'They speak so fast. He seems to have been in Munich and elsewhere in Bavaria, as far as I can gather. He says he has many documents if you want to check them.'

Behind them the queue had lengthened. The officer checked the papers again. 'And you entered Germany where?'

Edgar managed to look irritated and took back his passport. 'Look, it says here – Munich; by train, one week ago.'

'I see. You may board now.'

It was approaching six o'clock when the bus pulled away from the station, driving slowly through the town and over the bridge crossing the Rhine. Once they were on the Swiss side, they pulled alongside a narrow building, where their papers were checked by the Swiss police. Half an hour later the bus had arrived in Baden. It was seven o'clock and he was back in Switzerland, but felt little sense of elation.

'What time is the next bus to Zürich?' he asked the driver.

'A quarter past seven.'

'And do I catch it from here?'

'Yes.' The driver had turned off the engine and was locking up, anxious to leave.

Edgar put his suitcase down and settled on the bench inside the small bus shelter. The driver set off, turning around after he had walked past Edgar.

'I wouldn't make yourself too comfortable. It leaves at quarter past seven in the morning.'

* * *

It was 8.30 on the Friday morning when Edgar walked slowly across Basteiplatz to the small apartment above the hardware shop. He had thought about telephoning Basil Remington-Barber from Baden the previous night or when he arrived in Zürich, but had decided against it. A few hours' sleep in a small inn in Baden had cleared his mind and now the enormity of what had happened was hitting him hard. He needed time to consider quite how to explain this disaster to London: a debacle, they would call it, these people whose only experience of danger was dodging the traffic around Trafalgar Square on the way to their clubs. He would probably end up in Wales looking after munitions, if he was lucky.

Remington-Barber answered the door, looking as if he had seen a ghost. In the lounge Rolf and Henry were sitting around the table. It was a while before anyone said anything.

'Well, this is quite some reunion,' said Remington-Barber finally, sounding quite jolly.

'When did you two arrive?' Edgar asked.

'Yesterday,' said Rolf, who had now come over to Edgar and was shaking him warmly by the hand. Henry was half-standing, half-sitting, saying nothing and peering beyond Edgar, looking to see if anyone was behind him.

'Plain sailing?' asked Edgar, as he removed his hat and coat, and dropped them on to the armchair.

'Surprisingly so,' said Rolf. 'When we arrived at the station in Stuttgart I saw the train to Singen was delayed until four o'clock, but there was one to Ulm leaving almost immediately. From there, we found another train was leaving soon for Friedrichshafen. We booked into a hotel overlooking the lake and yesterday morning we took a bus to Konstanz. We crossed the border there using our Swiss passports then took a train to Zürich.'

'Where are they, Edgar?' Henry had stood up now and walked past Edgar into the hallway. He opened the door of the apartment, came back in and walked over to the window overlooking Basteiplatz.

'You promised me you'd bring Rosa and Sophia with you. Where the hell are they?' His voice had an urgent tone to it, louder and more broken than usual.

Edgar signalled to Rolf to stand by the door. 'Sit down Henry.' He led him over to the sofa and sat him down, then placed himself in the armchair.

'I'm afraid they're not here. I'm sorry.'

'Where are they?'

Edgar hesitated: he had rehearsed several versions of what to say in answer to this inevitable question and was quickly deciding which one to use.

'I'm sorry Henry, I really am… But they were arrested before I had a chance to get them out of the hotel. I…'

'Arrested by whom?' Henry had stood up from the sofa and only sat when Remington-Barber guided him down with a firm hand on his shoulder.

'Don't shout,' said Edgar. 'I promise you this is something I regret just as much as you do, but I'm sorry to say it was the Gestapo. They must have come to the hotel late on the Wednesday night. I'm not sure what happened, but because Milo hadn't made contact with me I decided to go down and find her at around one in the morning. As I went down, I saw she was being questioned in the reception area and I heard them say they were going to search the hotel in the morning. There were police everywhere. I went back to my room and remained there until seven in the morning. If there was any way I could have gone down to the basement I would have done, but every time I looked out the door there were police patrolling the corridor. When I went down to check out, I saw Rosa and Sophia being led away.'

'And you didn't try to warn them or anything?'

Henry was shouting so loudly now that Rolf shut the windows and Remington-Barber slammed the lounge door.

'I told you Henry, I just didn't get a chance, I promise you. The Gestapo were all over the place. I was worried that if I went down into the basement I could be caught and that would alert the bastards to search down there. I…'

Henry had begun to cry. It started as a gentle sobbing but within a minute had turned into uncontrollable weeping, tears streaking his cheeks. Remington-Barber stood awkwardly in front of him holding out a handkerchief, while Rolf sat next to Henry and placed an arm around his shoulder, but nothing would console him. He was grief-stricken and everyone in the room knew there was nothing to be said that could be in any way reassuring.

Henry did nothing other than weep for five minutes. By now, Remington-Barber had taken Edgar's place in the armchair. He held a glass of water and in his open hand were two large white tablets.

'Take these old chap: they'll help you rest and when you wake up it will be with a clearer head.' Henry looked at the tablets and took them one at a time. Within five minutes he was stretched out on the sofa, fast asleep. They waited another five minutes then carried him into the bedroom, which Rolf locked from the outside.

'He'll not wake for most of the day.'

'Well, before he does, we need to check something,' said Edgar.

They emptied all Henry's possessions on the floor and searched them carefully, paying particular attention to the trousers they had last seen in the hotel room in Stuttgart. The report they had found there was nowhere to be seen. As far as the Russians were concerned, he would have served his purpose.

'Well, that's a relief,' said Remington-Barber.

'Thank you Basil. I only told him half of it, you know.'

'Well whatever you do, better not to tell him the other half,' said Rolf. 'In the hotel in Friedrichshafen last night we got talking: I was telling him about Frieda, my fiancée in Vienna – about not having any idea of what's happened to her and all that. Henry opened up a bit: I can tell you he was absolutely set on rescuing Rosa and the child. He regarded it as a mission, the most important thing in his life. I don't think love or romance comes into it, he kept going on about how if he saved Rosa then he could save himself. I asked him to tell me more, but he said it was too terrible to talk about. It tortured him to even think about it. He said he hoped that once we'd rescued Rosa and her daughter, he'd find some sort of peace. He clammed up after that.'

'Were they killed?'

'The little girl was, Basil. Shot in cold blood, just yards from me. God knows what they've done to Rosa. In the...'

'Are you alright, Edgar? You seem a bit choked up yourself. Would you like a couple of these pills?'

Edgar had moved over to the table, his back to Remington-Barber and Rolf. For a while he said nothing. When he did, it was in an unusually faltering voice.

'Better not, we need to talk. I'll help myself to this Scotch, if you don't mind Basil. Rolf, you tell me what happened when you got back here. That's the most important thing right now.'

Rolf and Remington-Barber joined Edgar at the table.

'I did exactly as you said Edgar,' said Rolf. 'As soon as we arrived in Zürich I booked us into a small hotel on Löwenstrasse. Once we were in the room I told Henry to wait while I went down the reception and from there I was able to call Basil and he alerted my watchers. I stayed in the room with Henry for an hour, by which time I reckoned my men would be in position, so I told him I was going out for a couple of hours to find out where Basil was and to see when it'd be safe for us to come here. I said he could go for a walk if he fancied, but not to go far and certainly to be there when I got back. I walked off down Löwenstrasse. My watchers say he left the hotel five minutes later and went into a bar across the road to use the phone. He stayed in the bar for about 15 minutes and was doing his best to see if he was being watched. Then he left the bar and walked up to the station. He met up with Viktor by one of the suburban platforms and my watchers say they saw Henry hand an envelope over to him. They spoke for about five minutes then Henry made his way back to the hotel. When I returned, I told him I'd made contact with Basil and we were to come here and wait for you – and here we are.'

Edgar leaned over and patted the Austrian on the arm. 'Well done Rolf, well done. Maybe London won't see this as quite the total disaster I feared they might.'

'I suppose that means everything has worked out rather well in the end, eh Edgar?' said Remington-Barber. 'Rather against the odds I must say, but the going turned out to be in our favour. I've lost my cell in Stuttgart, which is a damn shame, but then they did last somewhat longer than I thought they would.'

'Can't you see we still have a serious problem, Basil?'

'Not sure I'm with you, Edgar. Tragic about the little girl and one wouldn't rate the chances of her mother, Milo or her brother very highly, but surely in terms of our...'

'Think Basil, think. Henry's the problem.'

'But he handed the document over to the Russians and...'

'Yes, but consider this: the Germans were clearly after a Henri Hesse from Switzerland. They knew he was the man who'd taken Rosa and Sophia from Berlin. No doubt they'll inform the Swiss, who'll take a very dim view of this indeed. The last thing they want is for one of their citizens to use Switzerland as a base to cause trouble for the Germans: they're not keen on biting the hand that feeds them, are they?'

'No.'

'Henry entered Switzerland yesterday on false papers, which buys us some time – but that's not a long-term solution. Either he stays hidden for the rest of the war, which to me isn't feasible or he returns to Geneva under his proper identity.'

'I see... And gets arrested by the Swiss, no doubt.'

'Yes,' said Edgar. 'And think then of the implications for all our work here if he starts to spill the beans. The Swiss will know what we're up to, so will the Germans and quite possibly the Soviets, too.'

'If he starts to spill the beans, surely.'

Edgar stood up, brushed himself down and loosened his tie.

'We're not going to be able to take that risk Basil.'

* * *

They left Zürich in the middle of the afternoon on Monday 7th April. Rolf, who was driving, had borrowed a Citroen TUB van from another of his contacts, and Edgar and Remington-Barber sat next to him in the front. They headed south then passed through Luzern, Sarnen and the valleys of Unterwalden.

They drove slowly: they were in no hurry, had no desire to draw attention to themselves and in any case the van made worrying noises when it felt it was being pushed too hard. 'Rather like a woman,' Basil had said, but none of them were in the mood for humour.

It was only seven o'clock when they arrived in Brienz and, despite everything, it was still too early. They would need to buy some time. They found a small inn with enough space to park the van at the back, in the shadows, and took it in turns to go inside, one by one. Though none of them would admit it, no-one wanted to be left in the van on their own.

Edgar and Remington-Barber were in the van together at around eight o'clock. The older man attempted to break the silence.

'Rum business this, Edgar.'

Edgar said nothing, but nodded his head. *Rum business, no question of that: messy one too.*

'Lord knows what'll happen if we're stopped.'

'I told you, Basil. You're a British diplomat: you have your papers. You're on Embassy business. They can't touch you or the van. Please stop worrying.'

'But if… if… anything goes wrong, all hell will break loose. Heavens know what London will have to say.'

'Basil,' Edgar turned around to face his colleague. 'Whatever happens will be more acceptable than the alternative. And, in any case, nothing's going to go wrong. Pull yourself together.'

They left Brienz at 8.30, as twilight turned to darkness, and drove along the north shore of the lake, stopping in a side street in Interlaken for another hour to let the skies darken further and ensure they hadn't been followed.

It was ten o'clock when they pulled out of the town, driving along the track across the north shore of Lake Thun. It was only a few days past the new moon and that, along with the thick banks of trees on either side of the track, ensured they were now driving in near total blackness. Rolf brought the speed of the van down to ten miles an hour. Shortly after they passed a sign for Steinbruch they spotted a clearing to their left, and Edgar told Rolf to pull in. *Wait here.*

Edgar checked his torch and revolver and disappeared into the trees. He was gone for five minutes. 'This'll do,' he said. 'The lake is just through the trees and there's a decent slope which'll help us. Rolf, reverse as far as you can into the trees then we can take the dinghy down first.'

Once they had placed the dinghy by the shore they walked back to the van.

'How far out will we need to go?' asked Remington-Barber.

'Thun is supposed to be one of the deepest lakes in Switzerland: five minutes rowing should get us out as far as we need.'

They struggled from the moment they hauled it out of the back of the van, the three of them manhandling it and dragging it through the trees. They paused twice for Basil Remington-Barber to throw up and, once they'd reached the dinghy, they returned to the van for the ropes and weights. By the time they pushed the dinghy into the seemingly solid lake it was 11.30 and the world around them was completely silent. Edgar and Rolf rowed until they felt they were far enough out.

'You do your best to hold the boat steady, Basil: Rolf and I will do the rest.'

'Shouldn't we... I don't know... say something?'

'Like what, Basil?'

'A prayer, perhaps? Seems the decent thing to do.'

'If you must, Basil. Be quick though.'

Basil Remington-Barber muttered his way through Psalm 23, pausing after the words 'still waters' and struggling with the 'walk through the valley of the shadow of death', sounding decidedly tearful by the end.

Then the deed was done. It took them less than five minutes to row back to shore. Back in the van, no-one said a word until they saw the lights of Bern.

'I didn't know you were the religious type, Basil.'

'I'm not, Edgar. Church every so often and all that, but nothing serious. Why do you mention it?'

'Knowing the whole of that psalm, off by heart.'

An ironic laugh. 'Forced to learn it at prep school. The chaplain would beat the living daylights out of you if you got one word wrong. Never imagined I'd have cause to use it, not like that at any rate. I was thinking while I was reciting it, you know. That reference to the "presence of mine enemies": who would you say his enemies were?'

It was a long while before Edgar replied.

'Everyone was his enemy, Basil. That, I'm afraid, is a consequence of serving more than one master.'

* * *

It had taken two days for Henry Hunter, whose body they had consigned to the depths of Lake Thun, to die.

Once Edgar had persuaded Basil Remington-Barber they had no alternative, they came up with a plan. They woke Henry up at two o'clock in the afternoon, when he was still drowsy, and made him drink some water, into which they had dissolved seven of the tablets. They were convinced he would not wake up, but one of them remained in the room with him all the time. Although his breathing became more shallow and at times he appeared to be on the verge of slipping away, he held on through Saturday and by the Sunday morning his breathing sounded stronger. They crushed a dozen tablets into a saucer and turned it into a paste with a bit of water which they spooned in his mouth, but struggled to get much of it down him.

Still Henry hung on. By the Sunday evening they were convinced they needed to do something else. Remington-Barber was in a terrible state, red-eyed, shaking and pacing around the apartment. He had convinced himself something was bound to go wrong and they would all be arrested, creating a diplomatic incident in the process. Rolf suggested he went out for a walk. Edgar and Rolf stood at the window watching him cross Basteiplatz and then nodded to each other. *We need to get on with it.*

Edgar removed his jacket and rolled up his sleeves, and the two men entered the bedroom. Henry was now stirring and making noises as though he were trying to speak. As Edgar approached him, Henry half-opened his eyes and his mouth moved.

'Come on, Rolf, quick.'

'He's trying to say something, Edgar.'

'Exactly: let's get on with it.'

The sounds coming from Henry's mouth were indistinct, but just before Edgar put the pillow over his face and Rolf held him down, there was one word they both heard clearly. *Rosa.*

There was a very brief and one-sided struggle, but they both agreed afterwards it was probably painless. *He would have been too drugged to know what was going on*, they assured each other.

'He couldn't have known a thing,' said Rolf.

Edgar straightened his sleeves as he turned to the Austrian.

'He knew too much.'

* * *

Epilogue

Rosa Stern was taken to the Gestapo headquarters in the old Hotel Silber building on Dorotheenstrasse, just south of the Schlossplatz and not far from the Hotel Victoria. She was in such a state of shock she did not utter a word. She sat very still in her cell, staring at the wall, her hands crossed neatly on her lap and her mouth slightly open, occasionally breaking into the slightest of smiles. A psychiatrist brought in by the Gestapo assured them she was not putting anything on. It was, he told them, one of the most extreme cases of catatonia he had ever seen. *Could she, by any chance, have been subjected to a serious trauma recently?*

'So she's gone mad then?' the Gestapo officer asked.

'You could put it like that: I find it's much more common these days.'

They tried for a fortnight, convinced that when she did speak she would have plenty to reveal. *Who was helping her in Berlin*, for instance? *Where had Hesse gone?*

But Rosa said nothing, sitting quietly, occasionally swaying very slowly as if listening to a piece of soothing music and once in a while mouthing something silent to the wall. In the end, a Gestapo officer stormed into her cell and held his revolver in front of her, but there was still no reaction. When he hit her hard around the face she didn't make a noise and stayed in the same position as she had landed on the floor. When he knelt beside her and released the safety catch she did not blink. He shot her four times, only stopping when his gun jammed.

* * *

Rosa Stern's first husband, Gunter Reinhart, managed to avoid suspicion. He was questioned on two occasions that April, but was able to persuade the Gestapo that Hesse was a mere courier from one of the many Swiss banks he dealt with and his contact with him was confined to the handing over of documents. *I wish I could help, but I really remember little about him... He was such an inconsequential man.*

Reinhart assured the Gestapo he had not had any contact with his first wife since their divorce in 1935 and it had been many years since he had seen his son. The last he had heard, Alfred was in France. The Gestapo officer assured him this was one of a number of unresolved aspects of this case.

* * *

Franz Hermann also avoided coming under suspicion. Because he knew the woman who lived opposite had already contacted the police, he decided to risk taking matters into his own hands. With his mother safely at his sister's in Brandenburg, he went to his local police station in Dahlem and reported the nurse he had hired to look after her had disappeared. *She mentioned something about her husband being killed and having to return to Bremerhaven, but now I'm not sure... And a very helpful neighbour told me she'd seen the nurse leave the house with a man and a young girl, and drive off in an Opel. I hope I'm not wasting your time, but I'm becoming very suspicious...*

The Gestapo officer in charge of investigating the whole business of Henri Hesse and Rosa and Sophia decided he believed Franz Hermann's account: after all, had not the lawyer reported the matter himself to the police?

Franz Hermann's good fortune only lasted until July 1944 when he was one of many thousands of people arrested after the attempt on Hitler's life. Although the Gestapo never suspected him of being a British agent, there was enough circumstantial evidence to link him with the resistance to Hitler and he was sent to Sachsenhausen concentration camp, where he was murdered in November 1944.

* * *

Edgar and Basil Remington-Barber agreed that as Marlene Hesse had been unaware of her son's intelligence activities, any contact with her would be counter-productive. She had waited until the second week of April before reporting her son missing to the police in Geneva. They could tell her nothing, but appeared to be very interested in what she could tell them: *could Herr Hesse have perhaps travelled to Germany? Could she provide a list of his associates in Switzerland?* She insisted she knew nothing and promised to let them know if she heard from her son.

Marlene Hesse's income disappeared along with her son. Edgar was adamant it would be too suspicious if any money was transferred from Henry's account at Credit Suisse. *The last thing we need: what if she tells the Swiss police and they try and track the money? They're good at that type of thing.* Madame Ladnier was prevailed upon to close the account and ensure there was no trace of it having ever existed.

Her reduced circumstances meant Marlene Hesse had to move to a drab bedsit in a block between two railway lines, earning a living as a cleaner.

* * *

Viktor was not altogether surprised Henry had disappeared after he handed the Rostock Report over to him at the railway station. He had long wondered when the British would discover the man they had recruited as an agent in 1939 had been a Soviet spy for many years before that. Moscow seemed pleased with the Rostock Report: it reassured them a German invasion was unlikely and Stalin used it as vindication of his conviction that reports of invasion plans were just the British being mischievous. Viktor was well aware that Henry's disappearance could cast doubt on the veracity of the report, so he decided to say nothing to Moscow: if they were pleased, why upset them?

As far as Henry was concerned, he assumed Edgar had killed him, which was what his service would have done in the same circumstances. It was a shame: he liked *synok* and he had been a good agent, but he had lasted far longer than Viktor had expected. In early June, he told Moscow Henry had been recalled to London.

Viktor Krasotkin's encounters with British Intelligence resumed in early 1944 when he turned up in Vienna, where he remained until at least the end of the war.

* * *

Rolf Eder continued to work for British intelligence. Edgar had been so impressed by him that when he became involved in plans for a clandestine mission inside Austria he had no hesitation in recommending Rolf. He slipped into Vienna in early 1944 and was still operating there when the Red Army liberated the city in April 1945.

* * *

Captain Edgar returned to London soon after Henry Hunter's death. The mission was deemed a success by those who pronounced on such things, though it was also acknowledged it had not been without its unfortunate aspects. Operation Barbarossa meant Germany committed itself to fighting on two fronts in Europe and British military chiefs were convinced this was a fatal error. Edgar was credited with having run a successful intelligence operation, helping to ensure the Soviet Union was at the very least confused as to German intentions and at best – thanks to the Rostock Report – convinced there would be no invasion.

Author's note

The Swiss Spy is a work of fiction and, with a few obvious exceptions, all the characters in the book are fictional. Having said that, the book is based on actual historical events and in that respect I have endeavoured to be as authentic and accurate as possible.

There was indeed a high-level meeting of senior German military figures in the Bavarian town of Bad Reichenhall in July 1940, where plans to invade the Soviet Union were first discussed, notwithstanding the fact the two countries were supposedly bound by a Non-Aggression Pact at the time. Hitler's Directive no 21 referred to in the book is genuine: it was released on 18th December that year and outlined plans for Operation Barbarossa, the invasion of the Soviet Union. The Rostock Report featured in the book is a work of fiction.

Operation Barbarossa began on 22nd June 1941 and Hitler expected to conclude it within just a few months. In the event, it ended in disaster for Germany. They failed to reach Moscow by the time the Russian winter took hold, allowing the Red Army to regroup and push the Germans back. The Germans suffered a crushing defeat in the Battle of Stalingrad in February 1943 and Operation Bagration in June 1944 was the start of Germany's defeat on the eastern front.

There is a good deal of evidence to show the Soviet Union ignored dozens of credible intelligence reports about the planned German invasion. Many of these came from their own intelligence services, including a copy of a handbook to be used by German troops in the Soviet Union, which was passed on to the Soviet

Embassy in Berlin by a German Communist printer. As for the British intelligence, Stalin was convinced these reports were disinformation, designed to provoke a war between the Soviet Union and Germany. He described them as 'English provocation'. So though the missions at the core of *The Swiss Spy* are fictional ones, the idea of British intelligence using other sources to inform the Soviet Union would be quite in keeping with what was happening at the time.

I have done my best to ensure details such as street names, the locations of embassies, railway stations, airports and other named buildings and places are accurate. Many of the hotels referred to in the book existed and, in some cases, still do. The Adlon in Berlin seems to be the preferred hotel in most Second World War espionage novels, but in fact both the Excelsior and the Kaiserhof, where Henry Hunter stayed, were equally prominent at the time. Both were destroyed by Allied bombing, as was the Hotel Victoria in Stuttgart, which had been the main hotel in the city.

Readers may wonder whether it really was possible to fly on commercial routes in Europe during the Second World War. The answer is that it was, most commonly if the departure or destination airports were in neutral countries. Muntadas Airport in Barcelona was a major hub for travel around Europe, as was Portela Airport in Lisbon and Zürich Airport. During the war, Whitchurch Airport in Bristol replaced Croydon Airport as Great Britain's main commercial terminal: the site is now a housing estate. In June 1943 a BOAC flight from Lisbon to Bristol was shot down by the Luftwaffe over the Bay of Biscay. All four crew and 13 passengers were killed, including the famous British actor Leslie

Howard. It was one of very few attacks on civilian flights in Europe during the war. The names of the airlines, the type of aircraft used and the flight details in the book are, to the best of my knowledge, accurate.

The Roman Catholic cathedral of St Hedwig was destroyed in an Allied air raid in March 1943 (it has since been reconstructed). Although Father Josef is fictional, a priest at St Hedwig, Bernhard Lichtenberg, was arrested for publicly protesting at Nazi policies towards Jews and the euthanasia programme. He died while being transported to Dachau in November 1943.

This is probably not the place to go into detail about the considerable complicity of the Swiss banks in the Nazi war effort. However, it is well established there was an active relationship, to say the least, between the Reichsbank and most of the major Swiss banks, including Bank Leu. Bank Leu was an independent bank until it became part of Credit Suisse in 1990.

To save fellow football fans the effort I had to go to, I can assure you the match between Sporting Lisbon and Barreirense that features in Chapter 15 did actually take place on the 9th February 1941 – and Sporting did indeed win 2-0.

I would like to thank my agent, Gordon Wise at Curtis Brown and his colleague Richard Pike for their help, encouragement and sound advice. Gordon rightly has an outstanding reputation as an agent and I realise how fortunate I am to be one of his clients. I would also like to thank my publishers, Studio 28, and especially its editors Rufus Purdy and Alice Lutyens. Rufus first saw *The Swiss Spy* when I mistakenly thought it was the finished article:

the fact he has contributed so significantly to its current state is testament to his editorial brilliance.

And, finally, my thanks and love to my daughters Amy and Nicole and my wife, Sonia. It cannot be easy living with a writer, not least one who wonders aloud how to kill someone and who, at times, lives exclusively in a world that existed more than 70 years ago. As a teacher, Sonia is a very astute and frank reader: draft chapters are returned with plenty of annotations in red biro, the occasional tick compensating for the more frequent exclamation marks.

Alex Gerlis
London, February 2015

Alex Gerlis

466

The Swiss Spy

Also available

The Best of Our Spies

Alex Gerlis's thrilling debut novel

France, July 1944: a month after the Allied landings in Normandy and the liberation of Europe is underway. In the Pas de Calais, Nathalie Mercier, a young British Special Operations Executive secret agent working with the French Resistance, disappears. In London, her husband Owen Quinn, an officer with Royal Navy Intelligence, discovers the truth about her role in the Allies' sophisticated deception at the heart of D-Day. Appalled but determined, Quinn sets off on a perilous hunt through France in search of his wife. With the help of the Resistance he finds Nathalie, but then the bitterness of war and its insatiable appetite for revenge, catch up with them in dramatic fashion.

Based on real events of the Second World War *The Best of Our Spies* is a thrilling tale of international intrigue, love, deception and espionage.

Read an excerpt now:

Chapter 1: Northern France, May 1940

The first time they saw German troops was around eight hours after they had left Amiens.

Fear had swept through the 20 of them, mostly strangers who had silently come together by happening to be on the same road at the same time and moving in the same direction. *'Don't head north,'* they had been warned in Amiens. *'You're walking into a battle.'*

Some of the original group had heeded that advice and stayed in the town. A dozen of them had carried on. They were refugees now, so they kept moving. It had quickly become a habit, they couldn't stop themselves.

A tall, stooped man called Marcel had assumed the role of leader and guide. He was a dentist, from Chartres, he told them. The rest of the group nodded and were happy to follow him.

Marcel decided the main road would be too dangerous, so they dropped down to follow the path of the Somme, passing through the small villages that hugged the river as it twisted through Picardy. The villages were unnaturally silent, apart from the angry barking of dogs that took turns to escort them through their territory. Anxious villagers peered from behind partially drawn curtains or half-closed shutters.

Occasionally, a child would venture out to stare at them, but would quickly be called home by an urgent shout. Some villagers would come out and offer them water and a little food, but were relieved to see them move on. Refugees meant war and no-one wanted the war to linger in their village. In a couple of the places, one or two more refugees joined them. No-one asked to join, no-one was refused. They just tagged along, swelling their numbers.

On the outskirts of the village of Ailly-sur-Somme a middle-aged couple came out from their cottage and offered the group water and fruit. They sat on the grass verge while the couple appeared to argue quietly in their doorway. And that's when they called her out.

'Madame, please can we have a word with you?'

She was sitting nearest to the house, but wasn't sure if they meant her. She looked around in case they were addressing someone else.

'Please, could we speak with you?' the man asked again.

She walked slowly over to the doorway. Maybe they had taken pity on her and were going to offer a meal. Or a bed. She smiled at the couple. Behind them, in the gloom of the hallway, she could make out a pair of piercing eyes.

'Madame. You seem a decent lady. Please help us.' The man sounded desperate. 'A lady passed through the village last week.'

There was a pause.

'From Paris,' his wife added.

'Yes, she was from Paris. She said she had to find somewhere in the area to hide and asked us to look after her daughter. She promised she'd be back for her in a day or two. She said she'd pay us then. She promised to be generous. But that was a week ago. We can't look after the girl any longer. The Germans could arrive any day now. You must take her!'

She looked around. The group was getting up now, preparing to move on.

'Why me?' she asked.

'Because you look decent and maybe if you're from a city you'll understand her ways. Are you from a city?'

She nodded, which they took as some kind of assent. The woman ushered the girl from inside the cottage. She looked no more than six years old, with dark eyes and long curly hair. She was dressed in a well-made blue coat and her shoes were smart and polished. A pale-brown leather satchel hung across her shoulders.

'Her name's Sylvie,' the man said. His wife took Sylvie's hand and placed it in the woman's.

'But what about when her mother returns?'

The wife was already retreating into the dark interior of the cottage.

'Are you coming?' It was Marcel, calling out to her as he started to lead the group off. His voice sounded almost jolly, as if they were on a weekend ramble.

The man leaned towards her, speaking directly into her ear so the little girl could not hear. 'She won't be back,' he said. He glanced around at the girl and lowered his voice. 'They're Jews. You must take her.'

With that, he quickly followed his wife into the cottage and slammed the door behind them.

She hesitated on the doorstep, still holding the little girl's hand. She could hear the door being bolted. She knocked on it two or three times, but there was no response.

She thought of trying to go around to the rear of the cottage, but she was losing sight of her group now. Sylvie was still holding her hand, glancing up at her anxiously. She knelt down to speak to the little girl.

'Are you all right?' She tried to sound reassuring. Sylvie nodded.

'Do you want to come with me?'

The little girl nodded again and muttered 'Yes.'

This is the last thing I need.

She thought of leaving her there, on the doorstep. They'll have to take her back in. She paused. I need to decide quickly. Maybe as far as the town, there'll be somewhere she can go there.

By the time they had walked down the path and started to follow the group, the shutters in the cottage had closed.

It was as they left the next village that they came across the Germans. They emerged from behind the trees one by one, with their grey uniforms, black boots and oddly shaped helmets, not saying a word. Slowly, they circled the group, which had come to a halt, too frightened to move. The German soldiers moved into position like pieces on a chessboard. They waved their machine guns to herd the group into the middle of the road.

She was terrified. *They're going to shoot us.* The little girl clutched her hand.

She breathed in and out deeply. Remember the training they gave you, she told herself:

When you're in a potentially dangerous situation, don't try to be anonymous.

Never look away, or at the ground. Don't avoid eye contact.

If you're in a group or a crowd, avoid standing in the middle, which is where they'd expect you to hide.

If you fear you're about to be found out, resist the temptation to own up. It's a fair assumption that the person questioning you or searching you will miss the obvious.

She heard shouting from behind the trees and over the shoulder of the soldier nearest to her she spotted two officers emerging. One of them was speaking loudly in bad French.

'We're going to search you then you can move on. Are any of you carrying weapons?'

Everyone around her was shaking their head. She noticed Sylvie shook hers too.

He waited a while in case anyone changed their mind. 'Are there any Jews in this group?'

There was silence. People glanced suspiciously at those stood around them. At the word *'Jews'* the little girl's hand tightened its grip on hers with a strength she could not have imagined. She looked down and saw Sylvie had her head bowed and appeared to be sobbing. She realised the extent of her predicament. If they caught her looking after a Jewish child, she would have no excuses.

'My men will come and search you now. I'm sure you'll all co-operate.'

Too late.

The soldiers spread the group out along the road and began searching people. Marcel was close and was searched before her. The soldier searching him gestured to him to remove his wristwatch. Marcel started to protest, until one of the officers walked over. He smiled, looked at the watch that had been passed to him, nodded approvingly and slipped it into his jacket pocket. Along the line, members of the group were being relieved of possessions: watches, pieces of jewellery – even a bottle of cognac.

The soldier who came to search her appeared to be in his teens.

His hands shook as he took her identity card. She noticed his lips moved silently as he tried to read what it said. One of the officers appeared behind him and took the card.

'You've come a long way.' He handed it back to her.

She nodded.

'Is this your sister?' He was staring intently at the little girl.

She gave the faintest of nods.

'She's your sister, then?'

She hesitated. She hadn't said anything yet. She could do now. They wouldn't harm a child. The little girl now placed her other hand around her wrist, stroking her forearm as she did so.

'Yes. She's my sister.' She replied in German, speaking quietly and hoping no-one else in the group heard her. Trying to appear as relaxed as possible, she smiled sweetly at the officer who was probably in his mid-twenties, the same age as her. She threw her head back, allowing her long hair to settle over her shoulders.

If you're an attractive woman – at that point the instructor had been looking directly at her, along with the rest of them – *don't hesitate to use your charms on men.*

The officer raised his eyebrows approvingly and nodded.

'And where did you learn to speak German?'

'At school.'

'A good school then. And does your sister have an identity card?'

It was too late. She should have realised this would happen. Does he suspect something? *She doesn't look anything like me. Her complexion is so much darker*. She had lost the chance to tell them the truth.

'She lost it.'

'Where?'

'In Amiens. A Gypsy stole it from her.'

The officer nodded knowingly. He understood. What do you expect? Gypsies. Don't we warn people about them? Thieves. Almost as bad as the Jews. Almost.

He lowered himself down on his haunches so he was at eye level with the little girl.

'And what's your name?'

There was a pause. The little girl peered up at her for approval. She nodded and smiled.

Tell him.

'Sylvie.'

'Sylvie is a nice name. Sylvie what?'

'Sylvie.'

'What is your surname – your full name?'

'Sylvie.'

'So, your name is 'Sylvie Sylvie?' The officer was beginning to sound exasperated. Sylvie was whimpering.

'I'm sorry, sir. She's frightened. It's the guns. She's never seen any before.'

'Well, she'd better get used to them, hadn't she?' The officer was standing up now. Not satisfied.

From the east there was a series of explosions followed by an exchange of rifle fire.

The officer hesitated. He wanted to continue with the interrogation, but the other officer was shouting out urgent instructions to the soldiers.

'All right, move on,' he said to her.

It was only when the soldiers disappeared back into the woods and the group moved on that she realised how petrified she was. Her heart was ramming against her ribs and cold sweat was running down her back. The little girl walked on obediently beside her, but she could feel and see her body trembling.

As the group walked slowly along the road, she realised she was stroking Sylvie's hair, her trembling hand cupping the child's cheeks, wiping away the tears with her thumb.

Not for the first time and certainly not for the last, she had surprised herself.

* * *

They had walked for another hour. Marcel dropped back at one stage and sidled up to her.

'And where did she come from?' He gestured at Sylvie, who was still clutching her hand.

'The couple who gave us water and fruit outside their cottage. The last village but one. They made me take her.'

'You realise…?'

'Of course I do!'

'Aren't you taking a bit of a risk?'

'Aren't we all?'

Marcel had spotted a forest ahead of them and said that the deeper they got into it, the safer they'd be. But, as she was beginning to realise was the case in the countryside, distances were hard to judge and the forest was not quite as near as it seemed. By the time they found a clearing, everyone was exhausted.

That night she found herself with Sylvie on the edge of the group, resting next to an old man and his wife. As the rest of the group slept the old man gave her his blanket, assuring her he wasn't cold. Sylvie was curled up alongside her under the blanket, fast asleep.

The old man had also given her the last of his water. He wasn't thirsty, he assured her. The moonlight poked through the canopy of the forest, the tops of some of the trees swaying very gently despite the absence of any breeze. The old man moved closer to her and spoke quietly: he and his wife had lost both their sons at Verdun and had prayed they would never see another war. He had tried to lead a decent life. He went to church, he paid his taxes, he had never voted for the communists. He worked on the railways, but was now retired. They could not stand the thought of being in Paris when it was occupied, so now they were heading to the town where his wife's sister lived, he explained. It was bound to be peaceful there.

'You look so much like our daughter,' he said, patting her affectionately on the wrist. 'You have the same slim figure, the same beautiful long, dark hair, the same dark eyes. When my wife and I saw you for the first time yesterday – we both remarked on that!'

'Where does your daughter live?'

The old man said nothing, but his eyes moistened as he held his hand over hers. The old man was kind, but there was something about him that unsettled her. As she lay down on the cold earth, a familiar yet unwelcome companion descended upon her. The memory. The old man, she realised, reminded her of her father. He too worked on the railways. The same dark eyes that couldn't hide the suffering. The same awkwardness. The reason she was here now.

She'd tried so hard to forget her father, but now the dark memories were stirred, she knew she would be troubled for the rest of the night.

She slept in short, unsatisfactory bursts as she always did when her father came back to her. At one stage she woke with a start, aware she must have cried out in her sleep. She looked around and noticed the old man's eyes, glinting in the moonlight, staring at her. When she awoke in the morning she felt stiff and cold. As the group moved off, she fell in with the old man and his wife, but the kindness of the previous night had gone and he ignored her.

* * *

'Come closer.'

It was later that afternoon and the group had paused at the edge of the forest, through which they had been walking all day. The old man who was calling out to her was now slumped at the base of the tree and had aged ten years in the past ten minutes. His legs were twisted under him and his skin was as grey as the bark he was resting against. His wife knelt by his side, anxiously gripping his right arm with both hands. He held his other arm out towards her, fingers urgently beckoning her to him.

'Come here,' he called out. His voice was rasping and angry. The rest of the group were moving off, leaving just her and Sylvie with the old man and his wife.

She looked down the forest path, where the rest of the group was now disappearing beyond the sunbeams. They knew there was nothing they could do for the man and were anxious to try and reach the town before nightfall. She could just make out Marcel, his short walking stick waving high above his head to encourage them along.

'Leave him,' Marcel had said. 'I warned everyone not to drink from the ponds. This water can be like a poison. He took the risk. We must move on.'

She hesitated. If she lost contact with the group she could be stranded in the forest, but she had made the mistake of stopping to help when the man collapsed and it would seem odd if she abandoned him now.

She knelt by his side. Around the tree was a carpet of bracken; green, brown and silver. His lips were turning blue and spittle flecked with blood was dribbling down the sides of his mouth. His eyes were heavily bloodshot and his breathing was painfully slow. He didn't have long to go. She recognised the signs. She would soon be able to rejoin the group.

'Closer.' His voice was now little more than a harsh whisper. With a shaking hand he pulled her head towards his. His breath was hot and smelled foul.

'I heard you last night,' he said. She pulled back, a puzzled look on her face.

He nodded, pulling her back towards him, glancing at his wife as he did so, checking she could not hear. 'I heard you cry out,' he whispered. 'I heard what you said.'

He waited to regain his breath, his whole body heaving as he did so. His reddened eyes blazed with fury.

'This victory will be your greatest defeat.'

* * *

Later that afternoon she realised how soon you become inured to the sights and the smells of war. They had a tendency to creep up on you, allowing time for the mind to prepare itself for what it was about to experience. But not the sounds. The sounds of war may be no more shocking, but they had a tendency to arrive without warning, imposing themselves in the most brutal manner. You were never prepared for them.

So it was on that dusty afternoon at the end of May, where the Picardy countryside had begun to give hints of a nearby but unseen sea, and where a small group of French civilians desperately trying to flee the war found they had walked right into it.

It took a few seconds for her and most of the others in the column to realise that the cracking sound a hundred yards or so ahead of them had been a gunshot. Maybe it was the shock of the strange metallic noise that seemed to echo in every direction, more likely was the fact it was the first time most of them had ever heard a gun. In a split second, she reassembled in her mind what she had just seen and heard. Moments earlier, the tall figure of Marcel had been remonstrating with the German officer. She could barely make out what he was saying, although she did hear the word 'civilians' more than once, as he pointed in their direction with his walking stick. Then there was the cracking noise and now

Marcel was on the ground, the dusty, light-grey surface of the road turning a dark colour beneath him.

A wave of fear rolled through the small group that had been held up beyond the makeshift German checkpoint where the shooting had taken place. *I know the area*, Marcel had told them. *I can handle the Germans.*

Apart from the woman with four children and three elderly couples, the group was mainly women on their own. All fools, she thought. All allowing themselves to be herded like cattle. All part of the reason why France had become what it was.

She knew she had made a terrible mistake. She could have headed in any direction, other than east. That would have been suicide. When she looked at where she had ended up now, she may as well have gone east. She realised now, of course, south would have been best. Due west would have been safe, too; not as safe as the south, but better. But to have come north was a disaster.

It wasn't as if she had been following the crowds. Half of France had been on the move and each person seemed to be heading in a different direction. She had made up her mind when she left home that she would head north and it wasn't in her nature to change her mind. She had tried it a few weeks ago and this was why she was in so much trouble now. It was crazy though. When she was a girl on the way to the coast for the only happy family holiday she could remember, they had passed through Abbeville. It had been an idyllic day, no more than a few hours respite on a long journey, but for some reason this was where she had decided to head.

The German officer walked over to where Marcel lay on the ground, the pistol still in his hand. With his boot he rolled the body over onto its back then nodded to two of his men. They picked a leg each and dragged the corpse to the ditch by the side of the road. A long red smear appeared where his body had been. The officer inspected his boot and wiped it clean on the grass.

One of the soldiers came over to the group and spoke to them slowly in French. They were to come forward one by one. They were to show their identity cards to the officer who had shot the man and, after they had been searched, they would be allowed to carry on into the town.

The light had not started to fade yet and beyond the checkpoint she could see the outskirts of the town quite clearly. Plumes of dark smoke hung over it, all remarkably straight and narrow, as if the town lay beneath a forest of pine trees.

She couldn't risk the checkpoint. Not with this identity card. The first Germans they had encountered had not paid much attention to people's identities. They'd been more intent on finding what loot they could lay their hands on. This checkpoint seemed to be more thorough. She had known she would have to find another identity and assumed she would get the opportunity in the town. She had not counted on coming across the Germans so early, no-one had. The last news she had heard was that they had not yet reached Calais. That is what Marcel had told them and now his feet were sticking out of the ditch in front of them, his blood now turning black on the surface of the road.

She edged towards the rear of the column, looking around her as she did so. She spotted her opportunity. The soldiers were distracted by dealing with the mother and her four children, all of whom were crying. No-one was watching the group. She leaned over to Sylvie, who was still clutching her wrist, and whispered that she was going to the toilet in the field. She would be back in a minute. The little girl's eyes filled with tears. Reluctantly, she reached in her pocket and took out the bar of chocolate. It was the last of the bars that had once filled her coat pockets and it was all she had left to eat. She pressed it into Sylvie's palm, noticing it was soft and had begun to melt.

'If you're a good girl and keep very quiet, you can have all of this!' She was trying hard to sound as gentle as possible. She looked around. No-one was looking at her. Towards the front of the column she saw the smartly dressed lady in her mid-thirties who'd told her she was a lawyer from Paris, heading for the family home in Normandy.

'You see that nice lady there? The one with the smart brown coat? She'll look after you. But don't worry, I'll be back soon.'

Still crouching down, she edged towards the ditch then through a narrow gap in the hedge. The corn was high in the field and not far away, as if expertly painted onto the landscape, was a large wood that seemed to taper as it spread towards the town. She waited for a moment. She was certain the Germans had not counted how many there were in their group, so hopefully they'd not realise one person had crept away. If they did come and look for her now, she was near enough to the hedge to be able to persuade them she was just relieving herself.

It looked as if she had landed in an Impressionist painting: the golden yellow of the corn, the blue of the sky unbroken by cloud and ahead the dark green of the wood. A timely breeze had picked up and the corn was swaying slowly. It would disguise her moving through it. If she could make it to the wood she would have a good chance of reaching the town under the cover of the trees and the fading light.

* * *

To buy *The Best of Our Spies*, visit www.studio-28.co.uk

Alex Gerlis

Printed in Poland
by Amazon Fulfillment
Poland Sp. z o.o., Wrocław